# MISS WOO COUNTRY

# David Peak

SilverWood

Published in 2016 by the author
using SilverWood Books Empowered Publishing®

ISBN 978-1-78132-495-0 (paperback)
ISBN 978-1-78132-496-7 (ebook)

British Library Cataloguing in Publication Data
A CIP catalogue record for this book is available from the British Library

Set in Sabon by SilverWood Books
Printed on responsibly sourced paper

Or could it be I'm no longer here?

*

Not six feet from me Colquahoon reads *The Times*. Glimpsing his tartan dressing gown from the corner of my eye's a matter of being drawn to the Highlands. The time I imagined Loch Lomond, I was on a loaf-shaped stone at the water's edge boldly wearing the cubist cardigan Mother could have bought me. I'm not sure they do them any more, but then they were all the rage and I'd been keen to have one. The imagination was of what some in here would call a fine day though I've rarely heard a sound explanation of what one entails. Colquahoon probably has many substantial definitions. I'm not sure how he's spelt by the way. Jugg told us some names in the language are written differently from how they're spoken. The one that stuck in my mind all those years ago was Featherstonehaugh, which Jugg said was pronounced Fanshaw. I asked him why – given it was written Featherstonehaugh – it was pronounced that way, but he couldn't or wouldn't explain. My continued insistence on knowing the full details led to me being sent to the headmaster – a Mr Lee so free of mispronunciation himself.

*

Words all at once yet they make no sound other than in here – here being the brain, mind, call it what you will. Words through the patio doors, across the flagstones, down the slope onto the lawn. This seductive light makes me want to go after them though I can't of course because of the legs, chortle. Jugg said also – not in the same lesson – walking was controlled falling, the control consisting of a foot extended repeatedly. More wonders of the body M'Lud. I might have said M'Lud aloud. It made Colquahoon twitch I'm sure of it. A woman comes to visit him – his wife? – handbag – hair of parboiled cauliflower. They say generally women fare better than men. She has striding legs. Maybe a Girl Guide in her day. And rather than commit murder she has walked briskly and taken deep breaths ever since. If she dabs her cheek to his in greeting, a puff of powder – only the obsessive would notice – rises above Colquahoon like thoughts used to be in comics. Maybe they still are.

*

Once the storm passed a hypnotic wind came through the patio doors, carrying with it the smell of the hedgerow. I doubt Colquahoon noticed. He's more a numbers man. Most times he crosses the dayroom without sound like a butterfly on a summer day. Is it summer? Or summer's? Jugg used to explain that sort of thing and then he'd make transgressors – of whom I was one – write it out oh a hundred times. I shall not in italics do whatever it is again. Such severity had its good points. For example I've never since spelt different wrongly. I used to miss out the first e. Jugg wore linen jackets whose pockets were dappled with chalk dust. I don't think he ever married, though he did have a number of whitened cats. They were in the paper when he died. Homes Wanted. Ten to one they drifted back. Cats don't settle easily elsewhere. The word's territorial. Like me. I was never one for roaming or for following in the footsteps of whoever. I was afraid something might happen while I was out of range of home. A certain oh no leapt to mind if ever anyone suggested a night away.

*

If only I could make it out to the patio under my own steam. It's an ache. Not an unpleasant one necessarily. I'm perturbed by Colquahoon's fixation on his *Times* when he can, in fact, get up and go out there if he wishes. Perhaps he'll occasionally cross his slippers or clear his throat. Any number of things. I heard Harry invite him earlier – Harry's good like that, though not with me evidently – for what he called a turn round the grounds. Old Colquahoon dug his heels in. I'm fine where I am, he said gruffly. I enjoy the occasional adverb even though Jugg said too many are a sign of laziness. I'm not even sure it was gruffly. I used it because it made the sentence scan in my head.

*

It won't be long – assuming Colquahoon follows routine – till he pops a toffee. The wrappers are a different colour depending on the flavour. He always looks down at the sweet as soon as he's taken it from the bag and then gives a jerk of the chin. He pulls at the wrapper's ends till the toffee itself is disclosed. He then pops it – that *is* the word – into his mouth, more often than not rolling up the wrapper with a movement in his hips to raise himself slightly and then putting it in his dressing-gown pocket. Prolonged observation has led me to conclude mint's his favourite. It's in the broader or elongated jerk his chin performs upon encountering the said flavour. You take a man like Colquahoon and he'll bring life into focus not with the creation of a symphony for violin but in the modified jerk at a mint toffee. The wrappers are green.

*

Oh. Hadn't noticed for once. Harry with the chemical trolley. I said to him the other day, I said: Harry, why I believe looking back I could have spent the whole of my life writing about you and this place and I might as well have done that as anything because once I'm gone I won't remember what I did anyhow. Harry has said he likes visiting Laugharne to think in detail about Dylan. The time we discussed it further I said to Harry, I said: How do you go about thinking in detail? I told him I'd tried thinking like that only to find my mind went off the rails just after leaving the station. I'm using similar terms to the ones Jugg used to describe my wayward abilities to Mother one school Open Day. Mother responded to Jugg by saying yes, I did have a head like a sieve and though Jugg never said anything I could tell he wasn't happy having sieves muddle his transport metaphor.

*

Colquahoon's nose reminds me of Monsieur Chandler who taught French with a look in his eye as he recalled student days in Montmartre. It was an early ambition of mine to emulate his life since it mostly comprised soft cheese, croissants, Mademoiselles. How long he lived in France and how many of the Mademoiselles were real we'll never know. He was Mister really but insisted on Monsieur for the lessons. He corrected in Red as did Jugg. I kept the exercise books.

*

Bees hum among the petunias. Father liked them – petunias, not bees so much. There was invariably a row of them at the front of the border in summer. He said to me one day life itself was only so many petunia seasons long so I'd best make the most of it. I have never, however – sorry Father – understood for myself what making the most of it entails. Once upon a time we found out he was making the most of it with Miss Woo up the road. Mother never put his meals down on the dinner table as carefully after that. She told me by way of explanation – using bee imagery herself – it was in a man's nature to seek out the nectar of more than one flower every so often and that if a wife was sensible she let the matter go. This was at a time when letting these matters go was more likely. I can't imagine K would ever have had such a view. Tangle with women and I'll thrash you, she said one leafy afternoon – there I go again – it might not have been an afternoon at all or leafy. More accurately we were on the banks of the river after a picnic. She wore boots. Yes, that was it. She said: Tangle with women and I'll thrash you. I thought for a second or two afterwards of – you guessed it – witty ripostes, but I just said okay then or something. Across the river from us stood the castle battlements. Earlier we'd been on them looking this way. I've been meaning to tell Harry about the castle because it's not so very far from Laugharne. Sometimes though if you wait to tell someone something you go off the idea or feel embarrassed you left it so long. Besides which, when Harry talks about Dylan you feel in your heart you should leave the topic to him. One day I caught him here at the patio doors looking out. He said he'd been thinking through some of the poems. I said to him how commendable it was he could think them through without having the text to hand, and this led to a conversation about how – though he loved Dylan's work – he wished he had poems of that quality in his own soul. I said: Not everyone has poems and he said he realised that but

8

all the same he wished he had. I made some comment then about the quality of care he gave, saying from what I knew of Dylan it was unlikely *he'd* be capable of such philanthropic behaviour. I'll never forget because then Harry shunted from the edge of the door-frame with his shoulder saying snappily: All the same... Later he said sorry, he'd had a row that morning with Cheryl. I said that's okay Harry, we've all been there, or something like that. The thing to remember, Harry told me, is Cheryl doesn't have time for Dylan. Not that she knew anything of his character; it was more she didn't have time for the amount of space he took up in Harry's head. Add poet to work and there can't be that much left it's true. He's the most dedicated. Comes in for every whist drive and sing-song. Did the CPR when Cholmondley collapsed.

*

We'd spoken his name phonetically for ages before one afternoon – leafy or not I can't remember – he shouted at us all saying it was pronounced Chumleigh, Chumleigh! We asked him why he hadn't pointed it out sooner and saved us embarrassment. Even Harry had always addressed him our way for heaven's sake. Cholmondley said in a dry voice – unusual among mucus folk – he'd been hoping against hope one of us would take the trouble to look into it. Colquahoon said why would we have looked into it if we hadn't realised there'd been a mispronunciation in the first place? Cholmondley was pronounced dead later that evening. Harry said there was no connection between the dispute and his death but on the quiet I think Colquahoon was disturbed by his having been the last one to argue. Myself, I've always been the sort to apologise as I go along in case the person I've had a row with dies before I see them again. Massive stroke.

*

Father was saying each of us has a skill and if we're lucky we can use it in what he called our professional life. Miss Woo's skill – folding herself into suitcases and small boxes – led her, he said, to be employed by a series of travelling magicians. It seemed he was giving Mother more information in the hope it would make her put the dinners down carefully again. His drift was that essentially Miss Woo was like everyone else on earth and

Mother thinking she was a threat in any long-term sense was erroneous. I quite wished he hadn't used the word erroneous because I believe it was the one that made Mother throw aside the tea towel and run into the bathroom. Father looked at me while she was gone and said if you can manage son, try not to have a Miss Woo as you get older. I told him I'd do my best, though I don't think I knew quite what a Miss Woo was.

*

Colquahoon was an accountant, he told me when I first came here, using the tone of voice he would have used if he'd been saying he had a gun. I remember being settled into this chair and hurriedly thinking what I might say in response to what *he'd* said. But thereafter he remained almost as quiet as he is now. Just beyond his shoulder, but more distant and in a combination of fawn footwear and recycled clothing, Jaundice stares at a small round mirror held eight inches or so from his face. It's Jarndyce really. James. What possessed his parents? It would be kinder for us to call him JJ I suppose, though Jaundice does tie in with the complexion. Harry said something about him having lost his mind in the Cairngorms. Sometimes people just decide not to function properly any more, he said. Anyway, he's ended up watching a mirror. I had a spell of something similar a few years back. Staring at myself I mean. I've been advised not to any more. It doesn't bode well, Harry said, citing Jaundice as an example. When I say he cited him what I mean is he nodded in Jaundice's direction and I felt that day me and Harry were friends. I'm hoping that of all the people here he thinks I'm the least troublesome. I've certainly done my best not to create fuss.

*

Fuss gives people heart problems Mother said. She certainly tried to keep fuss to a minimum over what came to be known between her and Mrs Chaffin as The Miss Woo Business. I didn't tell Mother I already understood things about life because she might have thought I was arrogant or trying to annoy her. Mrs Chaffin wore an arrangement of headscarf while doing the housework that resembled soft ice cream on a cornet. It liked – in league with her – to lean against the back fence nodding whenever Mother pegged out the washing. Mrs Chaffin's efforts to be discreetly compassionate if Miss Woo came up led to a hushed Iss Oo which I felt only Mother and me understood. Mrs Chaffin's own husband died of such a heart problem years before. One minute, she said, he was digging potatoes, the next...

*

Bees don't hum. It's their wings. I've been warned never to mention things like that to Colquahoon because in all probability he wouldn't let the Romance Of Intentional Inaccuracy linger. That's what I call it. K understood, and would allow embellishments because she knew they were only there to help boost a minimal self-esteem. It's hard to see how she and someone like Colquahoon would get on. I've come to the conclusion – it has to be said with the help of Harry – we seek out those who positively or negatively acknowledge our idiosyncrasies. We want always to be forgiven or – if not – then patiently and peacefully redirected.

*

When I'm around someone for a while – Colquahoon for example – I suddenly see them as if I hadn't come across a human before. The curiosity of shape and physical function astounds me. I easily catch my breath. It's like there's a planet from which I've arrived. Nothing about earth or the people on it are in any way familiar. My own language hasn't the scope to make sense of what I come across. Seen in this way, most of what's laid before me becomes inexplicable. There's an unwelcome desire to return to my part of the universe. Harry isn't so keen to talk about this aspect of my observations. I don't think he's ever woken to find Cheryl's taken on gross unfamiliarity. Or it could be such discussions inevitably keep him from the estuary at Laugharne, the shade of Dylan in the boathouse window, the call of curlew. So in respect of Colquahoon – or any of the others given the right circumstances – I suddenly find myself star-struck by, for example, the fleshy protuberances at the ends of hands. If we weren't all human we would probably find our shape grotesque or comical. In my self-examination days I'd often catch sight of myself in this alien fashion and wonder quite what nature had been playing at. I find it curious still that K seemed not to mind me much.

Not that we ever became completely physical. There were opportunities over the years, which weren't taken through fear or lack of motivation. It's something I'd like to remedy if ever our time comes again. I ignore my chair-bound status in this fantasy. Sometimes there's no pleasure to be had sticking with truth.

*

The nearest in physique to Dylan, Harry pointed out, is Major Gwillingington. Yeah, Dylan was short and overly plump too, Harry once said out the corner of his mouth so as not to offend and again giving me reason to suspect co-conspirator status: Short, plump and full of gorgeous poems. The gorgeous is mine. It isn't a Harry word. He has said he finds Cheryl spectacular but I think he used the term tongue-in-cheek because it had been round about the time he'd been telling me about her persistent lateness at the office where she works – Lambton, Lambton, Lambton & Lambton, Solicitors. He said it was as important in this instance to make sure one got the right number of Lambtons as it was to remember the Major's second ing. She's a personal assistant to the eldest Lambton – the senior partner. I liked the name so much when I first heard it I repeated it to myself as a mantra if ever things became unpleasant, which they can do in here from time to time, most recently when one of the newest arrivals attacked Harry with a table tennis bat. Harry was saying later how he isn't allowed to retaliate, however much he feels like it, and had reason to be grateful on this occasion for the bat's rubberised surfaces. Tobias Mawk – the new arrival – has been shackled by medication to an easy chair facing the office more or less ever since. If anything gets out of hand – which it shouldn't with medication – Harry can ring for help from a place of safety. A rectangle of reinforced glass allows him to keep an eye on things whenever he's in there. Fair play to him though, he more often braves our dangerous waters, coming ashore for a chat with anyone he feels might be safely marooned for the moment. He has a knack of drawing us away from self-pity towards a greater appreciation of how fortunate we are compared to other categories. In one of the far rooms they're so bad they have to be kept in high-sided cots wearing restraints, he said. No poems for them. He says there are nine rooms altogether. The first eight alternately male and female. We are five. The far room he was referring to is the ninth and least pleasant. People here – those who talk at least – say things like he'll be off to Nine at this rate, though to be fair I haven't heard Harry use it as a threat. And anyway, like he said, by the time you get to Nine you're too far gone to understand that's where you are. They don't segregate the sexes.

*

Honeysuckle. Since the storm its smell has intensified. Those out on the patio had something about them whisked in the wind – a collar, lock of hair, lock of wig, corner of a newspaper. I'm put in mind – though there's no connection I'm sure – of the work of the Impressionists. It's as if colour itself ruffled across the view. I used to have a postcard beside my desk at home showing Monet. K sent it when she was in Paris. Monet's standing with a pipe in his hand in front of one of his lily ponds. He's looking at the camera. Slight pot belly. Hat. Or was it a cigarette? Anyway it got me thinking about this business of sending rectangular pieces of card through the post with a picture on one side. Since the image on the card K sent started life as a photograph, poor Monet's in black and white even though he's probably the last person you'd wish it upon.

*

Harry says there's little chance of my regaining the use of my legs. The couple of times I've tried they've corrugated under me. Years ago I ran everywhere. Like a cat on a hot brick Mother said. Or a blue-arsed fly. Colquahoon has used the phrase 'like a greased whippet' but I've not heard it in any other quarter. I enjoyed the first time he used it. This was during the few days when he toyed with the idea of making a break for it even though we'd heard they have twenty-four-hour cameras here and in the corridors. The possibility of this makes it hard to relax though I think it's unlikely anyone watches full time. If there are cameras they're probably just to provide evidence if ever there's an incident, like Tobias and the table tennis bat. He was a professional player once. He's another non-speaker, though he did roar the day of the attack. He'll end up in Nine. Colquahoon said he'd detected a Russian dialect among the shouting. Trust Colquahoon to know not only Russian but dialects of it, I thought. It was a sign of my lingering resentment and self-pity. Harry said give it a few months and I'd feel better about things.

*

Though I've been nearby, I never made it absolutely to Laugharne. I have a revulsion about visiting places famous people lived. I never know what to do when I'm there. Harry reckons you can see the shed Dylan wrote in. I wanted him to think I was excited to hear about it so I asked him where the shed was and could you go in? He said no you couldn't, but you could see through a Perspex window. Luckily he had an emergency at that moment. I've since decided if he mentions the shed again I'll ask if he has any photos. I feel better when I have observations or questions in reserve.

*

K stalled me beside the river as I was indulging in a monologue. I broke off to ask what was up and she said: Shhh, a kingfisher – really just a blur of blue, it turned out, alighting on a twig. There's something about a kingfisher that makes you watch as long as you can, not speaking. When it was gone she asked me to carry on with what I'd been saying. I realised it didn't matter any more.

*

There aren't many books here given the numbers. Hardly any of us can be bothered anyway – Colquahoon's an exception – and what books there are tend to be dog-eared crime or westerns. Harry says the budget doesn't stretch so they have to rely on donations. There's one on the table left of centre of the patio and damp by the looks of it – *Apache Afternoon*. It's likely the publisher hoped an alliterative title might entice the reader. There was an Apache statue or at least of an American Indian outside the pub down the city centre, the last place I saw K. She insisted on buying the drinks and went alone to the bar while I found a table in the window. She'd said she'd probably be having Coke, ice and lemon while I'd opted for tomato juice with a splash of Worcestershire sauce. In terms of decor, both of us had been expecting a theme because of the statue but it turned out to be just an external curio. K, being on the right, would have been able to see along to the head of the harbour while I had my own dark view of the recently reopened office block, which had been re-clad in glass and was reflecting sodium light. We both started talking at once. I'd been going to ask how she felt about not turning up for her share at the AA meeting, and would people be annoyed, while she – having a clear run at speech so to speak – said how relieved she was we'd come here instead. She drained her glass in one and went out for a smoke. I watched her from inside, trying to imagine not knowing her. While she was away a barmaid came to wipe the table. I was realising how morbidly entertaining the world was. Lank soul music softened the background. A trio of men in suits laughed along the bar. Not so long before, I'd found a recording of T. S. Eliot reading 'The Love Song Of J Alfred Prufrock' and thought what an odd voice he had. I would quite liked to have gone up to him and said: Of all the people in the world I fear you're the least suitable to read your own stuff. I glanced out at K again. As she smoked she jigged from foot to foot. Maybe she was quietly regretting not doing the share after all. I supped from my glass. Beyond K and beyond the roadway, a series of fountains spurted tubes of illuminated water. In summer toddlers and what have you played among them. Beyond these another roadway – the other half of an elongated circuit – and immediately beyond this, the theatre, currently showing *Kismet*. K's ear was cold under my mouth. Or it was as I imagined it. I felt like going out and saying: We're supposed to be here together, but I held off. What was wrong anyway with her going out for a smoke and why was I so immeasurably anxious? I'm sure – if he knew more of me – Colquahoon would be the first to say I haven't been successful in my relationships. Not that there've been any except with K. The others were theoretical. Smithson used to say the anxiety might have had something to do with Mother leaving me on the 38a because she wasn't used to having a baby with her. I was found and held on to by a barren Rumanian couple for two weeks till the female of the couple saw sense and left me with a note on the doorstep of The Department Of Work And Pensions. But he would keep on – Smithson that is – about how being mislaid by a mother early on could well have created fearful attachments in adult life. I can see his point to an extent because even now any mention of Rumania renders me lightly suicidal.

I checked my watch as K glanced in my direction, hoping to gee her up about coming back in. A man alone at a table with tomato juice soon becomes an object of scorn. I wondered if I ought to hook a forefinger and rap it lightly against the window but I didn't want her to think me dependent on her. Smithson said more than once that in all his born days…and there he would leave a gap to stand for what would have been his conclusion. A part of me was thinking – and still can – one of his own difficulties was that he would on the one hand seek to explain and forgive my nature through his observations, and at the same time seem as if any moment he might throttle me. The part-funded therapy had been arranged through Doctor Mainwaring who didn't say outright so much, but hinted nonetheless, that the scheme was a golden opportunity for me to have quality sessions for a fraction of the cost. And if you have a golden opportunity you feel bad if you don't go along with it or find once it's under way any reason for complaint. Or, I decided, it might seem less critical if I picked up the beer mat and tapped the window with it instead of my finger. But I was afraid she might come in and say what did you do that for? How could I in all honesty say to her that I – I! – considered she'd had long enough to smoke and should now be back inside? Laying down the law – as she was wont to call it – never went down well and I see her point. Smithson said that if by the end of your life you can absolutely let people be themselves you've done more than most. So leave K out there as long as she wants, I thought to myself. In celebration I took a mouthful of tomato juice. I should have asked for ice too. It was beginning to take on the fug of the bar. K was framed between the edge of the glass and the edge of the curtain as I drank again. She exuded a dark rage, which overlaid the area around her so that downhearted passers-by became startled and ravens fell gasping to earth. They didn't really do this. It's what my mind made up. Actually thinking of it, my mind has had many untrue words in while waiting for others to finish doing something. Smithson said there were two kinds of person: Those who wait for those who don't and those who don't. It took me a while to grasp this. He printed it out in Comic Sans on a sheet of A4 and laminated it as a present for me one sultry afternoon. They were the sort of afternoons – surely – that would have inspired Eliot. He was 1888 to 1965. We did him in the fifth form. One morning I suggested to Harry he might think of taking up T. S. as an antidote to Dylan, but he wouldn't hear of it. He'd enjoyed 'The Love Song Of J Alfred Prufrock', but that's as far as it went. He'd had no desire to go and see the places Eliot wrote about and certainly wouldn't dream of thinking through any of his work, with or without the text in front of him. I have a copy of the *Collected Poems* at home somewhere. It must have K's fingerprints on because she threw it at me. She said it was no good quoting as a thin attempt to distract her from the truth, which was frankly that I was bol-locks. It wasn't a good idea to argue being bollocks was literally unlikely because it only made her retrieve the poems and throw them again. I avoided the temptation to remind her about my being left on the 38a to explain why I'd cross-examined her about a walk she'd had with Tom the day before. She said just because she was seeing me didn't mean she was going to ban herself from close-ish friendships with other men, especially Tom who'd she'd known a long time. I wanted to say what on earth does close-ish mean? These things could – can – cause me disquiet through the long night when a sleep disorder forces me to recall thoroughly. *Tom.* Even now the name makes me want to thump Colquahoon. I sometimes wonder if I'd have been better off generally thumping people for say a day and getting it out of my system. Oh, so you've walked with Tom have you? I'd said. Smithson maintained I have an excellent system when it comes to my neuroses. I keep them hidden till the person in question has become entangled and then up they come. I said: Thanks Doctor, it's good to know what's going on in here. The gesture I made towards my head was a waste because he was already gazing out of his window.

*

K stubbed the cigarette. She came back with evil in her eye. How's the tomato juice? she said. Looking back, I detect in her question a deter-mination not to see me once the evening was over. At some earlier time she'd discreetly arranged work in another part of the country, lodgings, a removal van. Ignorant of this, I glanced at her: It's okay, I said. Let me know how you're doing when you've got a moment. Like fun I will, she said. Then after a while I fingered the rim of my glass and asked how she felt now about missing the AA meeting. Wouldn't it have been better to have gone through with the share after all? She looked daggers at me and shook her head, not so much in answer to the question but as an appraisal, I felt, of my interpersonal skills.

*

This afternoon has been balmy since the storm. Our foliage is lush to the point of somnolence, our winds playful and warm, and oh the smell. There was a discussion among some on the patio a few days ago about whether dogs knew they were dogs. The discussion was stalled by Fiona coming round with the tea. Today it was bourbons again. Ones she buys from the market Sunday mornings. They purport to be real bourbons. I can't count the times I've overdunked and had to fish for the lower half with a spoon. Real bourbons have staying power. Anyway so they were discussing if dogs knew they were dogs. Atkins felt dogs did know they were dogs. Smetham felt they didn't. Kandinsky felt they knew some things but not specifically whether they were or weren't dogs. It was driving me potty listening. I don't mind philosophising providing there's at least a chance of arriving at an answer. Atkins said if they didn't, how come they scraped the door when they wanted to be let out? Kandinsky said he was making an error of reasoning because whether or not dogs scraped doors when they wanted to be let out didn't in itself prove they knew they were dogs. Smetham didn't say anything else. He was nibbling *Apache Afternoon*. In the previous few days he'd tried soil, a bin, plastic spoons, the dayroom upholstery and a corner of Colquahoon's *Times* when Colquahoon nodded off.

*

Not wishing to discuss her decision apparently, K looked out of the window for the first few minutes of her re-entry into the bar. She wanted to get another drink for herself, she said. While she was gone I shuffled nervously. I found it hard to relax when she was with me. I wanted to relax – I'd say I was less than an inch away from achieving it at any moment – but I couldn't get there. Smithson put it down to a combination of something and something – I can't remember what. One of them, he said, could be treated with drugs while the other might need keyhole brain surgery. I didn't get round to taking up either option, at least till I came here. Doctor Mainwaring isn't one for prescribing chemical or surgical procedures willy-nilly. She even said maybe I might go on more holidays instead to which I think I said give me the money doc and I'll do that very thing. I say I *think* I said that because to be honest it's getting harder to know what's happened and what hasn't, but even if it *did* I expect I said doctor rather than doc. Having drained her second drink as quickly as the first K put her glass down more heavily than she had before and said: Peter? I said Yes? She said: I've been meaning to ask how we are, I mean really. I said (I think): Do you mean you've been *really* meaning to ask how we are, or you've been meaning to ask how we are *really*? She went out for another smoke. Her exit prompted the men at the bar to look round in unison. I smiled and raised my glass. The one this end chuckled and turned back to his pint. The others followed as if the first was a leader. How I wished more customers would come in. If you imagine someone with their arms folded and then they raise one of the arms to smoke – well that's what K was doing outside. Of course I knew she was fed up about my fastidiousness, but it was a mechanism I found it impossible to lose. I was half thinking maybe I should go out and ask what the matter was. Sitting there like a tomato juice chump might not have been the best thing. Further glances on the part at least of the leader of the three men, and one from the barmaid, led me to believe they probably thought they knew what the solution to my difficulties was more than I did.

*

Time has almost no sound, a hum perhaps or the gentlest vibration. I was always satisfied and appalled by it, this business (I called it) of having to be two or three steps behind in my capacity to describe things even to myself. I was poised at the edge of a bluff above Laura Bay. Hardly anyone went there because the beach was hard to get to and there were no facilities – as they're called – anywhere near. A similar hum was passing through the thinly grassed limestone under my feet. K had climbed down to the sand.

She'd taken off her clothes and drawn herself into the waves. She stood, squeezing sea from her hair. The vertigo was exhilarating. Though I was glad later to get down I dreamed of going back up. I was wearing a coat that was too warm, as K pointed out as we were setting off that morning. I can count on the fingers of one hand the times I've been proved right in that kind of discussion with her. I wasn't in that sense a man's man. Not a man-at-the-bar man.

*

K came back in before she'd finished her roll-up. She was holding its stubbed half as she sat down. Actually you're driving me out of my mind, she said. You and a number of other things. Or, maybe it was you've *driven* me out of my mind. The latter would have suggested she'd reached the end of her willingness to be driven out of her mind as opposed to the former, which sort of suggested she might be okay with being driven out of her mind a while longer. I did my best to take a saddened mouthful of tomato juice. I knew she was right, whichever version she'd used, and I knew I was lucky for her to be there at all. A voice I didn't recognise said, weakly, are these 'other things' Tom? to which her face grew darker still. I was hoping she knew me well enough to know the question had been involuntary on the part of my inner child. Almost immediately she was off to the bar again, not asking if I wanted anything. I could hardly bear to watch any more.

*

Yes, an odd voice, but I daresay no one felt they should persuade him not to read his own work. *Let us go then, you and I.* I have the *Collected Poems* and its annotations still at home and whenever I opened it – like Prufrock himself I suppose – I wondered who it was who – in my hand – made elaborate notes and assigned complex meaning to the poem when really it's a thing of *listening*. Like I said to Harry one time, if you listen you might not get it straight away, not in the sense you could convey all of it to a third party, but its essence does attach itself forever to what I called the soul. Harry said: I'm not the biggest fan if you don't mind. There's no need to keep trying to persuade me. I chuckled and said: You're beginning to sound like K now and he said: Joseph K in Kafka?

and I said: No, my friend K, my dark lady if you will. He was again leaning against the patio door-frame and nudged himself from it. But then you see Harry – I said – I've used the dark lady allusion at the same time as having no idea what that was about so the allusion might not be accurate. I have a habit of building conversation on the thinnest information.

*

You couldn't get away with thin allusions to dark ladies where Bulwark (pronounced Bullock) was concerned because he would have the information chapter and verse. He was small, had a thick penumbral beard that belied his years and all year wore a duffel coat with the cowl raised. A joke went round college there was no top to his head and that the cowl was an extension to an enlarged brain. In there he had just about everything. Except romance. We suggested he shaved off his beard and cheered up but he believed when the time was right nature would reveal his life partner and sometimes here at night when owls tick and the clocks hoot forward I wonder if it ever did.

*

There's a quickness to our insides till we die they say and so it's impossible for as long as you're alive to be entirely still. We all saw what real stillness was like the evening Cholmondley passed. Jaundice came along with a magnifying glass to check the eyelashes. Not a sausage, he said before he and the others were ushered away. An already exhausted Harry had to get Cholmondley on to a trolley and wheel him out. Atkins and Smetham gave him a hand because the dead are unreasonably heavy. Even if you get half their body up ten to one the other half will flop back. As this one at last passed through the doors I remember thinking: There goes Cholmondley. I'd used the phonetic version for old times' sake. He was born, he lived, he died. It was he who said at breakfast one day the best proof of there not being a God was the fact there were billions of galaxies and yet according to most religious folk this God had seen fit to create people only on one planet. You could ascertain Cholmondley'd been working this out all night to see if it would earn him a respected place among us. He otherwise felt himself to be an emotional and intellectual outcast.

No, K said emphatically when she came back from the bar, Tom's nothing to do with it. I told her being driven out of one's mind was a psychiatrically inaccurate term anyway and asked exactly what she meant. Well, she said, where you're concerned there are infinite problem areas. Now's no time to be bandying infinity about, I said, thinking the men at the bar would enjoy it. The Indian outside gave me a look. Heap Big Mistake, he seemed to be saying. Wooden feathers reared from the far side of his head. In his right hand he held a carved tomahawk, raised as if he was about to attack passers-by. I asked K, loosely I felt, if it was that I'd never sought for us to become more committed to one another. This made her drain the latest drink too. In the surface of her glass a faint reflection of the leader of the three men looked towards my back. You couldn't honestly want to be more attached to me anyway, I said. I mean here I am Office-bound and officially unstable and though I've been told by Smithson and various others I have untapped talents, it seems they are destined to remain untapped. Attaching yourself to me would be akin to an ailing sailor mooring his schooner to the hull of the *Titanic*. Since I was expecting laughter from someone – hopefully K – I decided to initiate it by laughing myself. At the same time I raised my glass to the midpoint between table and mouth. There were speckles of the tomato juice at places around one side of the rim where I'd taken previous mouthfuls. It was as I was focused on these K stood and made her way unsteadily outside, this time continuing along the pavement till she was out of sight. I believe some kind of weight held me on the chair because the more I felt I should go after her the heavier I became. The moment was characterised by an infernal listing by the Indian of my defects of character and examples of the difficulties they'd caused me and others over the years. K herself would have said I choose to see that my difficulties have been created for me rather than owning full responsibility for them because such a view absolves me to an extent. Thinking about it now I feel envious of Colquahoon's parboiled wife. I said to Harry one time there are wives who have that kind of devotion and husbands who have that kind of devotion but not often a husband

and wife with equal devotion. Usually one of them's having to save their real thoughts for when they go to bed where they can snarl to themselves in darkness. Harry said I was showing evidence of ingrained cynicism. I was honoured because rarely does Harry share insights but then maybe it was something he could identify with in terms of marriage to Cheryl.

*

The envelope Father left me contained a note that said though he'd advised me against having a Miss Woo, his own had been the finest woman in the universe. Had he been alive I would have challenged this on the basis you'd need familiarity with the entire universe before you could reach such a conclusion, and furthermore I'd heard Mother say to Mrs Chaffin one time women hate it if a man persistently and wholeheartedly believes they're the finest though they don't mind if he says it occasionally in the heat of the moment. Given Father chose to impart this information to me from beyond the grave while being extraordinarily reluctant to enclose cash, I must assume he meant it as much as he was able to. In the years since I've thought I might like to find the real Miss Woo, but each time the idea came I reminded myself she was most probably dead too and, though she would be part of the universe in the sense of having had her atoms returned to it via cremation or burial, she was unlikely still to be the finest woman in it.

*

Poor Cholmondley and his considerations, like the time he asked (again at breakfast) what would happen if we moved at one hundred and eighty-seven thousand miles per second given light travels at one hundred and eighty-six thousand miles a second. Kandinsky felt you'd expand and disintegrate, basing his supposition on what he knew of the theory of relativity, which wasn't (by his own admission) much. Atkins said you wouldn't be able to move at one hundred and eighty-seven thousand miles per second. You'd run out of land to move across. Smetham didn't make a contribution. He was chewing the tablecloth. It was a day I ached and longed for someone to say perhaps they'd been having a look at *The Catcher In The Rye* and what did the others think? We studied it at college. Maureen came into the seminar room and threw it on to her table. Such was the patina thereof, it continued across the surface and fell at Bulwark's shoes. She explained she'd thrown it to take us by surprise. The surprise had been intended to elicit a conversation about how literature should seek sometimes to disrupt expectation. It's a disruption we need from time to time (Maureen explained) if we're not to stagnate. I've no intention of stagnating whatever, Bulwark said, the words falling from his beard. Maureen's dress had tulips from neck to hem. It was, Bulwark was to say later, an Art Nouveau extravaganza. He followed morning seminars with a steak and kidney pie, peas, chips and gravy in the refectory and always sat at the end of the third table by the window. If the space was taken he'd adapt willingly but didn't enjoy his pie half so much. He carried in his briefcase a wooden apparatus to support whatever book he was devouring over lunch. Two swivelling adjustable brass pegs enabled him to keep the pages from fluttering even if the refectory doors were open. He would pause in his meal every so often to ease back the pegs and turn to the next page. We were all jealous, all of us, because most of us had brought the books currently being studied while he – he! – was already familiar with them and could afford to ruminate instead on – among many, many others – *A La Recherché Du Temps Perdu.*

*

I can't for the life remember how soon Fiona will come with tea again. Her daily arrival's one of the certainties. Others include the hum of the laundry car. Atkins it was who schemed he was going to escape in a laundry bag but even the frailest of us realised no one would take a bag with a man inside and on the day in question anyway he did everything right except get into the bag. He was found beside other bags, curled up, his eyes closed. He was on Seven for a month after that. Kandinsky's said more than once as the laundry car arrives – he has no concept of when a joke's worn out – somebody go and check on Atkins! and this even on a day when Atkins is clearly working on his fruit bowl. The frames are pre-made. We weave raffia through till the whole bowl's covered and then there are plastic bobbles ready-made to fit on to each of five metal legs. They sell in charity shops. Major Gwillingington was a fervent weaver till he took up the dozing option. I said to Harry I said: If ever I get that way shoot me. Harry said actually wanting to be shot if you get that way means you're still reasonably well. I said: Thanks but no thanks, Harry.

*

Bulwark and me didn't necessarily like or identify with each other. All the same, after lunch in times of reasonable weather, he'd often request I join him for a wander round the college lake where it was occasionally his wont to point out wild flowers and benign waterfowl and proffer their Latin names. I didn't need to say much myself and so he was allowed full rein. He walked usually with his briefcase in one hand and used the other to embellish what he said. The earth path wound atop the contours beside the artificial lake. Bulwark passed behind any benches with people on and ran galoot-like if ever a swan pestered him. His father had been fatally attacked by one, he told me, and thus swans had become objects of fear. Moorhens, ducks, grebes, pintails, mallards, widgeons, coots, dabchicks – he was fine with these – so much so he would occasionally bring crusts – but at any hint of swan, Bulwark fled. It didn't matter to him he might embarrass himself or that girls laughed. He ran till the danger had passed. Peter, he said one swanless day, I have a confession. I replied languidly: Which is? Following a breath he told me he was in love with Maureen and if she didn't reciprocate he was going to kill himself. This declaration took place at the same time as a haul of crusts towards some nearby ducks. I scratched my head, not because I had an itch, but because it gave me a moment to think. Isn't she married to the Dean? I asked. Deans be buggered, Bulwark answered softly. I asked him (and, as it happened, a crow) if he had made his feelings known to her, hoping he'd say yes he had and that this might explain the tulip dress, but he said no, no, and then no more times till it seemed denial might become a permanent part of the landscape. I wasn't sure if I should advise him to forget it or if I should cite Father's posthumous appraisal of Miss Woo and suggest he took the bull by the horns before it was too late. Maureen could always turn him down and it can't have been the first time she'd had one of us take a shine. There she stood in tulips talking of literature. It was bound to happen. I said most of this to Bulwark,

25

going beyond my usual quota of words. Bulwark said he would certainly take my comments and ingest them or digest them over the weekend. The lake was placid that day. The waterfowl accompanied a vaguely rippled duplicate of themselves. Further along a swell of willow hushed the surface. I wished K was with me to offer Bulwark some even-handed advice, also perhaps to support me. I've realised to my detriment age surely doesn't wither boyhood. It's here as much as ever it was, even as the body becomes heavier, less reliable, digestively uncomfortable, twitched here and there, dry at the lips, itchy at the underside of its testicles. One of the inmates here – Kandinsky possibly – oh months ago – withdrew what he himself referred to as his love machine and offered it to Fiona. No more bourbons for you, she said. It lightened the moment and enabled Kandinsky to put his machine away without recrimination. I don't think he meant anything by it, but it is difficult when your body's coming to the end of its life not to make the occasional gesture. Fiona must have a catalogue of similar anecdotes. I remember the additional hush that fell over the dayroom and Colquahoon's critical flick of his *Times*.

*

After all it was only a hillside, only a monument. K said how much the vale appeared to have been steeped in watery blue. The shoulder of land probed the plain hundreds of feet below. We heard sheep on the wind, the occasional biplane drawing gliders to the correct altitude, the growl of what we liked to think were Morris Minors negotiating the narrow roadway running between hedgerows at this side of the escarpment. The monument had been erected in honour or memory of Q. L. Marjoribanks, a mostly forgotten author from the nineteenth century. K said one of the saddest things about death was you might not ever know people liked you enough to build a monument. We had a discussion then about how sometimes life is partly about the construction and maintenance of memory, giving the illusion it's longer than it really is in the same way (K said mischievously) as a ha-ha gives an unbroken view of the countryside though I told her I didn't think memory was anything like ha-has. We didn't speak much for the last few hundred yards. As ever the monument's stout door was locked against us. Far as I know it hadn't been opened in my lifetime. K would circumnavigate the base looking up, saying when clouds moved overhead it was like she was falling. I'm trying to think now of the last time we were there. In here these things become exceptionally important. Soon as we tired of the monument we would cross to the brass plate set into a stone block that pointed out landmarks and how far they were only we didn't bother reading it any more. Yes, I think on our last walk there we then crossed the hillside to sit at the far side above the quarry. Men from the nineteenth century dug here to get stone to build the monument, K said suddenly. This was information she'd found in a book she'd bought in a charity shop, which gave, she said, intimate details about life in the local area. I said to her I'd been walking round there most of my life and hadn't realised the quarry was formed when they extracted stone for the monument. K said: Not *just* the monument. I chose – yes it's coming back to me – not to ask what else they used the stone for because I was jealous she knew more than me. She went on: The contrasting lighter-coloured stone at the corners and used sporadically throughout the one-hundred-foot structure was quarried elsewhere and brought to the site. I glanced over at it as if to confirm what she'd said and as I did so I had a feeling of morbid attachment to her. I say morbid because though much of it was luxurious, moments like these hurt and yet I knew I couldn't be without her through choice. Neither of us had read anything by Q. L. Marjoribanks. I asked Harry one time if he'd mind looking out for anything by him or her even though I knew there was no way Harry would remember. It's an aspect of my character that mystifies me – why I request things when I know they won't happen. Even if Harry did find something I don't expect I'd read it. The plaque on the monument goes on to let us know Q. L Marjoribanks was best known for historical romances. I'm not sure what they are. Maureen said we should resist the temptation to categorise works of fiction because to do so was to open up the possibility of prejudice. Like with me and Q. L. Marjoribanks. So when anyone asked in the seminar what type of book we were going to be allocated next week, Maureen would say something like: It'll be roughly eight inches by five and on average about three quarters of an inch thick. I see why Bulwark admired her. However I believe he was making the mistake of transferring her literary mystique into the kind of life he imagined for them both, forgetting that even for the best of us mystique is a temporary condition; that come the water bill or gastroenteritis it goes by the board. But oh the love... Maureen said one afternoon leaving what I expect would have been a line of dots had the hanging pause been visible. Bulwark shook his head to himself. His beard remained stationary while his face swivelled within. It wasn't a negative shake I don't think, but a disbelief to himself that having heard these words, he adored her even more. I didn't say any of this to K on the hill because none of it had happened yet. At least I don't think it had. So much overlaps. Smithson said it was a wonder I got safely through any given day. I remember sighing for his benefit and saying yes well I thought so too. I've told Harry about the overlappings. He said being limited in my movement these days should help minimise them. By then I'd lost sight of what *them* were and he'd said *the overlappings you buffoon* and we'd had a laugh about buffoon and were joined by Kandinsky who said it had reminded him of the word *doubloon*, which in turn he said had made him sad about a Spanish girlfriend he'd had years before. Carmineta. Tumbling dark curls, he said. Days of dread. Nights of ecstasy. Atkins asked if by ecstasy he'd meant the mood-altering drug some people took, and Kandinsky – showing tolerance – said no, he'd meant absolute pleasure, bliss. Atkins nodded for longer than I felt necessary and even though I don't think any of us felt he knew quite what bliss was either. Smetham asked where Carmineta was now. It was a question of remarkable coherence given he was eating the cheeseplant. Kandinsky informed the hushed dayroom she was no longer with us. It was fun then to hear nothing but chewing. It was probably out of respect to Kandinsky's feelings Harry hadn't come across to relieve Smetham of the leaf straight away.

*

Maureen blew through her lips, up as far as her fringe, then said I was too colourful for this world and I said thanks Maureen and even wondered if I could cock a snook at Bulwark and fall in love with her myself notwithstanding the Dean. But I pulled away from those notions between drawing my marked dissertation across the desk and reaching the door beyond which stood Bulwark, who'd already retrieved his and was scanning the margins for codes of any kind from his unrequited love. I told him, with gravitas, I had a third but that Maureen had stressed this mark was based entirely on the content and didn't include anything for a quality she couldn't put her finger on that wasn't relevant to J. D. Salinger anyway but which she had really liked, as a person. Bulwark snatched the dissertation from me asking where did it say that forcing me to snatch it back and say it didn't say it anywhere, she'd been speaking off the record. You're making it up, he said and stalked away. I think it was stalked. Half Nazi you might say. I called after him *what did you get* but he swung wordless out to the quad. The following day at lunch it was when he still wouldn't speak to me but happened to have his dissertation on the table beside the steak and kidney pie. It had a first in green at the top of the page and beside it in Maureen's handwriting *Highly Commendable*. He ate his pie more carefully than usual and kept his eyes not on a book supported by his reading apparatus, but the sunken lawn of the quad where girls came and went. He said through beard and pie: Nothing will persuade me she said what you said she said about your work and I said for want of anything better: That's a lot of saids, to which he replied: I'm overwrought. This pie's rubbish too. I took this to mean he'd eventually forgive me, albeit with reservations.

*

Even though I didn't choose life, I was held up to be smacked by the consultant pediatrician who'd been called in to induce me because I'd been displaying an irregular heartbeat. Had I mastered language in the womb I would have said as much to him and Mother while the cord was severed and I was smothered in a blanket. The consultant went home for lunch. I lay beside Mother while she chatted about this and that, interspersing her comments with waggles of my cheek. My early impressions of the world were that it was white with perforations in its ceiling tiles. At the left side of my field of vision lay a curtain covered in what would turn out to be chrysanthemums. A few hours later these were pulled aside by a nurse who introduced us to Mrs Hodgkins in the next bed. Mother held me up to show Mrs Hodgkins. This would have been Paulette if he'd been a girl, she said, but being a boy he's Peter. Mrs Hodgkins held up a similar bundle. This is Alexander, she said. And had *he* been a girl he would have been Alexan*dra*. Mother said she thought both were lovely names altogether whereupon Mrs Hodgkins said she thought Peter a lovely name too. The respective bundles were put down. Life was tedious thus far. Mother breastfed me during which I liked to squeeze my hand into a fist in time with each mouthful. Alexander had a bottle. He cried often. Father came to the hospital after work. He pulled aside one edge of the blanket surrounding my face. He looks like you, Mother said though I wasn't sure if she was talking to me or him. I've wondered since if he was already seeing Miss Woo. Leaning down at me he smelt of beer and smoke. He then took a moment to lean at Alexander. Alexander's response – when wasn't it so! – was to cry inconsolably. Maybe he was taken aback by being born also. You can never tell. Some babies relish it. They can't wait to get cracking. Through a small window high in the opposite wall I could make out grey twigs and beyond these the top of a lamp post that, as the light shone, cast upon the twigs an orange web. It's raining as you arrive in the world, Mother said, but hopefully the sun'll soon shine. Mrs Hodgkins threw an apologetic glance at howling Alexander and said she didn't think he liked wet weather. On my way to be born I'd drifted mutely among planets, marvelling at the enormity of the universe, and it was to this glorious imagination I turned whenever these early hours on earth became too much. Mrs Hodgkins talked at some point about cracked nipples and that's why Alexander was having to face a disadvantageous start. His feet kicked in protest at the lower end of a blue all-over suit. It was odd even then to realise Eliot had come into the world in much the same way and I wonder if the tedium expressed in *in the room the women come and go talking of Michelangelo* meant that he too had been born, as it were, inadvertently. I ushered Harry over recently hoping to strike up a discussion about this but as you might have guessed he'd soon brought the topic round to Dylan and how he thought *Under Milk Wood* something he'd like to have read out – just an extract obviously –

at his funeral whenever that was and he rather hoped the reading would contain a reference to Mrs Ogmore-Pritchard. Oh that I could have written instead of working here, he said. He quickly reassured me this didn't mean he wasn't delighted to tend to us on a daily basis. But then looking round at Atkins, Smetham, Kandinsky and the like I fancied he might well have been making up this last part. I mean Colquahoon alone would give me the absolute willies if I had the job rather than Harry, who has confirmed in confidence the most difficult among us are those who display the fewest symptoms although he later conceded Colquahoon could be plotting rabid insurrection behind that *Times*. I haven't looked at Colquahoon in the same way since to be honest and sometimes I wish I was a bit further from him. Funny then but the moment I was thinking that another thought came in over the top of it like a wave against a sandcastle and the thought was: Where oh where is K, even though looking at it I can see the *oh* isn't needed. Bulwark would say putting *oh* and another *where* wouldn't convince anyone I missed her any more than if I'd put just one *where* and no *ohs* at all. In fact, he would go on, our desire to express the greatness of a thing often reduces its greatness. He'd said this as we were at two on the aquatic clock that was the college lake. It was a muggy, swan-free afternoon and we were the only people about. Mugginess hung among the bulrushes that rose from the water in clumps here, and to our left the ground led into a spread of mature pines that held its needle floor and aromatic shadow jealously. How are things in respect of Maureen? I said. He made a sound then – something like grshhhhh. I waited half a minute to see if this was going to be followed by words, then said: So I take it all's no further forward? He said no, all wasn't, snappily. It seemed, he went on, he was doomed to love her for all time with no return. I suggested that creatively such a non-return could be productive and mentioned Gerard Manley Hopkins who we'd been doing in an associated seminar. Bulwark ignored this and went on to say if it carried on like this much longer he might jack in the course so I said well that's better anyway than killing yourself, to which Bulwark replied he still intended to kill himself but not before he'd made the gesture of abandoning his studies, and by implication Maureen with them, so that he had at least some time to judge the effect of his withdrawal before taking that final step. We paused awhile to enjoy a bench set atop a mound close to the pine trees. The bench had been gifted to the college by the wife of the man who'd taught History here for over twenty-five years though this was before our time, our being Bulwark and me. I felt strangely conspicuous atop the mound that afternoon, thinking some of the students who lived in halls would watch us through binoculars. She gets me right here, Bulwark said, punching the side of his head. I was feeling even less talkative thanks to the mugginess but managed to say I could see it would be immensely difficult having feelings of that magnitude unreciprocated. It says it all in the books of course, he said, but that's not the same as when it attacks in real life. I thought this a clumsy sentence from Bulwark altogether and put it down to emotional distress. I suppose you can only pray really, I said, to which he replied he wasn't one for mumbo jumbo. Even if you don't believe in anything, I said, prayer can be useful. Spoken regularly, it can in fact adjust your inner temperature. I regret using the word temperature but it was the only one to come. Given the moment again I might well use *landscape* instead even though that's not quite what I meant either. You don't smoke, do you? Bulwark said. Taking a silver tin from his pocket, he opened it to reveal a number of ready-rolled cigarettes. Not me, I said. He said: Love has enticed me to take it up again after a gap. Today's Day Two, I'm finding it hard but I'm determined. I laughed slightly because I hadn't come across anyone determined to start smoking. It didn't hang well with the scope of his beard besides. When he'd taken out a cigarette and put the tin back in his pocket, he lodged the cigarette in his lips and carefully parted his beard on four sides before lighting up. He inhaled, arching his neck back to give the smoke direct access to his lungs. After fifteen seconds of not breathing he then leaned his head forward and exhaled. It makes me sick and dizzy, he said. I didn't say: Then don't do it, because I felt this would be too obvious. In a week or so I daresay that'll have passed, he went on.

*

Besides, said Harry, if I had my way I'd make your Eliot cut the line *Like a patient etherised upon a table.* I looked round thinking he must have been already in conversation with someone, Kandinsky perhaps, but no, it turned out he was speaking to me and that I hadn't heard any of the earlier part of what he'd said. It was an instance of a fairly regular occurrence already noted about me by others – but of which I hadn't myself been aware – called Dimming of Realisation. When Harry told me about the dimming I was annoyed no one had mentioned it before. He said that because most of the time I didn't seem to notice, they hadn't seen any point in pointing it out. With your condition, he said, this type of event is common and tends to increase over time. It'll mean, he added, you'll have a gradual sense of your immediate past being peppered with holes. My great-aunt had that, Kandinsky said. He has acute hearing brought on by a condition of his own, namely Overly Enhanced Auricular Reception. The enhancement thereof apparently increases as the rest of him decreases. So eventually I got round to asking Harry why he'd like Eliot to cut *Like a patient etherised upon a table*, especially since he didn't care much about him in the first place. He said he didn't have time now but he'd catch up later. He'd sensed in me I expect that if I was having a spate of realisation dimming it might not be the best time to carry on. Conversations about Eliot and the like demand concentration. During that afternoon – and in the absence of Harry – I thought about Eliot's phrase myself and could see that, yes, etherised wasn't a good word and, well, I probably wouldn't say *upon* because it sounded too formal. Besides we were told – by Jugg I believe – that simile was a poor way to express yourself. Once Jugg came into my mind I started to get angry. How on earth, I was thinking, could an evening – that's what Eliot had been referring to – be anything *like* a patient etherised on a table? My annoyance permeated the others, inciting Tobias Mawk to holler. It led me to call for Harry and tell him he should be careful which poets he mentioned. Yes, it absolutely was Jugg. Be wary, he said, if ever you find yourself saying so-and-so is *like* so-and-so. Ask yourself, he said, is it *really* like so-and-so? and if it is, does describing it in this way *add* to the original object or idea? We left class amazed, apart from Alexander who – as he boasted later – took such things in his stride.

It's explained how medication liaises with brain chemicals to effect subtle, positive change. I said to Harry as he handed me my pills and cuplet one day, I said: How do we know what these things might do in the long term? I went on to remind him the brain was a delicate mechanism I supposed it risky to tamper with. Harry said my particular ensemble had been around donkey's years and nothing but good had been said about any of them. Then how come most nights I dream of *Great Expectations*? I said. Not only that, but the ensemble seems to be responsible for forging a repeated rough and tumble between Mrs Joe and Abel Magwitch. I must have maintained one of my straight faces when I told Harry this because instead of smiling, he went off and – bet you anything – made a note. From then on he occasionally enquired after my *Great Expectations* dreams. The ones I made up were mostly based on Lean's 1946 film of the book starring John Mills as the older Pip. Young Pip I liked but not this older one. Some would say we're not *meant* to like him. And as for the grotesque older Estella! I said to Harry, and went into what was later described as a paroxysm. I hadn't liked her in the film nor my dream and I felt however much we weren't meant to like her Lean would have been better to have cast someone enigmatic to rationalise Pip's devotion. I was haunted by the marshes down by the forge and visited them in imagination to afford solace. K bought me a tape of the film for Christmas one year. You take a woman like K and she goes out and gets you something to magnify life while I might roam shops for days only managing to come up with the least suitable gift, bath salts you might say as a last resort, but never daring anything in the clothing line. Unable to watch the tape any more, I often enjoy a few remembered minutes of it during daytime. Pip creeping to the graveyard or him and Herbert Pocket fighting in Miss Havisham's garden.

Must be one hell of a story in Colquahoon's inner pages. Or maybe he's fallen into a state. States are something we're subject to yet none of us seem fazed by the variety of them, choosing instead only to adapt. Thinking back I suppose I first went into a state as I was walking home with

Ormerod. We were nearing the pond surrounded by willows where we'd heard there was a heron from time to time when suddenly – bless it! – the sky became triangularly crackled and next thing I was lying on the grass being wafted by Ormerod's imaginary exercise book. In that way he had, he asked, once I'd recovered consciousness and got to my feet, if we were still going to look for the heron. I told him I didn't think birds appropriate in the circumstances and he said oh okay then and went with me as far as my gate. Mother was at home with her feet up and resting her eyes. We went through the before and after and all I could say was the world had been fuzzier than usual prior to the incident. She thought it best to hold off from the doctor's till Father came home. I waited, hoping not to die, till five thirty only he didn't arrive and later phoned from the Moon and Sixpence to say he'd bumped into an old workmate. Peter's had a turn, Mother said. I didn't hear what Father said but Mother put the phone down as if it would bite her if she replaced the receiver quickly. Your father says it's probably nothing and you should get yourself to bed. I struggled up the stairs, some of my struggle feigned I guess, half hoping Ormerod would come to see how I was. My room faced on to the road. I watched boys with a greater life expectancy playing marbles. The evening tore with swifts and the chimes of ice cream. I believe both Mother and me thought Father wasn't really at the Moon and Sixpence. Since the Miss Woo business neither of us trusted him. The thing for fathers is that if they've ever had a Miss Woo it's unlikely anyone close to them will believe their Moon and Sixpence stories again. I watched Mother go next door to see if Mrs Chaffin was home. Mrs Chaffin knew about boys thanks to *The Popular Remedy Handbook*. The occasional seagull bewitched the evening. I think to myself now well *were* there seagulls? I mean were there? The dog from up the road wandered here and there, sitting down whenever he couldn't think of anything else. Maybe he was regretting not being able to play marbles. If dogs *did* know they were dogs there must be times they feel down about it. Oh for longer life and an opposable thumb, they might say. It was a wish of K's to have a dog of her own one day. She said it was easier to go walking if you had one because you felt you had company. She said this in such a way as to suggest she might be needing more human company while walking than she currently had. She could be accused of not quite saying what she really meant. We were along by the millpond. It was an evening of dragonflies and above us more swifts racing from one end of the water to the other and drawing from the surface a musty smell, something rich, heart-rending, something, K said, that altogether soothed her. Maybe ozone's a way to describe it, I said and she said no, that was totally the wrong word and I said: Yes I see that now though I didn't. It was my habit to accede to her sentiments after a brief internal struggle, if you like, whereby I tested the possibility of disagreeing and, finding myself without courage, eventually decided against it. You really are peppery, she said then and I said: Don't you mean papery? Although if she *had* meant papery I still wouldn't have understood, but it turned out she meant I was scattered in my thoughts and feelings. I said that was nothing like pepper and that furthermore Jugg would have condemned the simile. She tried to explain as we went along how the earth was issuing a peppery fragrance and that something of this must have made the word peppery come out even though now she thought of it she really felt there was something accurate in it about me. By then the moon had begun to pass among the trees making webs out of their twigs and leaves. I've got that job in the Faculty, she said. Great, I said. I remember using that exact word. We'd both recently finished at our respective colleges. Congratulations, I went on. But I don't want you coming in there making fun of me, she said. I'll have to concentrate. You have my word, I said. I didn't know right then that the following morning a letter would arrive saying I had to start very soon at the Office. Had I known, I may have savoured our walk more. It would be entirely valuable to live life twice, the second time with knowledge of how it had gone before so there was ever an opportunity to perceive irony. Have you heard from the Office yet? K said. I said I hadn't, and didn't expect they'd want me anyhow. She said there you go again and I said there I go what?

*

Colquahoon spent some of his career in banking, earning enough eventually to buy a home round here for his retirement. He told Kandinsky this months ago. Kandinsky nodded. To me it seemed the act of nodding was hammering into place the facts imparted to him. I was all ears then because I felt Kandinsky might reciprocate with autobiographical facts of his own. There'd been rumours of a far country and making money illegally. He shot people for a suitable remuneration, Atkins said. We each thought about this for a while. I'd say the consensus was Atkins had misheard or was making it up. Atkins himself had been a writer long ago. He'd had four novels published in his career, one of them making it as an adaptation to the small screen. Those were the days, Atkins said, though rather than reminiscing, it turned out this was the name of the novel and one-off television drama. The nudity caused a stir, he said. This was when a glimpse of breast shocked the entire country, and I had four pairs in the one programme. He shook his head and made a movement with his finger along his top lip. Kandinsky said he didn't think a television play having breasts was anything necessarily to be proud of and Atkins – adjusting himself in an attempt to placate – said he was merely mentioning the breasts because that was what hit the headlines. He'd have preferred it if the public had been stirred by the metaphysical content. The way Atkins's finger moved made me feel there probably hadn't been any metaphysical content really. Jaundice reckoned television producers in those days put a breast or breasts into a production to boost audience numbers, less so today when bodies were two a penny and with the Internet all kinds of parts were there at the click of a mouse. You mean porn, said Atkins. Jaundice huffed, at least that's what it sounded like, adding: I'm not that way inclined, thank you. It was a day controversy kept threatening to overwhelm us but invariably ebbed before damage was done. The various incidents of that time made me feel once again I wasn't suited to the environment. I decided to have it out with Harry. When eventually my chance came, he assured me he'd note my concerns and pass them on to the Administrator. I don't know if he ever did or whether the Administrator just hasn't got round to them. Time in here runs at a more elongated rate than elsewhere. Elsewhere inclines me to gaze past stilled men on the patio to the lawn and beyond the hedgerow to the world at large. I remember on the way here a packhorse bridge crossing a slow-moving river. The driver said on summer nights further along a ferry carried passengers to and from the public house on the far bank. I went there once with the missus, he said brightly. I wondered who the missus was. In a sense I'd always wanted one myself, in theory at least. Smithson declared to have and keep one required a selflessness he didn't feel I'd be able to maintain. I dared at the time to ask if there was a Mrs Smithson and he passed to the window, looking out while he explained there had been one but that she was now deceased. When I ask people if they have a wife and they tell me there was one but now she was deceased it makes me want to die myself. Smithson stayed at the window longer than could be attributed to one of his therapeutic pauses. In the end I told him I was sorry for bringing her up. He said it wasn't my fault but that in general it would be best if I left him to ask the questions. Otherwise we risk cross-contamination, he said. Though to invite entanglement is instinctive in us as a species, he went on, it isn't useful from a therapeutic point of view. I told him I saw that now. Suffice to say, he said – keen to continue doing what he'd said we shouldn't – Mrs Smithson was the world to me and for a long time after her passing my own world, in effect, passed too. I had to see a Therapeutic Specialist myself. He leaned against the sill in what had become a favoured pose. Even curiouser, he said – though I couldn't recall him having said anything was curious so far – *that* Therapeutic Specialist's name was Smithson. It was like – he said – I was visiting myself. I turned on to my side and looked towards his tweed back. I said to it: I'm sorry there's no Mrs Smithson these days. Sorry too if asking the question endangered the integrity of our sessions. Apart from this one turning-on-to-my-side I'll make sure everything stays above board from now on. Smithson said: Good, good, without turning. I believe he was surveying the town maybe with an underlay of memories about Mrs Smithson herself. She was the air I breathed, he said. Or breathe. Either was remarkable. Especially for a man steeped in Therapeutic Specialism, which – let's face it – so often tries to rationalise love itself as little more than a symptom. For years after her death I had night and day the sensation of her hand in mine, he said. And in bed her breath against my neck. She always slept against me from the back you see. And on the wind, especially in spring,

I catch her perfume. I said to him: It still happens you mean? He reminded me of what he'd said about my asking questions. In despair one night, he said, I looked out every photo I had of her and threw them on the fire. I wanted the haunting to stop however much I loved her. In the end a lost love has to fall into its natural place. A place that – yes – has significance but which is yet small enough to allow the continuation of everyday life. Mostly, burning the photos did the trick. She was never as powerful after that, but oh don't ever think that means I haven't missed her, oh God no. He opened the window then to take a breath before closing it again and settling onto his chair at the head-end of the couch. I turned back, hoping these observations about Mrs Smithson might make it all right for me to talk a little about K, though every time I'd tried till then led to him getting agitated. It's never easy hearing of devotions other than your own.

*

Bulwark eventually succeeded in smoking heavily. The sickness passed, and what had started out as a mild interest in tobacco soon became rigorous necessity. He usually lit up once we were at the far side of the college lake, though he liked to keep his habit hidden from any girls coming by. I use the word girls because it was how Bulwark referred to them. He knew they were beyond the age where to call them girls was politically or morally satisfying, but we both had taken up a silent contract to let the matter rest because Bulwark's character was more suited to the word. A spread of pines fifty yards inside the woodland perimeter was where he liked to smoke most. I could see – mostly thanks to Smithson's teachings – that in hiding while smoking he was in fact hiding from himself. If anything he blamed his relapse on Maureen's reluctance to become involved – for this is how he construed her deter-mination to continue teaching in the usual fashion even though he loved her. The Dean's out of town for a few days soon, he said. A conference. They're always having conferences. He took a drag. It'll be a good time to tell her my feelings. I told him I didn't think the Dean being out of town would have much effect on the overall result. He said that in some ways he agreed, but that if there was the slightest chance she felt the same, this tactic allowed her to take advantage safely. His beard

39

had lately led me to think more of Edward Lear. I'd skimmed through a book about him around the same time. At night when sleep evaded me I tried composing limericks about Bulwark's situation. I didn't get far because of the lack of rhymes. I asked our Professor of Poetry, Piers Smoon, about Lear and if he too thought him an extraordinary fellow – wishing Bulwark had himself been called Smoon to ease the rhyming – but Smoon insisted he hadn't ever given Lear much thought and therefore didn't give limericks much thought either. He hanged himself the next day. Though this might explain why he wasn't bothered about Lear or limericks, I still find myself resenting him for being dismissive of my interest.

*

Mrs Chaffin said Miss Woo was most likely a trollop. With what she knew of trollops, she felt men would always find it difficult not to give in to their charms. Mother said she wasn't helping and Mrs Chaffin said: It's as well to hear the truth Doreen. Mother was pegging at the time, damp vests, Father's pants, a universe of socks, her nylons, it was like parts of us usually hidden being put on show for the occasion. There's plenty of trollops where she comes from. Mrs Chaffin looked aside as if fearful of her own information. She was born here apparently though Dolly, Mother said. Mrs Chaffin squealed at something in her garden. Almost immediately a cat scratched over the fence and raced across ours. Then Mrs Chaffin said: It'll be in her genes though. Mother kept her eye on the cat till it had passed through to the next garden. Though there was a reasonably stout wooden fence between us and Mrs Chaffin, there were only three strands of wire held up at intervals by cancerous concrete posts between us and Mr Pervert. It was Prevett really but the joke had started when he was at school himself and it had stuck. I wonder how many other husbands have been ruined by her, Mother said, turning back to Mrs Chaffin. More than's good for her I'll wager, Mrs Chaffin said, pulling a face at me. She was aware I was being ignored and wanted me to have something to do. Interpreting pulled faces was always good for a few moments. The odd thing is people of her race are usually so polite and proper, Mother said. Mrs Chaffin shook her head and nodded at the same time. The worst type of trollops are, she said. That's why they cause havoc. A good day's housework would wipe the smile off her face. Mother cast a glance towards the rhubarb Father grew in chimney pots. I'd say the glance meant she was fed up now of talking about Miss Woo. Mrs Chaffin must have noticed because she said: Well Doreen, I'll be getting on in now but pop round for a cuppa later if you fancy. I didn't comprehend the world of cuppas. To stave it off I passed round to the front of the house to stand at the gate and watch the road stretching to infinity in both directions. The boys were still playing marbles. The dog from up the road padded off the kerb and started to cross. When a rare car came he stopped where he was as if considering suicide but moved on at the last moment. He was renowned for unruly fur and a solemn aspect to the tail. I'd tried calling but he always ignored me. I'm steering clear of uncertain boys, he seemed to say. I picked flakes of paint from the top rail of our tubular metal gate. I was all out of grandmothers. My last one had died weeks before. Father was hoping to get her three-piece walnut bedroom suite. He said the dressing table had two side mirrors that if arranged in the right way could show you hundreds of yourself. She'd been burned in the crematorium then put in an urn Father kept in the shed. This is what it comes to, he said. Remember that. I told him I would. And the petunias. I asked him if the greyish dust was really her. When the dog reached the far side of the road he sniffed at some nettles and wandered deep into the bushes. He belonged to someone who let him out when they went to work and most often brought him in when they came back. In the small pond to my right goldfish swam round for the trillionth time. A noise behind me turned out to be the door opening and Mother flapping the hall mat. You mind that road, she said. Funnily enough Mrs Chaffin's door opened just after Mother closed hers. She too flapped a mat. When she'd closed the door again I leaned against the top of the gate thinking about mats and how it must be irksome to mothers to have to stay home flapping them. I left the gate and scuffed back round the house. I walked along the central path, eyeing the vegetable patch and shed one side, the cold remnants of Father's bonfire on the other, and soon came to the privet hedge that marked the end of our garden. Through it in summer you might see Mrs Belvoir sunbathing. Mrs Chaffin had warned Mother about Mrs Belvoir many times within earshot of me. She felt if Father had been vulnerable to Miss Woo who lived up the road, how safe was he with a half-naked woman yards away. Mrs Belvoir's husband – Mr Belvoir – had worked on coal lorries for years and according to her was built like an ox so Mother didn't see Father taking risks. At the time of that conversation I held up my hand. It was how I felt I might get a word in edgeways but both Mrs Chaffin and Mother ignored me. I'd been hoping to ask what an ox was. The sun contrived just then to cast itself through the shed window, illuminating Grandmother. She'd wanted burning to make absolutely sure, I'd heard Mother say to Mrs Chaffin.

*

Another line Harry didn't like was: *Oh, do not ask, 'What is it?' Let us go and make our visit.* The rhyming was overly simplistic, he said. I said maybe its simpleness was meant to convey superficiality in respect of the narrator's intention. As I said this I had a sensation in my chest as if an ice wind had blown through it. Fearing I was about to die, I mentioned it to Harry who said it sounded like a mild panic attack. It might be bothersome, he said, but it won't do you any harm. I had the wherewithal in my panic to say to Harry I'd enjoyed the word bothersome, which wouldn't have been out of place spoken by Pooh. He said: Winnie The Pooh? And I said: How many other Poohs do you know? whereupon he had a laugh but not a real one. It was the kind you ushered in as a way of drawing to a close a conversation. Major Gwillingington (who was talking in those days) said his father had been friends with a.a. (as he called the author). I didn't like then to pursue the bothersome connection because it was such a thin reference to Pooh when it was likely if pressed the Major could have provided all manner of incontestable facts. Besides, the panic led me to be quiet for a time repeating the prayer K taught me. God grant me, it said, the serenity to accept the things I cannot change, the courage to change the things I can and the wisdom to know the difference. We were at the coast, eating beef and cheese sandwiches between her dips in a cold sea. It's the prayer they use at the end of AA meetings, she said. All this time and you've not mentioned any such prayer, I said. I make a point of keeping some things confidential, she said. AA is anonymous after all. In the pause we watched a wave thump to the sand. Sounds to me like you're getting into a sea-mood already, she said. I had another large bite, chewing with difficulty various reflections. As the water from the wave withdrew across a band of pebbles and after I'd momentarily emptied my mouth, I told her I didn't know I *had* sea-moods and she said: Oh yes, you go peculiar minutes after you set foot on a beach. I was halfway through the next sandwich before I mumbled: How do I know this apparent analysis of my mood in respect of the sea and beaches isn't rather *you* having a mood? After all, I don't feel I've given you any reason to suppose I'm in anything at all. Well, she said, for a start look at the way you're eating. I can hardly have a satisfactory view, I said, because for most of the time the sandwich is near or in my mouth. That's my point, she said. Sea-moods make you bite off too much at once. Sometimes I wonder why you profess to care about me, I said. I mean already this week we've had observations about the hair in my ears, my coughing into the mouthpiece when we're on the phone, the dried tomato sauce on my gardening shirt and how I never hold my head absolutely vertical when walking. K sighed through her teeth. There you are, she said, calling it a gardening shirt even though you don't ever do anything out there so you can get away with it being covered in stains. Each time a wave struck the beach it intensified a smell of seaweed. Taking care to nibble my sandwich, I felt it typical of K she had only made reference to one of my complaints, presumably because she felt I did have grounds for not liking the others. The only way you'd be justified in making any reference to my mood when I'm by the sea, I said, is that I sometimes find myself wondering why it is that such a variance of our usual behaviour – and by 'our' I mean human beings – is suddenly acceptable because we occupy a swathe of eroded rock between the ocean and what I suppose we would more usually call the land. For example, were you to remove your top now I daresay no one would bat much of an eyelid. But do the same in the supermarket... I let my next nibble act as punctuation. Trust you to bring it down to sex, she said. She took up then a stick of celery. I wasn't referring to your upper half in a sexual sense, I said, merely citing it as a convenient way of bringing home a point. I could have easily used, I suppose, you lying down in the cereal aisle of a supermarket and singing the national anthem but the example I gave sprang to mind first, maybe because here you are wearing a bikini opposite me. That's another point, she said, using her free hand to loiter through a Tupperware box of tomatoes, here you are on a beach dressed like you're at home. You know full well I feel the cold more than you, I said. We ate in silence for a time. I wondered if I should say I loved her. Though more often than not these days the phrase seemed to antagonise. And don't say you love me, she said, just because you think it might make things better. Nothing was further from my mind, I said, but you're right that I am thinking about A) how we got into this discussion and B) can I hope to find a way out of it soon given we're supposed to be having a *nice* day? Remember *nice*? It's the word you used when first mooting the idea of today's trip. Despite the beef and cheese I was visited by the voice of Jugg reminding me not to use nice because it was weak and tasteless. I could see it *sounded* weak because the n was indistinct and the ice too slippery, but tasteless I couldn't see and went home to look it up only to find it had been used by Shakespeare and Milton too, and so one moon night I wrote a letter of complaint to Mr Lee hoping to get my own back on Jugg for good and all but in the night I had a dream where another Indian – a Chief this time – explained in language suited to my age that of all human instincts getting your own back was one of the most futile and was one of the signs, the Chief said, of immaturity. *Do away with it for the love of Him In Sky*, he boomed, so loudly it woke me and there I was with the half-written letter saliva-stained where I'd fallen asleep with it on my pillow. In the morning, though I felt more rested, the voice of the Chief stayed with me and so the letter was never finished. I felt I might mention this to K if our conversation continued to get out of hand. She looked across the beach and said: Take those… I followed her line of vision to see a man and woman, younger than us, playing Frisbee while a dog bounded and barked between them. You wouldn't say either of those was uptight would you? I turned back, my head lowered. I lifted one corner of my next sandwich to reveal a marbled area of roast beef. We have neither Frisbee nor dog, I said. That's not the point, she said. She took up a cherry tomato and bit into it. She wiped away some pulp that had fallen to her chin. So what is your point? I asked. Well you and me have lost the art of fun, she said. Oh fun is it now, I said. I hadn't meant to say it like that. An elderly man with white legs and pot belly had come round the headland, paddling through skeins of water as each reached over the sand. He looked like he may have been a naval captain at one time. Thanks to Jugg it was too that I never got naval and navel mixed up. A navel captain would have been a different sort of man altogether. I laughed inwardly and in so doing felt myself liked by K again and so my mood lifted and as it lifted I realised yes, I *had* been in a mood since we'd arrived and a sea-mood to boot. I didn't have to say anything about the mood having lifted because I could tell K could *see* it had. We covered the picnic things with a tea towel and walked along the beach. Yes, I did feel foolish now because the temperature had risen and I was wearing more than most people. K folded her arms across her midriff and seemed to be watching her feet swing across the sand. Sorry for going on at you, she said. I said it was okay and reiterated to her that I had seen I was indeed in a mood when we first arrived and though it was a mystery, I could also see she was right about me having moods when we came to beaches. The improving situation between us inspired me to select a pebble and throw it into the waves. Moments later the dog belonging to the couple raced in front of us and hopped through the shallows, pausing before long with a paw raised. If this one knew he was a dog, he didn't seem to mind. Don't throw any more, you'll get him worked up, K said. I told her I didn't think I should take the dog into consideration when thinking about whether to throw pebbles whereupon K said I might annoy the couple if I did it again. I had to think carefully about this. I felt if this line of reasoning on K's part continued it could well mean *she* was in a mood after all regardless of whether I'd been in one myself. My insides seemed to be nudging upwards into my throat to say this. It would have been my way of asserting myself, but the Chief was there to persuade me to hold my tongue, not generally, but just about any critical observation K might make. We were almost at the elderly man who'd been walking ahead of us. The flesh at his waist was threaded with veins. If he had been a naval captain maybe he came to the sea periodically to recall his career more vividly, even though his legs now lacked command. K and me parted to pass round him on both sides. K said hello to him so I said hiya. I wondered if he'd resist looking at K in the bikini. Probably naval captains did it as much as anyone. K said matter-of-factly to me: You might get a haircut soon. It's sticking up. In between its early lying-flat stage and its later lying-flat stage there is, yes, a sticking-up phase, I said softly. That's right, she said, so I was wondering if we might not bother waiting for the later lying-flat stage and get it cut in the near future. I ran my hand across it. I'm not sure why. Had anyone been watching they might have taken it as a checking on my part that I had hair at all. I thought to distract us from the topic by finding a second pebble. The dog was upon me almost before I'd come upright. Some dogs, you look at them and you can see it in their eyes that if you had a mind to take them home they'd adapt instantly. This was a collie with streaks of white in its dark coat. Its lower half dripped. Each time I raised my hand as if to throw, it ran a little way into the waves. K said: I thought we'd agreed not to throw any more pebbles while the dog was here. I made no such agreement, I said, imbuing my voice with a softness I hoped would enable K to differentiate between a sea-mood and appropriate self-defence. I mean dogs ran for pebbles and sticks. That's what dogs did. This one was beginning to steam even as it waited for me to make my mind up. After a few more yards I indeed threw the pebble, but made it land further along the beach. Thank you for not throwing it into the water at least, K said. I'm glad you take some notice of what I say occasionally. Now you're straying into overly critical territory, I said. If it persists I'll be forced to conclude it's ninety-nine per cent you that's in a mood rather than me, who, let's face it, we've been focusing on until now. Another characteristic of these sea-moods of yours, K said, is that you elongate. For example, saying until instead of till. On the contrary, I said, I am just choosing to speak carefully because I sense that the wrong word in *any* context could cause you to get even more irritable. Oh so it's me who's irritable, she said. Excuse me, I said, but surely you admitted as much earlier. I was just trying to keep the peace, she said. At that moment I was envious of the naval captain, who'd caught up with us due to the slowness we'd adopted in this stage of our discussion. As if to suit the pattern of movement we'd chosen earlier when overtaking him, he slid between the two of us, his hands clasped behind his back. Nice dog, he said. Oh, it isn't ours, I said. I waved my hand casually in the direction of the Frisbee couple although the captain couldn't possibly have seen it. It just adopted us because of the interest we've been taking. Dogs need to be made a fuss of as much as anyone. I was always told to think of them as I would a child. The captain was several paces ahead and probably hadn't heard. K said: And now you're saying you've always been told to think of dogs in a certain way but I bet you've *never* been told anything about dogs let alone that. Of course I've been told stuff about dogs, I said. Over the years I mean. Stuff about dogs *has* come up. And even if no one has specifically told me to think of them as I would think of a child, it stands to reason given they are fairly sophisticated creatures generally that we shouldn't abuse them. Calm down, she said. She couldn't think how we'd got on to dogs anyway. I told her we'd got on to dogs because she'd complained about me throwing this one a water-bound pebble. You always turn things round so they look like my fault, she said. I'm wondering if you do it with everyone. I don't always turn things round, I said, though it sounded flimsy by then. I'd been feeling sad about the captain's enormous shorts. The feet too, which were extraordinarily broad, again tending to highlight the thinness of the legs. All of a sudden K scurried to one side, ran heavily into the water and fell against the first large wave. The captain came to a halt, turning to face the sea himself. Strong swimmer your young lady, he said. I acknowledged this as I walked on. Water is her element if any of them are, I said.

*

Or should it be *is*? There are times I've wanted Jugg and his MA (Oxon) on hand. I asked Colquahoon a few weeks back Why Oxon? He mumbled about Anglo-Saxons. Then I thought I should ask Harry in the hope of clarification but thinking about asking Harry and asking Harry proved to be different things. We must get used to the brain having more of a free rein than would normally be suitable. Jaundice has a condition that allows him to recognise objects and to know the name for an object but then not be able to associate that name *with* the object. One side of his perception triangle's missing. Harry said they've tried to replace the missing side chemically, but this is a hit and miss affair and even if it does one day end up restoring the triangle a penny to a pound some other condition will have manifested itself. Life is a death sentence after all. Trying to restore triangles to those who've lost them is not unlike trying to hold a surfeit of balloons. I was kind of hoping when I said the balloon thing to Harry he might tell me I was still several short of the problem myself but all he did was scowl and walk away. Being hideously self-centred I took this to mean he thought me a lunatic, but it could have easily been a headache or an argument at breakfast with Cheryl. K used to tell me off about it. She'd say I could only relate to things on the basis of my own experience and that if I was to improve our relationship I'd have to learn how to see things through *her* eyes too. The pizza cafe was busy. She always ordered quatre fromages even though I'd given speeches on more than one occasion about how weary I was of ordinary things being given French names. She picked up with her fork an olive from the side-dish and flicked it at me. I moved my head. It fell beyond me to the floor and rolled to the foot of a local television presenter who was eating with a companion. The olive that is. K had been asking earlier if I felt it appropriate to ask for his autograph. I said I thought he'd probably prefer to be left alone. Besides, I said, what was an autograph and why were we keen to have them? Don't get Freudian on me, she said. I told her I didn't see Freud had anything to do with it. Well, she said, it's just that if I ever want to do an ordinary thing like ask someone famous for their autograph you start theorising. I'd hardly say being a local TV presenter makes someone famous, I said, besides which I've been thinking about fame too and wondering what it is and why so many of us wish we had it. Not only that (I said, waving my own fork) but then why so many who do have it seek to conceal themselves by disguise or isolation. I won't be coming for any more pizzas with you, she said. She then prepared to hurl a subsequent olive. Please don't do it again, I said quietly. We are above an age where such a thing is amusing or playful. She held the olive up. It was black, pitted. Do you ever look at an olive and ask yourself where it came from? she asked. Italy or somewhere like that probably, I said. No, K said. I mean *exactly*. Which tree, which branch of which tree, which twig, how far along the twig. I asked if she was okay. She said yes, she just wanted me to have a taste of what it's like. I'm not following, I said. And yet you so often do, she said. She ate the olive. She then carried on eating pizza. Her front teeth shone. She'd always looked after them.

*

Soon as my heartbeat regulated I was taken in a taxi with Mother, Alexander and Mrs Hodgkins who it turned out lived near us. Against Mother's shoulder I watched the world recede. It was still raining. Down to my left Alexander lay horizontal in his mum's lap. I was worn out, as if this was my umpteenth attempt at existence. The taxi driver was saying he hadn't seen weather like this for many a year and if it kept on much longer there'd be flooding down the water meadows where his sister had tea-rooms. As he braked to avoid a cyclist, Mother and I lurched forward. You will be careful won't you driver? Mrs Hodgkins said. Alexander's been sick. I must have missed this. I checked him again. Sure enough a line of white ran from the corner of his mouth. I turned back to the window. Your sister has the tea-rooms? Mother asked in a voice that started fairly high and ended even higher. Me and my husband used to go there in our courting days. We loved the macaroons. Really? How long ago are we talking? the taxi driver asked. About five years, Mother said. Oh old man Grayson had the tea-rooms then, the driver said. My sister only took over about three years ago. You can't get a good macaroon like you used to be able to though, Mrs Hodgkins said. The taxi driver said right enough, the world was going to the dogs. I enjoyed the word dogs even though at that time I couldn't have known to which objects it belonged. Like Jaundice, I suppose I lacked triangulation. Tell you what Doreen, you must come round for a cuppa when you're settled, Mrs Hodgkins said. It might be nice if Peter and Alexander got to know each other. It's important for youngsters to have playmates. It helps get them ready for the world. A sociable baby's a happy baby. I believe everyone was stunned to hear so much from Mrs Hodgkins, none more so than Alexander who'd turned his eyes to her. This is the age at which you can be amazed and regurgitate simultaneously. More milky liquid ran down his chin, pooling against the ruffle of his blanket. The silence of Mother and the taxi driver was maintained till they were sure Mrs Hodgkins had finished speaking. If you go down there again, the taxi driver said, say Frank said to say hello. I felt this an overly complex way of going about things. I will, Mother said, though heaven knows when now we've got this rascal. A sensation within I put down to early guilt. Mrs Hodgkins wanted to know if my father was good with babies. Mother held me further away from her. We'll have to see, she said, each word accompanied by a bounce. It had become evident bounces were something babies had to endure from the outset. I knew if I smiled as Mother bounced me it was likely the bouncing would increase so I turned my mouth down. And is diddums going to cry? Mother said. Diddums heralded a bout of waggling while Mother held my face close to her own. For all I knew at that moment, life was this one journey with Frank, Mrs Hodgkins and Alexander. Back against Mother's shoulder I watched more shops, more shoppers, and at one point what would prove to be a church with a graveyard, pass. Mother nudged Mrs Hodgkins. That's where his grandfather's buried, she said. Mrs Hodgkins ooh'd. What a small world Doreen, so's Alexander's. How long ago? Oh twenty years, Mother said. His too, said Mrs Hodgkins. I managed to get my head round again to have a look at Alexander. A bubble swelled from his nostril. You know what I think Doreen? I reckon it was fate you and me ended up in beds next to each other. I wasn't surprised when Mother found this comment difficult to respond to. I could tell by minuscule movements of her head she was thinking of something else to say. What about your husband? she said eventually. Is he good with them? Who? My Raymond? Mrs Hodgkins said. He's been so looking forward to having you home hasn't he? She'd changed the person she was addressing midway, confusing Alexander. He's been busy for weeks decorating the spare room. He found stork wallpaper. We believe it's in the baby's interests to get him used to his own company straight away. We've got a book. *Baby and Me* by Doctor Whatsit. Oh, I've heard of it, Mother said, using her amazed voice, they say it's good. It is, Mrs Hodgkins said. There's nothing about babies you won't find in there. Alexander's amusement succeeded in bursting the bubble. I'll lend you my copy, Mrs Hodgkins said. No need Mrs Hodgkins, really, said Mother. I'll get my husband to look one out for me. Mrs Hodgkins patted Mother's knee. Well you just tell me if he doesn't, she said. A sensation in my stomach of being drawn backwards as the taxi slowed. This is me, Mrs Hodgkins said. Here we are Alexander. Funny how quick journeys go when you've got someone to chat to. It is, said Mother.

*

Harry says when the mind's held back in some areas it compensates by becoming more acute in others. Hence the heightened sense of Bulwark along by the river on one of our out-of-college excursions. I can't sleep or eat, he said. I took this to mean he wished to discuss Maureen. Each day, he went on, I resolve to do something about her, be proactive, but then each day passes without anything happening so by night-time I'm little more than a Hamlet pacing the battlements. A dog nearby watched a pair of ducks swimming beyond the weir. It appeared to be wondering if it should bark. It had probably seen ducks before and felt this time, perhaps, silence was best but I'm only guessing till such time as we find out for sure if dogs know they are dogs. I mean for a start it's hard to imagine they know they're dogs unless they've some kind of mind-language to do the knowing in. I remember Kandinsky arguing one time he sometimes thought solely in pictures, without words at all. I had a go at this later but wasn't sure – for example – if I'd pictured a sheep without the word sheep coming as well. This may be the solution, Kandinsky said eventually. Though dogs might not have language, there's nothing to stop them seeing a rabbit in their mind if there's a rabbit in the vicinity. But I don't think they'd be able to see a rabbit in their minds *without* there being one.

Atkins said he didn't see where rabbits came in. I took his point. Suddenly the dog looking at the ducks sprang away from the water and raced along the path. It was chocolate brown and short-haired. If only all dogs were as lithe and handsome as that, Bulwark said. I said: Steady on, or something. He didn't hear. He would often blot out the introduction of topics that might take him away from himself. Maureen tells me she and the Dean have a similar one, he said, and so I understood why he'd mentioned it in the first place. I said to him: When did you have time to discuss dogs with her? He perked up. We were chatting about semiotics outside the refectory. We'd started on Barthes and it went from there. She's enormously gifted. I imagine us in a winter sitting room being woo'd by crackles from a log fire. I appreciate I'm enriching the fantasy, Peter, but the temptation to do so is huge. I scratched my eyebrow. I wanted more than anything to know how they got from Barthes to Maureen's dog. Aren't you hot in that duffel coat? I said as Bulwark came to a standstill at the edge of the path. I'm not criticising, I said. I've had the same problem myself. I'm only trying to gain another perspective on it. Bulwark seemed to be plumbing the deeps of the stream. No, I'm just right, he said. I told him, yes, usually I was too. Only the weatherwoman had said this was going to be the warmest day of the year so far and probably even I wouldn't consider a coat. Bulwark cleared his throat. He said he had a low blood temperature and almost always felt chilly. You could at least put the hood down, I said. He nodded as he thought about this, but didn't follow the advice. What *was* love anyway? I asked myself as we walked on. The smell from wild garlic was sweetly overpowering. I felt if Bulwark bothered to ask, I'd say I loved K, but then even as I thought this I asked myself: Well did I? It was time someone came up with a chart so you had a decent chance of assessing if you really did or you really didn't. Probably someone like Barthes was useless at working it out. I thought for a moment, hope against hope, Bulwark said, that the dog we saw just now would turn out to be Maureen's though I remember her saying it was black not chocolate, and yet you see how stricken hearts hope against hope? I even dreamed the Dean was killed in a mountaineering accident. I asked if the Dean climbed. Bulwark said he didn't know. He'd merely given him an interest to enable his accidental death to be more likely. It's hardly proactive to hope for accidental death, I said. It seemed for a moment, as Bulwark paused above the stream that he might throw himself in. It surely wouldn't have been fatal but I daresay he would have seen it as a gesture. The embarrassing thing, he said, was that when I bumped into her I'd been on my way to the toilets, but I could hardly say. I knew those toilets. Two doors side by side in the foyer of the refectory. Somehow, Bulwark said, talking about Barthes in those circumstances made me want to go more than I did before. I nodded as if that had been my own experience when in fact I'd only heard of Barthes in the slimmest of circumstances. So, what did you do? I asked. So say Maureen inadvertently saved the situation. She was on her way to meet the Dean who'd promised to take her to a garden centre for hostas. I suppose you could look at it, I said, that if you were with Maureen full time, you'd only have to worry someone like yourself might come along any moment and attempt to whisk her off to hostas new. I haven't as yet tried whisking, he said. I know, I said, but I take it that's your eventual plan assuming the Dean doesn't perish on the slopes. A duck quacked long and loud. I was in time to see Bulwark's duffel coat stoop as he picked a stone from beside the path. He lobbed it into the water. For as long as we were on semiotics I wanted to hold her in my arms, he said. It was time, I felt, to stop discussions, to abandon analyses, to *be* rather than think. He opened his briefcase and brought out an inauthentic pasty. He unwrapped one end and took a bite, chewing for a considerable time. Anyway, he said between mouthfuls, thanks for listening. I can't think of anyone else I can talk to. Love's lonely. It is, I said. I missed K when I said that. I'm not sure if I missed her because I missed her or missed her because Bulwark had erupted her within me. As soon as she'd erupted to her fullest she died back again and then I didn't miss her so much. I'm not sure what was happening between us at the time. There were any number of default settings. Bulwark opened out the pasty wrapper as if he was about to undo it further, but then quietly retightened it and returned the pack to his briefcase. From the pocket of his duffel he took his cigarette equipment and rolled himself a fat one, wolfing smoke as we headed deeper into the gorge. My lungs call Hooray every time, he said. Maureen thought it a bad idea I should try to start smoking again. She said the Dean used to smike a pope till a few years ago. She did! She really said smike a pope! I said in my mind, I said: Maureen how nice to hear a spoonerism from your moist lips. Of course I didn't actually say that. They aren't moist anyway. I just always feel lips you're in love with should be. Instead of any of that I laughed, waiting for her to laugh too, but guess what? She didn't even notice what she'd said. I said: Really? even though I was miffed because he'd asked me to guess what but hadn't allowed time for me to do it. Being green myself, I foolishly asked if what she'd said was, in fact, a Malapropism whereupon hood and beard shook for too long. No, Peter. Spoonerism. She'd inadvertently transposed the initial sounds of the two words. A Malapropism would have been if she'd mis-used a word that sounded similar to the intended word like the time my mum suggested she get lamented flooring in the study. To be a true spoonerism though, he said, less melancholy now, the transpositions of initial sounds would have resulted in a comical phrase such as the proba-bly apocryphal shoving leopard in Spooner's reference to our Lord. I made a sound meant to indicate laughter though I wasn't amused. I was still reeling from my erroneous correction and how even though he wouldn't mean to, Bulwark would remember it and remind me whenever an opportunity came. He took another crackly draw on the cigarette, making out one of the advantages of re-smoking was it gave you added protection from midges. I asked him how come he was saying it was an added protection given we didn't have any other type of protection. He told me if I was to get on in this world I should try to lessen this resent-ment of mine. I said: What resentment? my tone suggesting, I suppose, that maybe I *did* have one. As the path narrowed so we fell into single file, Bulwark's duffel just ahead. I could have grappled him into the river easily. I folded my arms to lessen the risk.

*

Smithson ventured I'd been variously damaged as a baby and this had warped the emotional course of my life. He said think think think think to see what I could come up with, other than the Rumanians this time if I didn't mind. I told him I would, of course I would, though I worried I might be granting baby Peter what adult Peter hoped to be reasons. So much annoys a baby. It's hard to isolate incidents that might have annoyed it more than was acceptable. For example, the day Mother first left me with Mrs Hodgkins and Alexander and went shopping. I was waggled by Mrs Hodgkins through our front room window as Mother went down the path. The first time this took place I felt I might never see her again. Mrs Hodgkins then put me in one arm and Alexander in the other. She said to us: Wave boys, wave, even though our arms were trapped by shawls. Sometimes Mother would stay behind with me and Alexander while Mrs Hodgkins went shopping. It was becoming clear neither my father nor Raymond were much use in baby maintenance. Alexander was still an entirely miserable boy who took pleasure in vomit. When Mother had passed out of view Mrs Hodgkins put me and him together on the sofa and swung wool at us practically till Mother returned. As well as her basket of shopping she brought home another mother altogether and a third baby. Here's Mrs Tintwistle from a few roads along, she said to Mrs Hodgkins. Just had a baby herself. And this speck of nothing is K. K was held above Alexander and me. As soon as we'd taken a look, she was swung out of our field of vision and replaced – as if we hadn't had enough already – by further wool. Mrs Tintwistle has only popped in for a moment, Mother said. She'd see us again soon. It was hard to understand who Mother was talking to. Mrs Hodgkins stopped the wool-games momentarily to say cheerio to Mrs Tintwistle and K. Mrs Tintwistle was taking the world out with her. I turned awkwardly to Alexander to see if he felt the same way. There's another playmate for you wicked boys she said, though Alexander and me were perturbed at being called wicked when to our knowledge we hadn't done anything untoward.

*

If you keep one of the tablets on your tongue you get a gentle tingling. Strictly speaking we're meant to swallow all of them using the water we're given, but often I keep the tingling one there as long as I can. The number of tablets has risen steadily. There are four now, each a different colour. I've developed a tongue movement that can in effect hold on to the tingling one while letting water carry off the others. Harry hasn't a clue. Too full of Cheryl or Dylan. Apparently the eighteen straight whiskies didn't happen. That's what he was telling me the other day. I said what do you mean Harry? even though I'd heard the real story myself. I asked him what he meant because I knew he'd enjoy someone being interested. But guess what, he took one look at me and went off. I was worried about it for ages – why he did that I mean – but then new worries came to take its place. I've only just remembered now. It's rare you meet someone who doesn't annoy you some of the time. K herself said her idea of a friend was just someone who annoyed you less frequently than others. She raised her eyebrows. I think this meant I was on the cusp of being relegated. We were on the towpath by the canal. It's a nine-mile stretch we walked occasionally, catching the train back from the station at the end. Or we might catch the train there and walk the other way. It was in the back of her mind maybe one day to buy a boat and live along there – it certainly seemed peaceful the times we went. You got the odd hoodlum but they weren't frequent enough to ruin illusion. Between villages the number of moored boats would lessen, the canal lined then here and there with bulrushes, home once upon a time to a heron. K entered a photo she took of it in My Bird Of The Week, from *Wildlife Monthly*. She came second, usurped by a golden eagle. I said at the time I didn't see how anyone could hope to come ahead of an eagle even if – as this one – the photo wasn't that good. The highlands to the left and right were blurry I felt, though K said that might just be the print quality in the magazine or – more likely – an effect to give the illusion of the eagle's speed. She won a book token for coming second. I told her book tokens filled me with horror, I didn't know why. She said she hadn't been going to ask. She bought a book on Photographing Birds with her prize. I said it was just like her to use a book token she'd won for photographing birds to buy a book on photographing birds. In summer the canal loomed ahead while willows and whatnot ran along the other side of the path. She stopped many times to talk to those who lived on the narrowboats, on one particular occasion a man who made his spring and summer living as a Chandler. I said to them as they were chatting my French teacher had been called Chandler. K said later I'd interrupted because I was jealous of her talking to the man. He said next time I'm along I could have a look inside, she told me. I said that would be handy given she was half thinking of getting a boat herself one day. She could look upon it as research. K shook her head. I asked her why she was shaking it again especially as she seemed to be shaking it a lot lately. She said I was pretending not to be jealous by actively encouraging what I least wanted to happen. I said: Excuse me but how do you know I'm not being genuine about you having a look round his fine boat? She said: Well there you go again when you say his *fine* boat. I can tell you're jealous. I'd really like to know, I said, how you manage to glean jealousy from what was, after all, a complimentary statement not about the man so much but, yes, his boat. We walked on in silence. I was viewing the surroundings trying to find a way back from what I'd said. I knew she was right but couldn't bring myself to confess entirely. Luckily a person came by wearing what I thought of as Woo clothing. I said to K: You don't often seen that on a towpath. She said see what on a towpath? I pointed backwards at the lady who was walking in the way oriental ladies do sometimes, mostly I suppose because of the tightness of the kimonos. I said as much to K. It's not like to you to be racist and sexist in one sentence, she said. We stopped for buns. We were halfway through them before we were able to talk calmly. I explained that though I didn't feel I'd *actually* been jealous of the Chandler I could agree something had happened to my insides while K had been speaking with him. I hazarded a guess it was because he had such a decent job while I had the Office but otherwise didn't really know what I wanted, not in that chandlery type way anyhow. You could make a start by being a Reasonable Peter, she said. I couldn't tell if this was a serious comment because she'd immediately taken another bite. Soon after this she asked if I knew why they were called Chelsea buns. Neither of us had a clue though we agreed we'd look it up. She rang a few days later to say the Chelsea was a type of currant bun first created in the eighteenth century at a bun house in Chelsea. I said: Hmmm, that's interesting, but she ended up blaming the tone of my hmmm on something in me that hadn't come to terms with the Chandler and his boat. I told her I really hadn't actually given either of them a thought since the day of our walk, thank you.

*

The distant past has a naive, monochrome aspect, as if the sense of being alive then was inexorably different, though Smithson said sitting by a willow at the edge of a stream in the eighteenth century would be essentially the same as sitting by one now. He strolled creakily across the room to look out of the window again. I say creakily because he'd had his old rugs taken up and hadn't yet replaced them. To be frank you seem to occupy yourself with thoughts that aren't interesting, he said. It's no wonder girlfriends get bored frankly. First of all I told him I hadn't said any girlfriends got bored. Secondly there'd only been the one and thirdly he'd used frank and frankly close together. I noticed, he said, but felt it too late to correct myself. He sighed out of the window. The rooftops were covered by thundercloud but it wouldn't break so tension remained with us for the entire session. Sometimes, he said eventually, it's like I'm not sure what Therapeutic Specialism's about. It often presupposes a future we might not have or a past we've probably rearranged anyway. I leaned up. I asked him if I should come to the window too. This must have snapped him out of it because he said: No, no, stay where you are. There was a menace in the way he'd spoken, but I let it go. If you can't have a bad day as a Therapeutic Specialist it's a poor job. I told him this in the hope he'd feel he had permission from now on to be any way he wanted. I had a notion it would lead to a more democratic healing process. For so long our sessions had had as their dynamic the assumption that whenever we might disagree, it was his opinion that overruled.

*

*I grow old... I grow old... I shall wear the bottoms of my trousers rolled.* Bulwark said this to himself as we passed to the east end of the lake. In his case I guess it was to do with a disgruntlement Maureen wasn't yet his. On the basis this might be what had prompted him, I asked how things were going on that front. He said he'd left a typed note in her pigeonhole outside the staffroom. But we're beyond childhood, I said

58

gently, including myself to take the heat out of the criticism. I know, he said without looking round. He was scuffing through the short grass to make known how forlorn he was. I'd say we were beginning to doubt the early stages of love made people feel well. Maybe, I said, swishing a stick I'd found – it had teeth marks a third of the way along – maybe we should re-evaluate our feelings in what we could call the Romance Department. Tell me, are you or are you not a virgin? Bulwark glanced at me. He then restored his gaze to a point four feet ahead of his brogues. I was brought up to believe I should save myself for Miss Right, he said. So even though there have been opportunities, I've resisted. Good for you, I told him. But I was wondering if the force of your desire might be causing gloom rather than the Maureen situation per se? I don't get you, Bulwark said, which more or less corresponded with a feeling in the pit of my guts I didn't entirely understand what I was getting at myself. Let's use an analogy, I said. Bulwark threw a stone into the water. Let's, he said. Let's say, I said, you didn't like pork pies. I don't, he said. I've learned what goes in them. Ears and what have you. I said never mind the specifics now. I'm using pork pies as a tool in my analogy. He sighed. The stone had made a ploop in the deeps and sent circles from the point of impact. Get on with it, he said. I refused to say more till I'd found a stone of my own and thrown it further than his. My great-grandfather once threw a rock and hit a pike, Bulwark said. From the side I could make out only cowl and beard, an area of beard at the front glimmering with margarine. So anyway, I said, let's say you don't like pork pies. The thing is if you didn't eat anything for a long while sooner or later you'd eat a pork pie whether you liked them or not and however many ears they had in them. The instinct to satisfy hunger ensures survival. I don't see what pork pies have got to do with Maureen, he said. Think man think, I said, inadvisably. I'd said it because I couldn't remember where pork pies came in myself. By commanding Bulwark to think, I had fingers crossed he could come up with the answer and save me further embarrassment. A flurry of girls passed either side of us, laughing about something one of them had said beforehand. Infidels, Bulwark said under his breath. Though I wanted to criticise his language, I held off because I was sure it was born of an unbearable sense of his own inadequacy and fear. I'd found this to be true in most cases where a man has been disrespectful to women. Another month and I'll kill myself, Bulwark continued. If I leave a note addressed to you, can you then make sure it's forwarded to Maureen? Why not address it to her directly? I said. I thought of that, he said, but if that happens we are involving another party – a postal operative – and I really don't want anyone but you and Maureen to have any hint of this. I'll write the note to Maureen, put it in an envelope and then put *that* note inside a separate envelope addressed to you. Your job post-mortem will be to make sure she gets the inner note. You should hand it to her when there's no one else around. Other than that you might like to see my belongings are forwarded to my parents up North. I'll leave an address on the mantelpiece. I'll give you a key to my bedsit and a key to the front door of the building the bedsit's in when I next see you. I'll also leave on the mantelpiece a list of phone numbers of the people who need to be informed. Excuse me, I said, but one minute you're talking about my only post-mortem job, then the list lengthens. Not only that but on the one hand you want nobody to know and on the other you're providing innumerable contactees. You're being illogical. Are you sure you want to go through with it? What's more, if I do as you ask people are going to be coming up to me after you've gone reprimanding me for not stopping you. Oh I can't see them being that insensitive, he said. It's a well-known syndrome that you can be deep into a conversation about the structure – let's say – of suicide before you realise the sadness of having the discussion at all. Look, I said, there are some amusing aspects to these talks, but you can't expect me to keep quiet if I really start to believe you're going through with it. Besides, we spend all this time planning suicide as if it mattered a hoot what happens once we're no longer conscious of life. If you're really serious you should just go and throw yourself off a cliff today and not bother with all this detail. A blue dragonfly abbreviated among the bulrushes as Bulwark and I continued what was beginning to feel like an infinite circuit. Soon he was saying all this talk of suicide was making him want another roll-up so we turned from the lake and made our way into the shadows. It was only when he was well through his smoke I remembered what he'd said earlier. So what did this typed note say? The one in Maureen's pigeonhole? Bulwark cleared his throat. It said: Maureen, before I die, whenever that may be, I need to say I love you. I didn't sign it. I went and got it back ten minutes later. Luckily it was still there. It was too direct. Anyway the Dean's pigeonhole's next to hers and he might have noticed it himself. I was getting angry with Bulwark and the endlessness of the difficulties he was having over what some would regard as a trivial matter. Hoping to make this known, I took a larger stone, throwing it further than either of the previous ones. Steady on, he said. Is it because of what I said about my great-grandfather? I said not at all, not at all, sounding somewhat like Prufrock. I just saw it to one side of the path and instinct took over.

*

It was on the news – the name Maureen was destined to die out altogether within twenty-five years. It stuck in my mind because as the item was talked about so I pierced and ate one of those tinned plum tomatoes they serve with scrambled egg and toast. In addition to this, one may have cornflakes, eaten first, a glass of fruit juice and then, at the end, a cup of tea. Something in my medication has increased my appetite though there's little chance of appeasing the increase. I suppose it's good I can't eat as much as I'd like because my immobility would quickly lead to weight gain. A medication intended to solve one problem often creates another. We've had discussions on this issue. Occasionally we've drawn up rough plans to redistribute our medication if only we can find a way of doing this under Harry's nose. I've told one or two of the others of my ability to keep aside the tingling tablet and probably if this skill could be shared by all of us we would in time be able to stockpile enough to make redistribution feasible, but as usual in here the mere drawing up of an idea can take weeks and is usually subject to the gentle anarchy that dominates most of the time. Some among us – Tobias Mawk, the Major, Smetham and, as far as I remember, Jaundice – have their medication intravenously or intramuscularly so they couldn't be party to any scheme we procure. Plus we'd have to be wary of whistleblowers – I fear Colquahoon's to be watched in that respect.

*The immeasurable suffering of the world is lightened by infinitely small acts of human kindness.* Q. L. Marjoribank's quotation is etched above the locked entrance of the monument. It came to me just then because I was sad suddenly at how picky I've been about Colquahoon. I keep meaning not to be then find myself doing it. K's the least critical person I've come across. I asked her about this once as we were looking over the vale near the monument one May evening where the world was the more peaceful for a bleating of lambs. I said how come I never hear you banging on about people the way I do, about their foibles and whatnot. She said whereas she wasn't so sure I did it as much as I made out, she would say the serenity prayer made an absolute difference to her attitudes when the chips were down, plus of course her attendance at AA meetings. Ah those, I said. I said it like that because I'd been concerned about a Gareth R she'd mentioned as having an admirable serenity himself. She had previously explained how he believed that though he really must adhere to the first principles of recovery – that is, regular meetings and a regard for the necessity of working the Twelve Step Programme – he should also ensure his life thereafter continues to be expansive rather than restrictive. He sounds a hoot, I said. Out of the bleating came the groan of a plane, which, as it eventually lulled overhead, seemed too slow. I watched it with the blade of my hand against my forehead, trying in that way to be excused for the remark I'd made. K added: It's good to be tight to the programme when you first stop drinking, Gareth says, but after a few years expansiveness should be the byword. I told her he certainly seemed to love the concept. The plane hung high above the fields. I said to K never had there been such an evening. Rich milk blossom on hawthorns the other side of the fence stood out against the green hues surrounding them. I touched K's knee as if about to alert her to something. The skin was cool and blushed pink where it was at its tightest. I was wondering if we would ever go beyond amiable celibacy. So what job does this Gareth do, I said. He's an artist, she said. He paints. I had a feeling he might, I said. But since we're meant to be anonymous, K said, I'd be grateful if you kept it to yourself. I told her I'd try. As well as enjoying the evening I was wondering if there would be any advantage in storming off. The trees at the beginning of the wood were a good three hundred yards away, which would mean I'd be plainly visible to K for the entire duration of the storming. This, in the end, was what made me hold tight to the rail of the bench. You should know better than to be jealous of anyone I mention at meetings, she said, noticing my white hand. He's there like me to maintain recovery, not to seek out people to have love relationships with. It wasn't jealousy as such, I said. A youngish Peter spoke before I had chance to warn him not to. I laughed to show her I was over it. It's no good making the laughing sound as if you're not bothered because I know otherwise, she said. You make many assumptions, I said. I was craning my neck to observe a bird of prey hovering above the slope beyond the fence. I disliked Gareth, I decided. I turned my attention from the bird to K's profile. Does he exhibit? Gareth? I shouldn't really say any more, K said, looking at her shoes as she rocked them under the bench. But I might as well tell you he likes to set up his easel down the harbour and give it what ho. What's what ho? I asked, surprised. I'm not sure, she said. It just came out. All of a sudden and for no reason I could immediately tell, it was as if I smelt Miss Woo on the wind. I realised later it must have been K using the word ho, which has an oriental sound. He doesn't do boats I hope, I said. I believe boats are included but they're not his main focus. He says he's mostly captivated by the physical evidence of the harbour's industrial heyday. I like your heydays and your what ho's, I said. I touched her knee a second time. That was it, because a rumour arose some time before or after this that Father had once been with Miss Woo here in the shadow of the monument, though this detail may have been supplied by imagination. K said, as if to herself, we ought to go there more often. The harbour. Do you mean you and Gareth or you and I? I said, hoping to mimic Eliot. I saw immediately that to do so was wasted because I don't believe K ever heard him reading 'The Love Song Of J Alfred Prufrock'. Another bone to pick with Eliot was J Alfred. Putting the initial letter followed by a fully expressed middle name was toffee-nosed, I'd tell him. Mind you there are probably reasons for it

I don't know. My knowledge though wide is paper thin. Yes well I'd like that, I said. We spend too much time staring into space. I see it as meditation, K said. I hate meditating as you well know, I said. A minute or so into it demons intrude. Well don't let them, K said. Thanks for the tip, I said, but if I could not let them, I wouldn't have needed Smithson. My mind, as he once put it, has a mind of its own. You ought to become an addict, K said, then you could go into recovery. Yes, Miss Woo, her spirit, her smell. Suddenly I felt I'd like a Miss Woo of my own, despite or because of Father's warning.

*

Mrs Chaffin said she'd seen her one time at a show in the town hall. The Amazing Leonardo had put her in a box and sawn her into three pieces. She was later reconstituted to the delight of the crowd. I can see how hard it must be being up against a woman like that, Mrs Chaffin said as she fought the wind with a sheet she was trying to peg to her own line. Every night for months afterwards torn sheets flapped in my darkened bedroom and through my dreams.

*

K said on the way back through the wood Gareth had told her she could go down the harbour by appointment if she wanted to see him work. I suggested if she persuaded the Chandler fellow to moor his boat there she could kill two birds with one stone. In the early part of the wood, we passed through a spread of beech. I told her I was sorry. I'd built Gareth and the Chandler into an unholy alliance but couldn't she see it was because I was fearful of there ever being a time without her? She said if you're not careful you'll bring about the thing you fear. Just there we came across a woman and a long-haired Labrador and the conversation branched into dogs, not so much this time if they knew they were dogs, but with some of them, K said, they could often look like they were smiling. Then you get other breeds, pit bulls and what have you who seem as if they're in a foul mood altogether. Just up the slope through the trees we came again to the area of level ground, the site of an Iron Age hill fort. You usually tell me about ancient peoples heating milk with stones taken from the fire about now, K said. I was saving it, I told her, after you expressed annoyance about them before. You do have a thing about time, she said. I said: Well yes, time is something that interests me. And it's the idea too of ancient peoples surviving through the year using their skills, many of which are lost to us now. Gareth says people who have an excessive interest in the past or the future are struggling to deal with right here, right now, she said. And how would Gareth classify excessive interest? I asked, not unreasonably. Well, she said, I happened to mention my friend – that's you – is always saying he can sense people from the past and gets a kick out of them when he's low. I was at a loss as to why I was a he all of a sudden. Sometimes I wonder why you're with me, I said. About now in the walk I'd start to feel tree-weary. A widening noise became someone riding a motorbike. I told K I didn't think it should be allowed. The list gets longer, she said. But we come here to be in nature and to breathe fresh air, I said. Say what you like about ancient peoples, but everything they experienced would have been natural to the earth itself. You could say motorbikes were natural to the earth because what they are made of has been fashioned from materials arising from the earth too, she said. Arising isn't one of your words, I said. You're not catching vocabularies from Gareth I hope. He does have good language skills, she said happily, it'll be because he's artistic. When you've come through an illness of addiction, it can bring out the best in all kinds of ways. She paused for me to say something. When I didn't – mostly because I'd almost run out of language myself – she reminded me that most often when we passed along this part of the path I recalled a time when one of my class-mates – Howard if she remembered rightly – had fallen out of a tree and broken both arms. Nothing was farther from my mind, I told her. Besides, it was Horace and wrists.

*

I hear the snapping sometimes. Smithson said it was possible for us to get this sort of echo resounding through our minds, especially at night. He was at the window looking over town. I was on a new therapy couch he'd bought from a catalogue. If ever things were going badly he remin-ded me it was so many pounds a week for so many weeks. One hundred and four most likely. It had an adjustable headrest. Flat was nought.

Almost upright, eight. Three was best. With three I enjoyed from time to time a seagull passing or the journey of a cloud. I told Smithson the boys with me told me to run home and tell someone what had happened to Horace and that I was proud to have such a mission. I have to be honest too though, I said. Horace went white. I was scared he might be sick. Though proud to be the messenger, I was also glad to be leaving the area. Ah, Smithson said, a fear of vomit. I had a case before, oh four or five years back. Did you cure him or her, I asked? If I'm to maintain his or her anonymity I'd best not say more, he said. He twirled from the window. These things are rarely cured as such though we may may discover ways to deal with the fear. You said two mays, I told him. He said yes, he'd been going to emphasise the second to indicate the discovery wasn't certain. For some reason the emphasis didn't come, he said. I hope it isn't the beginning. I asked him of what. He told me then of his grandfather's syndrome – whereby the brain on occasion fails to make an emphasis asked of it. I don't know why I fear it really, Smithson went on. It's not like a gradual inability to emphasise is going to make a great difference to life. It probably rules me out of a more professional acting career but then I'm happy with this. A hand movement suggested 'this' was Therapeutic Specialism. Though I'd been going there for years ostensibly to discover the root of a pernicious malaise, at that moment I don't think I'd ever felt more content. It was maybe down to a smell of biscuits from the bakery on the ground floor or to the hum of Eileen in the outer office. She was due to be getting married soon, she'd told me that day. To Ron. Ron's cooking for me tonight, she said as I was leaving to wait for Mother. I opened the door, passed over the landing and began the familiar descent of the thirty-six stairs and three further landings. A hurried clopping behind me as I adjusted myself at the front door was Smithson, now out of Therapeutic Specialist mode. I'm off for a spot of lunch, he said. I called after him as he walked away that I'd heard people mention spots of lunches but never quite knew what they were. He called back – probably to be the last one to speak: Give vomit some thought won't you? Because there were pedestrians and then suddenly Mother between us, I didn't answer.

The intensity of memory's something I keep meaning to ask Harry about. He probably won't know if it's safe or not because I've heard him say we should never be surprised about what brains do. Especially when they're medicated, I said loudly. Which pill of mine does it I'm not sure, but through the day it's like there are hands across the top of my head. My occasional anguish comes as a sensation of wooden struts bound to my left and right side. In quiet moments the faintest tremor runs along my spine. Kandinsky told me he thought it was selfish to spend so much time thinking about what was happening to me physically. I said it was all very well of him who can meander if he so wishes to the bathroom and back or play table tennis with Atkins. Straight away I wished I hadn't said it. I apologised at teatime. He said it was okay and gave me one of his sardines. Since there were only three to begin with, I said are you sure and he said yes have one, so in keeping with a new leaf I'd turned over to do with accepting the kindness of others, I waited while he slipped it from his plate to mine. Smetham beside me refused to eat his sardines even though earlier he'd consumed the cap of the brown sauce dispenser. This misfortune led to me being able to replace the one sardine Kandinsky had given me plus give us each another one. Which meant he had four while I had five. It was, to quote Atkins, Sardine City for some. The accompanying salad came with chopped lettuce, sliced radishes, sliced spring onions and sliced beetroot. We were allowed two slices of bread each, smeared with margarine. In all our born days we hadn't seen such a spread, though even as we said it – repeatedly in some cases – none of us were being authentic. We hated the sardines, the salad and bread ration with its margarine. It was agreed later that evening we'd get up a petition for Harry requesting we were never served that particular meal again and after a month or two we handed it in. Despite this we still have sardines weekly. The day they're due the smell of their approach becomes manifest. I said to Harry last time I said Harry did you ever pass on that petition, about the sardines? He said yes he had but because the food came from a central kitchen in town that supplied many facilities, not to mention other places like this, there was little to be done about it. I said isn't it odd Harry people say not to mention other places like this even though by merely saying so they have, in fact, mentioned them? It's one of the mysteries of language sure enough, he said. He shunted himself from the door-frame and went back to the office. His going back at that moment had been his way of ending the conversation. Sometimes he's just not up to it. Either he will have had another row with Cheryl or else he suddenly goes off the boil. He's said more than once going off the boil happens regularly. That's when you're most likely to see me away to Laugharne or off to climb the Sugar Loaf, he said. It must be nice to be able to choose to do things like that. I said to him. How high's the Sugar Loaf? What he hadn't realised was that this was the first time I'd heard a reference to the Sugar Loaf and I'd guessed – because of the one in South Africa – this was a mountain too. About two thousand feet, he said. And does Cheryl go? Harry laughed. I took his laughter to mean probably she didn't do mountains. No, Harry said, it's just me, a backpack, a few sandwiches and a bottle of water. We take it the sandwiches aren't sardine, Kandinsky said. None of us were sure why he said we, unless it was that the original sardine incident had involved him too and by using we he was paying homage to the solidarity we'd shared. Never has a sardine passed my lips, Harry said, switching himself to the office. Major Gwillingington told us soon afterwards – and this surely must have been one of the last things he said aloud – he'd once caught a sardine off the coast of Sardinia and something about this – he wasn't sure what – gave him the giggles. He'd told the story many times as guest speaker at dinners years before and it had always raised a laugh. When he'd finished speaking, Atkins asked him if that was it. The Major asked him what he meant. Atkins said: Well it seemed like you were going to tell us a funny story but then all you came up with was an anecdote about a sardine, which as far as I can see had nothing funny about it. To avoid a fight, Kandinsky told Atkins maybe you had to have been there to see the funny side. This made it worse because Atkins said something like why on earth would I want to be in Sardinia? Kandinsky had no answer because it hadn't been his joke to begin with, plus Atkins was displaying an inaccuracy it would be difficult to explain without losing energy.

If Fiona ever does come with tea I'll ask if she can spare an additional biscuit. I am, for want of a better word, peckish. It's not good we're each allocated our two biscuits or our three sardines or our two slices of bread. I would like more sometimes, less at others. To be overly regulated makes me feel inhuman. Jugg told us biscuits were a pleasing part of life's punctuation. Fatty put up his hand – I can see it as if it were yesterday – and said: Please sir what do you mean? I feel I should apologise for thinking of Fatty as Fatty but the fact is that's what he came to be called at secondary school and it stuck with him to the last day there and – who knows – beyond. Anyway, leaving aside for the moment the rights and wrongs, he asked Jugg what he'd meant when he said biscuits were part of life's punctuation. I saw in my head one of the problems of being a teacher was you might mention life's punctuation one time and be understood and the next you might mention it only to see an arm go up. Jugg walked dustily to the window – we were on the third floor – then used the teacher's trick of saying to us while not looking at us: Who would like to answer Paul's question? Some people probably wondered who Paul was. K raised her hand. Jugg must have seen it in the window's reflection. Yes girlie? he said. K said: Please sir you mean if life is to be regarded as a story in a book then biscuits and suchlike can be seen as the punctuation in that book. You could equally have said sweets. You're nearly right girlie and yes, I could have said sweets. He turned to face us again. So now let's return to hyphens. Alexander put up his hand and asked if they were a type of snake. To my mind he hadn't looked any different from one day to the next since we were born. We'd spoken about it. He'd said if you took a photo of someone every day for the whole of their life and stuck each photo on the wall in a line, you wouldn't be able to see a difference between one photo and the ones either side of it yet the very first photo would be of a newborn and the last a corpse. Enough of that laddie, settle down, Jugg said. He didn't send Alexander to the headmaster for saying the snake joke even though he'd sent me there for asking about pronunciation. Maybe this was because as well as his genius Alexander had a good smile. I found smiling hard. K said I looked as though I was waiting for someone to shoot me. Maybe it's like Smithson explained, I can't smile because I feel guilty for my sins although, he added, as yet we've no clear idea exactly how many sins are perceived by your psyche and besides, how many of them actually were sins and how many were normal boy things you perceived as sins because of the way you were brought up. It wasn't that bad, I said. All that happened really was Father making the most of it with a Miss Woo. Oh and there was a bus incident. Incidentally, I forgot to say, Smithson said suddenly, Eileen tells me she saw a Miss Woo performing with a Mr Abra Cadaver up North somewhere years ago. It stuck in her mind because of the Abra Cadaver man who could pretend he was dead. That was part of the act. Eileen says Miss Woo came into it in another part of the act when she would spring out of a hold-all Abra Cadaver had previously beaten with a sledgehammer. Aren't our talks supposed to be confidential? I asked him. He told me that Eileen, being the secretary, was exempt from the confidentiality clause because it was she who had to type up the notes. I didn't realise they were typed up, I said grumpily. I was hoping to put across I wasn't happy about it while at the same time indicating I understood on some level notes had to be taken. I can see now because of the various things I hoped to convey, I could have chosen a better way than grumpily to say it, but I daresay Smithson was used to me being in a mood on occasions and besides, allowing me to be grumpy meant he could veer from protocol if ever he had a mind to. I suppose it could have been another Miss Woo altogether, I said. Hmm, Smithson said, I can't see there being two, both of whom work as assistants to travelling magicians. As I replayed this in my head I had a feeling of regret, of shame even. It was just the sort of thing people say that can make me want to curl up and die.

*

Alexander lay in his carrycot one side of the sewing machine. I hung in rubber straps from the door-frame. Mrs Hodgkins was at outpatients having something off. Whenever Mother was about to speak, she glanced at the opened curtains. Mrs Chaffin was pulling faces at me. Mother said: Are you sure it was her? Mrs Chaffin shook her head at the same time as saying: There was no mistake. She was in the co-op buying cheese bold as brass. I didn't think they ate cheese, that's one of the reasons it stuck in my mind. I suppose she's entitled to eat cheese even if she is a harlot, Mother said. What bothers me more is her being in the co-op. She ought to know there's a chance of bumping into us this far down. The woman has no staples, Mrs Chaffin said. Mother sipped from the bone china cup. Father had bought the set ages before. It's got everything you need, he told her as he handed her the box. I hadn't yet been born so I didn't witness the presentation directly. I was told the story the day after Mother broke many of the items, variously describing Father as each struck the wall. There were marks on the paper to this day. She looked at the cup now. Each sip is like drinking out of that woman, she said. Then don't use it, Mrs Chaffin said. What and let her think she's won, Mother said. Illogicality made my straps twist. Quite soon I was looking into the kitchen and soon after that at Mrs Chaffin who pulled another face. For a while it was kitchen Chaffin, kitchen Chaffin. Still you have Peter, she said. He's bonny. He's got an appetite right enough, Mother said, glancing at me. My nipples are paying. Did you use that cream I told you about? Mrs Chaffin said. Yes, but it hasn't helped, Mother said. Besides which the rate he sucks at me it's not likely any cream will. Probably Mrs Chaffin would have looked into the corner of the room, foreseeing a time when such vigorous feeding would have transformed into a dependent nature for which I'd need the help of a Therapeutic Specialist. I've never liked anyone on my breasts, baby or not, Mrs Chaffin said. She shared a giggle with Mother while I took another spin. I was hopeful that when Alexander woke I'd be given something else to do, though pastimes for babies were for the most part second rate. Occasionally I saw through the front room curtains. The world was bounded low down by privet. Above it stretched the ridges of houses opposite. A crow perched at the end of one looked about itself in amazement.

*

Where did soil come from? I've a feeling Atkins initiated this topic having fared badly in the dogs discussion. Kandinsky asked did he mean where *did* soil come from or where *does* soil come from? He feared the second was easier to answer than the first. Atkins said he quite agreed, but yes, he had meant did rather than does. It's a tricky one all right, Kandinsky said. There was a tone to his voice as if he wasn't comfortable being in agreement with Atkins. You see, Atkins went on, mostly now for the benefit of Smetham chewing his own lip, you can sort of see soil replenishment would be down to the decay of fallen leaves and what have you, over millennia, he added proudly. Kandinsky leaned forward and said: But you're wondering where soil came from originally? Yes, I am, Atkins said. He paused a moment, tilting his head forty-five degrees. You see, things that grow need soil, and yet I presume a large part of a soil's composition comprises decayed vegetation. I wish you'd stop saying you see, Kandinsky said. He began to get ill because a great-great-uncle of his became a well-known artist. He'd tried it himself but his basics weren't good enough. Trees particularly. An art dealer friend from way back told him there was little hope of him making it on the back of his great-great-uncle anyway. Harry agreed this sort of thing could bother people in the short term but didn't think it could lead to the mostly clinical condition suffered by Kandinsky nowadays. Kandinsky was sad about art specifically in relation to his great-great-uncle and, by degrees, to art in general. He often resorted to corners to think it through. Well anyway, Atkins was hurt because he believed he'd only said you see twice and if Kandinsky was going to jump on him over such a matter it was no wonder he was here. A little beyond them all at the time a robin alighted on the patio. I'll never forget because Harry shushed them while it hopped and looked about. A robin! Atkins said loudly. It flew into the hedgerow. Now look what you've done, Kandinsky said. Atkins yawned. You've no proof it flew off because of me, he said. It didn't fly off when Harry shushed us. That's because shushing's a natural sound, Kandinsky explained, like the movement of wind through trees. And indeed yes the sound has a somnolent quality. K would become seized by the notion of going to the coast and if I was sensible I agreed without my usual dilly-dallying about what time did she think we'd be back? and similar questions. It took two hours to get there, the last mile of the journey giving frequent glimpses of the ocean. We're here, she always said as we drew into the car park. So I see, I always said. Most times we went there the car park – out of season, a large field – was overseen by a man in a beige overcoat who we learned was the farmer to whom the field belonged. Each car was a pound. Fuck sheep, he told K. The grass made a particular sound as we walked through it to the gate on the far side. Overhead the air was serenaded by larks. That's the word I used most times because it seemed that's what they did. You shouldn't use poetic language for what larks or any other bird type do naturally, she said. I believe it was because she was just happy to be back there and simply heard the birds rather than trying to describe their song. It was something drummed into us by Jugg remember, I told her, though drummed was a bit strong. He'd only suggested we listened carefully to the world in case we next wanted to say anything about it. By now we were up and over the first gate. The edge of the land half a mile ahead cut into a flattened sea. A line of trodden grass led to the next gate. It's good to be here again, I said, breathing in just afterwards. Are you sure? she asked. Yes, why wouldn't it be? Well, she said, it was in this field we had that row. What row was that? I said, a little sharply. About Tom. Really? I asked. I don't remember. We walked on. The path was elongated sorrow. We'd rowed because she'd told me she came there one time with him and how he'd had field glasses and friends who'd done a Ph.D. on the Theory and Practice Of Coastal Birds. I feel, I'd told her at the time, all I do is prowl in that ornithologist's footsteps. He isn't an ornithologist, she'd said. His friends are. The grass around us that day was a deeper green than I'd seen before. I would have used the word emerald if she hadn't said that stuff about language. Maybe it was an effect of the light, which was more vivid than at home. Actually I didn't want you and him to have been here together, I said. It was only the once, she said, but I was so impressed by it, I thought I'd come with you. How kind, I said. The rusted metal stile led to a steep track. As we made our way down so the land rose on either side and further still became low areas of crumbled rock. K said she could smell the sea. I said me too. She had under her arm a towel, her swimming costume rolled within it. I had a hand basket containing food, water and what have you. I believe ten thousand years ago this coast overlooked not

73

a sea as today, but a lush vale, I said. But if there hadn't been a sea, would there have been a coast at all? she asked. I'm not sure, I said. I wished I had been. The incline's steepness necessitated a leaning back. We were passed by a woman and a dog struggling upwards. Let's hope the tide's not right in, K said. The cove's covered twice a day. I thought it looked as though it was on its way out, I said, you know, when we were driving along and saw snatches of beach. I wanted to be right about this to counteract Tom's field glasses. Besides that dog just now wasn't wet. That doesn't mean the tide wasn't in, she said. Maybe it had an aversion. The path divides into two just down here. You can either go to the beach or on one of the lower paths. Me and Tom went along there. We saw guillemots. I thought about guillemots while K stopped for a cigarette. We were on a rounded stone that protruded from the grass to one side of the path. It too was loaf-shaped. You could in fact chart life from the point of view, say, of significant stones. This one was warm beneath us. K unearthed a tomato and cheese sandwich from the basket, unwrapped it and began eating and smoking alternately. Occasional smoke-veils sweetened the air between us. I could hear the sea below. You shouldn't eat and smoke, I said. It can't be good for you. It's interesting when people say things can't be good for you, she said. I'm not sure what it means. Okay, so we feel we *know* what it means, but does anyone ever follow it up to see if it's true? I didn't answer, not only because I'd become content, but also because I knew she was again making fun of the way I talked sometimes. When she'd finished her sandwich, she rested the cigarette on the rock and took off her boots. She handed them to me and with a nod indicated I might keep them and her socks in the basket. I wondered if Tom looked at guillemots and thought only of guillemots. The reason I was wondering it was because I couldn't recall ever looking at things in nature without hoping K or whoever I was with had *noticed* I was looking at things in nature. My life, as Smithson pointed out again and again, comprised a series of manoeuvres undertaken on the basis they were being observed by others. Spontaneous you aren't, he said. I've been informed thus by other parties, I said. He turned to the window and leaned against the sill. I can't imagine it would ever have been otherwise,

74

he said. The day pressed humidly against the window. My hair was wet where it touched the cushion. You may have been made afraid of something and proceed too carefully through life in case you prompt whatever it is to happen again. I raised my head and put my hands under it. One thing bothering me about Therapeutic Specialism, I said, is that it's good at such speculations without necessarily making any firm connection to events that may – or may not – have instigated the situation. By the time I reached the end of this sentence I was exhausted. I hadn't really understood what I'd meant. Smithson cleared his throat – a sign he hadn't understood either. His forehead moved a little further forward. When I think, he said, of the fuss those people made when they started work on that new supermarket, about how the town didn't need another and how it would directly threaten the livelihoods of small shops nearby, well it shocks me now to see its car park filled to capacity by those same protesters. The world has gone awry, he said, twisting from the window and settling himself on the wicker chair out of sight. I do wonder where it will all end myself, I told him. In the last few years things have advanced too quickly, Smithson went on. One wonders what else there is to be discovered before we blow ourselves up. I chuckled to myself, not about the end of the world, but about how enthused Smithson had become now he'd veered from my woes. Quietly at the same time I was thinking about chicken casseroles because I'd been leafing through a recipe magazine in the outer office before my appointment. Eileen had bought it for Ron. He's getting in practice for when we're in the matrimonial home, she said. I fancy the chicken casserole in there, I said, not because I liked chicken or casseroles particularly but because I feared gaps in conversation. Yes they can be nice, Eileen said. She sighed. I'm not much of a cook though, it has to be said. If it has to be said then it's good you've said it, I told her. She stared at me as I handed the magazine back. I was surprised because I felt working there she must have come across any number of human traits by now. Ron's doing me a steak tartare tonight, she said. He'll have popped out in his break to buy the ingredients. He's in Engineering. I knew someone in Engineering, I said, although I'd actually heard about him at second hand from Alexander. He makes things called spacers day in day out. On a lathe, I added. Ron's in management, Eileen said, although he's done his share on the factory floor. I got stuck again with the conversation and toyed with the idea of bringing in Isambard Kingdom Brunel, but even though Ron was in Engineering I couldn't think of a way to mention Brunel without floundering because really I knew little about him except for a grainy photo in the museum. He had a large hat, I remembered, and stood next to an enormous chain. Waiting that day in Eileen's office I had what was to become a common experience of time elongating either side of me, so barely could I remember coming through the door and hardly could I imagine passing from there into Smithson's therapy room. I was however satisfied to see how happy Eileen seemed about Ron and the steak. I crossed my ankles and glanced down at them before looking up again as Eileen made notes. I'm not sure if she had actual notes to make at that moment or if she was pretending. After another two or three minutes she said she was trying to persuade him to do a fruit salad while he was at it. I asked her if it was in the recipe magazine. She said no, she was sure Ron would be able to rustle one up out of his imagination. I said I didn't associate fruit salads with rustling. She appeared to make another note. Maybe the office area was part of the therapeutic space and Eileen had been briefed to observe idiosyncratic behaviour or speech on the part of waiting clients. Once I'd thought this I went off her and Ron and concentrated on the room itself rather than trying to continue conversation. The wall to the left was hung with framed certificates. In the corner a rubber plant stood in a sturdily decorated jardinière. Then the desk and Eileen. A filing cabinet occupied the next corner. The top drawer was A–F. The next drawer down was RECEIPTS ETC. Below this was G–P. The bottom drawer was labelled MISCELLANEOUS. Each time I was there I wondered should I ask about Q–Z, and could I do so without revealing something about myself? It could have been that to ask was good, that *not* asking was something of concern. Infinity came under the door as a prickled breeze while I waited. Eileen eventually said trouble was Ron did love his profiteroles so probably no amount of persuasion on her part would make him do a fruit salad. She smiled at me. Men! she said. I told her that though I could see

Ron's stubbornness over fruit salad was an expected trait, I did think it less expected that he was so keen to cook for her regularly. I examined this notion as it were in my linked hands and felt it worthy of a sane person. Before Eileen could answer a brisk turning of the consulting room knob stunned us both. The opening door disclosed the doctor, who directed me to join him and then held out his hand as usual towards his sanctum. We were discussing fruit salads, I told him as I got to my feet

*

On the gnarled upper segment of Colquahoon's finger sits a gold band that over time has created an indentation. The wait for him to turn the page is something of a game. I've noticed how often it's true things hardly ever happen if you're anticipating them, as if anticipation itself creates an energy, which in turn stifles possibility. I mentioned this to Harry one time. He said it's all in that saying, about a watched pot never boiling. I said I'd been hoping for a more intellectual overview. I had to apologise later. I wasn't comfortable at how pernickety I'd been. He said that was okay and how about a jigsaw? *The Haywain* hadn't been done since last year. He pointed to one of the larger tables in what was called the Study Area and said if I liked he could position me in there so I could have a go. It hasn't happened yet. I'm not sure anyway about *The Haywain*. Bulwark used to go on about how its over-representation in the decorative world embodied the Human Crisis. I think of it with capital letters because of the tone he used. We were circumnavigating the lake on a winter's afternoon. In shaded areas the previous night's frost clung to individual blades of grass. Maybe because of the poor light Bulwark for once was having his cigarette as he went along, smoke and cold coming out together, clinging to his beard and duffel-coat hood. So long has passed with me being in love with Maureen, he said. My doctor says if I hang on the feeling will pass. I told him I hadn't realised it had gone so far as to require medical attention. It's only the college doctor, Bulwark said, but I thought I ought to say something because it's affecting my studies. I received an ordinary second for my dissertation about Descartes in the philosophy module. Normally it would have been an upper second, even a first. Yes well I remember your other first that time,

I said. I probably shouldn't have looked but I did. I was a minky bit jealous. Oh no need for jealousy, Bulwark said. There's more to life than marks. We were parallel as we moved along the humps and hollows, though because of the diversity afforded by the terrain I often moved up while he moved down and vice versa. I asked him what sort of things he meant. He said well probably love though he wasn't having any luck at the moment and, he said after another drag of his cigarette, kindness overall to our fellow beings. I have to say old boy I've observed many kindnesses on your part. Kindness probably won't get me far though, I said. A brief discrepancy in the earthworks meant us passing downwards and upwards simultaneously. We were glad of this. Don't eschew your qualities Peter, he said. We chuckled. Though nothing was mentioned I'm confident it was because he'd managed to get an eschew in. He'd been meaning to since a few weeks before when Maureen used one. I see you in some kind of world capacity, he said. Something connected to the mind sciences, health, you know. Along with basic qualifications they look for an indefinable something and I'd stake my life on you having more than your share. When someone compliments you on your indefinable somethings the urge is strong to have them defined. As my foot landed upon the ground just then I started thinking about K. As soon as she'd appeared in my mind she passed on again and the sticking and unsticking of our shoes at the lakeside reawoke me to the current time and situation. I'm not sure what to say about Maureen, I said, to take myself away from the centre of attention. If you're being made to suffer perhaps it's time to abandon her and look elsewhere. Bulwark smoked wisely for a time then said love cannot be abandoned nor can it be looked for elsewhere. I would have thought you'd know that by now. Do you mean by now as in being at college or by now as in 3.45 pm? I asked. He sniffed. It was sometimes his way of laughing. I was pleased because the witticism had carried risk. I'm hoping to find out by hook or by crook if she might be amenable to an affair, he said. I mean no offence to the Dean but he doesn't seem a passionate man. Maybe Maureen has hesitated so far because she feels I might want to take her entirely as my own. She might not want to leave the old buffer even though things have chilled between them. So anyway that's going to be my next tack. I'll suggest an affair. I put my left hand into my pocket and pulled out my right. I'd been having one in because of the cold, but keeping one out at all times for expression. You say the suggestion of an affair's going to be your next tack, I said, but other than in a daydreaming sense I can't recall you having made a first tack. It might be Maureen's oblivious of your feelings. Though you say you perceive otherwise, you must surely know by now how easily a person in love misinterprets the language and behaviour of the love object. I glanced at him to see if he'd understood my use of *you must surely know*, which was meant to pay him back for the similar phrase he'd used. I mean I can't count the number of times I've been made to look a fool because of that particular syndrome, I added. No offence Peter, he said, but you do tend to have more syndromes than most.

*

I heard some such from the doctor who came regularly to check up on me. Mrs Hodgkins would bring Alexander round so, as she said, the good doctor could do us both. We were laid on the bed upstairs while the doctor examined us with the end of his stethoscope. Having finished Alexander and covered him in his shawl the doctor had a go at me. A few minutes later he unclipped the ivory-coloured ends of his instrument, folded it up and put it in his pocket. He said to Mother who was standing at the end of the bed: He's doing not so bad so don't worry yourself but there are one or two things we need to keep an eye on. Mother was alarmed. What sort of things? I wriggled my legs in the hope someone would cover me. It's nothing specific, the doctor said, but he might – just might – have a touch of Hagendorff Syndrome. It was in Mother's nature to wring her hands at news of a syndrome rather than ask what it entailed. Will he need medicine? Not at this stage, the doctor said. Thankfully, then, Mrs Hodgkins covered me. The doctor was in the act of leaving as he'd made this remark. Alexander and I listened as both sets of footfalls descended the stairs. Soon afterwards came the click of the front door. Mrs Hodgkins was coochy-cooing Alexander. Alexander was jealous not to have a syndrome of his own. Weary the footfalls of Mother as she re-ascended. She came in, picked me up and waited while Mrs Hodgkins gathered

79

Alexander. It was a cause of resentment that Alexander was forever being gathered rather than picked up. What's Hagendorff Syndrome? I haven't heard of it, Mrs Hodgkins said quietly. I guess it was quietly because after all it was me not Alexander who had it. A while later we were taken downstairs. Mrs Tintwistle arrived soon afterwards. She'd run out of sugar. All three women laughed because they're heard in magazines and on television about people coming to borrow sugar but this was the first time it had happened in life. When the laughter died, Mother asked Mrs Tintwistle where K was. Roger's with her, Mrs Tintwistle said. He's off work with his nose. Alexander and me caught sight of each other across the expanses of our mothers' shoulders. Alexander was pale despite a clean bill of health. He bubbled at me for a moment then was twisted away by Mrs Hodgkins. You have to mind noses with babies, she said. Oh but you can't guard them against every germ, Mrs Tintwistle said. It's not healthy. I felt Mother was keen for Mrs Tintwistle to go. She took me into the kitchen, poured with one hand some sugar into a cup and took it out to her. It was held at arm's length for Mrs Tintwistle. I'll bring you some back, Mrs Tintwistle said. Don't worry, Mother said. If I can't spare a bit of sugar it's a poor job. Isn't it Peter?

*

The time Harry overheard me mention Mrs Tintwistle he butted in to ask if I was sure I'd remembered correctly. I told him I appreciated his concern but hadn't he realised names from moons ago could have an odd quality, like Jugg. He asked who Jugg was. I explained about the lessons, leaving out Featherstonehaugh. And he had two G's? Harry asked. I fear he was being polite. Yes, I said. Maybe even three. Harry shook his head. Jugg's one thing, he said, but Tintwistle? I told him I'd have a think about it but only to get him off my back. I had a feeling he thought that because I was in here there was a chance I had the details wrong or had exaggerated or imagined them, which I daresay on occasions with other of his charges might be the case. Take Atkins's insistence last month that in the night he'd been woo'd by Ingrid Bergman. She'd become humanly embodied enough to hold his hand. K liked the part where Rick broke down when he first saw Ilsa Lund again. I wish you were more like that, she said, K, not Ingrid Bergman. I said what, in black and white and a heavy drinker? There are some attempts at humour you know you shouldn't have made even before they're fully out of your mouth. But it's true, I do tend to be reserved in the passion department. Colquahoon told Kandinsky one time the man who played Sam couldn't himself play the piano so the music had to be dubbed while he fingered the keyboard. Atkins wondered why they hadn't just found an actor who was also a pianist because in his opinion Dooley Wilson wasn't up to much as an actor either. Too self-conscious. And that way of craning his neck when he was about to – as it turns out – mime. Gentlemen, gentlemen, Harry said when he heard this eruption. If you continue I'll be switching off the DVD. Smetham stopped chewing long enough to say that would be a good move on Harry's part because frankly he couldn't give a damn. No one but Colquahoon dared point out the inappropriateness of the part-quotation. But blow me if Smetham hadn't even realised it had been a quotation in the first instance. There was our equivalent of uproar.

*

So yes, K wished I was more like Rick. I said it was typical of girlfriends worldwide to wish I was someone other than myself, and then I was prompted by the look on her face to reduce my criticism to her specifically. I've discussed it with Smithson though not in reference to K as such, more an age-old, probably mistaken impression that such was indeed the case. Smithson leaned against his windowsill and said: But Peter, why, there will never be another you in the history of the universe, to which we heard Eileen in the outer office give muted thanks. Turned out she'd had a spat with Ron and thus, Smithson proclaimed, she wasn't fond of males right now. He said Ron had gone out again in his break to fetch the ingredients of a prawn and mango dish he'd seen on television but so say Eileen didn't like mango, at which Ron – having had a bad day – took umbrage and threw the spatula across the kitchen, which was why – Smithson said proudly – I called it a spat in the first instance. He enjoyed it when on the rarest occasions, his words took on a life of their own. He said it had something to do with how the brain worked if given free rein. Let words alone and they'll be ballroom dancers, swinging here and there, connecting, reconnecting. The movement he made to unstiffen his neck at the window was a sign he wasn't happy with his images. He'd started out well with spat and spatula but the temptation thereafter to take control in the light of this linguistic accident threatened to end dancing altogether. I wasn't in the mood, stuck there and hair-wet on the dralon ruing a sensibility that had brought me into Therapeutic Specialism in the first place. The sky was monochromatic within each frame, reminding us, Smithson added, the world could be monochromatic too. I believe that was one of the things Eliot was on about in 'The Love Song Of J Alfred Prufrock', I said. Smithson growled deep in his throat, so deep it might have been his chest. That's not what I meant at all, he said. I twisted on the couch. But you've just said life could be monochromatic. I was pointing out that surely Eliot was partly referring to such a condition in his poem. You shouldn't try to get one over on me, Smithson said, languishing against the view. I'm not, I said. It just struck me all of a sudden how like parts of 'Prufrock' your comments about the world were. Then, having said 'all of a sudden' I realised with the same speed Smithson's argument was an attempt to get me away from Eliot and the poem because he didn't know of it and was hoping to avoid me finding out. After a lengthy silence – Smithson often allowed these on the basis it would give me time to search my soul – he said: I can't see prawns with mango anyway, I told her. I mean prawns are prawny, mango isn't. Against my better judgement I pointed out it would be helpful to me overall if he'd refrain from thinking through recipes while trying to relieve my mental hardship. The most curious sight then was Smithson shaking with silent laughter either at what I'd said, or something arising from the recipe; then again, as has happened many times, he may have been reacting to something in the workaday street. For a while afterwards – prawns having been saturated for the moment – we each remained quietly going through our own thoughts; maybe wondering if any of them were worth an airing. I'm sure I was on K again – she's so often the default of my interior world. I was thinking of the time we visited a churchyard for the sake of it not only in winter but deep in a midnight when hoar frost hung about the yews. It had started with her saying about ghosts and if I was the sort to be scared of them. I'd told her I couldn't be scared of something that didn't exist. We'll go at midnight to a haunted churchyard then, she said. I said: Actually we'll just be going to a churchyard. There's no possibility of it being haunted. The churchyard in question was out of town. On the way she explained she'd come across references to it in a book on the paranormal. I'd be interested to know the components of 'paranormal', I said. She said well, aside from poltergeists, there were UFOs, crop circles and Mysterious Human Phenomena. On the way in the car I was telling her I disliked books that had the word mysterious in the title because you could bet on there being nothing mysterious within. She laughed, but it was a fleeting thing and soon we were pointing through a mist that hung around the single-track road. This is a causeway, she said. The land either side floods at certain times of year. The church we're heading for stands on a raised ridge of land. The one before this was Saxon. Canute may or may not have popped in. I'm spellbound actually, I said to K. I had little idea about this side of you. Or King Canute. I saw him only with waves. That's because you're self-centred, she said, changing gear as we negotiated a bend. You won't ask anyone anything unless it's towards your advantage. I rubbed my nose. A lack of sensation in the tip due to the cold had led me to suspect it was running. I usually keep a tissue in my pocket, but today there was none. You're right, I said. So say it goes back partly to my mother and the Rumanians. It was as if the fabric of my life had been torn asunder. K shook her head. No one says asunder, she said. It was that sort of an incident, I told her. We were almost entirely enclosed by mist. We were reminded as one of *The Hound Of The Baskervilles* though we didn't know we were reminded as one till months later when it came up. Mist rolled over the car as we moved ever more slowly forward. You'll never guess who else is buried there, K said. That singer from the sixties. Bloke. Sideburns. Green trousers. Appeared years afterwards in floor wax commercials. It's odd when you do this, I said. Not only that but it's extraordinary you remember small things about people but not their name. She said never mind, we'd have a look while we were there. She couldn't quite remember where he was now. I asked her why he'd chosen to be buried in such an out-of-the-way place.

Don't know, she said. Maybe his family are from around here. She opened the window a little, a sign she was about to have a roll-up. She didn't often have one in the car but on this occasion I'd have said it was probably because she wouldn't want to disrespect the churchyard. I enjoyed the smoke as a little of it came across. I was reminded of Basil Rathbone. As we carried on in our quest, I had a sensation of love strong enough to make my legs and arms burn. A friend of K's from before (I think she meant Tom but didn't like to say) had asked her why she thought ghosts a particular size anyway? If they exist they could be dots, the friend said. I liked this idea so instead of saying something like Oh really? I concurred with the friend. It's in this fashion I've gained my extensive, largely irrelevant education. Yes, I went on, if you have the capacity to be a ghost at all then why bother maintaining an old size? Think of the inefficiency. The car crept for another ten minutes. Going uphill a little further on meant the mist thinned enough for us to see a few yards. K pulled in beside what became a lychgate. You seem to know this area, I said. I take it you've been here quite often. Don't start, she said. It wasn't with Tom, though I can't see it would matter if it had been. She opened the door into claws of night and climbed out of the car leaving me a mooncalf in the seat. I'd paused to think more about love. Come on. What are you sitting there for? That was K speaking from the lychgate, her own outline and the tip of her cigarette quietly visible. I'm reviewing what little I know of Basil Rathbone, I told her, though it wasn't true by then. As I got out of the car she told me he was born in South Africa but his parents were British. It was the sort of thing I disliked because other than his name and the fact he played Holmes, I knew hardly anything. Did he indeed, I said, timing the words with the creaking lychgate as we passed through. It was nice in some ways to have the thicker parts of the mist swirl our legs as we walked forward. So where are these ghosts? I said brusquely. If you're going to keep moaning there's no point us being here, she said. My waved arm itself created a maelstrom in the mist ahead. I hardly think me asking about ghosts given that's why we're here is reason enough for you to accuse me of moaning, I said, not sure I'd formed my sentence well. The tower's not high, she said, but it was up there one of the sightings took place. We reached for each other's hands simultaneously. I think we both felt embarrassed at first and wondered whether we should keep on with it, but as we moved forward our palms bonded. I said to her: Have you remembered the name of the singer? No, she said. Maybe we'll come across him, I said. I'm not looking specifically, she said, but yes, we might. I'm hoping so due to a lingering intrigue, I said. He also played saxophone, she went on. In the singing world it's as well to have an additional skill, I said. The footpath beneath us was unbearably soft. We'll be passing round the side soon, she said. There are yews further on. The person I was with before came another time too to do night photos. Oh? I said. I can't remember you mentioning that. It was when you were in one of your states so I didn't, she said. It's interesting though, I said, you keep mentioning the person you were with but you don't give a name. Does it matter? It was just someone from meetings. I don't know his surname. He dabbles in the occult as well as photography. It was odd I thought how often dabbles and occult came in the same sentence, and then using all my courage I stopped asking further questions. I told K sometimes it was like I didn't know her at all. She said that was one of the results of not making a firm commitment. I suggested we shouldn't use the word firm where commitment was concerned because commitment implied firmness in itself. Jugg used to mark us down if we used an adjective or adverb when the sense of the adjective or adverb was *in* the noun or verb itself. K said this was just the sort of chat she'd been hoping for. She let go of my hand. She was re-lighting her cigarette, making me realise I'd been wrong about the disrespect. It was odd not liking her just then and yet thinking life without her wouldn't quite work. I skipped a little. Out of the blue also I remembered the yellow fog that rubs its back upon the windowpanes, one of the lines early on in Prufrock except this was more mist than fog and it wasn't yellow. Perhaps his was born of a time when pollution in towns and cities was more visible. Father had mentioned pea-soupers they'd had when he was young.

*

Alexander said no, he absolutely wasn't in love with K. I'd been convinced otherwise. I didn't tell K of my suspicions at first. Smithson believed the reason was that deep down I feared I was wrong; that these worries were another manifestation of what had become known between us as the Rumanian Effect. Is it good for a Therapeutic Specialist to use the term Deep Down? I asked, in sport more than anything. He was at the window miming a pipe. He'd got a part in the dramatic society's production and practised at every opportunity. There are more technical terms, he said, but in view of the weather I'm allowing myself to be colloquial. May the fifth is my favourite day of the year. Light develops a luxurious tinge and all about us spring flowers peek above the surface of the soil. I reminded him it was the sixth. You weren't here on the fifth, he said, so I mention it now. What I really mean anyway is that if you were to take every day of every year of my life you'd probably find May the fifth – or thereabouts – was the most affable, generally speaking. He stepped aside, looking as if he might return to his chair at the end of the couch, but instead moved to the next window along. It can't have been nice for your friend to face such an accusation. I felt it best to get it out in the open, I said. You've always told me honesty reduces the chance of an inner sickness developing. Yes, but as with all my advice it's necessary to tailor it to specific circumstances, Smithson said. A guns blazing approach will often backfire. It took a while of mimed pipe to calm himself. My eyes were heavy, sticking at the lids whenever they closed completely. Each time I opened them he'd be standing with his back to me. The sky was virtually empty of cloud. Smithson took the pipe from his mouth. If I'd been the friend in question, he said, I fear it would be a long time before I felt the status quo had been restored. I see that now, I said. But the clues were there. I put them together and bingo. It doesn't do to become paranoid over the emotions of those closest to you, Smithson said.

*

I could feel nothing in my left hand though it held a wire basket. In my right I could feel a wire basket though there was nothing. K had wandered to another aisle. She'd said something about dried basil and garlic granules. At night she sprinkled them on olive-oiled toast with sliced tomatoes. I walked from one aisle to the next thinking it would be better if I came across her accidentally so she wouldn't think me grave or neurotic about the mixed-up hands. Oh there you are, I said when at last

I found her. She said: Did you get the gherkins? and this I saw as an opportunity. I was on the *brink* of gherkins, I said, when an odd thing happened. I would have laid money on it, K said. I didn't like the way she wasn't looking away from the herbs and spices display as she spoke. She said she was wondering whether to get Herbes de Provence to mix with the basil. I took some Herbes de Provence and stared at the label. You know me and anything given a French name, I said. Why can't they be just herbs from Provence? They won't be from Provence anyway. Watford more like. I put the jar back. I'm not sure strictly it *was* a jar. It was two or three inches high and slender. Jar's too big a word. The hand that held the wire basket but which felt as if it was holding nothing had gone cold. It was as if I was being erased. What about thyme, I said. K made a sound in her throat. Thyme's no good for that, she said. It's not the right flavour. Okay, I said, keep your shirt on. I looked at my hand hoping to inspire her to follow my gaze but she wouldn't have seen anything unusual. My heart quickened. She said casually to the upper row of mixed spices that we had previously identified as being most likely to contain excess salt: I saw Tom just now. He was buying a loaf. I looked round, not directly, but in bread's general direction. She said she'd been passing along when suddenly a hand was on her shoulder and there he was. It was nice to see him, she said. I expect it was, I said. It must be, what, ages since you last met? Why did you put a question mark at the end of that? she asked. I was missing the days when both hands worked to specifications. I didn't realise I had, I said. If I did it wasn't a question so much as one of those modern inflections. She said: What modern inflections? What are you talking about? I'm not sure I can put it succinctly, I said, but I'd heard making statements using the tone normally reserved for questions was on the up among younger folk. I swear you invent things, she said. I had to agree it had a made-up quality though I did in fact remember something of it, in a newspaper perhaps or magazine. K was drifting towards, among other things, passata, tomato puree and packs of chopped tomatoes flavoured with herbs. I didn't think you bought packet chopped tomatoes because of the preservatives, I said. Just because we're walking among them doesn't mean I'm buying any, she said. We moved on in silence till we were in pickles. So how was he? Tom? I said. I was staring at the gherkins I'd failed to buy. It numbed me to think how many gherkin jars there must be worldwide. It has to end sometime. Not just with gherkins either. Gherkins are only the thin green end of an inexorable wedge. Which was it you wanted? I said. I raised one of my hands a little and rubbed its knuckles. These are the ones, she said sweetly. Now my forearms ran cold. I keep meaning to try one, I said with what I believe was a squirm of the shoulders. This is exactly my point, she said. You're the only person on earth *meaning* to try a gherkin. Other people try them or don't. I can't see, I said, why my intention to try a gherkin at some point should cause you a problem. As long as you can enjoy them freely yourself. That seems to be the only criteria. She exhaled through her nose. It's criterion if there's one, she said. You're sounding like me now, I said. I was just helping you understand what it's like, she said. But, I said, you've helped me many times. I don't see a need to continue it. Anyway, are we getting gherkins or not? Only then did it fully come to me we'd left the herbs and spices area without buying garlic granules or basil. It may have been because we'd been distracted by the topic of Tom. I looked around myself in one sweep. Is he still here? Tom I mean? No she said, he was rushing back to work. He said he'll give me a ring one evening. One evening! I said. These syllables struck pickle jars in front of me. Sometimes I wonder if you two really split up. Now don't get in a pickle, K said, then laughed. She hadn't used pickle because we were in the pickle aisle, but thought it interesting it had happened. You'll always have a Tom to worry about, she said. You're afraid to let your own connections take hold. That's a bit strong, I said, though she might have had a point. You can't treat everyone as if they're fellow members of AA. It's nothing to do with AA, she said. Just an observation. You fail to take into account Tom and me broke up. If things had been okay we wouldn't have. I might try these. They look more central European. That's where gherkins ought to come from. I told her I didn't care where they came from or ought to come from especially since I hadn't tried one. Stop worrying about Tom, she said. Remember how old you are. I was told by Smithson certain reactions in the human mind are biological and as such firmly rooted in humankind's collective spirit, so ordinary procedures such as remembering how old I am would be ineffective. K took a jar of central European gherkins and put them in her basket. Why we needed a basket each was a mystery. I still couldn't feel the one I was holding with the hand holding it. I felt that once my panic had dimmed a little I might even enjoy the phenomenon. Life could too easily grind along fulfilling only its own workaday expectations. Now Greatness, do we need anything else? I most often called her Greatness when I was hoping to be forgiven. This time it was for the Tom incident and, to an extent, the gherkins. I didn't want to be jealous, that's the point. I wanted to be the kind who could pass into a cafe unexpectedly to find a Tom having coffee with K without batting an eyelid. I've boiled it down to sex, I said as we were venturing – as Tom and K had previously – into Bread. You've boiled what down to sex? she asked. Well because you and me don't have a full physical relationship it might be my psyche is afeared in case another man – Tom or whoever – comes along one afternoon and seduces you. That would be nice actually, K said, but I don't see it happening. Do you mean, I said, you don't *see* it happening or you don't *want* it to happen? And who would it be nice with? I meant nice generally, she said. Not with Tom. We didn't have much of a physical relationship ourselves. But yes it would be nice generally and non-specifically speaking with an anonymous person from time to time. I saved these words to an inner hard-drive for later. I don't know if you realised, I said, but you didn't get your herbs and your garlic granules. It's almost like something on your mind made you forget. That happens to me whenever I'm really worried about something. We were being passed by a woman I recognised from the checkouts. The previous day we'd had an incident with one of the plastic bags kept for customers at the tills. I said hello, with a wink intended to remind her of it. When she'd passed, K looked after her and said who was that? Anamika, I said. We had a thing with some bags. I don't know if I increased the number of bags to minimise the incident, make it less specific so to speak, or whether I thought K might feel jealous if I upped the quantity. It could even have been genetic. K said: Oh and began making her way again, I felt, to herbs and spices. I followed, grateful my hands were back in the right order. Just behind her here I had that same coldness in the forearms. She'd told me before people had to be careful with love because nine times out of ten it was only the manifestation of a mild mental illness – that is, you never really knew if it was love in the pure sense. She went on to say that in fact if love had any kind of *capture* involved it wasn't love at all. Turned out she'd heard these things from Gareth at her meeting. I said to her you certainly have a lot of people saying a lot of things at meetings. She said yes she did and she was grateful because it kept her grounded. You're a woman not a malfunctioning Airbus, I said. She said this wasn't a topic to joke about. To divert criticism I said now I came to think of it I was always repeating things to people Smithson used to say so maybe I was being a little harsh about the whole Gareth business. A little? K said.

*

So you're in love with her but haven't bothered to make advances. Am I reading you correctly? Smithson had imbued the r's of correctly with a growl similar to Jugg's whenever he was reading John Macnab to us in class. You're on the right track doctor, though 'bothered' isn't right, I said. The times we've started to be sexual we either become distracted by another topic or else we laugh. I sensed rather than saw Smithson rest one elbow on the sill as he continued his theatrical pipe. You find physical relations between consenting adults humorous? The small clouds could themselves hardly bother to make their way across the windows. You seem determined to talk of sexual matters Doctor, I said. This must have been about the time I'd first noted Anamika because I was remembering how she'd scanned the ingredients of my chicken stir-fry that morning. This also therefore must have been in the latter days of my connection with Smithson. It's unnerving how irregularly the cauldron of time simmers. Kandinsky has said linear time's an illusion anyway, granted to human beings only so they can make some sense of a chaotic world. Atkins, I remember, said enough of that Kandinsky and pass me a biscuit would you old boy? They'd decided they were going to put rivalries aside for a P. G. Wodehouse afternoon. I'd be delighted dear fellow, Kandinsky said. Biscuits were nibbled. The discussions had become wearied earlier

90

by the introduction of Cholmondley's Mole Detector, which he had tried to patent in the sixties. Nobody had wanted to fund him. Kandinsky said it was typical that when you had a good idea no one was prepared to stick their neck out. Atkins wanted to know why people would want a mole detector anyway. Cholmondley said: To detect moles. People with lawns for example. And sports fields, Kandinsky added. I was surprised because ordinarily Kandinsky didn't like to attach himself to idiosyncratic proposals. This it turned out much later was because he too had had problems with moles at his country home. We were aghast – even Harry – at the realisation Kandinsky had ever owned a country home, but it turned out he hadn't. He'd been an under-gardener in one. Almost everyone laughed.

*

Another day he explained to Atkins it was 'bison' even when there were many of them. Atkins being Atkins spent a while citing other members of the animal kingdom in the hope of catching Kandinsky out. I wondered at the time if I should chip in because we'd been through these things years before with Jugg, but for some reason I'm wary of trying to impose a greater truth. People don't thank you for it. You hope they might to begin with but then they don't. Colquahoon said he'd looked them up once. They were large wild oxen with shaggy hair and a fatty hump, commonly called buffalo in America, and furthermore, Colquahoon went on, I believe the same principle applies there, i.e. buffalo rather than buffaloes although I could be wrong. Looking at Colquahoon that day I could tell he was thinking he was right even as he was saying he might not be. Major Gwillingington (this being in a wakeful period) said we were ignoring an even greater curiosity, i.e. oxen. Smetham wondered why everyone was saying i.e. Just about then Harry came in looking like death because Cheryl had been in an accident caused by one of the younger Lambtons. She was okay but needed stitches in her upper arm, he said. We mused upon this long enough to make Harry think we were respectful of his difficulties, then launched back into oxen. I again wondered if I should mention Jugg because of what I'd been thinking about Oxon. I was beginning to sense an anxiety throughout the dayroom, which spilt on to the patio where innumerable wasps plundered flower cups. Our own subdued gardener had it about him to arrange terracotta pots left and right of the patio. Flowers in them dripped blooms, the fuchsias most of all. Of course mention blooms to Bulwark and his ears and beard perked up, hoping for Leopold. He believed *Ulysses* a great but awful book. I counted eighteen paces before asking why. I hadn't even been going to, but suddenly didn't want him hurting any more than he already was. Well, have you read it? he asked. I told him I'd had a go but only reached page two. There you are then, he said. But that's just me, I told him. As he glanced over, shreds of smoke escaped his beard, presumably from the cigarette he'd had a while before. If we assume, he said, a book is a contract between writer and reader then by not helping people beyond page two the writer's broken his part of the contract. But that was just me, I said again, this time changing tense. We were walking the ridge of an earthen bank to the right of where, during excavations for the lakeside, the Roman pottery was unearthed which was now displayed in the college foyer. The range of fragments suggested occupation over two centuries. But, Bulwark continued, there has to be a way of writing about the richness and complexity of life without becoming inaccessible. I mean look at that *Finnegan's Wake* bollocks. I stumbled as I followed the bank almost as if the profanity had struck me. Excuse me for saying, I said, but it's not like you to run down literature. I'm in a mood about it today, he said. I had a feeling you might be because of your lack of contributions in the seminar, I said, though to be honest I put that down to your troubles in the Maureen department. Don't call her the Maureen department, he snapped. By using the word department, I said softly, I was hoping to suggest not only Maureen, but things associated with her. Such as the Dean. I was pleased at the way I was therefore able to condemn mildly his anti-matrimonial ambitions without being too obvious. Even so, Bulwark continued, in searching for a word to describe *Finnegan's Wake* I don't believe bollocks falls far short of the truth. Though I secretly agreed, I decided to play devil's advocate. It was something you had to do if literary conversations were to have longevity. I was about to start playing it in fact when Bulwark sighed. Sorry I snapped about the Maureen department, he said. I told him it was okay and that I couldn't begin to understand how difficult it must be to love a woman apparently so rigidly attached to a Dean. And let's face it, I said, the Dean will have cash, prestige, and there's the Jaguar. I know, it makes me sick as a matter of fact, Bulwark said. When I look at Maureen in the cold light of day I can see she probably won't want to give up life in Academia for more simple pleasures however much she loves me. That's why really the affair idea— I felt I had to stop him there. You don't actually know she does love you, I said, folding my arms and hoping we'd soon get back to Joyce. No you're right I don't, not actually, but I'd lay odds on it, Bulwark said. When I stand next to her there's a vibration made by both of us as we struggle not to give in to our physical feelings. I have to confess though, he went on, that if she were to lunge I doubt I'd resist. We were absolutely fighting our way now through midges. I can't see Maureen lunging, whatever her feelings, I told him. By nodding in a certain way I was led by him into the trees to have another smoke. We stood in the fragrant shadow, me picking up a stick to whack a fern while waiting for he who puffed and shook his head and dreamed. After a while he gazed into the middle distance. Joyce definitely wasn't fulfilling his authorial contract there either, he said. The way I see it Peter is if you're hoping to draw the reader into a new way of reading, you need to do it more gently. Fair enough *Ulysses* is pivotal – pivotal – in the way it introduces us to the psychology of Man and the psychology of writing, but apart from the driest of literary folk – I count myself among them – who has read it completely and, more than that, who has understood its importance? Certainly not Joe Bloggs. I glanced aside as if to acknowledge Mr Bloggs but Bulwark didn't notice. I can't count the number of amusing things I've wastefully mimed in life. I was feeling a little stuck in the trees, which is why I'd had a go at the glance in the first place. The intensity of some people holds you to the spot, giving you little time to do anything while they talk but imagine ways of escape. The Molly Bloom part was good though, I said at last. Bulwark sniffed. Then he smoked. Thought you said you only got to page two, he said. Molly's at the far end. That is correct, I said, but I did flick through at other times and I came upon her. Yes, I've studied her myself on occasion, he said, and much as I admire Joyce's effort, would it have ruined it altogether if he'd used punctuation? I mean you wouldn't blame Joe Bloggs for giving up at that point even supposing he ever got that far. Though this was another opportunity for the Bloggs mime, I didn't bother. Even if it had succeeded, the placing of Bloggs's name in this instance didn't afford as much comedy. I tend to agree with some of what you're saying, I told him, though I'm having a hard time concentrating. I haven't been feeling well. Bulwark held the cigarette an inch from his beard. Really? Yes, I said. I have a syndrome. Hagendorff to give it its full name. I've had it since I was a baby. When Bulwark said casually he was sorry to hear it, I registered a disappointment he hadn't asked for details. I decided to give him some anyway. Yeah, I said, it's hard to put a finger on but there are days where I'm headachy, washed out and altogether subdued. The worst thing about it I suppose is it never gives me anything dramatic enough for other people to appreciate fully what it's like. When I looked towards Bulwark he started to walk out of the trees. It's something I don't feel I'll ever get used to that most of the time people love talking about themselves, but hardly ever like it if something they've said reminds you of something that you then try to talk about. Come, he said, let us continue our perambulation. We came up the side of the first bank, turned right and followed its undulating summit. Cash *and* a Jaguar, Bulwark said, I think to himself. I'm only guessing about the cash, I said. He is a Dean after all. But the Jaguar I've seen. Well, we both had, sleek, dark blue, often parked in a reserved space next to a building known colloquially as The Priest's House. While we're on the topic of Maureen, I said, or no, it's not about her at all really, though there are connections. Just get on with it, Bulwark said. Okay, well you know Jennifer Hough? Yes, he said, what about her? Well I've noticed she looks at you a great deal. I'd say she has the hots. Bulwark took a casual drag. Hots? What are those? They're where you fancy someone, I said. Never heard of them, was Bulwark's response. But even supposing it's true why would someone have them for me? I said, to please him mostly, it'll be the intellectual in you. Not everyone's into looks. Not that you don't have looks but I don't think it's the entire motivation in this case. I started noticing her noticing you in the refectory. It must have been the day you announced you were going to partake of apple pie subsequent to your main meal. Aha, he said, you used partake there as an echo of Pumblechook's tone when he came to dinner at the forge in *Great Expectations*. Dickens was at great pains to ensure we understood Pumblechook partook of pudding rather than just eating it. Nothing gets past you, I said, though in truth I hadn't realised the Pumblechook connection and frankly was still mystified when I got home and looked it up. It was never enough, I felt, to spot a connection unless you were able to explain what value the connection had in terms of the book or, say, other works by that same author or other works contemporary with them or indeed the whole of literature since the written word began. I'm not sure if I said any of this aloud to Bulwark. I remember looking at the ruffled fabric of the lake and the scattered waterfowl upon it and wondering at the same time, as I often did, what life was really about. Quietly, under his breath to be exact, Bulwark was playing with the sound *Jennifer*. After a while he mumbled: The hots you say? Well well.

*

Some here get them though not as often as in their younger days and without there necessarily being a person to attribute them to. Harry was saying Dylan had them for any number of woman much to his wife's anguish. She came to terms over the years with the fact Dylan's grubby genius was likely to attract a legion of admirers, he said. He was leaning against the door-frame in such a way as to suggest he wouldn't mind a legion himself. Another poor Cheryl day. He told me in confidence marriage was like that, sometimes you loved, sometimes you didn't. I'd seen much the same principle in action. It came to light Father had taken Miss Woo to the pub a few days before. It was an accident, he said. He'd been on his way to the Moon and Sixpence and there she was, looking at the menu in The Star Of Bengal window. He'd mentioned it only because they'd been spotted by Mrs Chaffin who'd now come round specially to let Mother know. Once the row had died, Father said snappily he was going out and Mother said snappily to make sure he didn't take any women to any pubs this time. Alexander and I bounced in our harnesses. Mother had offered to look after Alexander while Mr and Mrs Hodgkins were given half-price haircuts and manicures at the local technical college by students who did it as part of their training. Bouncing at all made us feel grim, especially Alexander who was simultaneously having to wear pink. One of his aunts had guessed he might be a girl and his blue was in the wash. Only Mrs Tintwistle arriving with K saved us. K was deposited in a rush basket on the chair opposite Alexander and me. It became evident she enjoyed eating her toes. This was something me and Alexander hadn't mastered. We had to assume therefore it was a skill particular to girls. Mrs Tintwistle flopped into her chair and took the cuppa offered by Mother. She's been a scamp today, she said, glancing in at K and using one hand to adjust the frill of the basket. I haven't known whether I've been coming or going. It's been bedlam here too, Mother said. He's been seeing that Woo tart again. Your husband? Mrs Tintwistle said. I thought that was all in the past. I don't like it but what can I do? Mother asked rhetorically. I can hardly stop him going out. Some men are more trouble than they're worth, Mrs Tintwistle said between sips. Roger's off work with his knee this week so I can keep an eye on him. But he's generally no trouble in that department anyway. Mother said Mrs Tintwistle should thank her lucky stars and that for her part if there ever was a next time she was going to find a dumb, blind, legless husband. She laughed hysterically. Mrs Tintwistle followed suit, but for the look of it I felt. K had almost her whole foot in by now.

*

Whenever she was fearful she'd say the serenity prayer. She hung her hand over the side of the ferry despite Health and Safety though she couldn't, as she'd hoped, reach the water. I had one eye on a seadog whose manner and outfit troubled me. He'd asked the boatman for a ticket to the Lower Dock so I knew at least his time with us would be short. Despite a dusted sky and soft wind K was chilly. Pools of cooler air lay about the surface of the harbour even when it had warmed up elsewhere. So, I said as casually as I could, I can't imagine you've brought us to a ferry for no reason. How soon are you going to unravel the mystery? The roll-top of the seadog's sweater had seen better days. K said couldn't she suggest a ferry ride without me getting hot under the collar? Ah, I said, but then there was your phoning out of the blue, the insistence it should take place today and that little sound tagged on to each of your words. I swear you make things up as you go along, she said. The other time you had that little sound, I told her, you denied everything for ages then said you'd met Tom in the museum cafe and had – what was it? – low-fat seed cake. I remember wondering at the time why you'd bothered to give the cake its adjectives even though they were irrelevant to the main thrust. Well spotted, K said. She brought her hand back up over the side and laid it in her lap. It curled upon itself like a spider hit by a newspaper. I have seen Tom again as it happens, she said, but it wasn't in the museum. What a relief, I said, jerking my chin towards the seadog who was sitting with hands clasped to his knees. I was admiring his gumboots. Where then? I asked. I didn't look at her, hoping she'd see how casual I was these days. He came to the flat for coffee, she said. I remained with my hands between my legs. She said: He was just passing and hoped I didn't mind. I said: And was there anything particular he wanted to discuss with you? Her brow corrugated. If there was it certainly didn't come to light. He had his cup of tea and a couple of biscuits then he was off. I asked what sort of biscuits considering there didn't seem to be any last time I was round her place. She said did it matter? I told her I was hoping to build an accurate picture of the event instead of making up details myself, something she'd chastised me for on many occasions. Anyway, she said, I thought I'd mention it so you know you've nothing to worry about. I flashed my brows at the seadog. He'd know having nothing to worry about wasn't reassuring. Water either side of the boat reminded me of Monet I think it was. *The Bridge At Argenteuil.* Jugg had a framed print of it to one side of the classroom door. It was there to remind us, he said, but in the time I was there he didn't say of what. If I tell you now it'll remind you falsely, he said. If you reach leaving day and it hasn't reminded you of what it is I'd like you to be reminded of, there's something lacking. Several of us felt it unfair to suggest we should be reminded of something by *The Bridge At Argenteuil* but not tell us what. Later I had a feeling he might have said it should remind us of something because he wanted to appear enigmatic but that actually it wasn't really supposed to remind us of anything except, say, boats, rivers, bridges.

If ever Harry reaches me with the trolley I've a feeling he'll suggest I become more focused. He dislikes anything haphazard because, he says, haphazard equals inaccurate. Assuming he does say something along those lines I feel I ought to respond by suggesting that, on the contrary, it's often through the haphazard one *discovers* accuracy. Yes, I might well say that, though I'm not sure of its overall veracity. If we concentrate – I might say – on the accurate too often, it could easily create a barrier between us and enlightenment. Yes, the word enlightenment could persuade him I know what I'm talking about. I'm fed up of people coming in over the top of what I've said or done to provide what they insist is a more accurate interpretation. Harry might say my reasoning's defensive, bordering on the paranoid. Now, we don't like it – any of us in here – if ever what Kandinsky calls The P Word's bandied about. He himself is able to cite historical instances where a person deemed to be paranoid turned out *in the long run* to have predicted accurately. The notion of the long run's important because too often people expect things to have relevance and accuracy from the outset or at least soon afterwards. I'll say to him, I'll say: Harry we must look at this and see how we can best modify that expectation. Kandinsky's sensitive about this area of things because he happened, he said, to read some of his notes (upside down as he sat at Harry's desk) and saw 'paranoid' underlined. He later came to believe however it was a specific diagnosis rather than just Harry's opinion. This offset his fury a little.

*

I wondered if I should say the area reminded me of the marshes in *Great Expectations* but I worried I might have said it last time; even the time before that. The estuary shone below hills at the far side. I like coming here, K said, not because it's beautiful because really it isn't, but because of something. I was walking with the help of a stick I'd found. It too had teeth marks. I glanced at K, waiting for her to say what the something was, but she didn't often concern herself with the need to explain. There was a tidal surge along here several hundred years ago, I said eventually.

I saw it on TV. Many villages along the banks were wiped out. She held my hand. Sixteen o six, she said. I told her I didn't know the exact date. Yeah, she said, sixteen o six. There's a plaque in a church the other side of the estuary. I was there once. With Tom. I told her she and him seemed to have gone most places. He liked walking, she said. There'd been no rain or a higher tide for a time. The edges of the salt marsh were cracking. I hadn't worn the right shoes. They believe two thousand people perished, she said. That many? I hadn't realised, I said. But don't you think perishing sounds preferable to dying? The flask in the haversack dug my ribs. I was planning to enter a phase of self-pity. Our hands were perspiring though the weather wasn't particularly warm. I can't imagine anything worse than being caught in a tidal surge, I said. K said she'd heard drowning was a good way to die. Till we hear from someone who's drowned, let's say the jury's out, I told her. If any death can be said to be good, I'd opt for hypothermia. You're snug and sleepy then you die. K let go of my hand, passing towards a low wind-shaped hedgerow. When she was there she appeared to look through. Then she came back. I was checking that pool from last time, she said, the one with the ducks. I asked her if there were any today. I was bored of my own question because I didn't mind if there were or not. Smithson said tiring of ducks was a sign of depression. He went on to say you could substitute most waterfowl, indeed animals of any kind for ducks in what he'd said. He'd used them mostly to tie in with what *I'd* said. Me and K walked on beside the estuary, weaving through tussocks of rough grass. Sometimes, I said, I believe you might have had a better time with Tom than you have with me. I had a *different* time with Tom, she said. Since the tide seemed to be on a vague diagonal we were getting closer to the water, the ground becoming softer underfoot. They found Neolithic footprints along here, I said. I know, she said, adding, to my surprise: I suppose you enjoy walking with me. I explained to her Smithson used to say the idea of enjoyment was entirely specific to the person concerned. Thus, however much *I* might enjoy it, I said, millions of people might not enjoy walking with you at all.

*

I was a stiff child – not in the sense of being precociously aroused, more in the way Alexander meant as we were eating our buns. Your mouth, he said, doesn't have fluidity as you chew. If you don't fix it there could be trouble later. Girls don't like anxious people. For the first time I revealed to him details of the Rumanian incident. He said after this that though he could see such traumas might predispose a person to anxiety, he – and Smithson I believe – were of the opinion all anxieties were thereafter chosen rather than suffered. The hems of his shorts were too wide. We'd been packed off to the copse a hundred yards up on the other side of the road by Mother and Mrs Hodgkins, who felt we must learn to fend for ourselves in case of nuclear war. Mrs Hodgkins had been reading how Aboriginal boys in Australia were sent into the bush to become men. She'd modified the ritual by insisting we should be back straight after the buns. I lay back and looked into the trees. Yes, I knew what Alexander had meant about being stiff. I'd already discussed it with Smithson who said let's deal with one thing at a time if we may. Alexander, after his own opening bun and before any biting of his second, melted to the ground beside me. He said anxiety was also in the way I walked, which could be like a Grenade Guard. Quietly he brought from one of his pockets two cigarettes stolen, he said, from his mum's bag and did I want one? I said no. He lit his, holding it gingerly between thumb and first finger. I realised I'd thought of it as gingerly because he was wearing a ginger coat some at school admired. I was drawn upwards by the swell of the leaf canopy and fancied myself becoming one with it so that soon I too might rustle in the wind. Girls are a mystery on the whole, Alexander said. You think you've got the hang of them then find you haven't. I said I'd been told as much myself. Smithson's always on about them. The thing is though Alexander, there's nobody for me but K. You haven't said anything before, Alexander said, taking a ginger puff at the cigarette. I was holding on till I was sure, I told him. He was shocked enough to sit up. Does she know? I said there was a resonance between us she was sure to have noticed if she was half the girl I imagined. Words were coming ahead of me. Some of what I'd said I hadn't known till I heard. You know Horace likes her? Alexander said. I said calmly I'd heard on the grapevine something to that effect. But I explained it didn't matter what Horace felt. It was only what K and I felt that mattered. I can tell it's serious the way you said K and I, he said. I told him I'm sure she would say Peter and I if the matter came up, which is why I'd used it plus I'd heard rich and royal people say the same. I intend to check its grammatical correctness with Jugg at the soonest, I told him. I fancied digging a hole in the bank to one side of the path, lying in it, getting Alexander to cover me and remaining there for eternity. It's a shame he's called Horace, he said. But then Alexanders aren't thick on the ground either. He was drawing smoke into the back of his throat and making it come out of his nose. It was something he'd copied from a comedian his mum liked. Funny things comedians, he went on. They say things and we laugh. They say things and I *don't* laugh, I told him. It'll be connected to the stiffness, Alexander said. You're scared if you let yourself laugh too much you'll open the floodgates to hidden sorrow. Smithson again, I said, except he doesn't call them hidden sorrows because they aren't. Hidden things are what makes us ill he told me. I was uninspired. It didn't seem to matter much if you were well or not. If Horace had an ordinary mum he wouldn't be trying to subsume his neuroses in the love of a woman, Alexander said. I sat up too at this stage. Anxiety was making the ground even more uncomfortable. You cannot, I said, class all loves of the Horace type as symptomatic of an illness. Alexander smoked a while. But Horace is a cheesy boy, he said, and the love of cheesy boys does have a psychopathic component. Add this to the mum factor and you've got a recipe for disaster. If you'll forgive me Alexander, I said, some of what you say seems to be at odds with what you said just now. You seemed to be saying that once you know you're anxious all anxieties thereafter are chosen. It was only then he remembered his second bun. A curl of smoke left his mouth as he opened it to take a bite. You're right, he said. It's hard making sense consistently. Join the club, I said. I'd been worrying for some time about my incoherence where girls – K specifically – were concerned. It was like I ended up saying to her the opposite of what I meant. I'd sort of decided to write things down and give them to her so there'd be no mistake. The thing about Horace, I said, is he's unlikely to try hard with K. I can see him building up to it sometimes but then it's just as if someone lets the air out of him. That's because of his mum, Alexander said. He's inadequate in her shadow. She is this town's best poet after all. And then there's the father running off to sing in West End Musicals. Poor Horace hasn't stood a chance. And all this is on top of the height thing. I understand your sympathies, I said, but don't call him poor. It makes me feel you think he'd be better with K than me. Not at all, Alexander said, it's just the way his life's already fallen apart to an extent. We moved on then to talk about life itself and what we understood of it. Alexander said on balance he was glad he was here. So was I, I said, otherwise I'd be talking to myself. I believe at that moment we liked the copse a little more. The air was tainted with garlic and above us a wood pigeon called. Looking up, Alexander wished he knew more about birds. Unless it's robins or a jackdaw, I'm fucked, he said. And who'd be a sparrow anyway? I said.

*

Our smallest songbird, the goldcrest, is dull green above, buff white below with a distinctive orange or yellow crown stripe. K was reading from the book she'd brought along. Thereafter for several minutes we checked the bushes. How's your mental health? she asked. I glanced at her, raising my brows at the shift in topic. Reasonable, I believe, I said. But I have a theory the more healthy we *think* we are mentally, the less we are. Like Economists. The reason I've asked, she said, is you seem unusually distracted. I guess she was right, though I wouldn't have been able to say what I was distracted by. She asked if everything was all right at the Office. I told her everything *was* if I didn't count Henderson. She raised one eyebrow and asked what he was up to now. Oh I said, it wasn't so much what he was up to, more a certain je ne sais quoi in his attitude towards me. He fails to keep an analogous exclusion zone between us whenever we're on the same shift. K was tickled. I don't suppose you mean analogous, she said. It sounded okay at the time, I said, but perhaps you're right. *Henderson.* Whenever his name came up it was like someone had lain their forearm under my heart and jerked it upwards. It appeared he either gelled his hair excessively or else it was false altogether. He wangled the meatiest files. He might be jealous of you, K said. If he is I can't think why, I said. It might be he considers himself devoid of your charm, looks and instinctive way of dealing with problems, she added. We were approaching the highest rampart of the earthwork. Is there a Mrs Henderson? she asked as we came to the top. He talks of little else, I said. She makes his sandwiches, not always to his liking. She insists on cheese three times a week. He craves Emmental, receives Cheddar. I sighed to indicate the internal connections I was making between Henderson's problem and my own life. He should say something to her, K said, hauling herself on to level ground. No sense in martyrdom in matters of cheese. My heart was running quickly as I reached the top behind her. And before we go any further, she said, please no mention of the ancient peoples or roundhouses. I scanned the tree-covered plateau. You generalise too much, I said. Besides, the cheese was mostly metaphorical. I might have been saying to you in a roundabout way *I* crave Emmental and receive Cheddar. K said that for some people accepting a cheese they don't crave is a syndrome they wish to remain in because it gives them what they see as an adequate excuse for self-pity.

*

Whenever I feel myself drifting, I try to paddle back into port. Moor myself squarely and maybe clear my throat. Internal sound helps. The worry would be you see, according to Harry anyhow, too much drifting might one day result in my losing sight of land altogether. There are some advantages to that he said in the sense that eventually you wouldn't be aware you'd lost sight of it, but all the same it would mean you'd most probably be on Nine. Nine's not so bad, I told him, it's Ten I wish to avoid. Harry chuckled, turning to the window. He could hardly bear not thinking Dylan things. He said it might have been the word curlew or the smell of Caitlin or the fishingboat-bobbing sea. The room took a breath, a moment of moments, the briefest interlude and yet it took eternity and all the while I drifted towards and then to the inside of Harry's skin. A dropped spoon brought me back or maybe it was Fiona coming round. I have an exceptional memory for unexceptional things. I sometimes try to take hold of memories as if they were physical. I might grasp an edge but always it slips away. In some ways that's like the sea itself, Harry said, which was a surprise because I hadn't realised I'd said that part aloud. Yes, I said, it has led me to believe death is something of a reunion with the Great Ocean. Harry liked that idea. Yes, I said, me too, but then I begin to wonder if there's any point saying things in the long run if they don't end up being written down. Harry waggled his head. Well, he said, I suppose the point might be things like that can add minutely to life itself even if they're not written. I mean here I am for one going to be taking your words home and who knows they might end up being regurgitated to someone else. Cheryl maybe. I was hoping you wouldn't say Cheryl, I said. No offence but you've said she doesn't like Dylan. The chances are if she doesn't like him she isn't going to be impressed by Great Oceans. I could tell Harry was tiring by the way he hoisted one leg at the knee and began to retie his lace. When it was done he returned his foot to the floor. I'd better get back to my desk, he said, I've got a report to write. If it's about me remember to explain I was only trying to live in anticipation of miracles, I told him in jest. He gave me a closed-mouth nod as if considering the entirety of the universe, his packed lunch, both.

*

Words begin the moment I wake, creating an extensive catalogue. K says it's something she needs to beware of for herself. Her own catalogue, unchecked, can lead to a condition called Stinking Thinking because, if you like, she said, the mind's default setting is towards self-destruction in an addict. I crossed my legs. I didn't care that normally I would have regarded it as a feminine gesture. I was also holding my cup like Noel Coward. We were in the Harbour Cafe. It can't have been long after our walk on the earthworks. It's interesting, I said, you still call yourself an addict even though you haven't had alcohol for years. I cleared my throat. I was trying to rid myself of a news reporter's tone. The principle is this, she said. She took up a handful of peanuts. She ate one, two, three, four, five, one at a time. I felt she was never going to say what the principle was. You get that with some people. They think if they hint they know what a principle is there's almost no need to explain. Eventually I had a peanut myself. Over K's shoulder fragments of light criss-crossed the harbour. I was ninety per cent happy. The other ten per cent was wrapped up in not being sure what the future held either at the Office or in a medical sense. I'd been able to track the Hagendorff Syndrome spreading like frost across a windowpane. You must stop this, I said. Saying only the first part of a sentence. I took a Coward-like slug of lemonade. It's hard to explain when you're not an addict yourself, she said, but if you have an illness of addiction it never goes away. It doesn't matter how long you've been without whatever substance it is, you reawaken a craving if you take up whatever it is again. So, I said, pausing long enough to try the peanut trick but not having the confidence to maintain it as long as she had, you're saying if you took alcohol you'd be ill again? K sighed. As sure as eggs is eggs, she said. I just thought you didn't do it any more because you didn't want to, I said. Oh I don't want to, she said, not often anyhow. To the left of her right hand was a plate that held in contempt a slice of mince pie. I was waiting for her to eat it because she'd asked if I could get her one, which I felt at the time was a large part of why we'd come into this particular cafe. The proprietor was known for her pastries. I nodded towards the slice minutely and with a sense of the aeons of injustice my soul had endured. There was a time, I said, when you could really only get mince pie in the Christmas Season. Now there's a free-for-all. I chuckled because I'd hoped to reminisce though I had no real idea about what. I'm saving this one up, she said, before you ask why I haven't eaten any. Nothing was further from my mind, I said. I'm not always the detective. I saw you eyeing it, she said. I scratched my brow, detaching at the same time a strand of hair. Eyeing's a strong term, I said, too strong for anything related to mince pies. Though I confess on many occasions what I say has a loaded edge, it would also be true to say you constantly look for loaded edges even when there aren't any. It's something Henderson does too and it gets my goat. The gentleman on the next table along glanced at me through crimson eyes, his jacket reminding me of the one Jugg used to wear. I believe he'd been startled by Goat. The human ear will often prick at anything it regards as deviant to the situation it's in. An experiment carried out by an American university established that the word milk uttered repeatedly in a cafe will hardly provoke a response from those within earshot whereas dagger would. As ever and wearily in my mind I wondered if I should discuss this with K and, as ever again, I decided not. She'd criticise my diversity and inattention. Mind you I've never before seen a mince pie with a glacé cherry on, I said. Yeah, K said. I'll take it off when nobody's looking. You have a right, I said, it has been paid for. Rather than applaud my stance, she asked what glacé cherries were anyway. I told her I felt it was when they were iced with sugar and suchlike. I hadn't meant to say suchlike. You mean the same as candied, she said, as in candied peel. I said I thought so. She said well why use the word glacé when they could say candied? They'd save a word. I don't expect they're bothered, I said. But perhaps if you check you'll find good reason why there are two words even when, nowadays, we feel one would do. I then asked if we really had to have this sort of conversation. She said she couldn't think what I meant because surely this was an ordinary encounter between two people over coffee. I said first of all I wouldn't say this was an ordinary encounter and second of all I had tea. She said she thought I was on a build-up to one of my cafe moods. I told her I *wasn't* on a build-up to one of my cafe moods even if I supposed I knew what cafe moods were. Well for a start, she said, when you're not building up to a cafe mood you're happy to accept that every now and again you have them. The fact you're not happy to accept it now is a sure sign you are, in fact, building up. I shook my head. There's no need to use the words 'in fact' I said. Especially since on this occasion there would be little doubt it is you, not I, who's in a mood, cafe or otherwise. I had a feeling one was starting as we walked here. There are things you do when such a mood is imminent that you don't do any other time. Oh really, she said. I'd be interested to know what those are. Well, I said, you fold your arms when walking. Then there's the chewing the ends of your hair, not all of the time, but in bouts. I can't think where you get these things, she said. If you were in a recovery programme they'd suggest you might be para-noid. I scratched my nose to hide a feeling of being wounded, got up and went to the counter. I ordered a slice of lemon cake, three quarters of which remained on an ochre stand. I turned to K thinking to check if she'd like a slice to go with her pie. Somehow she was already outside smoking. Now that was another thing Henderson wouldn't like. He said smokers should be forced to confront their own lungs. We'd had this conversation by the drinks machine and I'd said I didn't think you could force people to confront their lungs precisely because as a society we were collectively responsible for creating God knows what pollution and it could well be we inhaled as many toxins walking down the street as we ever did from a genial cigarette. I'd used genial not to defend cigarettes as such, but K's enjoyment of them. Henderson prickled. I'd rather you didn't take the Lord's name in vain, he said. I'm sure, I said, that if there is a Lord and he's all he's cracked up to be – even supposing he is a he, which I doubt – then I imagine he wouldn't mind in the least having his name taken in vain. It's only people like us who have a problem with it. We're small you see, I said triumphantly, and we *think* small. Henderson turned to the machine, programming in coffee white with sugar. He watched the entire process of the drink being dispensed before turning to me and taking a sip. He was known throughout the Office for answering rhetorical questions. The most recent was when I'd said that morning what kind of weather did he call this? and he'd gone on to explain in precise meteorological terms. My wife and I are Christians, he said now. We'd be grateful if you refrained from belittling our beliefs. I missed the button for coffee white without sugar and had minestrone. I turned to him when I'd taken the cup. I don't reckon I've belittled any beliefs, I said. He sighed before heading off. Work was hateful again. I'd been in the middle of filing the resource notes and then was planning to collate something though I couldn't remember what. I put the failing memory down to an expansion of the Hagendorff Syndrome. When I re-entered my cubicle fifteen minutes later there was a heart-shaped silver-foiled praline on my desk. I watched it, hoping a reason for it would come to mind, but in its silence it remained inexplicable. I sat at my chair, pushing the praline aside and gathering the resource notes. It wasn't that I hated the Office itself, just the kind of work that achieved things only for other people while providing us with hush money. Smithson it was, who said this was an attitude I'd grow out of. You keep, I said, expecting me to grow out of things I'm glad to have grown into. He turned to survey the city. You took a misguided footpath somewhere along the way, he said.

Had Jugg been there he would have pointed out it was I, not the footpath, who was allegedly misguided but then I'm sure, in that affable way of his, Smithson would have said he'd transposed the adjective for literary effect. I said: Hush money in the sense we go home exhausted to our ready-meals and watch repeated TV, and in our tiredness be reluctant to take on the authorities. I'd believed it a moment before yet suddenly my view was nonsense. I perked myself up and began to eat the lemon cake with a fork, keeping an eye on K simultaneously. The only thing between a smoker and looking crazed is the cigarette. I remembered other times, collective times, when we may have walked the harbourside just here dressed against the cold or arthritically uncomfortable in the heat, and even though I was still with her then, I missed her. Almost to the extent of abandoning the cake and going out there. Then I took a moment to remember the praline and to wonder who'd left it and what motive they might have had. An admirer who remains anonymous has charm. I was of course assuming it wasn't just a lost or abandoned praline, of which there must be some in the world. I'd put it on the shelf above the back of my desk thinking to unwrap and eat it would amount to a betrayal of K. I've loved no one else since time began. It's beginning to look as though it'll stay that way. You say that to people and ten to one they'll question it or think you mad and yet in some ways it's the most comfortable condition. Stupidly I can't remember what the weather was like that day. I remember the cafe well though. It causes me pain as a matter of fact because it's looking like I may never go there or any other cafe again. As I edge towards Ten this probability unhinges my soul.

*

Harry says Dylan's writing day could be shorter than most people's. More often than not he'd go to Brown's Hotel or his parents' place. His work would ferment for weeks. In his younger Swansea years he'd walk from Cwmdonkin Drive to Worm's Head and fall asleep on the slopes of the Outer Head, more than once becoming stranded by the tide. You're a labyrinth of information, I said. Yes, Harry said. I've been to Worm's Head, with and without Cheryl. The best times were without. Not only doesn't she like Dylan, she isn't keen on the coast. How can someone not like the coast? I said. Oh I don't know. It's not quite true anyway, Harry said. It's more she prefers long flat coasts with vehicular access and chocices. Worm's Head's rugged and hard to get to even on foot. I was doing well, I thought, not asking precisely where Worm's Head might be. I'd enjoyed too Harry's sarcastic pronunciation of the h in vehicular, the tone he'd used reminding me of a person from the deep south. I found in it further criticism of Cheryl. Though love's often initiated by noble gestures, it flounders mostly on insignificant details. I guess I'm saying I suspect all might not be as well between Harry and Cheryl as I first believed. The longer a mind's left to itself the more likely it is to realise truth. Bulwark was the first to suggest this on one of our circumnavigations. I held off from letting him know I'd glimpsed truth since I was small, if not very small. Bulwark went on to say he was brought up to seek truth only to realise later all he need really do is allow it to seek him. Once it knocks, he said, my part is to be brave enough to let it in. These words marked the beginning of an acceptance in him that perhaps Maureen wasn't going to abandon the Dean in his favour. I also wondered, if this was indeed the case had my mention of Jennifer Hough anything to do with it? In recent seminars she'd looked at Bulwark less than she had before, for sure, but I felt it was boredom and impatience rather than a cooling and if only she could have a sign he was even half interested she'd perk up. I came closely alongside him and thrust back the cowl of his duffel coat. Remember me telling you about Jennifer? I said, noting the hideous contrast between skin and beard. He gave me a look before restoring the cowl. I remember you saying something about the hots or whatever they're called in respect of someone, he said, but I hardly remember the name. I leaned down to pluck a stalk of grass. No, I went on, waving the blade in front of me, what I suspect's going on is you *are* interested in Jennifer but because you've made a song and a dance about Maureen you're afraid outright acceptance of another's feelings would indicate an insincerity about you. Bulwark said: If I'd known you were going to turn into Freud I wouldn't have suggested this perambulation. I took the grass from my mouth and threw it aside. An area of my tongue was bitter. Jennifer's a nice girl I'm sure, Bulwark said, but there you have it: *girl*. It's Maureen's womanliness

I admire. His beard gave womanliness an upholstered sound. There's a greater age difference between you and Maureen then you and Jennifer, I said, so in a sense Jennifer would be the more natural choice, added to the fact there's no hint of a Dean. Love's not logical, Bulwark said. His quickened pace condemned my immaturity. I was thinking how what had just happened was part of my life now and could never be undone. The smallest incidents have this quality. It made me realise I ought to make sure as many elements of life as possible had kindness and significance so that later I could look back on a kindly significant life. Ahead, Bulwark was almost all duffel coat, his legs swinging lovelessly below in mauve corduroy.

*

There was talk the other day of what Kandinsky called The Simplicity Theorem. Atkins perked up. He enjoys a theorem to while away an afternoon. And what does this theorem involve? he asked. He crossed his legs and put aside his compendium. It involves simplicity as the name implies, Kandinsky said, but the theorem itself isn't simple. That's so often the way with theorems, Atkins said shortly. But carry on. Tell us more. We're spellbound. In fact no one was the least spellbound. I took it to mean Atkins had used sarcasm to get back at something he didn't like about Kandinsky. Things hadn't been the same between them since the famous ancestor. Smetham had been holding up his own arm and seemed to be considering if it would be worth a bite. He said: Thank you Mister Kandinsky but I believe there have been many simplicity theorems in the history of mankind and hardly any of them has been A) simple or B) useful. Having said this he did indeed approach his own arm with an open mouth. I just implied that myself thank you Mister Smetham, Kandinsky said. You have a habit of repeating what I have already imparted. Never mind squabbling, Atkins shouted. You haven't actually told us yet what this theorem of simplicity states. It states, Kandinsky said fiercely, that every situation has at most four elements. Reduce whatever it is into those elements and there you have it – simplicity. Smetham removed his mouth from his arm or his arm from his mouth. I've heard this one, he said, and unlike some other simplicity theorems it might work as long as you adhere rigidly to its rulings. Kandinsky jerked in his chair. I took this to mean he hadn't been aware there were rulings and how come a man who ate himself knew of them? Smetham went on: This particular theory originated in an essay written in the late forties by Gregori Underlutz. He used it to explain how the Second World War could have been avoided. Kandinsky shook his head. He had a feeling now, as had I, Smetham was making this up. And how, Kandinsky said, again with an edge, did Underlutz say the Second World War could be avoided using the theorem? It was Smetham's turn to shake his head, this to indicate surprise that though Kandinsky was claiming to be familiar with the theorem, he hadn't heard of this use of it. Atkins made a sound with his tongue against the roof of his mouth. You ought to be on Nine, both of you, he said. Since he didn't seem to be needed in the conversation any more, he re-gathered his compendium and looked at it. He tapped a pen against his false teeth. It reminded me of the previous day when he'd said the brain is fooled early on in the application of false teeth into believing there's something edible in the mouth and so produces an abundance of saliva. One of the wonders of incarceration is that over time one hears most topics discussed or if not discussed, touched upon.

*

I was at position three on the couch. Smithson wanted me to say whatever came into my head. As I waited to see what came into it I realised I'd only really be capable of *making* things come. Eventually there was the weather, something appertaining to red squirrels and another curiosity I'd been rehearsing about time travel. None of it, I could see, was about me particularly so I blocked each topic. Smithson was miming his pipe by the window. In him I witnessed the miracle of life. No wires, nothing mechanical, yet he was able to move independently for an average of seventy years. I knew nothing then of course about how soon he would be grave-bound, uttering a silent *Still Attentive* to visitors and passers-by. He had the misfortune to be devoted to Therapeutic Specialism yet hopeless at it, at least in the traditional sense. Funny isn't it, he said, how sometimes you can see tomorrow more clearly than yesterday. It is, I said, not sure what he meant, but I thought we were waiting for me to say whatever came into *my* mind. We were, he said, but you're taking an inordinately long time about it. Excuse me Doctor, I said, but you did say you wanted me as far as possible to let my thoughts run out by themselves. Saying I'm taking a long time about it implies I should have more of a hands-on approach to the exercise. Smithson smacked his lips against the pipe-stem. But you can't have been empty-headed for this long Peter. It isn't possible and even if it was, it wouldn't be natural. I did have some weather, squirrels and time travel, I said, but they didn't seem to be what you were after. It's hard to let things come into our minds without thinking. Smithson glanced round. It might be for *you,* he said. He turned back. How odd it was to be human. I didn't say this opinion aloud because again it didn't seem to be the sort of thing he was looking for. Instead I laid my hands at my chest and linked my fingers. It was indisputable I'd spent too much time thinking since birth and that I'd better start helping and considering others soon. This notion made me sit up, half turn and adjust the headrest to position four. A gull swooped across the window then lulled this way and that, prompting Smithson to take an imaginary rifle and shoot at it while making a sound between pipe and teeth to indicate gunfire. Gulls should be on the coast, he said. It's our fault. All these takeaways. I nodded even though he couldn't see me other than maybe thinly in reflection. I had the ability on days like that to go to another place in my mind, trusting that if Smithson wished a return he would alert me. It was something like going to sleep yet nothing like it. In moments I was standing hands against my waist, with Alexander beside me likewise. We'd come to the sea but couldn't manage not to be gruff to start with. The idea was we'd rekindle our friendship because Alexander had been a scoundrel – by his own admission – in his admiration of K though he swore nothing had happened between them. Uncannily our hands came out of our waists in unison. We could go nearer the water I suppose, he snapped, though it looks from here as if the sand's wet and I haven't really worn the right shoes. Me neither, I snapped back, raising the left one. It happens a lot. Odd how neither of us thought it through even though we knew we were coming here. It must have been an unconscious desire *not* to be near the sea, Alexander said sarcastically, though our conscious selves have done their best to override it. We shouldn't really stand about thinking about thinking, I said, when we're at such an ancient coast, home of Pliosaurs and what have you. I'd added the what have you because I wasn't sure if there'd ever been such things as Pliosaurs and, even if there had been, if they would have had anything to do with coasts. Turned out from what Alexander said I was right they were something to do with coasts but wrong in that he didn't think this particular stretch a good habitat for them. They had powerful jaws, he said as we wandered left. We were heading for an arch of rock that gave access to the next beach to the east. The thing about beaches is that they inexorably prompt you to walk along them. We dreamed of women in bikinis but saw none because it was too cold and even if we had seen some we were both the sort not to look directly. For my part, among other considerations, I would have thought it a betrayal of K. Besides, Alexander said, having heard the discussion telepathically and deciding to bring it into the open, there comes a point when you realise women in bikinis aren't any different from women *not* in bikinis. You mean naked? I said, surprised. No, he said. I waited in vain for him to expand. The headland to our left was precipitous with gulls. About three quarters of the way up the rock face a climber wearing all the gear and a red hat clinked among a mess of ropes. K tells me you came here with her loads of times, Alexander said. Yes well it was her idea all along, I said. She'd originally read of it in a bird magazine. One of her old boyfriends came here with her to start with. Alexander said, after a pause: I'm surprised there are so few people about, though I suppose it is on the chilly side for mass visitation. In a way I prefer it like this, I said. It makes it easier to imagine our primeval past. Alexander's glance was his way of condemning my use of *primeval* alongside *past*. Sometimes however we allowed ourselves days off from persistent exactitude. Alexander laughed. He was waving vaguely left. Don't know if you remember, he said, but K gave me a coloured print one birthday of Rupert Bear lying on top of a rock like that one there. He's looking out at an emerald sea wearing his red coat and yellow checked trousers. Yes, I said, I remember. In fact I was with her when she bought it. She thought it was very you. Well it is, Alexander said, returning his hands to the rear of himself. She has a knack. Me, I'd go shopping for a week and still not come up with anything suitable. I fear generally women are much better than us at gifts, I said. The sea was lulling against the extremity of the headland as we passed into the cavernous space within the arch. We looked up and around. We could have stood there years and not seen a single change. Smells salty, Alexander said. It would, I said, this being the coast. The rocks scream of geological time, I added. Alexander said he knew what I meant. I told him it didn't seem five minutes since we were babies. Quashing surprise at my non sequitur, Alexander scoffed and said not to remind him. He hadn't thought much of babyhood. Me neither, I said. You never quite knew what was going to happen next. You didn't, Alexander said. It was decent of him to continue the second person singular despite what Jugg had always said about being careful with it. Once you're in it boys and girls it's hard to get out, he'd said, so keep an eye. We will sir, we said. Over time we'd come to realise saying We will sir loudly soothed his anxiety and on the whole meant fewer people had detention. It was nice we had K with us all the while though, I said to Alexander. Through childhood I mean. Yes, Alexander said, but I often wonder if a person should have a girlfriend they've known all their life. With one you've met more recently you open yourself up to new experiences. I was slightly alarmed at this. Sadly even the slightness of it didn't prevent it becoming audible. As we were coming out the other side of the archway I thought to myself it might have been better on the whole never to have had a girlfriend at all. With K it was sometimes as though she had a torch illuminating my thoughts. Once fully clear of the arch and its shadow Alexander and me again put our hands to our waists and looked about ourselves. We wanted to be here yet not here at all. We'd remembered we were meant to be rekindling friendship and yet neither of us knew how to go about it; maybe we'd been hoping the coast itself would submit us to its own repair. Alexander said: Has she made you any of her flapjacks lately? I asked if he meant the thick syrupy ones. That this was a poor question went without saying. That's the ones, Alexander said. She has bouts of making them, I said. Shortly thereafter we reach what she describes as a Flapjack Ceiling and she makes none for months. Mention flapjacks during that time and she'll look at you as if you've got a screw loose. Course then you're led to adopt a squeaky voice while you protest that under other circumstances she *loved* the topic. Once you get squeaky with K, you've had it, Alexander said. He picked up a pebble, examined it and threw it into the sea, or at least into the area where the thinnest remains of each wave continually arrived. I keep thinking I'll reach an age where squeaky no longer occurs, I said, but then wouldn't you know it, just when I think it's over, back it comes. Like hiccups, Alexander said. Not *much* like hiccups, I said. Of course if K were here, Alexander went on, she'd say your squeakiness is a sign of you not being sure of your ground. I was about to answer this squeakily when I realised he'd made the entire topic my responsibility. People do this in preparation for a betrayal. I'm not sure about that, I said, I mean there is a case for saying K likes to be right and will defend herself through to lunacy. I veered from Alexander at this point to stop myself talking neg-atively about her. It might have got back to her and then Alexander's case for betrayal would have been much the stronger. It can be hard sometimes *not* saying the odd bad thing about your girlfriend, but thereafter there's usually a mild disquiet even if you're absolutely convinced of your case. We walked parallel for a while, neither of us wanting to be the one to prompt convergence. It's the sort of day where I'd like to wander for infinity, Alexander said. He threw another pebble. I said in that case we'd need infinite sandwiches. During his next pebble Alexander explained he'd meant infinity in the metaphorical sense. But is there any other? I snapped. Later on I suggested that war did funny things to people. Dylan managed to avoid it for the most part, I said. I believe he was exempted on medical grounds. Wow, Alexander said, adding how odd it was you had to be well enough to kill and be killed. Rejoinders were stalled because a roundish blob alerted us to a creature offshore. Alexan-der regarded it with aplomb. Seals come in along here, he said. I saw then that a war was still raging between us, possibly – most likely – about K. My heart sank. I felt I would always prefer to be the one endangering a couple than to be the subject of endangerment myself. That's a grey seal, Alexander said eventually. People muddle them with harbour seals.

Whenever anything like this cropped up I would wonder how creatures of all shapes and sizes came to be the way they were. The only way to find out absolutely would be to go back through the history of earth a day at a time and witness all the changes, except that the changes would be so minuscule it might take hundreds of thousands of years to see any difference. K said our short lifespan was a fail-safe that nature introduced into the human experience to prevent us knowing all things. I said to her though that the accumulation of knowledge *could* be passed from generation to generation. It's not like each individual has to find out everything from scratch. I looked for signs I'd got somewhere with my argument. She was on her feet examining the tendrils of a pussy willow. Spring's on its way, she said. I was remembering this the same time as being irritated with Alexander for knowing his greys from his harbours. It's looking at us, I said. Oh they're inquisitive creatures, Alexander said. He continued walking, letting go so to speak of the seal, probably because he wanted me to think he was utterly familiar with them. One popped its head out last time I was here with K, I said. She told me it was saying yes, yes, yes, yes, over and over. She said it was a seal of approval. I managed to laugh, looking then at Alexander hoping he'd do the same, but instead he said: Seal of approval? What did she mean? I hurried to a nearby pile of seaweed, stooping as if to examine it. They used to harvest this, I said. There was quite an industry founded on it years ago. This was of course in the days before beaches were regarded as places of leisure. Yeah, K got some tangled round her legs one time, Alexander said. I looked at the sea, mildly critical of it. With that and the rip tides it's a wonder anybody goes in, I said. And I read the other day we're due an invasion of jellyfish. Alexander didn't stop as such, but I did detect minuscule tremors in his feet associated with slowing down. How can we be due an invasion? He asked. They've come on the Gulf Stream, I said. Before we know where we are we'll have millions clogging our southerly shores. Alexander shook himself, his head remaining still. He said: Jellyfish! This comment enabled us to walk on for a considerable time without speaking. I paused at a rock pool, dabbing into it with a stick I'd found. When I leaned directly over it I was greeted with a shimmering twin. For a little while I tried opening my eyes before the twin could open his. Then a shimmering Alexander appeared beside me. Look, he said, sorry about shouting out jellyfish and not sorry at the same time about my feelings re: K past and to a certain extent present – though lesser oh God yes. When a person tells me they feel less about someone than they did before I tend to think they mean they feel more than they did before. Alexander coughed deeply enough to further disturb the surface of the pool. I mean I realise you and K are like clampets. I believe you mean limpets I said. Yeah, sorry, Alexander said, but clinging to each other rather than rocks. We're not clinging to each other, I said. It's more we're clinging side by side to the same rock. And I'm sort of on that rock too, Alexander said carefully, but below you two or at least further round, with a larger space between me and K than you and her. I loathe crustacean talk, I said. In unison we thrust ourselves upright, our twins doing likewise. A man had appeared along the water's edge with a dog, an inverted copy of which bounded along the sand beneath it. Alexander said what he didn't understand about erosion was how if you followed it through, the implication was that one day there wouldn't be any land left. I suspected the reason he'd brought erosion up was to move on from K and our feelings for her. The man with the dog raised his left arm and said how'd you do before stepping forward. One of the things dogs learn early on is the difference between sea and fresh water. It could almost be these skills were on the point of becoming instinctive so that soon they wouldn't try drinking sea in the first place. This one was wet through to the shine and beneath its nose lay the thinnest smile. Momentarily I wavered towards a suspicion dogs did know they were dogs, occasionally at least, and not only that but that they were content being so. The worst case scenario for me had been that they not only knew they were dogs but also resented humans for *not* being dogs. We loped along the sand, Alexander and I, not dissimilar to dogs ourselves, though older ones from whom the bounce was fading. The air was joyful around me and it struck me that yes, the coast was making me better regardless. I was also remembering something from 'The Love Song Of J Alfred Prufrock', the part where he wears flannel trousers and walks along the beach, hearing mermaids singing, each to each. Jugg wouldn't have taken kindly to that rhyme any more than he would have enjoyed *Should I, after tea and cakes and ices, Have the strength to force the moment to its crisis?* though he may have pretended to like it just to be on Eliot's side so to speak.

*

The last time I'd listed my fidelity concerns, K had said I should repeat: *This too shall pass.* We'd been high above the river on a ledge worn over generations. K had used a nylon line she'd brought to anchor herself to a tree some way from the edge. Meanwhile she unwrapped sandwiches of fish paste, which to be frank I told her I hadn't had for years mostly because of the long distance and suspect manufacturing processes between fish and paste. You'll fuddy-duddy yourself into an early grave, she said. That's as may be, I said, but there are toxins. They were on TV. Oh well let's not eat at all, she said. She took a bite. I regarded the sandwich put aside for me. Should I dismiss what I knew of toxins so I might share food with my friend or should I stand my ground and go hungry? Several hundred feet below the river an omega wound between wooded islets. It was said three Cavaliers had killed themselves by leaping from here horses and all during the reign of one of the Charles's. I doubted the tale generally because surely the horses would have seen the edge coming and reared up. And if it had happened I didn't think it fair on the horses themselves, to be drawn thus into the despair of their riders. I was telling this to K when she admonished me for using phrases like 'to be drawn thus' and I told her I got into a mode in lofty locations once nausea and vertigo had subsided. In the pause I gathered the sandwich and took a bite. The bread had softened in the warmth and the salty paste in it had become addictively pungent. I don't suppose one will do me much harm, I said. *Any* harm, K said. You spend too long each day up your own bottom. For me it's a place of safety, I told her. I was already inclined to take a larger bite even though I knew the creation of this tendency was purposeful on the part of those damned manufacturers to make me eat more and more. Does it say which sort of fish the paste is made of? I asked. I didn't look at the jar, she said. If you get chance check later I said, not that I'll be able to do anything about it by then but I expect if

118

we could see the whole process from fish to paste even you wouldn't eat this. K said: Remember you're not anchored to a tree. I took another bite. Those manufacturers knew a thing or two about the desires of the palate. K said besides, she found salty things appeased the residual fancy in her for alcoholic beverages. I can see why, I said, the saltiness has quite a kick. This is also why I like crisps, she said. I told her I'd wondered, then reached over and touched the back of her hand as it and sandwich moved to her mouth. There are hard-boiled eggs in the bag too, she said. If you have one make sure you put the shells in the tub I brought. I felt happy then, notwithstanding the world's machinations. Deftly I folded the remaining part of the sandwich into my mouth. The eggs, it turned out, had been placed in an old egg box to prevent premature cracking. I tapped one against the rock. The mosaics of shell I removed and put into the aforementioned. This is just the location for hard-boiled eggs, I said. A second smaller tub held a few spoonfuls of salt and, having been intoxicated into it by fish paste, I bit off the top of the egg and put plenty on. How's Alexander? I asked suddenly. If you mean am I embroiled with other men, K said, the answer's no comment as usual. If you *mean* how is Alexander then I'm not sure. Yeah, one minute he's omnipresent, the next rare as hen's teeth, I said. He's an independent spirit too. I can't see him at home in an armchair with a wife and two kids. It would have to be a big armchair, K said. I ignored her. I'd been hoping my Alexander speculation would ease the fear I had in that direction. Thinking about it now, she said, it's probably salmon. I guessed it would be, I said. They creep in wherever fish paste comes up. I saw something on TV the other day. About how bears wait beside waterfalls so they can grab salmon heading upstream. The urge to leap is strong because they're on their way to spawn. The salmon I mean. One bear – you'd have died – well he nearly fell in when he released one paw from the rock to lash out. Adult bears bring their young along to watch so they can learn what to do. The programme was also partly about the laborious and complex preparations film-makers have to go through in order just to get a minute or two of footage. About here I stopped speaking to ascertain if K was listening. It must be scary for the fish, she said eventually. Coming out of the water to be faced with bears. Maybe you're right, I said, though I don't think there's any evidence salmon can be fearful. About the most you could say is that there was an air throughout the film that the creatures involved accepted their place in the scheme of nature. So salmon can't be fearful but they can have acceptance? K's question was the more disturbing for a munching either side of it. A tightness spread across my scalp. Simultaneously I realised again how far I was above the river. Let's not get into one of these, I said. It's too nice a day. I am prepared to accept I don't think through things before I say them so I hope that'll do for now. It was during the bears. I got carried away. You often do, she said. It can be endearing. Thank you, I said. I imagined my own suicide, adding the touch of making sure I still held part of a hard-boiled egg as I fell. Smithson has said these images are the result of an inordinately profound self-pity and that it casts a pall into my vicinity whenever I'm in that mood. I remember asking him, in that case, what did he advise? He said he didn't think it appropriate or useful on this occasion to advise me because the learning thereof wouldn't sink in. I had to become sick and tired of self-pity, so sick and tired I'd initiate a change in behaviour myself. A change that emanates from within rather than without, he said, will more often endure. Again he tossed the jelly bean I'd given him earlier. He'd been trying to catch it in his mouth.

*

It was the day Gerald – or the man I came to know as Gerald – passed my gate as I half watched the dog from up the road. Gerald paused in his walking by, raised his trilby to scratch the crown of his head and said that of all dogs on earth the one I had an eye on was by far the scruffiest and to judge by its mouth, the most downcast. He's left out all day while his owners are at work, I said. Gerald's pinstripe flapped in the wind. He looked as if he could do with guy ropes. If people aren't prepared to make provision for dogs, he said, they should be banned from having them. He has a routine of sorts, I said. About now he goes off through the hedgerow to who knows where to do who knows what. He'll be gone about an hour. And what of you? Gerald said. Why are you standing there like a lemon? If I knew more about the lifestyle of lemons I might protest at the comparison, I said. I probably didn't say anything like it. My brain endeavours to make the past interesting. I'm actually just watching the world go by, I added. And then I believe there are beans for lunch. Gerald took a pace backwards. Beans? My word! I was used to this way adults had of talking to youngsters. To conclude the theme I said yes beans, clutched the tubular gate, climbed on its lowest rail and swung backwards. Father had said not to do this because it ruined the hinges. And later on Ormerod's coming round, I said. Ormerod eh? Gerald said. Unusual name! He's an unusual person, I told him, swinging once twice three times. Well it's nice meeting you, Gerald said. You can call me Gerald. I've got a bookshop. You might have seen it. Today I've had to slip out naughtily to go to the dentist. I asked him if it was the shop called Books! And he said yes it was though the name was provisional while he and Mrs Aldridge thought up a better one. So you're *Mr* Aldridge, I said. Sadly not, or rather I'm sad she's not Mrs Mulwhinny, he said. I swung again. I was confused. Mrs Aldridge is a widow, Gerald said as if to explain. Works at the laundry. Momentarily I wished I was a dog myself so I might wander through the hedgerow in the wake of the other and do for an hour whatever he did. Well whoever you are I wish you good day, I said. Gerald smiled. I bet you're the sort of boy who likes a book. I am, I said, though currently I'm not reading any. My last had a Mohican in it. Good, good, Gerald said. The best ones do. I felt then something wasn't right because my last book *hadn't* had a Mohican in it and I wondered if Gerald had been equally loose with the truth when he'd said the best ones did. The word Mohican sounded odd right then. Mother was calling from the back door thinking I was out there when in fact I was out here. I'd say those beans are ready, Gerald said buoyantly. I'll let you get on. Pop into the shop next time you're passing. He raised his hat by grasping either side of its central crease, jerked his chin in what I took to be a wry gesture and scuffled off in gritty leather shoes. By the time I got round the back Mother was at the fence with Mrs Chaffin. They were oohing about a man from down the road who'd stolen three bars of chocolate from the local shop and run off only to be caught later by the police. Neither Mother nor Mrs Chaffin knew what the world was coming to. I felt I'd like to go up to them and announce my having met Gerald but then I remembered Mother saying many times not to talk to strangers, men especially, because, she said, they were up to all sorts, none of it any good.

*

Each time K comes to mind it deepens a missing of her. I tried Harry with it a few days back but all he said really was every one of us in here misses someone or something. I deflated. But the fact is you can't know someone else's sense of loss as well as you can know your own. I also detected in Harry a sense he missed Cheryl even though he's with her. I wondered if I should follow this line but by then he'd already lost the look in his eye that indicates he's up for psychology. And missing someone's a curious sensation, not unlike hunger but less easy to satisfy. I guess even Colquahoon misses the supposed Mrs Colquahoon. You have to assume of course part of missing someone is in fact *not* missing them or even not liking them particularly. Just someone gets into your blood then it's a job to get them out again even supposing you can at all. I had this with K right enough and if I wasn't bound to this chair I most certainly would want to sort it. You have to sort things, Smithson used to say. No use leaving issues to flap in the mind. In a rare moment of exposition, he explained he'd used flag imagery because there was one at half mast above the Council House. Looks like a dignitary might have died, he said. I told him I'd buy a paper on the way home and check. As I was saying this I knew I *wouldn't* buy a paper. I'd seen on my way down there the headline: DOG MAULS PENSIONER. The reporter had chosen to say PENSIONER rather than man or woman to imply the dog had picked a pensioner so it could achieve optimum cruelty. Course, in reality dogs can't be cruel to people. It's only people who can be cruel to dogs. In fact Father used to say humans were the only creatures capable of cruelty at all. He was in the living room behind his own paper when he said this. We were in the thick of the Miss Woo business so how he thought he had a right to mention the cruelty of others is anyone's guess. Some boys up on the estate, he said, nailed their dog to the floor. He took a slug of cider.

By its ears, he added. Mother was alarmed. I could tell by an additional click in her knitting needles. Whatever got into them, she said. Father put aside his newspaper, partially at least, and crossed his legs. From my angle they looked unutterably bony within his trousers. The thing is, he said, most children – especially boys – go through a phase of inflicting pain on animals. Nailing your dog to a floor's going beyond what's normal, but you can bet it's part of that same pattern. The dog in this case survived, though the father of one of the boys has had it rehoused to avoid any possibility of a repeat and the boys themselves have been given a caution. I was just to one side of Father's chair. I'd been hoping to mention Gerald. I felt if I said he had a bookshop, probably Father at least might say it was okay he'd stopped to say hello outside and if that didn't work I thought I might throw in Mrs Aldridge. You'd think nailing dogs to floors would get them more than just a caution, Mother said, increasing the number of dogs involved. It's the way these days, Father said. It's because the community no longer doles out its own justice. When I was a boy if I'd nailed a dog to a floor you can bet my dad and the neighbours would have made me regret it. Suddenly Mother stopped knitting to wipe the corner of her eye. If only you hadn't, she said. Father reopened his newspaper. Now come on Doreen, you said you wouldn't. I can't help it, Mother said. I keep thinking about you and her. At the pictures for example. Father sighed: We never went to the pictures! Sensing we were on the verge of another flare-up I hurried out, flying up the stairs in two bounds. I'd decided to go to the window in my room. I liked doing that, especially when the weather was milky and the dog up the road lay half on half off the pavement with his nose against the gutter cobbles. I squinted for a while to see if Ormerod could be prompted by this to come round but somehow the thought of wishing he would come guaranteed he wouldn't. Luckily through the creamy light K arrived or rather K's mother, hand in hand with a K who'd been transformed. Adults take it as read every child wants to dress up. It was the same with Alexander and the Wild Bill Hickok outfit. You *will* wear it, Mrs Hodgkins had said, yanking his hand, because your Uncle Neil was good enough to get it for you. I don't think anyone knew who Uncle Neil was even supposing he existed at all. Mrs Hodgkins invented uncles to help back up objectives she wasn't confident about. Anyway, I was looking down on K. Pink taffeta swelled from her waist and a pink top stretched to her neck. Mrs Tintwistle knocked. The Miss Woo discussion stopped. Mother went to the door and let them in. We were just reading in the paper, she said, about boys nailing dogs to the floor. Dog, Father said. Yes I saw that, Mrs Tintwistle said. I know someone who knows one of the mothers of one of the boys. He's also attacked sparrows. Father rustled his paper. Told you, he said. As I came to the bottom of the stairs I was thinking why sparrows. Larger birds like crows would probably be easier to catch. I supposed it to be that I must be subject to the same genetic urge for cruelty myself. As I arrived in the living room, K flumped to the sofa. The tutu rose up hiding the lower part of her face. With my internal structures aflame, I ascertained once more the early stages of love. You'd think his mum would give him a hiding, Mother said. For a while there was silence. Many of us I imagine were wondering at what point Mrs Tintwistle would say why she'd come. At last Mother said: How's Roger? Mrs Tintwistle's mouth moved oddly. She began to cry. Mother fetched a hanky. After a blowing, Mrs Tintwistle said Roger had had bad news. Mother said she was sorry to hear that and did anyone want a cup of tea? Before she could set about it Mrs Tintwistle announced Roger had a disease of the bones, which would cause him pain for the rest of his life. Mother clutched the arm of the chair. Father turned the page of the paper but I could tell it was only because he wasn't sure what to say. Why haven't you mentioned it before now? Mother said. Mrs Tintwistle told us he'd had tests a while ago but they hadn't wanted to worry us till they were sure of the diagnosis. A bloke at work had something like that, Father said. I think when we all watched Father, it was in anticipation of his revealing what had happened to the bloke from work. Instead, he took a pen and began studying the crossword at the back of the paper. When I looked at K she moved one side of her mouth down at the same time as moving the other side up. Her nose and cheeks were the colour of peaches. Why don't you take K upstairs and show her your puzzle, Mother said. I hardly wanted to show it to K because I'd been hoping she'd think me beyond puzzles. When I'd first seen the title Baboons of the Serengeti the hairs had gone up on the back of my neck. So anyway, soon I was in my bedroom with K, showing her the lid of the puzzle, which stood just to one side of the table on which lay the completed outer frame of the puzzle itself. Father had said that was the way to go about it. K was there with her hands in front of her like she was about to begin a ballet. These are baboons, I said, indicating the lid of the box. I know, I've seen them in a book, K said. The Serengeti's in Africa, I said. But I daresay you have that in a book too? I do, K said. Try not to get in a pickle about it. Me? A pickle? I said. K sat on the edge of the bed. What else have you been up to, she said. I told her I'd been looking out at the dog who, despite other kinds of neglect, had yet to be nailed to a floor. The afternoon inveigled itself through the surface of the window. Time, I decided, might come to a standstill soon. K laughed. I assume it was all this talk of dogs and baboons. I saw a man the other day, I said, leaning against the sill. He has that bookshop in town. K said: The one called Books!? That's right I said, but it's just temporary while he and Mrs Aldridge think up a proper name. I might want a bookshop when I'm older. I'm going to sit in an armchair wearing half-moon glasses and wait for people to come in. I'd been hoping K might join me at the window. That isn't much of an ambition, K said. For the umpteenth time I had to quash a desire to mention Mother leaving me on the 38a. I can see it won't generate much of an income, I said, but that'll be more than compensated for by people coming in day after day wanting to know things. Well, K said quietly behind me, I wish you every success. Something told me by the way she'd said this she wouldn't seriously entertain me as a full boyfriend unless I sharpened my ambitions. The man said to pop in next time I'm passing, I said to the window, but the thing is – and I don't know about you K – whenever anyone says I should pop in next time I'm passing I suspect they mean that on no account *should* I pop in. Mum says older people who say pop are only doing it to make you feel safe so they can molest you, K said. It was almost like the dog from up the road had heard as it raised its nose briefly to regard me at the window. I made a laughing sound. I wasn't amused but wanted K to think I'd already

125

thought of and dealt with that possibility. Oh he has a Mrs Aldridge, I said. A recent statistical survey says bookshop proprietors are the least likely to molest you anyway. The dog's nose moved back towards the gutter. So next time I'm passing I might well pop in, I said brightly. If you do, see if he has anything on poltergeists, K said. I told her I would and at the same time my heart reckoned it would scour the earth for poltergeists. Are they the ones who throw things? I asked. She said they were, but that they did other things too. I will ask for you obviously, I said, but I do worry about poltergeists. Why if you were dead would you want to misbehave? I can think of a hundred better pastimes. K said such as? which I was anticipating and depressed about. Well, I said, trying not to sound impatient, for a start I'd go and have a look at Antarctica. I can't see there'll be much of an opportunity while I'm alive. It's cold there, K said. We did it last week. It's almost twice the size of Australia. I don't see the point of learning somewhere's twice the size of somewhere else unless you know how large the second somewhere is, I said. I was only half concentrating because some boys up the road had put a coat on the kerb to act as a goalpost and the dog was being used as the other. K went on to say a Norwegian team was the first to reach the South Pole in 1911, a month before the British team led by Captain Scott. K was like that. If you mentioned somewhere, she always knew more about it than you. One of the reasons I'd developed a bond with Ormerod was that – bless him – he hardly ever knew more than me about things. Captain Scott and his team were eleven miles from safety when they died, K said. And when – fifty years later – some of the tins of food were recovered from the site, the contents were still edible. You've been studying it carefully, I said. It's India next week, K said. The dog didn't even mind when the tennis ball being used in the game struck its nose. From my point of view, I said, the sooner you get on to India the better. You're grumpy, K said. I told her I was having a bad day because I was behind everything trying to catch up rather than in front. I don't know what you mean, she said. I turned from the window at last, fingering instead one or two pieces of Baboons of the Serengeti. Sometimes you would see a piece and think it part of a baboon but it would turn out not to be. On the other hand there were pieces that you felt could never in a million years form part of a baboon and yet that's exactly what they did. When I'd told K I felt I was having to catch up rather than being in front, it tied in with this conundrum. Do you want me to help with the puzzle? K asked. I told her not right now, this fingering of pieces was more incidental than purposeful because I wasn't used to having girls in my room. I realised then I was doing the same as Mother who'd said dogs not dog. I'll go if you like, K said. No don't, I said. Anyway they're probably talking about your dad downstairs. What with his bones. Funny isn't it how some dads go on and on while others malfunction at the soonest opportunity. His own dad had the bone thing too, K said. That's my granddad. I never met him. He was in Paraffin Sales. My dad said they couldn't have him cremated because of the added fire risk. I think you'll find your dad was pulling your leg, I said, using this as an excuse to look at one of them. I don't know, K said. I did wonder though. He's always making things up. Like when he told me about the Abdominable Snowman. I looked at her face to see if she was making her own joke but she was quite serious. I took it she was either teasing me or that she'd made a genuine mistake. If you really want to, she said, you can sit by me. I explained I was okay with baboons. Just before you came, I said, Mother and Father were embarking on another Miss Woo discussion. K swung her legs under the bed. Sorry to hear that, she said. I don't think my dad's got a Miss Woo. He says Mum and me are enough to be going on with. Yes, it's odd how some dads say that and others wreak havoc, I said, and what's worse it's likely to mean I'll be damaged in later life not only because of that but also because of my being left on the bus. K said: Oh yes, the 38a. Anyway, don't worry about it. My mum says babies get left on buses all the time, especially the newest ones. I turned from her, going to the window again. Football had ended to make way for a game of throwing dirt at Mr Gravelle. He was Gravel to most of us. Hey K, I said to the window, do you ever get the feeling you're not here? I get it all the time. They're making me see a Therapeutic Specialist. K was quiet for a while. Eventually she said: I'm not surprised you feel peculiar. You spend too long staring out of windows at dogs. Not *just* dogs, I said.

*

At twenty miles a day, Cholmondley once said, it would take us thirteen thousand years to walk to the sun. Atkins said we wouldn't be able to do it because there was no air and anyway, when we got to within a certain distance of our destination we'd be incinerated. Not only that, but Cholmondley's current life expectancy wouldn't even get him to the top of the troposphere. Cholmondley explained he'd been talking hypothetically, which is what scientists did. They hypothesise, he said, and then see if the evidence supports that hypothesis. But, said Atkins loudly, saying the thing about walking to the sun wasn't a hypothesis. He's right Mr Cholmondley, said Colquahoon, who should have known better. It was otherwise an afternoon of freesias brought in at her own expense by Fiona. The perfume seduced us. Atkins said it reminded him of a girlfriend he'd had and how he'd proposed to her on a bridge over a stream in the wild hills. He said being younger then, he'd believed the pastoral nature of the location was bound to make her say yes. And did she? asked Smetham. We all looked at one another. I felt Colquahoon wanted to explain to Smetham how the structure and tone of what Atkins had said had quietly let us (the listeners) know what the outcome was without being explicit, but even he couldn't have borne the measure of arrogance such an explanation would have implied. Instead he garrumphed at the newspaper and Atkins returned to his compendium, shifting uncomfortably. Myself, I have never shifted uncomfortably without knowing that's what I'm at. I scratched my head. That bit at the back and side where there's a dent. Yes, I said, carry on Doctor. Before I do, Smithson said, I want to be sure you aren't going to keep interrupting. You certainly can be, I said. It was because I was distracted both by what you said about the flag and a dent I hadn't noticed before to the side and back of my head. Smithson reached round to stroke his own. Well yes, Peter, self-consciousness is a useful tool only when utilised in the correct way. Yours seems to stultify you. He removed the pretend pipe from his lips, passed over the room and consulted the dictionary he kept on a small shelf at the far side. At length he came back and resumed his former position, taking up the pipe once more. That is, he said, it dulls your mind, causes you to appear foolish or ridiculous, when I know for one this is far from the truth. Now we could if we so wished go through the numerous historical occurrences that have brought about this self-consciousness but then I wonder is it worth it? Wouldn't it be better to find a simple cognitive behavioural tool you could use to keep it at bay?

*

He had toyed with an idea for a booklet for his clients he was going to call: *Sanity At Your Fingertips*. Putting it to one side of my mind, I followed into the wood where Bulwark was already deep into a cigarette. Even supposing, he said, I could bring myself to develop a relationship with Jennifer I wouldn't be able to consummate it due to troubles down below. I haven't told anyone ordinary before. Only my doctor and mum. I said: Your mum?! He went on: I'm working on a theory the reason I've been loving unattainable Maureen is that my problem is less likely to be discovered. See, you're not the only one who can make evaluations. I grinned without opening my mouth. I've noticed in the years since that if ever a man mentions sexual dysfunction it's almost impossible not to glance at his groin. Yes, Bulwark went on, holding the tree, it's likely to last the rest of my life. I have low somethings. I'll have to take medicine. I haven't so far because there's no one to do it with. But come the day… He took a draw on the cigarette. I told him I hadn't realised there were such medicines although I had. Either I find myself claiming not to know something I do or vice versa. I'm glad you've told me, I said at last, and it surely helps explain some of the severity of the Maureen situation. Bulwark oscillated. Don't think for a moment I don't love her though, he said. I told him I wouldn't. It's just that I can't see *why* it was her particularly. As he was smoking and smoking we chose for a change, though nothing was said, to make our way through the wood rather than taking the shorter route back to the outside. The needled ground yielded underfoot. On more than one occasion a pigeon slapped through surrounding branches. So when you were telling me moons ago you'd had many opportunities, I asked softly, did you mean you'd had *no* opportunities? Exactement, Bulwark said. Well I was just guessing because of what you've now said about troubles down below, I told him. Bulwark chuckled. We're old enough not to say 'down below'. I suppose

129

we are, I said. At that moment I spotted someone ahead and almost at the same time realised who it was. Bulwark must have spotted her too because without a word he veered on to another path. I was stuck for a moment because when I listened to my soul it said go on in the direction I would have taken and don't let Bulwark's veering distract me. Quite soon and with little effort I was alongside Jennifer, glancing at her to say hello and going on a little faster so she wouldn't think I'd been in pursuit. A pace or two further on her voice behind me said: Peter? I slowed till she was beside me. Why yes, I said, a piece of him. One of the good things about college was you could quote without anyone thinking you were a noggin. I asked if she was okay given not many people ventured this far and wasn't it strange, I wouldn't have been there either had it not been for the vagaries of Bulwark who just now had decided to return to the outside world by a more direct route. You're ranting, she said. Yes, I told her. I'd had a strong coffee in the refectory just now. I don't touch it, she said. It used to be that even one at lunchtime would keep me awake at night. Caffeine has a long half-life. So I made a decision never to have any. It's toxic to parrots as well. When I asked if she had a parrot, she gave me a look. Swirling with this I decided to say I'd been thinking of cutting down. She said it wasn't good enough to *think* of cutting down as this strategy was used by many only to fend off possible criticism. Each footfall erupted a smell of pine. I've come here for a think, she said. I've been in recovery from a thing about your hairy friend. I told her I'd guessed she had one, and was sad – in a way – she was now in recovery from it. She gave a grunt. It was obvious he wasn't going to play ball, she said. There's a rumour going about he has a thing for Maureen anyway. Though surely he realises she's married to the Dean. I fear, I said, he's chosen to ignore Deans, though in his defence I believe he's coming out the other side – going by what he was saying recently at any rate. We walked on in silence. I couldn't separate naturally from her till another branch in the path came. In the meantime we heard an owl and, somewhere far away, the laughter of girls. You're quiet in seminars, she said, just when I thought she wasn't going to speak again. Yes, I said. It's because I always have two ideas, mostly opposing, and I can either not think of which to present or, even supposing I can, find I've run out of time. Like my father always said there's no evidence my head has been screwed on. She said softly: We should mind what we say to our children because it can affect the way they interact with the world later. Yeah, I said, I see that. And would you believe it, Mother left me on a bus when I was a baby. Jennifer jumped. Oh I can't say I blame her much, I said. I mean she'd discovered not long before that my dad was having a thing with Miss Woo up the road. I'd manipulated chronology without wanting to and felt shame but soon the shame wore off and I found myself wanting to lie more. I remember Bulwark saying something about how in Gothic novels a set of truths or situations could exist that didn't have to exist elsewhere. Was she Chinese? Jennifer asked. Apparently so, I said. She could fold herself small enough to fit into suitcases and became a favoured assistant among the travelling magician fraternity. Jennifer said: My grandfather's skin was too big. When he swam it wafted behind him like a separate creature. It frightened children. He was banned from the pool. Some people said if he could have worked through those disadvantages, he could have made a living out of it. As it was he ended up in Shoe Sales.

*

Mother walked quickly due to another Miss Woo discussion with Father; so quickly, that the dog from up the road – who'd looked like he might want to follow at one stage – turned and plodded back to his spot by the hedge. We had only moments to greet Gravel passing along the other pavement. As usual he carried a shopping bag patterned with diamonds of leather. Mother eventually slowed. I came in to land. At more or less the same time she let go of me. I was wondering, I said, if we could call in the bookshop while we're in town. Mother asked which and I said the one called Books! Oh, I've seen it, she said. You'd have thought they could come up with a better name. It's temporary, I said, till Gerald and Mrs Aldridge think of a proper one. What do you want with bookshops? Mother said. I'm on the lookout for poltergeists, I told her. She asked if they were the ones who threw things. I said they were, but that they did other things too. With a sigh Mother looked at her watch. Two minutes, no more, she said. I'd been allocated this amount of time for other things. The last occasion had been when a stall advertising the circus had been by the town hall and I'd been allowed to see myself thin and fat in a scaled-down hall of mirrors. I'd asked the circus man what the point was of a hall of mirrors and he'd said there wasn't one and that there were many such things in the circus, which was coming to town for a thrilling Four Days Only. I'd promised myself from then on never to ask questions of people wearing sparkling waistcoats. Oh and we have an elephant, the man called after me. I turned back to wave even though I'd lost interest. Suddenly from having been full of circus, a bell alerted me to our entrance into the bookshop where Gerald was a pair of shoes resting on the surface of a leather-inlaid desk. The shoes opened, Gerald's head being disclosed between them. Why it's you, he said. His suit fluttered as he came towards us with hand outstretched. I expect you're his mum, he said. Mother stood back as she shook his hand. You know him? she asked. Yes, said Gerald. We had a chat by your gate the other day. That's why I said about Gerald and Mrs Aldridge, I said quietly to her as I wandered to the nearest shelf. Mother told Gerald she remembered only that I'd been on about poltergeists. Gerald said another boy he knew came in regularly wanting Egyptians. Few people know, Gerald said, but Egyptians used to hook peoples' brains through their noses. Some of the spines before me had their title printed narrowly at the top, others going lengthways. Gerald clapped as he ended the silence brought on by the brains and came to me. You won't find poltergeists in this bit, he said. These are novels. Unpopular novels at that. If you want Poltergeists you need to come this way. There might be something in our new section. Coming this way involved a pincer-like placement of fingers atop my head and an increasing pressure that led me to turn and stagger in a north-easterly direction towards a shelf one side of a doorway. Through the doorway I could make out one corner of a table covered in an oilcloth. The cloth would smell, I decided, of romance. We've named this area provisionally The Mystic Sciences, Gerald said, pointing to the shelf. We'll probably call it something else once we've made up our minds for good. I *like* the term Mystic Sciences mind you. Mrs Aldridge isn't so keen. I told him it seemed Mrs Aldridge had a monopoly on decisions generally, at which

132

he made a noise, something like Ho Ho, which I fancy unsettled Mother even more. It's not easy meeting new people. For a while you think they might not be odd, but more often than not they turn out to be. Smithson said we might as well act on the principle everyone's odd in some respect. Though of course, he said, if everyone's odd then by implication, no one is. He turned abruptly to the window. I fear this was because once again he was chuffed at how he'd put things. I did think at this juncture of mentioning Smithson to Gerald, introducing them so to speak, but before I could work out how to do it, Mother was reminding me the two minutes were more than up. By the time I'd phrased a question about the nature of time, we were back on the street looking for chops. I said to Mother as sadly as I could I seemed to have missed out something because one moment we were in the bookshop then suddenly we weren't. While we're on the subject, Mother said, what's this about you having talked to that man and Mrs Oldbridge? You shouldn't chat to strangers, she said, unless you know them. I explained about my first meeting with Gerald, corrected her about Mrs Aldridge and the fact she hadn't been present and assured her I felt there was no risk of my being molested, statistically at any rate. I might *not* have said this because I was still anxious about the time-lapse incident as I stood with my nose against the butchery counter thinking critically about Egyptians.

*

In time Mother became easy enough to leave me there while she went shopping. I'd watch her set off along the pavement, then flop inside where Gerald would be whistling to make any potential customers think him a whistling man. He paused in his whistle this time to turn on his heel and lean forward, holding his knees in his hands. I haven't shown you my back room, he said. I said no he hadn't, though I'd glimpsed and smelt the oilcloth. I've a notion that if there are books around you'll be happy, Gerald said, but to complete the picture one should always have access to tea. Mother's often making a cup, I said. In the searching so far we'd not come across anything with Poltergeists. I was feeling guilty whenever I saw K, even to the extent I felt I ought to broaden my search and then maybe I could just pretend I'd got it at Books! Gerald had scooted ahead through the door beside Mystic Sciences. Come, he called, you and I must imbibe a cup of the noble brew. I'd spotted on the wall just beyond the oilcloth a golden clock. I must have been aghast because I arrived loudly enough to make Gerald turn. I see you've noticed, he said. It's hard to miss, I told him, hoping this wouldn't sound rude. What are those? Birds? Well, yes, it's a Bird Clock, Gerald said. I detected impatience. He stood near the clock, his left hand opened by way of indicating it. You will note that where there would ordinarily be numerals to indicate the hour, here we have twelve feathered friends. One needs obviously to specify the number of minutes in the usual way, he said, but to those in the know you can simply name the appropriate bird rather than the hour. For example, you'll see it's now almost twenty-five past chaffinch. I said I hadn't realised what type of bird it was. Why yes, it's one of our most colourful, Gerald said. I didn't like it when people said it was one of our most colourful as if this might help remind you of what they were like, when in fact you hadn't a clue. I apologised and said I didn't see the point of a clock in which so much added work was required. It's just a matter of getting used to it, he said. Not so long from now I'll be saying goodness it's ten to owl and you'll know *exactly* what I mean. The additional thrill of this clock is that on the hour, the mechanism plays the song or call of the particular bird whose time it is so to speak. I got it in the Midlands on one of me and Mrs Aldridge's Bumper Weekends. He was by now back seeing to the tea while I sat at the table. I'd say you were a spoon and a half boy, he said, holding up the sugar bowl. If you did you'd be mistaken, I told him. Father says if I never have it I'll never want it. Gerald said he thought that a wise approach. I don't think he was happy however to have his prediction thwarted. He half-thumped the bowl down. I don't take it either, he said, but Mrs Aldridge likes a spoon now and then. One of the joys of Mrs Aldridge is you can more or less discover a different woman each time you meet. Monday she'll like onions. Tuesday she won't hear of anyone suggesting she *ever* liked onions. When I told him I thought that might make shopping difficult he said well yes, long-term shopping, certainly, but whenever it's my turn I just meet the needs of the day in question. Today for example she's coming to my place and wants me to get Cumberland sausages and potatoes on the way home in readiness for sausage and mash. The other day she said on no account did she like sausages, Cumberland or not. I touched the hot cup I'd been given. We have them once a week, I said, usually Wednesdays. Not Cumberland though. Ordinary. We have mash too but Father also likes mushrooms, gravy and the dreaded onions. Gerald hadn't realised he hadn't been sitting down till then, and suddenly gave in to the urge with a look of surprise. He then had to get up again to fetch his tea. These things happen as you get older, he said. He laughed and said back to me 'dreaded onions'. I can see you have a future ahead of you Peter, he said. Something in the Arts I wouldn't wonder. I said I was hoping for a bookshop. He said: Oh don't. It may be a great thing philosophically but there's no money in it. I didn't say anything then because I had a feeling he was only halfway through. I've been lucky, he said after a sip. My father was a wealthy man. When he died and then of course my mother, I had enough behind me to set up this and not to mind much if I didn't sell many of the blighters. It also gives me the freedom to indulge Mrs Aldridge on our Bumper Weekends. She's a costly soul. It's not just the entry fee to wherever – she's recently been through a stately home phase – there are those numerous little things that in themselves don't sound much but which add up to even more than the main event. She's now started going on about the canaries. I glanced over at the clock. Not the bird, he said. I told him I hadn't looked at the clock for that reason. But I did say – just to show him I'd got the hang of the system – it was now almost twenty-five minutes to robin. Yes, he said, but that's the easiest. So as I was saying, the bookshop here's an indulgence. I love books. They love me. Oh and by the way I've searched extensively for Poltergeists and drawn a blank. That's okay I said. Thanks for looking. It was for a friend. A girl I'll wager, Gerald said.

*

She'd asked what I wanted to do. I said I couldn't think. She said there was an exhibition about insects at the museum. I said it sounded great. The word 'sounded' I associate with a lack of conviction. We arrived about lunchtime. In the foyer was a scale model of a dung beetle. K asked if I was sure I wanted to go on. I told her I'd never been more sure of anything. The beetle was made of metal plates welded together. I touched its surface. I said idly if they were all as big as this, the exhibition should be terribly informative. K said she guessed the rest of the exhibition itself would most likely comprise life-sized insects. This dung beetle was a one-off to draw us in. We scuffed up the steps into the main foyer, which once upon a time had been home to a Spitfire suspended on wires. Whether it had been taken down so as not to distract from the exhibition, K didn't know. She stood umming and ahhing and eventually peering towards the gift shop in the corner. Hopefully she was recalling our long-ago Tutankhamun pencils. Well, at least we made it somewhere, she said. With hands in pockets I said indeed we had. And there we have it, she said. Though I guessed what she was going to say I asked her what she meant. It's when you say 'indeed', she said. It suggests you don't want to be here. I do, I said, mostly because I'm with you. She said didn't I think that was codependent? Maybe, I said, but I was yet to find a more reliable system during close-knit relationships. She must have been caught then by the smell from the small cafe to one side of the space because she said we could start by having a drink. We moved into the cafe and stood looking up at a menu attached to the wall. I think I was the first to spot Alexander. He was more or less face on, a pamphlet opened on the table in front of him and a cup of something to his left. Then I was concentrating on the menu board when K said with a little intake: Oh here's Alexander. He perked up at his name and became delighted as he spotted K. We'd better join him, K said. Bring me a large usual. Then she was gone. I took my time buying the strong Americano and my elderflower pressé with ice and wandered over that way. I maybe myself sounded like a chaffinch as I greeted Alexander, put down K's coffee, sugar tube and wooden stick and clinkled into my seat, which had been gashed across the middle at some point by what was probably a craft knife. K asked Alexander if he'd come for the insects, he said no, no, he'd taken to spending lunchtimes here. The Office can be a nightmare as Peter will confirm, he said. Though I did indeed confirm the description, I added that I had no idea he came here to the museum. Ignoring me, he regarded K softly and said: What about you? Well, K said, we decided to do something cultural on our joint day off. We're starting with Insects. I shan't be going to any of the exhibition myself, Alexander said, though I've heard good things about it. K shivered. There's a section about Creepy-Crawlies on the top floor, she said. I can't wait. Alexander took a sip of what seemed to be herb tea. I said to break the tension what happened to the Spitfire? and Alexander said he'd heard it had been taken down for restoration and I said something like wonder how you go about taking down a Spitfire and where do you have it restored? It's gone to that place by the canal, Alexander said. They do all kinds of restoration there. I know the one, K said. The young man who'd served us had come round to the front of his counter and appeared to be looking for things to do. I felt I might alert him to my gashed seat if his difficulties continued. K reached over to take up the pamphlet Alexander had been looking at. Local Walks? she said. That's not you! I'm researching for me and Miriam, Alexander said. Miriam? K asked. A woman, Alexander said. She started working here in the museum a month ago. She's an Archivist. I sat at her table one lunchtime. Turns out we're both keen on local history. She suggested we might go walking round the older parts of town once a week. I told him I thought it sounded a good idea. I myself had been wanting to do something similar for years. K was saying she hadn't realised there was a Miriam on the scene and Alexander said to say she was on the scene made her sound more than she was and K said she'd have to get on with someone pretty well before she started walking round town with them. She laughed then and said: Even Peter's a struggle. I watched myself stab Alexander with the coffee stirrer. I knew at the same time I was meant to be objectifying the feeling, taking it – as Smithson once said – and wrapping it tightly like a gift, which I should then offer to whatever God I had. You don't often hear of Miriams these days, I said and yet it's a good name. Yeah, she's cool, Alexander said. She was married to that zoologist. Died a couple of years back. I said I thought zoologist should have another O in. I looked to the young man for support. His black pinafore and white shirt were wasted. No one had heard the zoologist comment. I sat back and sipped elderflower. I'd mistakenly got sparkling rather than still. I was partly observing K and Alexander in case anything passed between them at a body-language level. We'd seen a French film not so long before where the hardly-shaven male lead was quite happy when his wife flirted with the gardener who was Gallic with a muscled body. I'd prayed for a while afterwards to be like the husband myself. What did he die of? K asked after too long a gap. In gaps you can often detect subterfuge. He was caught in an avalanche, Alexander said. I didn't mean to laugh. K wouldn't speak to me on the way home. I explained it wasn't the zoologist's death or the avalanche that had tickled me but the waiter, who'd suddenly turned full circle on the tips of his shoes. I guessed he must have been a dancer who worked at the cafe to make ends meet. It's time you got over the Alexander thing, K said eventually. You've had practically your whole life to work on it. I asked her how she could make the leap from an avalanche to me being jealous about Alexander especially now he was seeing a Miriam by the looks of it. Maybe it was K who was jealous, I went on. With K, if you upset her, you have to wait quite a while before she's over it and even then she'll store a mild resentment, which lays atop previous mild resentments so that eventually a generalised resentment becomes substantial. We were having prawn curry that evening. I hadn't realised flies were such complex creatures, I said, hoping to distract her. But I've yet to understand their purpose. Most things you can sort of see why they're on earth, but flies? I left my voice on an up-note. K scooped another forkful. When she'd swallowed, she said: From now on I don't want you to refer even in the slightest to any jealousy or suspicion you might have. I need to say this because I'm at the end of my tether about it. I took up some curry myself so I might not seem to rush into a response. Before I go into detail, I said at last, I just want to put on record I didn't say anything about you and Alexander though of course I acknowledge there have been examples in the past of me being unreasonably jealous. K shook her head to herself. I don't want you even to be *reasonably* jealous, she said. Even supposing you ever have grounds. Okay, I said, generally speaking I admit if I see Alexander and you together I feel uncomfortable but I'm working on it and am confident of a full recovery in due course. If you were being treated for an addiction, K said, I'd suggest you made an inventory about the problem, read the inventory out to someone and then prayed to have the problem taken away. Good idea, I said. I'll write one straight away. Can I read it to you when I've finished? Like I said, K said, if you were being treated for an addiction it would help but you're not and there's the shame. One side of me wants to reassure you about people like Alexander. Another wants to thrash you. I looked at her and my arms cooled. Despite this she wanted to leave almost straight away, even turning down the latticed apple pie I'd been defrosting. I was at a loss to understand what had happened and stood at my window after she'd gone. Somehow the night had misted. The street lights were casting dimmed orange veins through it.

*

Maureen said the term beautiful was lazy because it couldn't be universally applied. Beauty, she said, is an entirely personal concept. As she moved to look out of the window the lines and folds of the tulip dress revealed graceful truths. Bulwark was to say at some point if he was going to describe her he'd have to resort to the terminology of nature. He was leaning back as he negotiated the downward slope of one of the hillocks while I leaned forward scaling the one behind. Fog restricted the view to a few dozen yards. The laughter of girls from within the halls of residence was amplified as it came across the lake. How are you with her nowadays, anyway? I said. He said he was taking it slow but things were yes significantly better. After an anxious few steps further down the hillock he asked if I'd managed to speak with Jennifer the other day. I said well yes, it felt rude not to once I was passing her. I was surprised you left me to go on alone, he said. It was rather you who left me, I said. I make it a rule not to divert from an original direction if the person I'm with changes theirs. It's to do with managing my tendency to be dependent, which in turn arises out of that business of my mother leaving me on a bus. I expect I've told you. You have, Bulwark said grimly. I was thinking he needed to abandon this habit he had for grim replies if he was going to have any luck with love at all. Before I could work out how to put this, he asked if I'd ever considered being evil. I had to ask him how he'd meant because he'd taken me by surprise. He said well all these years he'd been what he thought of as good and nothing had come of it so he was now giving consideration to evil. The trouble with that, I said to his descending cowl, was evil would take a lot of work if he was going to engage in it full time and, besides, I'd be interested to know how it was going to manifest in daily life. Well, he said, as if he'd been waiting years for someone to show interest, I've been littering here and there. Only small scraps as yet. The experiment's twofold: one is to find out if it really *matters* in the long term if we drop litter, you know, to the environment and that bollocks, and two is to find out if, by doing the opposite of what I deeply believe, I can, over time, *change* those beliefs. You mean, I said, you want eventually to believe it's good to drop litter? Yes oh yes, metaphorically speaking at any rate, he said. When I've perfected littering I'm trying theft. I glanced about the fog for something useful to say. The waterfowl had become soundless. Don't you think though, I said as I was coming down and he was going up, all this might be a reaction to the women thing and those troubles below? He cleared throat and beard. Actually Peter, a sustained period of evil can alleviate impotence. It was in a book. There was a chapter on Goats. I told him I'd always been in awe of writers, especially those dealing in non-fiction, because they seemed, for example, to have the patience to write chapters on things I'd barely be able to string together two words about. Goats being a case in point. Oh goats are potent symbols of evil and the like, Bulwark said. I felt his adding 'and the like' indicated he wasn't committed to the idea of his own downfall. But I did say: And after theft? He said he hadn't got that far in his mind, but that he was going to give the first two a go and see how they went. I've got a feeling, I said, some of those late-nineteenth and early-twentieth century novelists were interested in the concepts you're referring to. Bulwark chuckled sharply. I can see *you're* going to do well in your exams, he said sarcastically. I told him I'd been trying to read the critical books suggested by the tutor in this other seminar group but often found I wanted to fall asleep early on in a chapter, especially if I was reading mid-afternoon. He told me he used to have similar problems till he started the System, which required him to eat a portion of dark chocolate five minutes before reading commenced. And when chocolate alone wasn't enough to make him alert, he would then have a cup of maté, the traditional South American infusion made by steeping leaves of yerba maté in hot water. I was feeling chilly what with the fog and was simultaneously missing K, but all the same put aside my troubles to tell him I'd not heard of maté. He said to think of it as another stimulant, like tea or coffee. Strictly speaking it should be served with a silver straw from a shared hollow calabash gourd, he said, but I use a cup. Two helpings drunk slowly through the afternoon in league with the earlier chocolate help me to read even critical tomes with barely a yawn. You're an intriguing fellow, I said, picking up as we went along the tenor of his language, and there's no doubt you'll go far in the Academic world, though I have to say I can't see you doing terribly well with intimate relationships. I fear that myself, Bulwark said. As does my mum. How is your mum with the evil thing? I asked. She doesn't know of it yet and neither should she, Bulwark replied. And besides, he went on, I doubt I'll bother being evil at home. My plan is to do it somewhere else then be normal in the evenings. I said: Do you think it's possible to be both evil and not evil without one infecting the other? And if you're truly going to find out if sustained evil behaviour can change your core beliefs I feel you're going to have to give the evil itself more commitment. Bulwark scaled several mounds in silence. Then as we were continuing in our circumnavigation, he said: One of the things I appreciate about you Peter is how often you make me change my mind about an issue even though I might have thought before how it was absolutely the thing. I asked him if this meant he wasn't going to be evil after all. That's right, he said. I don't suppose I can really live with Mum and be evil at the same time. I hadn't thought it through. You were spot on. It's a shame you don't achieve the same incisiveness in your Academic work. Now if you don't mind, I feel like a smoke and to be temporarily alone and dream my dreams of Maureen.

*

K reminded me (when she could bear to mention the subject again) how wise nature had been in its creation of insects. Couldn't I see that such a force would go even further with humans? A speck of custard remained at the corner of her mouth from the slice she'd been eating. Though I told her I supposed she was right, it was because really I didn't want to chat about nature right then. The wind was making it hard to concentrate. The man who'd arrived at the cairn after us was leaning forward at forty-five degrees. He reached down to pat the collie streaming beside him. Nice one Misty, he said. Even though we were two thousand feet above fields below, and despite the wind, we could hear more bleating. I said to K you're in a lofty mood this afternoon. It's the location, she said. Indeed we were gods just then. These rocks, I said, will have been here millions of years. I imagine they've become exposed as the elements eroded the mountain. K glanced at me as if to suggest my comments had been expected. Then she looked at her watch. Three hours to get up here, she said. The pamphlet says allow two to get down. She'd picked the pamphlet up at the cafe we'd had breakfast in before setting off. It had been my first Panini. K had the full English, which I now wished I'd had myself. Along with us at the top, other than the man and dog, were two women, one with a handbag, two teenage boys and a man and a woman in waterproofs. Everyone was looking into the egg-blue distance. Ravens rocked above the outcrops as the pamphlet said they might. If it's going to take two hours, I said, we'd better set off soon. But that'll still leave us another hour and a half to wait for the train, K said. I like margins, I told her. I didn't think I'd win the argument. An anxiety in me hardly ever abated. That's a shame, she said, I was hoping to have a nap. When I told her oh well I'm sure it wouldn't matter if she had one, I was thinking I wouldn't be happy with it. Where are you going to lie down though? I said. It's risky with people around. We'll go further along, she said. Besides, you're here. There's hardly anything worse than being on a mountain in a mood because you know come what may you're going to have to make your way down again. I know I'm here, I said, but you seem to be assuming I won't want a nap myself. You never sleep out of doors, she said. What was worse was how she then finished her custard slice and licked the tips of her fingers. But, I said, there's nothing for me to do up here if you're asleep. You could relax yourself, she said. It'll benefit mankind. Soon we had packed our things and made our way to the end of the plateau, in among the ravens I thought it, K finding a roughly human-shaped and sheltered area of stunted grass to lie on while I perched on the rocks themselves. I said about infinity and how it was easier to imagine in places like this, but she already had her head resting on the folded coat. For a while thereafter my arms goosebumped as I thought about time. I was distracted by the earlier dog who'd wandered along and was standing a few yards off, its fur now streaming right to left. I held out my thumb and first finger and rubbed them. Hello Misty, I said. The dog looked towards its distant owner, then wandered away in a lugubrious manner. K made no sound. I wondered what other entertainments she had lined up. I scrambled over and took out the pamphlet. This was the highest point for forty miles. The mountain comprised mostly old red sandstones laid down in the Devonian period, which lasted 63 million years, from 416 to 359 million years ago. Putting aside the pamphlet, I searched through K's bag and came across a slab of flapjack. Its syrupy nature was ideal for hiking, she'd said. I ate slowly, thinking of the Devonian period and wondering what periods came before and after it. The flapjack had sultanas and toasted almonds. As I ate, so weariness receded a little. She was right. I'd never been able to sleep out of doors. Night was the only time suitable for it. To indulge in it otherwise was harmful to health and wasteful to experience.

*

Smithson explained it was not beyond the realms of possibility for someone to imagine their whole life, convinced it's actually taken place, but really they might be in a dream, a state of psychosis, or something similar. You see, he said, the brain has magnificent power and complexity. Well yes, Doctor, I said. I'm beginning to realise that. It was a clear day, a breeze coming through the partly opened windows. Since it was his birthday, he'd brought doughnuts to eat as the session progressed providing they didn't interfere with the therapeutic process. As he looked over at me to check, the sun caught a rime of sugar on his mouth. Now, do go on, he said. I told him I couldn't remember where we'd got to. He said: You were telling me about your resentment towards Alexander. I said: Oh yes, even though I couldn't remember anything about it but then Smithson, knowing I had low self-esteem, sometimes took me to a topic he preferred, counting on the fact I wouldn't dare contradict him in case I was wrong. He yawned without shielding his mouth.

Mrs Smithson had an Alexander, he said, though that wasn't his name. Really he was a Malcolm. When the soon-to-be Mrs Smithson and I started courting it was Malcolm this, Malcolm that. Malcolm ice-skated for the county. Malcolm could open jars with one hand. Malcolm's stepmother came third in the Miss Universe competition. I interrupted to tell him Ormerod had told me there was no point having a Miss Universe because as far as we knew there were no humanoids beyond our own planet. Miss World was plenty. Smithson took a breath out of the window. Though Ormerod is right as usual, he said, to pursue that line would take us further from the point. He shunted from the sill, snatching up his doughnut for a second bite. When he'd chewed and swallowed and returned to the window he explained Malcolm also had a sports car and once trained as a sous chef in a posh London Hotel. In the first few years of our marriage I was obsessed with him, he said. The man dominated my life. And then blow me if one day out of the blue we didn't hear he was getting married to someone from Scotland and was, consequently, moving away. The late Mrs Smithson was invited to the wedding. She went. Without me. Although I wished I'd gone the moment her train. Drew away from the station. I rubbed my forehead. I said: Why are you leaving pauses between words? I hadn't realised I was, he said out of the window. I took my own bite of doughnut, chewed at length, swallowed then said: You could be revisiting feelings of the time and becoming emotionally hesitant. Smithson took up his pipe for an imagined draw. Therapeutic observations are best left to the experts, he said. He glanced round to ascertain I agreed that observations would be best left to them, then returned to his survey of the locality. The whole time she was gone, he said, I imagined she and Malcolm getting together, even at the expense of the new bride and horrified guests, but, *but,* what in fact happened was Mrs Smithson rang me both nights she was away and returned on time carrying a small box containing a slice of wedding cake. I expect you were mortified, I said, guessing he was about to say something similar himself, to find out your lurid fantasies had no basis in fact. Smithson put the pipe aside. Though I wouldn't have used the term lurid, I would say that yes, I was ashamed of where my head could take me when I was brushed by love. He came to sit in the chair to the rear of the couch. I take it, he said, you've grasped what I've been talking about and how it relates to you? I have, I said, though we mustn't forget you're older than me. Smithson chuckled. Age makes no difference to the severity of emotion, he said. All people, however young or old, have an Inner Buffoon. First sign of love, and out it hops.

*

Gerald was hanging signs from strings on which in capital letters was written SALE! Apart from the three he'd already put up there were two posters in each window either side of the front door carrying the same message. He said: Wait while I finish then we'll put the kettle on. I sat by the front window. I was finding it difficult to be in the same world as corned beef and yet Mother and every other housewife for miles made something with it once a week. Gerald must have noticed me watching them pass because he told me to remember each had at some point been an object of passion. He paused in his erection of the final sign as he said: Take Mrs Aldridge. Although not a mum in the strictest sense, to me she's the finest woman in all of Christendom. That might not be true for any man but me, but it's one of the ways in which this world works. When I asked him where Christendom was he carried on as if he hadn't heard. He'd taken several lengths of tinsel from a cardboard box. Soon he was pinning them round the inside of the window frame. I said to him wouldn't people confuse it with Christmas? He told me tinsel had more than one reference and anyway it wouldn't do any harm to bemuse customers. When he'd finished he stood wide to admire the effect, turned and headed into the back room. I called after him to ask if he'd seen Mrs Aldridge and he said they'd had a rush on at the laundry so no, it had been a while now, but one of the pleasures of mature relationships was romantic delays didn't bother anyone. A rustle turned out to be his hair poking round the door-frame. At your age I expect you struggle if you don't see K for a day or two, he said. I wouldn't go that far, I said, though things flatten, certainly. When I next looked, his head had gone. Instead his voice called: A boy like you shouldn't be having anything flat at all. Except of course in a literal sense. While he was saying this Alexander and his mum passed the window, though to be fair while almost the whole of Mrs Hodgkins had been visible I was only able to deduce Alexander by a bobbing of hair along the lower run of tinsel. Just after this came Mrs Tintwistle and some wisps I took to be K. I was diverted from thinking more about it by Gerald swerving through the door with mugs. I remembered about the non-sugar this time, he said. He suggested I bring my chair so we might sit approximate to each other by the desk. He put his feet up as before. No, he said, being with someone like Mrs Aldridge is free of the anxiety you experience at your age. I can easily bide my time till she chooses to come in next and of course in that way there's ever a surprise element, which is pleasing in itself. She's an angel of the first order. He sipped tea and took a look at the shop as if to get the measure of his happiness. Incidentally, he said, when someone comes into a second-hand bookshop it's important to make them think A) they are not being observed and B) they have all the time in the world to look round if they so wish. I thought I'd give you a few tips given what you said about wanting a shop of your own one day though God forbid it should come true. Promise me you won't do it unless you're in a viable position! I said I promised. After a while of tea, he said: I don't suppose K would be interested in séances. He'd turned the sentence into a question at the last moment. Once we'd sorted out what séances were, I told him I was sure she *wasn't* interested in them, although I had no idea either way. He said he'd thought for a moment she might be because of their connection with poltergeists. An aunt of mine was always trying to contact the dead, he said. She made a living out of it. I said nothing because I'd suddenly remembered K and Alexander. I hadn't felt uneasy till then and didn't feel uneasy soon afterwards, but right then I did. A prolonged chirping from the back room I took to be eleven o'clock. Ah now see if you can guess which bird that was, Gerald said brightly. If you get it right I'll leave the clock to you in my will. The curious thing was I knew it was a blackbird because I could recall them all, but I couldn't bring myself to tell him because I didn't want him to feel he was under obligation about the will. I said: Reed-warbler? Gerald laughed with his hand in front of his mouth. Not only wasn't it a reed-warbler, he said, but there aren't any reed-warblers on the clock face. It sounded like one, I said. Ormerod does impressions. He's an all-round boy, your Ormerod, Gerald said just before or just after another sip of tea. I could tell he was missing Mrs Aldridge. I hoped she'd pop in soon for his sake. Yes he is, I said. Again an unease about K, Alexander and their mums passing along the street. My own had gone to buy kidneys and stewing steak for a pie she was going to make Father so long as he didn't use the words Miss and Woo one after the other again. She'd been mentioned last evening and Mother had decided to put her foot down. So in my All Inclusive Sale, Gerald said suddenly, every book has a twenty per cent reduction. If – but only if – a person buys five, they can have the least expensive free as well as the overall twenty per cent. I'm hopeful it'll create an upsurge. The other day I saw two free-standing shelf units in a junk shop. I'm wondering if I shouldn't use them on a daily basis out on the pavement. I'd only put the cheaper books in them because no doubt criminals would see it as an opportunity to help themselves, but do you know, part of me doesn't even mind that? There are worse things than to steal books – unless of course the criminal intends to sell them on for profit. But yes, the cheaper volumes will go out there. If I get the shelves I'll buy a couple of hooks to secure them to the shopfront during the day. What do you think? He'd asked this to give himself time to swig. I was lightly composing a reply when he said: One day, I'm hoping, Mrs Aldridge might leave the laundry and work here. I'm sure she'd find it therapeutic and the lack of dampness would be a blessing. Besides, she's been saying for some time when life settles she's going to write that book, and being in here should help her no end. When I asked him what book, he said the term 'that book' was meant to indicate not a specific book as such, but one she'd previously said, in theory, she might work on when she had time. She could call it *The Life And Times Of Mrs Aldridge,* I said. Gerald nodded. That could be a fine title if it were to be autobiographical, he said, but from what she's said it's more likely to be a murder mystery set in the suburbs. He adjusted his shoes on the desk, sipping between times. The silence was beguiled by a seethe of the shop's volumes. When you're older you can give me a hand on Saturdays if you like he said, that is if your mum doesn't mind. In my experience some mums do while others are only too glad to have a breather. Mine likes as many breathers as possible, I said. How much older do I have to be? I'm not sure, Gerald said. I'll mention it when she comes to pick you up. I mean there's no guarantee you'll have to be older at all. I was saying it for want of anything else. That's happening more and more these days. With a sigh he got up, pushed his hands in his pockets and walked to the right-hand window, leaning forward to see as much of the street as possible then going to the door, opening it, stepping outside. I couldn't understand why he hadn't gone to the door in the first place. Much later I learned one of the conditions dealt with by Therapeutic Specialists was a tendency in some to do an inefficient, illogical thing just before they did the efficient, logical thing. Gerald was now rising on to his toes and back again. He turned after a few moments to wave me out. The street had dogs and a spread of agonised mums faced with bargains or so I thought till I mentioned them to Gerald and he said I shouldn't say such things. I told him I'd made it up anyway and for the most part made everything up and he said though that was well and good on one level, wasn't I worried people might not know what was really going on? We were both scuffing as if to scuff up customers and soon Gerald turned to explain where he was hoping to put the Outside Shelves if he should end up getting them. That's the one drawback of an inheritance, he said, knowing which purchases are necessary and which frivolity. I noted as he was speaking he was choosing not to categorise Mrs Aldridge's Bumper Weekends. I was still hoping she might come along so I could see why he yearned for her but at the same time I realised I'd never yet seen the someone someone else yearned for without being disappointed or freakishly amazed. Gerald finished imagining shelves, turned again and held out his hand. I felt a few spots of rain, he said. I said I hadn't so far though maybe that was down to me being thinner and shorter. Gerald rushed inside leaving me there like one of his lemons. Soon afterwards a woman came along cupping her hand against the far window. It's open, I said. She looked startled but asked who I was. I told her in detail, ending with: And I expect you're Mrs Aldridge. Then you expect wrong, she said. Gerald's inside somewhere, I told her. She withdrew from the window sighing enough to steam it. Well, when you see him tell him you saw Mrs McKintosh, she said menacingly. I don't have the time to stop now but I will do, tell him, *very* soon. When I'd located Gerald in the back room cupboard and reported the incident I included the menacingly. The look on his face made me think I shouldn't have. He stepped out, glancing at the ceiling. Listen Peter, if ever you're on the pavement again and I'm in the shop and she comes along tell her I'm not here. Even if you are? I said. Especially then, he said. She was once a companion. We had a falling-out. In the time we were apart I developed a separate companionship with Mrs Aldridge. Beckoning me, he crept back through into the main shop and looked towards the windows. She lives out of town so she doesn't drop by often, he said quietly, but when she does... It's funny both of them are Mrs Whatevers, I said. I went back outside. A dog in the back of a parked car looked across and barked. Because it had poodle qualities, curls of fur around its face trembled. Mother was hurrying along the opposite side of the street. The sadness of Miss Woo was still on her despite the pie plans. She came hotfoot to me, in a fluster it turned out because she wanted to know why Gerald wasn't keeping an eye. I've only just come out, I said. In her basket was a paper bag, a reddish brown wetness leaking through it. By the time she took me inside Gerald was on a small stepladder, dusting larger volumes that lay along the top shelf.

*

He left *This Curious World* in his will instead of the clock. Sometimes when K came round she would take it out. On many occasions an anxiety hung between us and the book would usher in a muted argument. It might be better if we went out rather than hang round here, she said one time. That's true, I told her. There was something about anxiety that made me want to develop it. I'd tried K's serenity prayer. It's not so nice out, that's the problem, I said. I know. I walked here in it if you recall, K said. She was at the same time examining whatever page *This Curious World* had opened on to. I asked again if she wanted me to hang up her coat. There's no point, she said. Either we'll be going out or I'll be off home again. The pain of the latter part of this information circulated through me. It's like you've already made up your mind, I said. It's not that, she said. But you're in a mood. You need to be active. I tried to look startled. I don't feel I am, I protested. She hadn't even looked up from *This Curious World*. Okay then, so tell me what you've been doing today. I shook my head. I don't see what that's got to do with anything but if you like I'll list my activities. On days off I stay in bed longer so it was, what? half eight when I climbed out. I heard the rain but wasn't daunted because I knew you'd be coming. After this I went to the shop for milk and bread so you'd be able to have a hot drink and toast if you wanted. I was soaked when I got back. I dried my hair and had a cup of tea. How's that! I shook my head again in case the first hadn't registered, then went into the kitchen to steady myself. I came back when I was sure I could manage. K asked if I was better, I told her I couldn't be because that would imply there'd been something the matter in the first place. K said we never get on when the weather's bad. I told her that was a shame. It is, she said. But all the same, I said, I did want to protest at this idea everything was down to me and my moods when it could easily be down to hers. I'll go now anyway, she said. I don't want an escalation. She took her coat and was gone. I went to the window and watched her pass along the pavement. The wind was bringing down leaves. The dog from up the road looked at K as she passed, sniffing the air afterwards, his tail low. I stood at the curtains till she was out of sight. I turned in to the room and flicked through *This Curious World*. Rain flushed through a broken drainpipe next door. Come back, I was saying to myself.

*

Atkins has said walking the wooded earth and its hillsides was the finest thing, finer even than his novels or the adaptation. Smetham asked if he was going to talk about breasts again and Atkins said he didn't think he was; this was more a musing about the nature of his having wandered for much of his life. Human beings are meant to be on the move, he said. We spend too much time glued to desks staring at computers. Kandinsky laughed. He explained that when Atkins had said glued to desks he'd imagined it literally. I wish you wouldn't mock me the moment I open my mouth, Atkins said. He glanced at his compendium. Yes, he went on, me and my wife often used to walk to The Hill. Any of you heard of it? Whenever Major Gwillingington's medals jingled we weren't sure if he was indicating yes he had or was having a dream. The Hill's actually a mountain, Atkins went on. Kandinsky said: Why call it a hill then? Atkins said it wasn't he who was calling it a hill, but the Middle Saxons. Harry had been over by the windows and said, maybe to help Atkins out, he'd heard of it and indeed it was a mountain though only just beyond the height necessary. And which height would this be? Kandinsky said. I believe he was trying to catch Harry out and in a way Atkins too. Colquahoon butted in to say it was where the land rose a thousand feet above the surrounding terrain and that, of course, was about three hundred and five metres. You and your metres, Kandinsky said. Atkins stretched his feet in front of him and put his hands behind his head. Yes, whenever things go tits up in here, he said, I remember Judith and me walking the lower slopes, hearing the chirrup of larks, the distant lowing of cattle, the creak of the picnic basket. You're making this up, Kandinsky said. He was the only one still drinking tea. Just for him Fiona had made a cup with leaves in. It reminded him, he told us once, of holidays in Ireland. On the contrary, Atkins went on, we'd pause at the gate then lazily climb over it before tackling the diagonal path that led, by degrees, to the majestic summit. If I might say so, Colquahoon piped up, you are overindulging the descriptive elements. It might be one of the reasons Mr Kandinsky feels you're making it up. Florid language can give that impression. Atkins stayed quiet a while then said: Once up there we could see virtually into the next county. Judith loved it. She had her late mother scattered there. Smetham asked did he mean her ashes? Atkins sighed. Colquahoon said it was a mistake to think you had someone's ashes to scatter. There would be a residue from the coffin and maybe even parts of the person cremated immediately beforehand. You're asking for a thump, Atkins said. He didn't look to be honest like he was getting ready to thump anyone. Judith talked to her mum whenever we were up there, he went on. Though Colquahoon said nothing, his eye twinkled. Smetham said he'd heard there was a small crematorium just beyond Nine for people who didn't have relatives. I'll probably be going there, he

151

said. You're welcome to my funeral service. I'm having 'All Things Bright And Beautiful'. Harry knows. It's in his book. We each maybe turned to Harry to make sure not only that he had a book but that Smetham's request was in it. Harry nodded though I had a feeling he was thinking about Cheryl. Kandinsky said he'd heard you could get yourself liquidised these days as an environmentally friendly alternative to cremation or burial. You become, he said, a small quantity of a green-brown slush containing amino acids, peptides, sugars and salts and soft porous white bone remains, which are easily crushed. The slush can be recycled into the ecosystem by being applied to a memorial garden or forest. Or, of course, it can be put down the sink. Atkins said he wouldn't be going down any sinks. You'd be slush! Kandinsky said. What would you care! The following silence continued for over a minute though I might have got that wrong. I'm hopeless at time, as K was fond of pointing out. I'm always saying things were five minutes ago when actually they could have been half an hour or less than a second. Harry said there are medications that realign one's sense of time but that they're too expensive at present. Someone in Switzerland developed them, he said. Yes, I said, the Swiss have a monopoly on that sort of thing, to which Harry said I don't believe the person who developed them is Swiss, only that she was in Switzerland when she did. People should rot naturally, Atkins said. I can't be doing with liquidation. Well, Kandinsky said, we liquefy as part of the decomposition process anyway. It was about then Tobias Mawk began shouting. He rocked in his chair, fighting his restraints. When this sort of thing happened those of us witnessing it would look elsewhere. None of us had taken to him. Right people, Harry said, clapping his hands as before, let's talk about something life-affirming. Atkins chortled. I think that's the noise he made anyway. In excitement he stretched his slippered feet. I was saying life-affirming things before, Harry, but this shower of hooligans started on about death. Tell them Harry, tell them. I was rooting round memory trying to find out where the conversation had gone wrong but my brain was in a tangle. It was like I could reach a place halfway down the thought but not get to the bottom. Jaundice put aside his mirror and stared forward as if he was about to speak. The strain was enormous. When we each felt we could bear it no more, he restored the mirror to its usual position and his face relaxed. It tickles me what the head can get up to when left to its own devices. I said as much to Harry who'd restored himself to the door-frame giving me the impression yes, something had gone wrong with Cheryl. Where wives were concerned, he told us once, there was ever the possibility of things going wrong and it could be additionally painful if you were the sort to live in fear of conflict.

*

Gravel, having doffed his cap, glanced at the emptiness behind him and said: Isn't this road a blessing since the bypass! Father said yes, he certainly felt safer these days. Softly-spoken Gravel went to church which is why he used words like blessing. Father leaned on his spade. He liked to have it with him to make it look to passers-by not only that he might soon be doing something horticultural but also that despite rumours, he wasn't the sort to associate with foreign women. His Anti-Miss Woo Spade, Ormerod called it. The dog from up the road had wandered down to see who might be talking. He drew to a solemn halt some yards away. I was wishing he would come near so I could reach through the gate. I remember, Gravel said, when there were lorries up and down here day in day out. Oh yes, Father said. Many's the time we'd be woken in the night by one. Mother was in my bedroom window, breathing on the glass. She moved a cloth in yellow circles. She'd told Mrs Chaffin all men were the same and that women were better off without them. Mrs Chaffin said too true though she had to confess to missing Mr Chaffin. Our front garden was much like everyone else's. Father had eternal plans for a pagoda. I was dying to swing on the gate. The dog scratched itself. Mother had said it was best not to stroke any dog you didn't know because they might have fleas or bite you. Father said or they might have fleas *and* bite you. He'd been pleased with this till Mother'd asked if *she* had a dog. Imagined voices were using italics suddenly. Jugg said they were a sign you weren't composing sentences properly in the first place. I laughed at how easily these ideas gathered in the sky, glooming it in some areas, brightening it in others. Decent petunias you've got there, Gravel said. His wife had run away with the lemonade man but nobody mentioned it. Yes, Father said, they get better year on year. Had Ormerod come I might have asked if we could head into the trees further along. The stream had rainbow trout. Very small ones but trout none the less. I'm a geranium man myself, Gravel said. Last year I had Highly Commended in the church fete. Love the smell. Just half a dozen in your greenhouse can be overwhelming. I like geraniums myself, Father said. I'm with you on the smell, but my wife doesn't like them. That's a shame, Gravel said. When his head lowered I fancied it meant though geraniums were okay as a topic, he didn't really want wives brought into it. A stubborn stain meant Mother's cloth squeaked as it moved. Bells from the church sounded the hour. I was trying to remember which bird would be singing in Gerald's shop. I had a feeling it might have been a wren. Gerald had said it made a huge noise for its size. He went on to say that when he looked at a wren sometimes he could hardly fathom how something so delicate could be alive at all. I coughed and took a few wasteful footsteps to bring myself back into the garden. Life was melting into itself. Gravel looked at his watch when the last chime sounded. I'm due down the surgery, he said to Father. I reckon I might have got that bug. Well I hope you haven't, Father said. He raised the spade and thrust it into the soil. The dog from up the road stopped scratching. In general he didn't respond confidently to situations or noises he hadn't encountered before. Me too, Gravel said. My encyclopedia says it can be dangerous as you get older. I sighed. I hope nobody heard it. It was because despite saying he had an appointment and despite having been warned of dangers by an encyclopedia, Gravel didn't seem in a hurry to get going. Father had said on another occasion he felt Gravel was on general lookout for lemonade men and that when your wife runs off with one it can make being on the lookout more time-consuming than it ought to be. Okay, Father said, I hope you have good news down the doctor's. Gravel shook his head. So do I, he said. I don't want this hanging over me for weeks on end. Father said it sounded nasty, more to appease Gravel than anything because he didn't actually know any of the symptoms Gravel had been suffering. I only noticed, as he was about to take step one on his continuing journey, that it was necessary for him to raise his left leg higher than his right. Father leaned on his spade to watch him go. Don't end up like that, he said. I said: All right. I'd put a pause between the two words as Jugg had suggested. He'd told us we must never use alright. It was acceptable however to use already rather than all ready. Father said threateningly so what are you up to today? Well, I said, in a while I'm wandering round the back to see how Grandmother's doing. All right, Father said, but only through the window. When I asked him as usual, why, he said, as usual, he didn't want to risk having her spilt. I asked him what it was like to be dead. He chopped his spade among the petunias. Nobody's sure, he said. If I can when I die I'll let you know. Thanks, I said. I happened to catch the dog yawning. At maximum his jaws had a greyish foam around the back teeth.

*

Bulwark's head and cowl turned while his body did not. You're a good fellow, he said, but I don't believe in spilt grandmothers. I told him he must have misheard because though certainly the potential for spillage had been there such an accident had never taken place. The cowl returned to face forward as its owner and I patrolled the eternal hillocks. He said as we proceeded downwards: I was generalising. What I meant was hardly anything you tell me about your life rings true. I was nodding behind him, pointlessly. I've been told that, I said. One of the dangers, he went on, of being steeped in literature, is you begin to ask yourself if there's any point dealing with truth at all? I was wondering – and while I continue to wonder I may veer into the trees for a you-know-what – I was wondering if this might be what's happening to you, no offence. None taken, I said boldly. But I assure you that while I see the dangers arising from a study of literature, Father really did keep his mother's ashes in the shed and I was certainly warned against spilling her oh, I don't know – a hundred times. I'd sighed through the oh-I-don't-know part to give myself a certain verity. If that's the case, Bulwark said, I'm envious. I've nothing but run-of-the-mill grandmother stories. And before you say anything I mean the stories are run-of-the-mill, not the grandmothers. You're lucky to have had abundance, I said. We were looping down from the side of a hillock towards one of his favourite areas. He was doing well in his determination to smoke heavily. Only the inconvenience of college hindered more progress to that end. He held his arms outwards as we descended. They're both dead, he said gravely. One of them kept tins of chocolates. She gave me one each time I went there. I liked to observe the world through their coloured wrappers. And Grandmother herself of course who looked best – if I remember right – in pale amber. He hurried the last few yards. Soon we were in the trees. Half crouched by pressing his back against a tree, he lit up. It's not that you're not a fine fellow all round, he said, nodding, but it's hard to know what's what with you. I rubbed my hands to warm them. Ormerod's said as much, I told him. He says it makes it difficult for others to know me properly, unless of course those others also like to play their cards close to their chests. Well yes that's right, Bulwark said. What does your girlfriend make of it all? J isn't it? K, I said. Oh sorry, Bulwark said. That's okay, I said. I waved one hand in front of my mouth to disperse the rising smoke. Anyway, she regularly gives me ultimatums. I understand why, he said. And I prefer ultimata. She says she wants me to become more attached to the real world, I said sadly. And how do you propose to go about *that*, Bulwark asked. It was like I was under attack. Suddenly I saw he was taking revenge on me for chatting with Jennifer that day. Well when I'm free of this place and I've finally done with my Therapeutic Specialist, I said, I'll get a job, settle down and become commonplace. I heard a sniffing within Bulwark's cowl. And what line of work do you see yourself in? I don't know, I said, if I want to be 'in' one as such. If the Office doesn't get me, K says I'd make a good investigator but I wouldn't begin to know how to start being one of those. Part of me wouldn't mind having a second-hand bookshop. Bulwark shook his cowl. No point, he said. You'd never make enough to live on, you have to make enough to live on. His repetition of the key concept entrenched its horror. I often wonder why it's hard to make enough doing good things, I said. For me, Bulwark said, it's because money naturally attaches itself to the immoral parts of life. I use the term immoral in its loosest sense of course. I repeated: Of course. Both words moved quickly forward, losing themselves in the pine wood.

Bulwark must have noticed this phenomenon because a slight change of angle in his cowl indicated he was looking towards where the words had gone. I hear on the grapevine Jennifer's going to work in Administration, he said. The cowl tipped forward. He took a draw on his cigarette. I suppose that means she'll be off to the capital. Maybe, but it won't be happening for a while yet, I said. You have plenty of time to get to know her better. I'm sure she'd like that. Don't jump the gun, Bulwark said. You have a tendency. For jumping it I mean.

*

At the same time as hearing the world through patio doors I'm remembering Alexander wedged in the school gate, his right and left hand high on the uprights while his right and left foot lay tight against the lowest points. Mums and janitors stood by. I said to him quietly: You really need to take the plunge and go in Alexander. It's the rule. K was already across the yard by the coal bunker. I stretched to wave. Go through and I'll give you sixpence, Mrs Hodgkins said. Mother ticked her tongue. Don't offer cash. It means he won't go in tomorrow either unless you give him another sixpence. She leaned down to the back of Alexander's head. Look at everybody having fun, she said. You'll have a lovely time too. Peter will be there. Mrs Hodgkins said: I don't want to push him psychologically Doreen. It might do more harm than good. Mother said boys were resilient and not to worry. Shall I give it another go? she asked. Really she wanted to shove Alexander into the yard because of her anxieties about Miss Woo. There was no evidence to suggest Father was still seeing her on a regular basis, but like Mother said to Mrs Chaffin a few days before, subterfuge lingered on the wind. I remember because Mrs Chaffin said getting involved with any man had that risk, not, she added proudly, that there'd been anything along those lines with her late husband. He didn't have it in him, she said. Or me come to that. Meek and mild were his middle names. So anyway, Mrs Hodgkins pushed against Alexander's back. It drew attention to the ginger coat. I wondered if this might not have something to do with his unwillingness to begin school life. An old woman in the yard looked towards us, aching to cane a child. Mrs Strachan's got her eye on you now, Mrs

Hodgkins whispered to Alexander. I'll make it a shilling. Mother drew breath. You're doing it again, she said. I know, Mrs Hodgkins said, but I can't think. I should have asked Raymond to bring him. He would have known what to do. If you don't mind my saying so, Mother said, saying it anyway, you're being soft. Alexander needs to go to school like it or not. He's always been delicate though Doreen, Mrs Hodgkins said. This is frightening the poor lamb. In the corner of Alexander's eye, a twinkled celebrity. It was like he'd been holding on at least till he reached the lamb stage. The person referred to as Mrs Strachan was making her way towards the gate. She had one hand inside a bell. Might I ask what's going on? she said. I felt that if I'd been fully under her jurisdiction at that point she'd have given me a good hiding for being in the locality. It's Alexander, Mrs Hodgkins said. He's nervous. Mrs Strachan took a step back, getting the measure of Alexander spectacularly. Perhaps if you go home now Mrs Um, I'm sure we'll have the problem resolved in no time. I can't leave him like this, Mrs Hodgkins said. The first day at school is a big moment in a child's life. I saw myself from above. I had an unquenchable hatred for plastic sandals. I doubted K would like them either. No, no, trust me, Mrs Strachan said. Mother took Mrs Hodgkins by the arm, pulling her softly away. She was too engrossed in the problem of Alexander to remember it was my first day too. The sky was triangularly cracked, making me wonder if things would ever come right. Mrs Hodgkins can't have been more than a moment out of sight round the corner before Alexander let go and rubbed his hands. Mrs Strachan told him he'd avoided the cane, but only just. I followed them into the yard. When we'd reached the far side she took her hand out of the bell, held the wooden end and rang half a dozen times. K was at the far side, one foot up against the wall. Turned out we were meant to stop what we were doing and form lines. In the classroom K sat in a double row of desks containing girls. I was only able to see an edge of her hair from where I'd been though the good news was that since we'd been allies during the gate crisis, Alexander and me were together in the boys' row. Mrs Strachan, pronounced Strawn (she said, having written it on the blackboard) sat on a high stool. She told us she was married to

Mr Strachan who was pronounced Strawn too. If you need proof of our marriage, Mrs Strachan said, here's the ring. She raised her left hand high enough for everyone to see, even Horace, who was on medication. We were told never to knock into him and he wasn't allowed heights or puddings or anything with nuts. He'd been named after the leading Roman lyric poet during the time of Augustus. Alexander whispered to me he'd had enough and didn't think he'd come tomorrow. I said as far as I knew we were supposed to go every day except weekends. He said if that was the case he'd be writing to the authorities although he could barely write and most probably didn't know who the authorities were. Mrs Strachan told us we were about to embark on a journey that for some would last thirteen years. Many of our heads fell to the desktops. Alexander's was not only against the desk, but rocking from side to side. Tell me when she's finished, he said. His whisper found its way to her. The craning in her neck had the effect of smoothing out, temporarily, her facial skin. We don't have talking unless we are invited, she said. Alexander sat up, adjusted his nose and settled back, wanting the thirteen years to pass. Another boy, not far from Horace, raised his hand to ask Mrs Strachan if we'd be doing sums at any point, because his mum had told him they could be fun. Mrs Strachan became her version of delighted and said certainly we *would* be doing sums but not today. Today, she said, is a getting-to-know-each-other day. Starting at the front row and working her way back, she wrote each of our names on the board when we had said what they were, then each of us had to go to stand in front of the class while what we looked like was associated with the name. K came early on. Her nose changed colour as she stood there. Sun through the window picked out the hairs between the tops of her socks and the hem of her skirt. This is K, Mrs Strachan said, revealing what she'd just been told. And here's her name on the board. Thank you K, that will be all. K returned to her seat. A wound marred the universe. It was years before Alexander's turn. I could see by Mrs Strachan's expression she'd marked him out for attention. And *this*, she said, is Alexander. We met earlier. Who can point to his name? Horace said he could see where it was, though none of us quite knew if he was standing. He'd been alerted by the X, he said. A survey by Mrs Strachan revealed Alexander was the *only* child to have one. No one's got Q or Z either, Alexander told her.

*

The last but one time Kandinsky cracked – though I wasn't here in those days – an upholstered chair was thrown through one of the windows in the study area. There'd been a management meeting afterwards to decide if he should be moved, but Harry – bless him – pleaded on his behalf and earned him a stay of execution. The best thing, Kandinsky said later, was no one had asked him to pay for the window and yet that's surely something that would happen out there. He pointed towards the wider world beyond the hedgerow. I told him I can't say I've ever thrown a chair through a window though if I was being honest there have been times I've wanted to, or something equivalent. Well, he said, maybe you should give in. It makes you feel better. Colquahoon said he didn't think feeling better was enough to justify broken windows and in the end there was a vote held though hardly anyone bothered to participate. Atkins conceded that yes he had an urge now and then to throw chairs but didn't we think it would be more appropriate to seek out someone at that point and discuss our feelings? Smetham said he'd once thrown a copy of *Lark Rise To Candleford* through an open window because his wife had refused to put it aside while he was trying to talk to her. Kandinsky said to Smetham couldn't he see that if the window wasn't actually closed there was no problem? Smetham said if he'd really broken the window – not that he could have anyway because it was a paperback – he knew it would have resurrected in his wife memories of an aggressive father. We each fell into an abused silence, tempered by the song of a localised bird.

*

How badly Gerald had been hoping Mrs Aldridge would come in because, he said, he was lonely lonely lonely (each beaten on the desk), a loneliness deepened by the thought that any day Mrs McKintosh might come instead and what would happen this time if she took us by surprise? I'd remembered from a previous visit a book named *What To Do In Tight Spots* in the Medical section and hurried to get it for him. He flicked through in what I felt was a token gesture before laying it on the desk and turning to me. It won't have anything on The Prolonged Absence Of Mrs Aldridge, he said. Although it should in an ideal world. In fact in an ideal world it would have every possibility, like those infinite monkeys. How about I make another cup of tea? I said to him, hoping he'd see sense: But that'll be our fourth. Fourth my bollocks, he said, getting up. My grandmother had nine or ten a day if she had one. Lots of people have a grandparent who did odd things, I said. Mine's in our shed. Father said she could balance on her head without using her hands. Gerald was already on his way into the back room. He called to ask how I was getting along with *This Curious World*. I said I was getting along with it though I hadn't looked at it in detail so far. He called that I should have another wander along the shelves to see if any titles else jumped out at me. I followed his suggestion, standing slightly back in case any of them did. I wasn't concentrating because I was thinking about K. Although thinking about her isn't the right phrase. It was more that something about her had set itself an inch from my forehead. I wondered what she might be doing and why I wasn't with her, albeit it was nice I was allowed to help Gerald – though help isn't the word because no one came in for the time I was there. If you go into a second-hand book-shop and find the proprietor doing something with books, be assured he's only been doing it for as long as he sensed you were about to arrive. From the back room a bluetit or a series of bluetits announced the hour. Give me a shout if Mrs Aldridge comes, Gerald called, and tell her I won't be two ticks. This was Gerald hoping to put across to himself, to me, and the universe, that he wasn't so intent on hoping for the arrival of Mrs Aldridge that he could be distracted from current tasks. When at last I looked at the books, I found myself by Fungi. There were fewer than a dozen in this section. One of them had a deep red cover, which made me take it out. The pages were interleaved with coloured plates. The Fly Agaric was one of the best. I must admit I'm imparting a future admiration of it on to a K-struck child who was mostly flicking through and half waiting for the sound of the door. Gerald was calling that he wished he'd gone out for biscuits because there were none left, none, anyway, that merited the term biscuit because they were now soft. He should have noticed, he said, and was sorry. The apology convinced me how difficult he was finding it waiting for Mrs Aldridge. He was shrouding himself in sound in the hope of not hearing his own despair. While down that end of the shop – prophetic in view of what had been said earlier – I was confronted by Mrs McKintosh, who had a hand cupped against the outside of the window as if she hadn't realised there was an accessible interior. I called in a half whisper to Gerald who must have known the situation by something in my voice. I heard moments later the click of the toilet door. Mrs McKintosh wore a hat Gerald had previously warned me about. An area of window was already stained by breath. I went to the door, sauntering I thought it, and stepped outside, stroking the recently positioned Outdoor Shelves. You again, Mrs McKintosh said. I said yes, I'd started helping Saturdays. Something in the situation – in the clouds drawn along by a blue wind – made me feel alive, but then I realised it must also have been because a sixth sense had recognised the imminent approach of K and Mrs Tintwhistle. The moment she noticed me K raised her brows to indicate she wasn't happy with the pattern of the coat she had on, which as it came into focus I could see comprised dolphins. I'm helping Gerald. Not that he's here, I said when she was in earshot. K said she'd worked that out and how was I? I told her I was reasonable in the circumstances. K said she wasn't going to ask what circumstances and she had said the word 'what' more loudly than other parts of the sentence. Mrs Tintwhistle suggested I came with them for half an hour if I wanted, only I'd better let Gerald know given he was in charge. Mrs McKintosh stepped to us, telling Mrs Tintwhistle she'd pass the message on to Gerald herself now she knew he was there after all. She then raised her brows at me. K said they were on their way to get something for tea. As we walked on, I was concerned Mrs McKintosh might forget to tell Gerald where I'd gone or else withhold the information maliciously. I didn't look up from the pavement till K informed me we'd reached the Fruiterer's. Mrs Tintwhistle went in. I said to K it was a miracle she'd come along and that I'd been struggling at the shop mostly because of Gerald's worries over Mrs Aldridge and now Mrs McKintosh. The Fruiterer's window had a display of apples, bananas and oranges. I told K I liked her coat and she said it had been half price and I said which half? and I suppose the attempted joke set things on a bad footing. She asked where my mum was and I found myself looking up and down the street before I said she was shopping, also for something for tea, although she was making an extra effort with food because this was the best way to counteract Miss Woo. It's a shame, said K, Miss Woo has to be counteracted, and I said I agreed since lately it was beginning to look like soon I might inhabit a broken home. My hair and the shoulder of K's coat were patted by Gravel going by on one of his likely trips to the doctor's. When he'd passed, K said she didn't want adults patting her and I, my hair wild, said I didn't enjoy it either. K said it was odd oranges were called oranges because it seemed the person charged with responsibility for naming them hadn't put any thought into it. I asked if she'd seen anything of Alexander since yesterday and she said he was in bed with a temperature and couldn't come out because, she said, originally Mrs Hodgkins had wanted to go shopping too. You spend a lot of time with Alexander, I said. Well, K said, having paused, for one he's close and for two he has a rabbit. I was astonished. In all the time I'd known him I hadn't heard of a rabbit. Oh yeah, the rabbit, I said. K raised and lowered her shoulders. It was like she wanted to shrug off the dolphins. Actually he doesn't *have* a rabbit. she said. I hoped Mrs Tintwhistle would soon come out of the shop. So why, I said eventually, did you say he had one? Well, K said, why did you say oh yes, the rabbit when you didn't know if he had one or not? Let's not talk about this, I said. Your mum'll be out soon. A bell from across the street shook the pavement, the windows. That's fruit done, Mrs Tintwistle said as she appeared. I've got a bit more than usual. Roger's under the weather. A glance from K confirmed this was the case. I would have said generally he'd always been under it; all that varied was the depth of immersion. K asked if *she* knew why oranges were called oranges. Mrs Tintwistle said it was probably because of their colour. When K nudged me it was because she'd not been serious about asking. Mrs Tintwistle went on to say that was most likely also why lemons were called lemons. K said she supposed bananas would have been called lemons if they'd got in first and nudged me again. Though I didn't like the nudging, Ormerod later said it hinted at a deepening connection. I dared to say to K: Surely they would have been called Yellows. We moved on to the Tobacconist's. The window was dominated by large cardboard cigarettes lying at angles. K said window displays were funny and though I had to agree, the reasons weren't clear. She knew windows had things in so people going by would know what the shop sold but it was like there was more to it than that. I again agreed because I wanted her to know she'd ever have my support. Mrs Tintwistle told us to stay where we were while she bought Mr Tintwistle's cigarettes though heaven knew, it was time he stopped. Money up in smoke, she said.

*

Atkins wondered why he always made that sound with his lips and extended his hand whenever he was trying to entice a cat. Kandinsky said the hand gesture was intended to fool cats into thinking there was food available and who knew, but the sound might be a long-term development from the sound of kittens, thus prompting a cat's maternal instincts. What if it's a Tom? Atkins said. Smetham said they ate cats in China and Korea and in some ways he envied them. The cats? Atkins joked. No, Smetham said in a measured voice. Atkins twitched his upper lip. He shivered. You wouldn't catch me eating a cat, he said. Well to be fair, Kandinsky said, that's because your experience has only featured domestic cats. But even here in the west there have been times when we've eaten them. I'm sure you're right, Mr Kandinsky, said Atkins, but I promise you I wouldn't eat a cat in any circumstances. Oh you would, Kandinsky said. I think what was irritating Atkins was the way Kandinsky was picking at the hard skin on his left hand. We've eaten them, he went on, in times of famine and war. I would lay any money on it that if I left you starving in a room with a cat or, come to that, any creature, sooner or later you'd eat it. Smetham laughed. When we looked over to him it was easy to ascertain it hadn't been a reaction to anything said. I don't expect I ever will be left starving in a room with a cat or one of your so-called creatures, Atkins said bitterly, and thus your supposition – Mr Kandinsky – will remain unproven. My grandfather ate eels, Smetham said. Atkins wondered – impolitely – what eels had to do with it. Well, Smetham said, since the Iron Age people have used rotting cats to catch eels in traps. It was Kandinsky's turn to laugh. I wouldn't eat an eel that had been caught using rotting cats, he said. As if his head had been transparent and his thoughts words therein, I could see he realised this seemed to contradict what he'd said earlier about famine and war. He cleared his throat and went over to stand at the opened patio doors. We should have a cat here, he said. Harry happened to come out of his office just then and had to remind Kandinsky this room and its environs were animal-free zones for hygiene and health and safety reasons. I was supposing that's all, Kandinsky said, I appreciate it's not possible. Atkins said: Do you though Mr Kandinsky, do you really? It looked for a moment as if Kandinsky might crack again. Colquahoon nervously unwrapped a toffee. I've said nervously because his hands shook as the sweet turned in his fingers. I do wish you'd all stop talking nonsense, he said. Day after day after day after day after day. He would have added days into infinity had not the insertion of the sweet brought the incantation to an end. Smetham said on the contrary though he sometimes disagreed with the thrust of most topics, he was always glad to have one come up. Otherwise we'd go bonkers, he said. But you are bonkers, Atkins told him. Not in an unpleasant way, but bonkers all the same. Harry interrupted to remind us offensive terms re: our conditions weren't allowed either. Smetham was biting his own hand. Even from where I was sitting I could see tooth marks when finally he took it out. I don't think you'll find the word bonkers anywhere in my notes, he said. I was sometimes tempted to enter these discussions, but always it seemed the topic had moved on by the time I had any relevant words in my mouth. Besides, what could I say here? I'd no opinion on whether people should eat cats and I wasn't sure if I felt Smetham was bonkers or indeed if it made any difference using correct terminology. True it probably wasn't a good idea to eat furniture, but then something about it made you know that no amount of physical or psychological treatment would ever stop it happening. Some people just have things, Harry told me once, and not all things have names. Only last year he had a man in for assessment who leaned his head against the wall to one side of the patio doors. He would start doing it after breakfast and stay doing it through the day, with breaks for meals and the bathroom. He died. Harry looked sad when he told me this. Yes, he said, answering himself, died with his head against the wall. It was when he didn't come to dinner we realised. I asked Harry what happened next though I have to say I wasn't really interested. Every next on earth adds up to death so you have to make an effort to bother about what lies between them. Well, Harry said, when I went over and touched his shoulder, he fell sideways. Rigor mortis. Harry said these last words as if they were to conclude the discussion and, true enough, he sidled past Kandinsky and went onto the patio. Once down by the hedgerow he stood on tiptoe. I concluded problems with Cheryl again though I do this too often. It's just that there are few things as easy to spot as the burden of a difficult relationship. I felt sad for him and would have liked a Dylan conversation. I previously tried to explain to Harry, however, something I find difficult, and that is whenever we think of Dylan or Eliot we think of them in this post-Dylan and post-Eliot world, which suffuses the topic with delicious nostalgia if that's the word, and then I wonder how Dylan and Eliot managed in a world that didn't have the enrichment of themselves. Though I was doing my best to put it across I could see bewilderment in the Cheryl eyes, and heard the chuckle of Major Gwillingington. You'll have to excuse me Peter, Harry said, but I'm not operating on all cylinders. Maybe write it down and give it me next time. I couldn't write it any better than I can explain it, I said. He made a face I recognised but hadn't categorised, though I knew it heralded a drifting on his part to the deepest parts of the room where, for example, the light or an occasional sun caught the surface of Jaundice's startled mirror.

*

Smithson flicked open the clasps of his briefcase, bringing out not as I'd hoped a treatise on the recognition and treatment of childhood disorders, but a cheese and pickle sandwich. It's good of your mother to permit outside sessions, he said. The mother in question was four benches along. Smithson had explained to her there was a distance established in therapeutic circles beyond which boys felt safe to talk freely. He swallowed a first bite. My *Man With Pipe* went well, thanks for asking, he said. We had an audience of over seventy for each of the three nights. It's not hard to see why actors go on stage. The feeling at the end of a performance is unlike any other. I didn't want it to end. Of course there are dangers. Public attention acts as a drug in some areas of the personality. I'd advise a fellow of your disposition, for example, to refrain from a life on stage however tempted you might be. Within a year you'd be caught up in domestic violence and drug abuse. He mimed the pipe once more, catching the attention of Mother who waved at us, breaking, Smithson was to say later, the therapeutic boundary though since we were outside for the first time and since she'd only waved once, he let it pass. Enraptured by sunlight, he took a valedictory breath. It's so necessary to get into the world when you've lost your life partner, Peter. That's the reason I took up the Dramatic Society. Each role I've had, if you like, is in honour of the late Mrs Smithson. Time for his next bite. I was thinking if I didn't see K soon I'd throw myself into the harbour. This tickled me to the extent I laughed aloud, prompting Smithson to warn me of the dangers of Incongruous Amusement. Outdoor sessions require great vigilance on both our parts though especially yours, he said, so we don't become distracted by what's going on around us. He was oblivious to the seam of pickle along his lip. I never know in those circumstances if I should point it out. So for now shut your mind to everything but my voice. And don't look at your mother. It's a shame we have her along at all frankly. As I looked at her and at the cerebellum hat she wore for the occasion I felt sorry for her. She was probably chewing over Miss Woo. I heard her say to Mrs Chaffin that once a situation like the one with Miss Woo occurred it was hard to think of anything else. So, Smithson said. Let's begin properly. How *are* you? I looked around myself. Luckily I soon saw Smithson hadn't been serious because he was smiling as he chewed his next bite. Upon swallowing he too laughed aloud. Well done, he said. You didn't go bananas when I asked how you were. But yes, I see on one level you're well, using the evidence say of flushed cheeks for one, but then there are many levels to answer this question on. Which do we choose? Spiritual? Emotional?

Cardiovascular? Many of us pooh-pooh the question with evasions such as fine thank you, how are you? We want *none* of that here. I had a feeling we didn't, I said. You know, Peter, he said – he seemed to be examining the imaginary pipe – I can *smell* her. It's one of the reasons I chose this location for our first outdoor session. I told him it was an okay location but I still missed the consulting room. Of course you do, he said, that's the point. Sometimes when he said things were the point, I couldn't seem to ask what they were the point of. Yes, he said, we'd come here when we were at loose ends. Mrs Smithson would have the twitch about her at breakfast time on my rare Sundays and before you knew where you were we'd be stepping along the dock. She loved cobbles, the old anchors and the narrowboats not to mention the hustle and bustle. Maybe when both of us looked up the quay it was to see if we could spot either of these last two. A man across the harbour was hauling an iron chain from where it lay on the quay through the doors of an old warehouse. It was about then I had a sensation in my head, like water running through it. This was followed by a pain in my left eye. She loved history, Smithson said. Social history you'd call it, or maybe industrial history? He'd turned this into a question at the last moment, his chin raised. Hardly a visit went by she didn't pop into the Heritage Centre for a memento, he said. Do you like mementos? I didn't know whether to answer or mention my eye. Love was upon him so I doubt he would have minded either way. In the end I nodded. The pain intensified. One day you'll be down here with a Mrs Smithson of your own Peter. Make the most of her. Mother had got up from her bench and was walking further along. I was thinking to myself: So there's my blood mother. We were stuck with whoever it happened to be. Mine was wearing what she called the Guatemala coat. When there was company, even distant company like this, she walked like Vivien Leigh. She would probably have given the world for there to have been no Miss Woo whatsoever. Ormerod said at a later or earlier time we could reduce Miss Woo to a concept, and that as a concept she was feared by mostly everyone on earth except, he said, by those who got a kick out of there being one. It was the day we were supposed to be feeding ducks and he accidentally threw himself into the water rather than the crusts.

Smithson took a breath. So yes, he said as if continuing a sentence, she would go in for a memento almost every time. I still have most of them. I cupped my palm against my eye. It was like I was holding in the pain. I don't know if it helped. When I next took it away, part of the harbour was blurred along the centre of my vision. Gradually, and as the pain at last began to subside, so the line of disturbance drifted upwards. By then Smithson was talking about a holiday with Mrs Smithson on the Algarve. The medical incident, though brief, had left me with a euphoria. Neither Mrs Smithson nor I, he said, were keen on foreign holidays, but we didn't find out till we'd been twice to the Algarve and once to Malta. What it was, neither of us wanted to confess about not completely enjoying ourselves for fear of upsetting the other. There ought to be a syndrome named after that. One Christmas she bought me a board game, part of which partly involved telling the absolute truth about something for the first time. On her turn she earned Honesty Points for telling me she didn't like the Algarve or Malta and could we do the Lake District? He took from his top pocket a handkerchief, patting it into the corner of one eye. We never did get there. A few years after her death I went myself. I was two thirds of the way up Helvellyn before I realised I didn't want to be in such a place without her. There's no pain like the pain of suddenly losing someone you love Peter. The fells were Mrs Smithson, and yet she wasn't there and never had been. It was a lonely descent.

*

I swung on the gate while the dog from up the road spiralled into position under the back wheel of a van. Ten to one, Mother said just now as she'd been beating the mat through the front door, it's somebody's fancy man. Why can't they do it privately? Mrs Chaffin – beating similarly next door – said she didn't think the van belonged to anyone's fancy man *because* they weren't making an effort to hide. It'll be a tradesperson, she added. Ooh hark at you, Mother said. Mrs Chaffin laughed. Then she said: You might think people are up to things because you've been in a state about you-know-who. It comes in waves, Mother said. The dog seemed from where I was swinging to be chewing the tip of his tail. I'd seen younger dogs worry over tails as if they weren't sure whose they were and how come they were so hard to catch. The dust that comes out of these mats, Mother said. Mine's not as bad as yours, Mrs Chaffin laughed. It's to do with you still having a husband and Swinging Harry over there. I'd been on the gate years. The more I thought about getting off the less likely it seemed. So far only Gravel had come by whistling because he'd won not much, just a few pounds he said, on the horses. Had the odds been better, it would have been hundreds, he'd told me. All the same it's enough for some cigarettes and my exotic biscuits. He winked and drew his hand through my hair. I'd heard him the day before telling Father about sure things at Lingfield. He'd tapped the side of his nose. The image came back as I swung and the world swung with me. You'll catch it if your father finds you on that gate again, Mother said with a sound I'd say came from the expulsion of air from her cheeks. If you must do it stay on the side closest to the post. When the wind was in the right direction a musty, sweetly unpleasant smell rolled upon the road from the brewery in town. Poor Mr Gravelle, Mrs Chaffin had said earlier. It was a continuing sympathy for his wife having run off with the lemonade man. There must come a time when you run out of people to run off with. I mean after the lemonade man, who? By now Mother had ventured down the garden. When she reached the fence she leaned out. Then she went back to the front door. Mrs Chaffin asked if the van was still there and Mother said it was. I can't think where the driver might be, Mrs Chaffin said. Did Peter see? He said he didn't, Mother said, but he's going to give me a shout when whoever it is comes out of wherever they are. The flapping of mat from Mrs Chaffin's had ceased. Ormerod said chores were designed to make us feel useful when we weren't and that life had meaning when it didn't. Though it was always good to see Ormerod, he could be a little bleak. Occasionally on the wind a sound of whooping boys escaped the trees. Sometimes Mrs Chaffin looked towards them wishing she'd had a child, especially since Mr Chaffin took his leave early on. So, she said, what are you doing him for tea? Fish, Mother said. Haddock. Somehow this confirmation bothered me even though I'd been with Mother to buy it and had been smelling it at intervals. I don't often have fish, Mrs Chaffin said. It doesn't agree with me. I'm all right as long as it isn't smoked, Mother said. The words smoked and fish failed to make sense. Though it was like this with language sometimes for me, Mother said the doctor had said it was part of the Hagendorff Syndrome and she wasn't to worry. Words came and went. I'd often fail to discard those which didn't fit what I was looking at or thinking about. With the fish Mother had bought potatoes and what she called greens. A hinge squeal made the dog look up. The boys had tried taking him with them earlier but he'd dug his paws into the tarmac. Did you do that homework? I swung back to find Mother looking at me. I told her I'd do it Sunday. We had to write an opening paragraph about our adventures on a desert island. I liked the idea of being marooned. I swung harder to shake off a sinking into clouds. Swinging back again, I glanced at the pond. It was my job to sprinkle fish flakes. I always gave them more than the pinch I was told to. You have to mind the bones, Mrs Chaffin said. Mr Chaffin almost choked on a bit of plaice. He wouldn't eat it after that. Yes, bones can be a problem, Mother said. When she gave the mat a last couple of extra-hard beats I fancied she was thinking she had Miss Woo in her left hand. But anyway, haddock's got less than plaice. And I usually ask the fishmonger to give it the once-over. Pervert came out of his front door, inclined his head, and sidled to the pavement turning right. Mother had said I should write out a hundred times it's Prevett because sooner or later she was going to call him Mr Pervert to his face. He doesn't mind, I told her. I was wondering how much longer I could bear the gate, the road. While I wondered, two men appeared further down carrying a carpet, which sagged between them. The back man had a cigarette. The dog got up and moved to rest against the hedge as if quietly remembering the world was against him. I alerted Mother to the carpet-bearers by an additionally zestful swing and what I took to be an appropriate hand gesture. By the time she was down with me the two men had loaded the carpet into the back. Did you see what number they came out of? she said. Not as such, I said. She called quietly to Mrs Chaffin it was men with something like a carpet. I wanted to say it *was* a carpet, not something like one, but calls from afar became the boys returning through the trees holding sticks aloft and causing the dog to bark once, gruffly and with a bored resonance in the back of his throat. Mother said: What if it was *her* rolled in that carpet? She's small enough! Come off it Doreen, Mrs Chaffin said, Miss Woo doesn't live down that way and even if she did I can't see any reason why she'd come out in a carpet. Well, Mother said, she could have been having saucy games at whoever's house she was in, got killed, and had to be snook out. Now you've gone mad, Mrs Chaffin said. Mother laughed. I was pulling your leg, she said eventually. Both legs by the look of you.

*

For some it's tough when the green light alerts us to visiting and through the door they come, sparsely it has to be said, but so far not for me, which makes the presumed Mrs Colquahoon even harder to bear. Harry says I should rejoice in her loyalty, not find reasons to resent either of them, which is a sign, frankly, he said, of my selfishness. I'd not heard Harry forthright before, at least where I'm concerned, and it made me not want to speak any more. He went on then about how sooner or later we have to forgive everyone because the human condition gives us no choice. Fiona was warmed by his perspicacity and told him he was wasted here. My father was a psychoanalyst, he said quietly to her. Maybe it rubbed off. It rubbed well, in that case, I said, interrupting a little. And tell me Harry, when you say 'was', do you mean he's no longer with us? Ten years now, Harry said, falling lightly against the frame of the patio doors. At his funeral my older brother read 'Do Not Go Gentle Into That Good Night'. Fiona paused in her teas to ask if that was the one which had the line *rage against the dying of the light* and Harry, though I could tell he was reluctant, said yes it was, except it was rage *rage*. Sorry, Fiona said. I've never been a great one for poems. Kandinsky asked gruffly if that was the case how come she'd heard of 'Do Not Go Gentle'? She said oh, somebody read it at a funeral *she'd* been to. Oh really, Kandinsky said. And whose funeral was it? Just an old friend of the family, Fiona said. Eighty-seven. Smoked till she was eighty-six. Atkins remarked it might have been the giving up that killed her because taken over a number of years toxins acted as a scaffolding. She didn't stop the gin though, Fiona said. Half a bottle every evening. Harry said wow. I used to get depressed whenever I had gin, Atkins said. We each waited I think for a while, hoping he'd elaborate. Though I was keen to stick with the conversation, it was inevitable the mention of alcohol should remind me of K. Just one drink and I'd be back out there, she said. I asked where 'out there' was and she went on to say the world of the addicted drinker was different from other people's; so different, it could be regarded as a foreign country and if she had a drink, just one, she would be back in that country. I wouldn't even need a passport, she said. She cracked herself up with that. She had to hold on to the Pasta Shelves as the public address system was announcing an offer on mulberry cheese. I like the way you laugh, I said, but I don't always find the things you find funny as funny as the things *I* find funny. She stopped laughing to tell me that was because I was riddled with self and started laughing again. I feared security guards. We should at least keep moving, I told her. But before we do, do you want the fettuccine or not? Because she wouldn't stop laughing long enough I took a packet anyway and flapped it into her basket. I don't suppose Gareth R would find your outburst conducive to recovery, I said. I'd been keen to get him into the conversation for days. K had been to a fair number of meetings recently without mentioning him. This, I felt, would give her an opportunity to fill me in on anything she hadn't admitted so far. When at last she did stop laughing – it wasn't till we were almost at Cereals – she said something like: You and your Gareth R's! What do you mean? I said. Is there more than one? No, she said, examining the ingredients on a pack of what were described as wheat pillows, but you do manage to find a name to worry about regularly so you could say they're all a Generalised Gareth. It was nice of him though wasn't it, I said, to say you could go down the harbour and watch him work if you wanted. When I said this it was with a view to her confessing she'd been down the harbour if that was indeed the case and yet I didn't think it gave any indication I was jealous or being what she described as Holmesesque. She sighed without looking up from the ingredients. Salt, she said. It gets everywhere, I told her. In my mind's eye she was at the harbourside, helping Gareth arrange his palette. Leaning over I could just make out the ingredients myself. Only a trace though, I said. She made a sound and put the pack back. And in case you're wondering, she said, no I haven't been down the harbour to watch him paint, no he hasn't even mentioned that again and no he hasn't asked me to his flat after meetings for coffee and sex. He has a flat, does he? I said. They're like gold dust these days. Suddenly K was again leaning against the shelving in fits. I asked if it was still the passport joke and, unable to speak, she could only nod. When she'd recovered for the second time she explained you'd have to be a recovering alcoholic yourself to appreciate its humour. I walked on to avoid any further mention of Gareth R. I didn't have a basket of my own. It seemed a good way of avoiding buying things. When it wasn't alerting us to mulberry cheese, the public address graced us with Bizet's *The Pearl Fishers*, one of K's favourites. She hadn't remarked on it. I hung around Pasta Sauces till she caught up though to my surprise she went on by. I called after her about the pasta sauces in case she hadn't noticed them but as I did so I felt foolish and like I wasn't human. I can't imagine how the incident gave rise to such a destructive and hopefully inaccurate idea. There was K, by now turning out of the aisle at the far end. The sight of her made me stop for a moment as if my mind was taking a photograph. She drew a luminescence behind herself like a comet through the night sky. I walked on. Jugg wouldn't have liked the simile. K was nothing like a comet. As I approached Bread I had a sense my feet weren't touching the floor even though, when I glanced down, I could see they were. Soon afterwards I was up to my ankles in nothingness and wondered if I should alert K, providing I could find her. She had the ability to vanish even if you'd seen her moments before. A security guard was apparently fixing his attention on a man in Bagels. I didn't think if I alerted him to my sensations he'd be sympathetic. I'd had it out once with Doctor Mainwaring about how I always seemed to get things people hadn't heard of. She said eventually I did indeed have some unusual neurological and perhaps psychological conditions that she hadn't come across much either, but that I should see this as a cause of celebration, not self-censure. Though I couldn't feel my feet and – by this time – shins, I was in pursuit of K without difficulty. I was citing to myself my nine times table, figuring if anything major was happening my brain wouldn't be able to manage. I hadn't as yet acknowledged to myself I'd had an incident in this same supermarket before. I was in time to see K going round the top of the aisle. She would soon reach the hot cooked chicken counter. If only she cared enough to wonder where I was, I told myself. Another Peter criticised the first for this sentiment because she was K altogether and even in my diseased state at that moment I wouldn't have had her any other way. I was about to turn towards Chickens myself when I bumped into someone who turned out to be Alexander. He beamed, I thought it, from head to foot. Isn't this interesting, he said, meeting in the supermarket and you, look, not even with a basket. I've only come for odds and ends, I said. Arms are all you need in those circumstances. He chuckled. No K? The chances of him seeing her if I said I was alone were astronomically large, I told myself, but only because right then I caught sight of a string of stars hanging from the ceiling as one of those decorations used to make shoppers think being in a large space searching for Stuff wasn't madness. I knew I had to be honest if I was to expect any further Gareth disclosure from K. Yeah, I said with a sigh. She's up ahead. You know K. Buys pasta without necessarily going to Pasta Sauces straight afterwards. She's not one of us really is she Peter? Alexander said, looking round in a generalised K direction. He was doing this, I felt, to put me off the scent. What about you? Oh I'm looking for something for tea, he said. He held up his basket. No luck so far then, I said. Yes, he said, well you reach a point when you live on your own of not being able to decide what to have without a great deal of thought and self-discipline. I was going to do Chilli Con Carne, but I had it three times last week. I have it about every six months or so, I said. I'll have to wait for another Chilli Con Carne moment to come upon me before my next bout. Mind you, I've enjoyed it much more since I've been sploshing lime juice onto it. We stared at one another. In the gap I remembered my fading lower limbs. I wouldn't have felt right telling Alexander about it though because he might have thought I was using incapacity as a barrier against his affections for K. It's the same for me with chicken stir-fry, he said. On day one I'm thinking I've never had anything so nice in all my life. By day four I never want to see another beansprout long as I live. He leaned over to grip the Bread Shelves, convulsed. Don't you start, I told him. When he'd recovered enough to speak he said it had been the beansprouts. I said I knew him well enough to have supposed that myself. He returned to seriousness more quickly than K. Yes, they've started selling ready-made stir-fry sauces in plastic pouches suitable for a one-person portion, he said. Oh that's handy, I said. If Marian comes round you could buy two. He said it was Miriam and as yet she hadn't been round for dinner. It's hard, he said, moving from a shared interest in walking and local history to the concept of a meal together. I patted his arm. Not at all, Alexander. Go for it. I expect she's waiting for you to ask. I'm not so sure, he said. She keeps mentioning a Harold. Not the one with the arrow in his eye! I said. I felt it was a fair response in view of my lower limb problem but as ever when I make a joke to Alexander, and even K most of the time to be honest, it was met with a look of perplexity. I don't like to ask, he said, but have you ever had a situation where someone mentions someone several times but doesn't give any more information? I pride myself on being able to work out things just by listening, but Miriam's a difficult case in that respect. I sighed. It was mostly because of my legs and because I was resentful at K for vanishing when I needed her. Anyway, Alexander went on, you know as well as I do the moment a woman looms I turn into a vagabond. Still, the walks are nice. I feel I'm seeing this town of ours for the first time. That is to say I've seen its expanse before, not its depth. It might have been inadvertently he reached for and took hold of a nearby malt loaf. He looked at it with embarrassment before dropping it into his basket. We're up to two a week now, he said. I asked if he meant malt loaves. He said: No, walks. What'll you do when the weather becomes unsuitable? I asked. He said: Sorry to say this Peter but it's typical of you to worry so far ahead. The thing is we'll keep walking day to day and when the weather takes a turn for the worse we'll think again. I know you're right, I said. K takes life very much one day at a time and often says to me not to climb on walls to get a better view of any approaching cloud. Alexander looked blank again. A metaphor, I said. She means not to search the future for signs of trouble. Just deal with what's happening right here, right now. You're talking as if I haven't known her my whole life too, he said. I am and I'm sorry, I told him. I don't know what causes that. Without even being aware of it we'd crossed several aisles. I was looking into a chill cabinet of prawns. I'm inclined towards economy prawns when the price difference is considered, I said, but in terms of quality the more expensive they are the better. Yeah, I'd say so, Alexander said. You shouldn't take risks with prawns. You have to ask yourself what corners have been cut in order to make them economy. The entire world has become vacuum-packed, I said. You shouldn't buy prawns in supermarkets anyway, Alexander said. If I had to buy some I'd go to a fishmonger. It's just the place. I then had to endure another half-minute at least of him propping himself against the chill cabinet. My inability to feel had extended to the level of my upper thighs. I discreetly tapped one with the nub of my palm. So, I said when Alexander had stopped chuckling, when's your next walk with Miriam? Oh well tonight Alexander said. We're going to do the edge of the heath. I hope enormously it goes well, I said. Alexander swayed. He might have sensed my use of enormously had hinted at an end to the conversation. I found myself poking him where the midpoint of a tie would have been if he was the sort to wear them. Now you ask Miriam round for dinner, I said. Do it before she goes off the boil. Alexander grimaced. I've no real evidence she's on it, he said.

*

So that's how 'Do Not Go Gentle Into That Good Night' came in. Oddly enough Harry had planned to take Cheryl to Laugharne during the holidays. I said to him I felt he'd indicated Cheryl didn't have time for Dylan and Harry said well no, she didn't, but she was okay going there so long as he promised not to drag her into heritage centres, churches or places like that. We all roared – at least imagination says we did – at our image of Cheryl saying this to Harry. You're going to have to forgo the boathouse this time then I take it, I said to him. Well you forget, Harry said, Laugharne's an attractive little place, right by the estuary, and well worth a visit even if you know nothing about Dylan. It was the day of the miracle of Major Gwillingington rising from slumber to tell us he'd attended one of Dylan's readings in the late forties. I bought him a pint afterwards, he said. This caused a fluster in Harry I hadn't witnessed before but in Gwillingington style, the Major was asleep again moments afterwards. Well he is *ancient*, Atkins said. Kandinsky believed the Major had simply arisen from his coma to stir the conversation. But he's not in a coma, Atkins said, keen to get one over on Kandinsky. I was being playfully figurative, Kandinsky said. Thanks to a gift of fruit given to us by a visitor, Smetham was enjoying an unskinned banana. Since it was taking longer to chew than it might otherwise, the conversation had been over for several minutes before he said he too had heard it read at a funeral and that the reading was followed by an extract of Mahler's Fifth. That funeral must have been a hoot, Atkins said. They're not meant to be hoots Kandinsky said, though I daresay Mahler *is* a bit glum for anything other than exceptionally solemn occasions of international, even global significance. I used to have it on CD, Kandinsky said. Fat lot of good that is, Atkins said. Kandinsky asked him what he meant by that. Atkins said he was fed up of people saying they used to have stuff because the fact was we didn't have stuff any longer. We were in here and unlikely ever to get out unless it was to move to an even worse place and that was the long and the short of it. None of us, I believe, enjoyed this, particularly Colquahoon who said he had every intention – assuming he didn't escape – of ensuring any official move was towards the lower, less troubled wards. Isn't that right Harry? Harry said the best policy was to take each day as it came and for none of us to concern ourselves with the future and to bring all our efforts to bear on resting. I looked from him out through the patio doors. All this thought of K. She hadn't ever been here so knew nothing of the patio, the lawn, the hedgerow. I wanted us out there together one afternoon, yes that would be the thing. My reverie was interrupted as Fiona at last brought my tea over with her version of a bourbon in the saucer and of course I knew only too well not to plan anything but the most cursory dunking. There you are Peter, she said. I see I don't get one, Colquahoon said grumpily, which was highly premature because she'd been on the point of returning to the trolley for his cup, which she'd already poured. Bless her though, she fetched it and placed it on his chair's side tray without mentioning his impatience. He too had a bourbon. Is this our life now, he asked? Fiona asked him what he meant but with the sing-song tone beloved of teachers with young children. Colquahoon turned purple around the backs and below the lobes of his ears. I mean, he said emphatically, are we to have teas and biscuits day in day out till the end? He had already forgotten his plans to reach less troubled wards. I can try and get some different ones at the market this week, Fiona said. I didn't realise they were a problem. Take no notice of him Fiona, Kandinsky said. The purple had spread round Colquahoon's neck. I wasn't referring, he said, to the type of biscuit though God knows they are an additional source of anxiety. It was more to the principle of us sitting here day after day being subjected to twaddle. Atkins leaned back in his chair, affronted. Kandinsky stared towards Colquahoon. Who exactly are you accusing of twaddle? he asked. Well yes, you lot mainly, Colquahoon said. It's not like we're doing you any harm, Atkins said. We're chatting like people do. It was a strange thing then that Colquahoon took what I believe to have been a Victory sip but that he overcompensated somewhere along the line, causing webs of tea to escape his mouth at either side and run from his chin into his lap. Now he's dribbling, Atkins said. We should all calm down, Harry said, having reappeared from the office. Fiona, get some tissues. Fiona did as she was told then softly wiped Colquahoon's lap, replenished his cup and said he'd need clean trousers. I leaned towards Colquahoon a bit to say I felt it could have happened to any of us. I have an instinctive need to side – for a while at least – with anyone harangued by a majority.

*

Following days of inconsolable rain, leaves have formed a mash across the paving and along gutters. The Office is heated of course, so in winter there's ever that gush of warmth as I step through the automatic doors to be greeted by Sutton in cap and braid. Now I've always been hopeless at responding to meteorological observations. Today Sutton says: Still chilly out there? and I say, reluctantly, well yes. I prefer this to the rain we had though. He has time to say a gruff me too before I'm round the corner negotiating one of several corridors, which culminate as if by bad magic in my cubicle and its praline. I take off my coat and hook it round the chair. It's feasible to have your feet up much of the day. My most regular visitor's Alexander who can't be in the same building as me for long without saying hello. In fear of this possibility I've hidden the praline in my bottom drawer. The view from the window's roof upon roof through a canvas of redundant chimneys. The rectangle of light blue on the horizon marks the beginning of the countryside. K and me went that way with binoculars hoping to find the exact spot but of course we couldn't and neither, by looking back, could we figure out which building this was when seen from over that way. Ormerod used to say there was a theory arising out of such consideration that he was going to call – temporarily at least – The Myth Of Distance. I switch on the computer, getting up a worklike screen. Occasionally I open the bottom drawer and take out the praline, sometimes hold it to my nose. Here women come and go, usually with files. I have a pile of the latter to the left of the computer. Quite a stack you might say. Alexander remarks on it whenever he pops in. You can bet his pile is ever on the right waiting to be taken elsewhere. I hardly ever go to *his* cubicle. The thought crosses my mind occasionally but I rarely follow it. Mostly hands behind the neck thinking about K. I picture her about to have a sandwich on one of our walks and yet then when the picturing's finished, I wonder what the point of picturing it was. I don't expect she ever pictures me, in that way at least. I mean she told me if I spent less of my life picturing things that weren't there I'd have done better generally. I said I found thinking about things that weren't necessarily there added richness. That's all well and good in the right circumstances, she said, but things can be overdone. Oh for sure they can, I said. We were passing along the harbour on a ferry. I'd said for sure they can because I wanted her to feel I agreed with her. And to bring myself more squarely into the day, I leaned over and would have let my hand hang towards the water if I hadn't remembered Health and Safety, a copy of whose Rules were tacked to the cabin. K shook her head. I can't count the number of times that happened. I most often passed it off as a sign of affection. So, she said, suddenly I felt, are you enjoying your birthday so far? I said indeed I was but then as long as she was there with me I didn't suppose it could be any other way. And you liked the book? It was rare for her to show self-doubt. I told her I *loved* the book.

Megaliths were my cup of tea. She turned her attention to the watered scenery. You're not yourself though, she said. What makes you say that? I said. She took a breath as though it was going to be a list. Well, she said, normally by now you'd have given a number of harbour facts. Though I then waited for the other things the breath had hinted at, there was only silence. At last I said to her, yes, normally that would be the case, but since she pointed out, on our last ferry trip, that my harbour facts were overly numerous, I'd decided to keep them to one side. This is what I said though really I believe the cause of my general quiet had been mostly that copy of the Health and Safety Rules. Life was being diminished through so many delights being banned. What's more, the banning of them created an undue desire to have a go anyway and almost as if it had a mind of its own my hand forgot what it knew and I kept finding it halfway to the water. The thing was, I felt the chill on my fingers as I sat in my cubicle smelling the praline. I've never been the sort to attract members of either sex – with the exception of K I suppose – but then that's more on her part an example of familiarity breeding, not contempt but anguished tolerance. The Peripheral Boy, Ormerod called me. So my fingernails touch the edge of the foil covering the praline and yet if I go all the way with it, so to speak, it will only be a matter of time before I do a Colquahoon and pop it into my mouth and then the point will have been lost. An unconsumed sweet is even more enjoyable than one you're eating. The computer flickers, reminding me I haven't done anything work-wise. The view through my window – at least till it reaches the light blue rectangle – is almost entirely grey even if it inspires notions of a colourful kind.

*

Sometimes it felt I'd been walking with Bulwark always. So this girl-friend of yours, he said suddenly. I say suddenly, but as he'd pointed out in the seminar a few days before, it was impossible not to be sudden when speaking. He'd irked Maureen because surely there was more to say about the book than that? For my part I felt it was Bulwark's way of getting back at her for remaining loyal to the Dean. As I walked muddily behind him I said: What about her? He said well, I hadn't said much other than bare facts. I told him I wasn't a great one for going beyond bare facts where K was concerned because to talk about her excessively when she wasn't present didn't seem right. You're a strange fellow, for sure, Bulwark said. It's a wonder anybody sticks with you. I think so too, I said, deadening any temptation he had to further criticise me, but the fact is we've been 'together' most of our lives. When he glanced round I had a glimpse of the pallor above and beyond the beard. As a scholar I'd say you intimated inverted commas round the word together as if it wasn't quite true, he said. I told him that, on the contrary, it was absolutely true, and that the inverted commas were meant to prevent anyone assuming we were together in what would otherwise be thought of as in a common or garden sense. I was relieved when the cowl faced forward again. And Alexander? Bulwark went on. I spent the next few yards trying to remember when I might have mentioned him, because I surely must have. Well me, him and K arrived on earth at more or less the same time, me and Alexander even sharing the same hospital room though not, I hasten to add, the same mother. K was born at home not far from where I lived. Both me and Bulwark started chuckling. On my part it had been a delayed reaction to my saying: 'I hasten to add', whereas Bulwark, as he later admitted, had been laughing at a cracker joke he'd read some Christmases before about a hyena who'd swallowed an Oxo cube and made a laughing stock of himself. He regarded it as an especially successful joke because whenever he remembered it he laughed again even though, so to speak, he'd heard it before. So what made you think of it now? I asked. It's hardly Christmas. He said it was one of the joke's aspects that it had a self-popping mechanism so you were never sure when your mind would be prompted to re-hear it. Anyway, Bulwark asked then, what type of road had it been where I lived, and though I was tempted to ask him why all the questions, I instead described the road, including both lemonade man and dog. Turned out Bulwark was one of the old school because he said you don't get dogs like that these days nor, come to that, lemonade men. You're right, I said. In the more modern world, Bulwark said, it's every lemonade man and dog for himself. Though I felt this was a non sequitur I let it pass and then, almost because I'd let it pass, we had to scurry prematurely into the wood because a swan near the shore had shown signs of interest in Bulwark himself. Once we were in the gloom and the person in question was smoking he said he wished he'd been born in a road like mine. The only dogs in his were pedigree and lemonade men, well, were few and far between and then they were Chablis men if anything. I waved away smoke, asking him if things were further forward with Jennifer. You're assuming I want them further forward, he said. Well yes, I said. I'm assuming also eventually you'll free yourself of your devotion to Maureen and that to a large extent your troubles down below will be at an end and of course that either Jennifer doesn't go away to work as you fear or that you're somehow able to go with her. Bulwark made a sound – probably derision – in his throat. That's a lot of ifs, he said, though I hadn't used any. But you're right I've been regarding her in a different way lately. She has a purity and though I've been drawn for so long to inadvisable passion, I must say her genteel ways are becoming more appealing. It was badly timed of me I guess to mention the grandfather with excess skin. Bulwark looked daggers at me through the smoke. I didn't realise you'd had conversations of that magnitude, he said. No really, we didn't, I said. The grandfather just came up. I can't even remember how. Bulwark snapped a pine twig. It wouldn't do for you to have leanings towards someone I'm interested in even if I haven't decided to go for it hammer and tongs. It was an unwise image in respect of a potential girlfriend. Its inappropriateness came I guess from his not having known one so far.

*

A voice – Gerald's – saying: I see you've found *The Young Gardener's Guide To Colourful Borders*. A little alarmed, I slid the book back into its space. I don't think I'd have been able to explain I sometimes pulled books out for the sake of it; to give, if you like, the impression I'd found something interesting, but really that day at least everything I did was thin mortar in a wall of K. I've always hoped one day to have a garden with Mrs Aldridge, Gerald said, reaching round to take the book out again. You know something Peter? I turned to him to ask what but before it could come out he said: I see us on Sunday mornings getting our gardening things together and going outside with our dog to spend the day tending our plot. Oh, you have a dog? I said, though I was being playful. No, he said, it was figurative. The page he'd opened onto had a plate showing tickseed, red hot pokers, a sunflower and a rough heliopsis. I resolved to have some of my own years from then. Gerald slammed the book shut and shoved it back into its space. I'm in cloud cuckoo land though of course Peter because currently she and I aren't speaking. She knows this man – let's call him Jim – from her night school. It's Jim this Jim that. I said is he figurative too? Gerald said sadly not. If you ever have a woman friend, he said, beware of her doing evening classes. I had a feeling, he went on, because the other night I saw her on her way there in the street. Dressed up to the nines she was. I imagined nines were the worst to be dressed up to and would have patted Gerald's shoulder had he not stood tall suddenly. There will be times when you get older, he said, when you'll wonder what it's all about. Life goes well for a while before – bang! He'd illustrated the last word by speaking it loudly enough to make a woman, who'd been on her way in, make her way out. He'd told me recently women in hats over a certain age were the least likely to buy a book anyway and I should remember these things if ever I came to run my own shop. I took advantage of his distress to make my way to the open door. I caught sight of my reflection in the side window and wondered for a moment who I was. It couldn't be guaranteed, Ormerod had once explained. Of course, Gerald said as he caught up, I wouldn't dream of saying she couldn't go to her night school. I just wish there wasn't a Jim. The more you mention him the less I like him, I said. He's married, Gerald said, but his wife doesn't do classes because she has a bad leg. I asked him what class it was as a cuckoo in the back room sounded the hour. Pottery! Pottery! Gerald said. If I've told you once I've told you a dozen times. As far as I was concerned he hadn't mentioned classes before, let alone what subject Mrs Aldridge did. It's why I'm suspicious, Gerald said, because you wouldn't expect people to dress up when they're going to be messing with wet clay. Strangely trying to escape him today, I took steps onto the pavement, standing as before by the external shelving. People would often stop to look through the books here but rarely bought anything. Gerald was soon beside me, his hands behind his back. He moved up and down on his toes like he was about to go on about Jim again, but then said: Odd things books Peter. Bigger on the inside. Take this Cowboy. He picked up and waved a paperback at me. In here we have deserts, canyons, cactuses, horses, saloons, gunfights, et cetera, et cetera, yet it's only this big. He held it close to me. Underneath the bravado, Jim was still burrowing through his mind. I knew I was right in my speculations when Gerald crumpled inwardly and said: I mean, pottery for God's sake! Why did he have to choose pottery? On the night she goes I sit at home hardly able to contain myself. Oh but here's me opening up to a youngster. I should know better. If you don't mind I'd rather you didn't mention any of this to your mother. She'll think I'm a buffoon and might even stop you coming. I told him I didn't think he was a buffoon in the absolute sense and that besides Mother appreciated the time to herself even though, I added, she also had plenty of time by herself through the week. Mothers need a lot, Gerald said, though I had a feeling he was making it up as he went along. His pinstripe fluttered less when he was having difficulties. It hung from his shoulders looking as if it had developed a mind of its own and couldn't wait to be free of him when it got home. I was thinking to myself I'd ever remember being here this Saturday morning and looked across the road to get the components of the view lodged in my mind. So here I am, I decided, and here's Gerald: me hoping K will be along soon and he hoping ditto Mrs Aldridge. It surely wasn't good so much life was taken up with waiting. At the same time my shoes sank into the pavement and the triangular crackling began. Gerald said later he was glad he'd been on hand to catch me because however much you might feel you're sinking into them, pavements are hard. Even longer afterwards Mother returned to collect me. She was carrying a laden basket. Gerald took her inside to explain about the incident. I heard Mother say something like it had happened before and that she felt sure now she should take me to the doctor's. I feel that would be best, Gerald said, you never know with this sort of thing. He'd started to say he had a great-aunt once, and would presumably have gone on to explain what had happened to her and how it had all turned out, but Mother pulled a paper bag from her basket and placed it in his hands. A pie for you, she said. I thought you could do with building up. And it's also to say thank you for looking after Trouble. Gerald took a breath before saying he didn't know what to say. I am partial to a pie, he said. Though it's a while since I've partaken of one this size. Mother patted his arm. Just don't eat it all at once, she said. You'll have a seizure. He said he would pop it in the fridge till later, which was strange because he didn't have a fridge at the shop and yet it reminded me that I too – in his position – would have said I'd pop it in the fridge till later. I felt he was like me in the sense if he hadn't wanted a pie he'd be unable to say so. In this way I supposed many of the world's pies were discarded before a bite was taken. I was otherwise hopeful the story of my funny turn would be taken up again. So anyway, Mother said instead, I hope he's behaved himself. He's been goodness personified, Gerald said. Mother glanced round the shop. I must have a gander one of these days, she said. Not that I have time for reading. She gave me a nod then, which involved closing and elongating her lips. Husbands and children prevent that sort of thing. The world was more or less back to normal in me. Only a few triangles remained. Then you must find time, Gerald said. Being so busy that you're unable to read means you're too busy altogether. He suddenly crumpled further. He was having difficulties engaging with Mother when he was quietly in agony about Jim. He held the pie in one hand. The paper bag it came in was clamped in the other.

*

Kandinsky huffed. Whenever people want me to be somewhere it's on the hour or half hour, he said. Jaundice beckoned to Harry who wasn't even looking and humorously suggested more tablets. Kandinsky's procedure for calming himself involved a stark stroll through the patio doors, all the way to the lawn. On his return, he faced Atkins with arms at his sides, fists clenched. The upshot is, he said, from now on I'm starting things or going places at arbitrary minutes to or past the hour. If people can't cope, tough titties. Colquahoon looked round. He seemed as if he might comment but then returned to *The Times*. Atkins was more determined: Do that old boy and you'll be out of kilter with everyone. Kandinsky appreciated his concerns but felt someone should make a stand. Besides which, Atkins added in that way he had when adding things, we don't go anywhere. We don't need time here. Time's for them. He nodded towards the patio. Jaundice told us his mother had given him a wristwatch as a boy and he hadn't taken it off day or night and in the end he had to be bribed with sweets because everyone knew – though he refused to accept it because of the eight jewels – the watch wouldn't survive if he wore it in the bath or the swimming pool. This led, to my surprise, not to a further discussion about clocks but to an astonishment on Atkins's part Jaundice could swim. Oh yes, Jaundice said. My father threw us in the river as children and said if we wanted to live we'd learn quickly. Really the water only came to our waists. He doesn't sound like the best father in the world, if I might make so bold, Atkins said. On the contrary, he was in the Air Force, Jaundice said. I wondered if I was keeping up with the conversation or if my condition meant I was missing part of it. Harry had been outside the patio doors all this time staring towards the hedgerow. Tobias Mawk had begun speaking in what Harry said were tongues some time before and though several of us had heard of tongues as a concept this was the first time we'd experienced them directly. He's in communication with the dead, Atkins decided a while before. Colquahoon stated that speaking in tongues was also called Glossolalia. Glosso what? Atkins said. He was in a mood because he hadn't heard of it in these terms. Glossolalia, Colquahoon said. Strings of syllables made up of sounds taken from all the sounds the person knows put together more or less haphazardly but coming out nevertheless as word-like and sentence-like units because of a realistic rhythm and melody. There are all sorts of reasons for speaking in tongues, all sorts of conditions that bring it about. (Apparently) After re-comfortabling himself, he said: I said apparently in brackets because no one's absolutely sure. It's one of those things that defy science. Like those people who wake one morning speaking a different language. Atkins said why yes, he'd heard of a woman on the news who woke up Chinese. Colquahoon said she probably didn't wake up Chinese as such, although he could believe she was *speaking* Chinese given other cases he'd read of. All this got me thinking about Miss Woo so for a while it was as if I'd drifted away altogether. Over dinner Mother had asked if she enjoyed English food. Father held his knife and fork just so as he took a breath and then said given she was born in this country it was hardly surprising that in the main she did, yes, enjoy the same food as the rest of us. Anyway, he said, we've done well for months not talking about her so why didn't we carry on? Mother said Mrs Chaffin said Father getting uppity if ever Miss Woo was mentioned meant he wasn't over her. It was in her book *Problems of Matrimony*. Father's knife and fork made their way back towards dinner. He looked as though he'd thought of something to say but had decided not to. Mention of my most recent collapse was overdue. Also my head was whirling about Friday's class when Mrs Strachan had needed a thin boy to stand at the front so we could do ribs. It was a toss-up between me and Horace, though Horace's stature in view of people being able to see him fully meant I moved into first place. I was to remove my shirt and raise my arms while an elected boy and girl counted them. The ribs. Luckily it was K for the girls, I say luckily but it was only marginally preferable to have her count the left side than it would have been for a lesser-known girl to do it. Because he'd failed on height, Mrs Strachan allowed Horace the right side. Twelve, said K after much tickling. Twelve here too, said Horace. So how many does that make? Mrs Strachan asked. Alexander put up his hand. Twenty-four Miss, he said. Good boy, Mrs Strachan said. In some people, she went on, there are two smaller ribs further down, but we won't count those. Sweat ran from under my arms. So if you'll stay there a bit longer, Mrs Strachan told me, I'm going to ask K and Horace to return to their seats. Luckily the amount of time between her suggesting she was going to ask them and asking them was short. She then told the class to turn to an empty page and have a go at drawing me from the neck down and waist up. My arms were hurting. It was explained later by Ormerod the pain was caused by blood draining from my arms and pooling at my shoulders. Listen Doreen, Father said at last, it really is time you gave up on Miss Woo. It ruins mealtimes. If you didn't get uppity it wouldn't be a problem, Mother said. But if you didn't keep on I wouldn't *have* to get uppity, Father said. All I know is,

Mother said, no one else's husband I can think of has been with other women. Father glanced at me. This was his way of criticising her decision to Have It Out in front of a minor. He was also seeing in that moment if I could be relied upon if support were needed. If you go to a bank and borrow money, Father said, you have to pay it back. But once you *have* paid it back the repayments stop. He continued eating. He had a twinkle in one eye. Mother quietly ate another potato. You can't compare what you got up to to having a bank loan, she said. Besides which you have to remember the interest. The point I was making, Father said, is that no one would expect anyone to go on making repayments beyond what the bank asked for, interest aside. As soon as the next potato had been completed, Mother said: Mrs Chaffin and Peter think you still see her. I transferred my feelings into the runner bean hanging from my fork. Then Peter and Mrs Chaffin are mad, Father said. I saw the house, the road, the town, the world, folded like a map by the hands of a god, and this I guess because I hadn't liked what Mother had said or Father come to that. From their and the god's point of view, however, I merely put the runner bean in my mouth. They were seasonal. Mr Prevett let Mother have a handful most weeks in season. Oh, Mother said, so your son's mad! I said: And Mrs Chaffin, remember. Luckily the woman herself arrived to see if we had any washing powder. Mother told her of course she could have some and Father asked how she was doing and Mrs Chaffin said well thanks and how were things at work and Father said things were fine all round and Mrs Chaffin took the paper bag of powder Mother had fetched for her and left. Soon dinner was finished. I went to my room and waited to see if Ormerod would call. I also had a think about K. In between these things I did three pieces of Baboons of the Serengeti. One of the baboons looked towards the puzzle's horizon from its perch on a half-finished tree. In the end because Ormerod didn't come and my thinking about K ran out, I decided to write her a letter, which would start Dear K. I couldn't think what to say beyond that without ending in an apology for the ribs even though Ormerod had already warned me not to go down what he called the Ribs Road. If a girl likes you she'll put up with you ribs and all, he said.

Smithson rubbed his nose and crossed to the window. I'd bet myself that would be his next stop. I'd been testing my precognitive abilities. I hadn't told him because he preferred me to remain inferior. This would have been Mrs Smithson's birthday, he said. We used to go to a schooner moored in the docks. It acts as a restaurant during the summer. In winter it sails to warmer climes. They have an idyllic lifestyle. I say 'they' but I don't know who 'they' are. It's specific in that we know *someone* owns the schooner and sails it, in winter, to warmer climes, certainly more specific than the 'they' referred to in sentences like 'they say it's going to be a cold winter'. He chuckled. But let's face it, he said, no one knows who that 'they' is either. I shook my head. I was on my way, mentally, to taking a break by thinking about Eileen who'd earlier told me Ron was doing duck. I'm not a fan of duck because it can be very fatty, she'd said, but I haven't dared say so after what happened with the mango. I laiad low the comic I'd been leafing through. Earthlings were under attack from an evil force. Smithson had recently put a selection of comics in one corner as a concession to me even though Eileen had said I was the only boy. I was leafing because I wasn't fond of comics though I did like the smell of ink. The spat with the spatula? I said. Eileen laughed. That's right! Has he been talking? The word 'he' had been accompanied by a chin towards Smithson's door. Not in a gossipy way, I said, more to point out how interesting it was he'd used the word 'spat' when it turned out there was a spatula involved. Eileen leaned forward. Every time I eat duck, she said, I see them quacking and bobbing. I told her I hadn't ever tasted a duck, not only because I hadn't but also because I too was upset by similar images. They're not something anyone has on a regular basis, Eileen said. As she pushed back a lock of hair I noticed her coloured fingernails. We had a joke, she went on, about how there probably won't be much duck on the menu after we're married. My neck ached with the effort of not looking at the next page of the comic. Despite finding my time on it difficult so far, I felt myself wanting to know if earth would survive. Eileen said: You're pale today. Have you been poorly? I told her there'd been one or two unusual instances but the doctor had assured Mother they were nothing to worry about. Eileen asked instances of what, which I'd hoped she wouldn't because I was always embarrassed if I got as far as the triangles. Mother calls them funny turns, I said. Oh you should chat to Ron, Eileen said. He gets them. She laughed. One of his is what he calls sticky feet. Suddenly he can't walk properly. Many's the time we've been going along the road and he'll stumble. I worry when he's in the kitchen with all the hot water and what have you but he says he never feels danger in any culinary circumstance. I couldn't wait for the sound of Smithson's doorknob. I can happily go into a conversation only to find myself, moments later, wanting out. Smithson saw that as more evidence of self-obsession. When at last the knob did turn and he beckoned, I put the comic and the fate of earth aside, saying to Eileen I hoped the duck went well. Smithson interrupted to ask if I'd heard what he'd said and I managed to say, what? About the boat? and he sighed loudly I felt and said that had been a while ago and that I must learn to concentrate. Anyway, he said, we went there for two or three birthdays and at least one wedding anniversary. Mrs Smithson used to say however many voyages you go on, you should occasionally return to the original berth. Since his role in the play, he hadn't been able to resist sucking the imaginary pipe now and then. One year I might go down there again and have a meal in honour of her. Do you think that would be odd? I told him I didn't think so. He said he might ask Eileen to go with him. Ron too? I said. Oh it's not that sort of thing, he said, just a Therapeutic Specialist taking his secretary for a meal. I'm sure Eileen would be the first to say it isn't necessary for a woman to be accompanied by her future husband on *every* social occasion. Besides which she knows the ins and outs of my marriage whereas Ron does not. He'd soon tire of reminiscence. As he turned from the window he rubbed his hands. He sat behind me. So tell me how you've been getting along, he said. Anything of note? I'd dismissed the rib incident. He'd only say something about the natural shyness of children. I considered then rejected the latest Miss Woo episode because it had been discussed often before. I tossed up then put down my collapse at the bookshop, but did consider for a while discussing books generally. It seemed there was every topic to choose from yet none. I tried writing to K, I said eventually, but didn't get further than dear K. Ah, Smithson said behind my head, what you should do is start halfway through. I asked him how I could start halfway through if I didn't know what the letter was about and though I couldn't see him I heard him nod. If I had a pound, he said, for every time someone's asked me that. You need faith, Peter. Faith that if you make the effort to start beyond the beginning, some force will not only see you through to the end, but will enable you, at last, to create a starting point. You must learn not to rely entirely upon yourself for answers.

*

We were on the turf either side of his headstone. *Still Attentive* in carved italics. I wondered where Mrs Smithson was. It would have been nicer, I felt, if they'd been buried together. But then perhaps she was cremated. That's what I like about our days out, K said, the bright conversations. We're merely visiting an old friend, I said. Rushing at it would be disrespectful. I've time for a roly-poly then, K said. I said yes though I hadn't realised till she'd taken out her tin she'd meant a cigarette. It was May. Daisies were legion through the grass. The sound too – almost as fond a sound as rising larks – of a distant mower. So, K said when she was safely smoking, have you decided where else we go? I haven't, I said. Only it's supposed to be your choice this time, she went on. I'm aware of that, I said. Options are percolating through me even as we sit here beside poor Smithson. You don't know people are poor just because they're dead, she said. As she placed the end of the cigarette in her lips and drew on it and as the tobacco crackled, I wished I smoked myself. You make assumption after assumption and hope you'll get away with them, K added. I'm not sure that's true, I said. I'd been picking daisies with a view to making a chain. Then I felt guilty for having uprooted such an intricate part of the natural world. To divert attention I said to K it was funny to think of Smithson one minute in his consulting rooms or down by the waterside with his briefcase and now here he was for all time. There you go again, K said, resurrecting death. Well it's interesting, I said to her. As I glanced over she fell back in a controlled manner till she was utterly horizontal and smoking upwards. We make all this fuss over the most trivial things and then phut, it's over. *You* make a fuss, she said. It runs in the family

192

I said. We try not to make one but then we do. We being who? K asked with a sniff. It was a non-specific we, I told her. And not only that but they – we – only exist in my head. Oh there, K said using a tone. Not far away a blackbird sang. Our surroundings hushed. How long do they live? K asked. Who? I said. Blackbirds, she said. I don't know, I said. Two or three years? That's a shame, K said. Don't take my guess as gospel, I said. Anyway, it's not a shame from the blackbird's point of view because they won't know greater longevity occurs elsewhere. K smoked awhile then said: When Gareth was first sober it was birds singing each morning that inspired him to carry on. Bit risky though, I said. I mean what if you came to rely on birdsong and one morning there wasn't any? He wasn't being literal, K said. He meant nature was coming back into his soul. When I said I felt that was a nice concept, my voice didn't sound like it was. It can be like that in the first years, K said as if she hadn't heard. I can imagine, I said. I was unhappy having said it because I'd remem-bered K saying once I lobbed that very phrase in to avoid having to find anything more useful. Among atheists who come into recovery it's common to find a higher power in nature, K said dreamily. I'm saying dreamily despite Jugg because her voice did have a quality just then. I had a fear of it being the result of thinking about Gareth. I put the fear to one side remembering Smithson would have told me to, though all the same I consigned the enigmatic painter to a few moments' canvas-ripping. What's your higher power? I asked her. I've heard you refer to it but haven't grasped it. It changes, she said. In the beginning it was a child's god, you know, an old man with a beard, but over time it's changed. Into what? I looked over the city below and before us. The idea I suppose had been for the dead to have a view. I wish I could say, K said. It's not specific any more. It's a feeling. The word feeling attached itself to Gareth. I said in my mind to Smithson please help me rid myself of suspicion once and for all. K then asked if I wanted an egg sandwich and I felt guilty about the Gareth thing. If we have one now, will we have enough for the rest of the outing? I asked. That's just the word I used in my head about today, K said. Outing. It goes with egg sandwiches. It does, I said. And in respect of your question, K said, yes there are plenty of sandwiches though only two egg. Oh I said. It looks like it might be quite warm later, K said, so I thought just a couple of egg we could eat early on then cheese and tomato for later because they won't go off. You're magnificent with sandwiches, I said. One has to take account of the climatic conditions, she said, especially when those conditions tend towards warm. Cold isn't so tricky although if you've got soup or something you have the problem of Thermos flasks. I never suspected we could have such a measured conversation, I said. It has come upon us, K said, maybe because we are in the vicinity of the good doctor. I reached round to touch his stone. In my arm was a horror of Gareth. To diminish him I said to K that going back to her earlier question, I was now wondering if our next stop might not be the lake. K threw aside the roll-up and propped herself on a forearm. You said last time you weren't going there again so long as you lived, she said. As I've explained before, I told her calmly, I found us bumping into your Tom distressing, especially when the hug occurred, but now I want to show you I'm easy with the world. Smithson advised me to wear it like a loose overcoat. Wear what? she said. The world, I told her. And don't say my Tom, she said. You do it on purpose to hurt yourself. I didn't want him confused with other Toms, that's all, I said. From the forearm K took herself into a sitting position, pulling over the rucksack then and taking out a package, which held – at the unwrapping – two sandwiches. I said to her wasn't it extraordinary egg sandwiches smelt bad but tasted nice. I mixed mayonnaise in with the egg, she said. Further proof, if any were needed, I told her, of your culinary and adventure expertise. For a while we ate and looked about the cemetery and the world. I do like it here, notwithstanding its associations, I said, or maybe because of them. Gareth's parents are here somewhere, she said, looking around. They died in a leap from a bridge over the river. That must have been devastating, I said. A note said it was because they'd failed as parents, she said. Though I didn't want to upset her about Gareth I felt I had to say leaping from a bridge was the worst failure of all. Is that why he drank? I asked. She explained terrible events didn't *cause* drinking as such, though someone with an addictive predisposition might well use them as a rationale for its continuance. I love it when you talk like that I said, distracted momentarily by a jackdaw hopping nearby, maybe in pursuit of a sandwich himself. He really does look, K said, like a plumpish gentleman in an evening suit. As the sandwich came to an end so serenity deepened and I began to hope me and K would be doing this for years, but simultaneously there was a darkness between us exemplified by Smithson's headstone and, on my part, Gareth R. Then I remembered Tom and the incident at the lake that time and how I'd just told her I wanted to be easier with the world, but even thinking it caused an old pain to crawl upon me. Maybe not the lake after all, I said. And we did the museum not long ago. Zoo? I don't fancy zoos today, she said. Nor, as it happens, ever again after last time. Really, I said, it seems we've run out of city. What about the woods? she said. You haven't mentioned those. I'm not in a wood mood just as you're not in a zoo one, I said. With the sandwich done, she was preparing another smoke. All the same she asked me why I wasn't in a wood mood given I was always saying how much better I felt once I was in them. I don't know, I said. But I feel definitely I want whatever we do to be about just you and me. Isn't most of what we do about just you and me? she said. And hasn't it been that way since time immemorial? Okay, so I'm not gregarious, I said, as you've often pointed out. It would be an exaggeration, she said, to accuse me of pointing it out often. But most people, it is true, do things with other people now and then. I rubbed the sides of my mouth. It was a calming strategy Smithson taught me. He also said never to say the first thing that came into my head. I don't remember you saying when today was being planned you wanted there to be more people, I told her. Had you said that, we could have made other arrangements. We could have had Tom along. Or Gareth. K shook her head. I see it now, she said. I asked her see what? Well you said about the lake to give the impression you were over what happened there, but really it's like I said you're trying to hurt yourself by going again even though there was never anything for you to be hurt about in the first place. Well, I said, I'm a complex being, as this fellow here – I patted Smithson's marble – was keen to point out. The only good thing right then was the hopping of the jackdaw as he patrolled what I had come to see as his zone of consideration. After a long while of thinking songs, K said: I've enjoyed this first leg of our sandwiches all the same. Oh absolutely, me too, I said.

*

A face framed below and at the sides by dark greasy hair against the pillow. Come in, it said. I already had. Take a seat. It was one of those tubular affairs reminding visitors not to stay long. Flowers in a vase on the cabinet had a card saying Get Well Sooon, Mum. I guess the extra o must have been an accident. I've done the same with a's. Then I found myself staring beyond Bulwark. This was the tenth floor. Grey filled both windows. For a moment I thought I might jump out. Emulate Gareth's parents. But they were the sort of windows that only opened an inch. Bulwark seemed to be regarding the circular one in the door I'd come through. You're lucky to have a room to yourself, I said. I'm not private, he said, but due to my snoring and the recent death of Mr Scull who occupied this bed before me, I was put here you might say for my own safety as well as to maximise the nocturnal comfort of others. His words smelt of liniment. We're missing a lake, I said to lighten things. Rarely for him he smiled and said: I'm hoping you won't go there again till I'm back. If I am back that is. Oh I wouldn't, I said. Not even with Jennifer? Bulwark asked. I had a feeling he might get round to that. Of course not, I said, only she did tell me – I bet you'll be pleased – that if I ask and you agree she wouldn't mind coming to see you. Bulwark grunted. If she wants to see me I'd rather it was more than 'wouldn't mind'. You have to make allowances, I said. She'll be hedging bets at this stage. Just because someone gets shot doesn't mean you make a beeline for them. I felt bad mentioning the shooting this soon. That's another thing, Bulwark said grumpily. If she's only coming because of what happened she'd best stay away. I rubbed my mouth, coming across as I did so a flake from the bacon and cheese puff I'd had on the way here. An occasional one stalls the blues. Bulwark was struggling to sit up more. I went to one side, lodged my hand under his arm and helped. On the cabinet, at the foot of the flower vase, was a paperback called *Things To Cheer You Up*, which I guessed his mum would have brought in too. Whenever a book suggests it has things within to cheer people, I open it with a determination not to let it work. Anyway, the author will have chosen things that cheered him or her and it's misguided to presume it'll work universally. Beside the book was a slab of Turkish delight chocolate with one segment missing. I expected you to be attached to equipment, I said. There's no need, Bulwark said. The bullet passed through my torso without damaging anything important. But surely it's all important in some respects, I said, otherwise it wouldn't be in there. When I laughed I truly believed I'd brought Bulwark into the vicinity of a rib tickler. But this time the face remained impassive. The surgeon said people were fairly safe, he said, unless it went through the heart, brain or a major blood vessel. I jerked my chin. Surgeons eh, I said. Never ruffled. Would you want them to be? Bulwark said. Silence then while a seagull passed. Bulwark leaned towards me. We have to work out a strategy, he said. First couple of days I didn't think about cigarettes. Felt ill. Today I've been having fantasies. They might as well be Daisy Buchanan. You'll have to grin and bear it, I said, at least till you're mobile. They've probably got a room. You'll be able to hobble off down there soon. Bulwark leaned away. I could smell K where she'd held me earlier. Whenever she held me lately it was like we were never going to touch again. I'd linked it to Gareth or a resurrection of Tom. I reached into my bag. I brought biscuits, I said. Cherry Creams. Someone was raving about them in the supermarket. They're half price for an introductory period. I don't like succumbing to offers normally but I remember once upon a time you saying you liked cherries. Bulwark said: A cheap biscuit's just what you want when you've been shot. I waited in vain for his eyes to show amusement. I'll put them on here for if you change your mind, I said. Bulwark intercepted the packet, said cherry creams under his breath and put them on the cabinet himself. I'm being cared for by a Greek Consultant, he said. Mr Opopopopapalous. I had to write it down. I said to him I hadn't seen many Greek Consultants and he said they were rare in this country. That was the end of the conversation. They aren't chatty unless they're listing gruesome facts. Consultants I mean, not

Greeks. I believe, I said, remembering something Smithson once told me, the dedication necessary to become a consultant rids them of social skills. This one snaps, Bulwark said. If you ask an awkward question or get your facts wrong, he snaps. Maybe he just sounds snappy because of the nationality difference, I said. I wouldn't take it seriously. Oh and by the way did you want me to bring in any of the work from college? Or has someone already done it? Do you have the textbooks with you? Bulwark's head shook, scraping the pillow. Questions, questions, he said. My head can't cope right now. Anyway, like I said, I'm not even sure I'll be coming back to college. I wanted to say he shouldn't let being shot by the Dean put him off, but saw it could be regarded as a fatuous comment. They say, I said instead, the bullet was found lodged in the cypress. Forensics located it by plotting its trajectory based on where witnesses said you were standing. Bulwark nodded. Hopefully there will be a plaque or something in time, he said. It's a wonder I hadn't given up glancing at him to ascertain if he was joking or being ironic. He was merely reaching weakly to the cherry creams. Open them would you? he said. All these years alive and I still haven't mastered biscuit wrappers. I took a while then to do as he'd asked, finding whenever I left a vacancy in my mind it filled with K and an imagining of she and any number of males. But what will you do, I said, fearful of the delay, if you don't go back? Well, Bulwark said, I'm hoping to write a book. Mum says the family solicitor's on the case and there's a good chance I'll win compensation. This would enable me, of course, to write the said book. I chuckled lightly. When Bulwark asked why, I explained he was one of the few people I knew who'd call it the said book. But then, having explained this, I proffered it as a working title. The beard nodded. The Said Book, he said. For once you might have come up with something useful. With people like Bulwark you just don't bother to admonish them if they patronise you. With others, the admonishments are in wait for them to say the wrong thing. We paused in our deliberations, me for some reason leaning back as well while a nurse came in to replenish Bulwark's water jug. Everything all right? She asked. Ticketty fucking boo, Bulwark said.

Colquahoon's eyes are at an angle as if he's looking over the top of a pair of spectacles. Half-moons they would have been, if they were there. He's said before he's lucky that of all of him, his eyes have remained the most robust. Then being Colquahoon he went on to explain robust's origin, with reference to Shakespeare and Milton. He was in full flight as the person I take to be Mrs Colquahoon arrived. She brought that day a Thermos of oxtail. She sat and watched him drink half a plastic cupful. That, she said, would put hairs on his chest. This led later to a discussion not with Colquahoon, who after the visit and soup had a nap, but with Atkins and Kandinsky. Atkins said he couldn't bear it when people said things like it'll put hairs on your chest because it seemed they were speaking in clumps of words rather than crafting individual ones. Kandinsky – though I felt he was sad to admit it – knew quite what Atkins meant. A silence ensued as they came to terms with the shock of agreement. After a while Atkins said – as if putting one foot into a bath to test the temperature – they're the sort of things people say in public houses? He'd intimated a question mark at the end in case Kandinsky didn't think they were the sort of things people said in public houses at all. I reckon you've hit the nail on the head there Mr Atkins, Kandinsky said to everyone's relief. Across these foolish sayings come with the pint as it slides upon the bar. Ah, Atkins said, the Foaming Pint, although it's me putting the capitals to make up for something about the way he said it that would otherwise go missing. Quite, Kandinsky said. Some of the others looked across to see if they could grasp what it was he'd said quite to, but he merely took one of his navigations of the dayroom before coming to a standstill more or less where he'd started. I should say now, in the presence of you all, I'm forbidden pints foaming or otherwise. Have been for many years. Down the hatch is another one, Atkins said, out of embarrassment at Kandinsky's confession. Kandinsky appeared relieved to have us diverted. I'm not sure down the hatch fits in with the type of thing we're after, Mr Atkins, he said. What do you mean? Atkins said. How is this'll put hairs on your chest different from down the hatch? It just is, Kandinsky said. Atkins snatched up his compendium. I'd like to hear you justify that in a court of law, he said under his breath. Jaundice glanced over from his mirror. Smetham halted a hairbrush halfway to his mouth. In the pub, he said, they also say things like how's the wife? Personally I feel that's different again, Kandinsky said. But Mr Kandinsky, Atkins said, almost before Kandinsky's last word had ended, there's no point saying personally because we know it's you, you uptight polony. The room erupted into amusement. Suddenly Harry was at the door saying gentlemen, gentlemen, we ought to keep it down for the benefit of those sleeping. But Harry, it's afternoon, Atkins said. Then there's nothing sadder than someone who spends their life saying but Harry or but whoever. Looking about ourselves we realised that yes a good fifty per cent of us were in what Harry calls the Land Of Assisted Nod. The Nod part a biblical reference, Colquahoon once informed us. Things calmed when Fiona arrived with the tea trolley having – as in the best reciprocations – cherry creams from the corner shop rather than the Sunday market bourbons because she'd got there late that week and the man selling them had already packed up and gone. Each time I bit into mine I remembered Bulwark in the hospital bed and yet using every last scrap of self-control I managed not to take the memory further, at least on that day. These biscuits are pleasant thank you Fiona, said Colquahoon, who'd gone into nibbling autopilot upon waking from his nap. For a few minutes the room filled with sipping and munching, the occasional semi-choke – crumbs were a pernicious culprit – birdsong from outside and if I remember correctly, a breaking of wind from Major Gwillingington and I was thinking that this was my life, this is where it has reached and suddenly all that went before was remarkably brief even though upon inspection, individual days could seem eternal. Fiona had come to crouch beside me as I enjoyed a second cherry cream. How are we doing? She said. I took a moment to think because it's the hardest question. The biscuits are good, I said. I like the bourbons, but it's always nice to have a change. It's also nice to know they still make them. Cherry creams I mean. They take me back. Oh? Fiona said, squealing, where to? Nowhere that matters, I said, which is the strange thing. I laughed. You'd think if the brain has the sophistication to restore you momentarily to an earlier time, it would make it somewhere significant. You would, Fiona said softly. I loved her then, in that way you can sometimes though even this brief romance led to guilt about K. And what about the tea? Fiona said. I looked into its surface. Fine thanks, or shall we say fine within the parameters? We couldn't do without you Fiona. That's nice to know, Fiona said. She has evocative dark hair. So it's okay for me to put cherry creams on my list occasionally? she asked. I looked at the end of the biscuit I'd been eating. Why yes, I'd say so, absolutely. As far as I'm concerned you can put anything on the list you like. I fancied she blushed. Atkins said after his most recent sip: How about that'll keep the wolf from the door? Kandinsky made a sound not unlike a horse on a cold morning and said: Mr Atkins, forgive me but you don't seem to have grasped the exactness of the topic at all, even though – and *this* I find hard to believe – it was you who started it in the first place. When it began I was pleased, you know? I thought here at last is a topic I can get my teeth into but since then you've insisted on coming up with sayings people don't use in public houses, well not especially anyway. Atkins shrugged. It was your lurid confession Mr Kandinsky. It put me off. Glad you can see where you went wrong, Kandinsky said. Smetham said then: Is it like where people say set them up Ted? Kandinsky sighed. Yes, that is the sort of thing Mr Smetham, whoever Ted might be. He's my late brother-in-law, Smetham said. Loved *his* pint. Well, Kandinsky said, if he's your *late* brother-in-law I suggest we leave him to one side. Atkins was half up from his seat before holding himself a moment and sinking back. No need to speak ill of the dead, Mr Kandinsky, he said harshly. Whatever Mr Smetham's done, he doesn't deserve that. Smetham looked perplexed. Whatever I've done? What do you mean? It slipped out, Atkins said. Take no notice. Strange, isn't it, Kandinsky said, how ready Mr Atkins is to admit things slip out where Mr Smetham's concerned but he won't make the same admission in respect of myself. Alerted by the tone of his question I looked to him to realise that of all of us here, in Assisted Nod or otherwise, he'd been addressing me.

*

201

We caught early sight of Gerald taking the key from his pocket to unlock the shop. The string on which the key was tied was only just long enough to reach the lock and this led to him being squashed against the door to the detriment of his hat. God love and save us, I heard him say when the door finally swung open and the bell sounded. Even from yards away the smell of books enticed me. Mother said she was going to leave straight away because she had things to do, waved to Gerald who was busying himself in the gloom and clicked off down the street. Even though he knew it was me I was glad he said: Aha! Peter! as I came in through the door. Earlier than planned but welcome. A bluish yellowish mark had appeared below and to one side of his left eye. I went to stand at a fond spot on the shop carpet. It was the place to be while I either wondered what to do or was given instruction. Nothing much is of your own volition when you're a child. There's no sense asking if you'd like me to pop out the back and put the kettle on, Gerald said when he'd untangled himself from hat and coat and hung not himself but both items on the stand by his desk. If there's no sense then please don't do it, I said. Ormerod had urged me to practise being quaintly sarcastic. It can get you out of situations, he said, although care is needed because it can also get you in them. I'd already had one situation so far that day because I'd woken to shouting from downstairs. A glance through my window revealed the dog from up the road must have heard too because he was standing diagonally with his tail between his legs. You could look at a dog sometimes and know he was fed up by that same manouvre and the shape of his mouth. Set foot in this house again and you'll be sorry, Mother was saying and Father was saying if I set foot in it again kill me with my blessing. When you hear your father going out for what will become the last time, it's surprising how little goes through your mind. I dressed with shaken legs and an odd stomach Ormerod told me later was somatological trauma. It seemed strange the Miss Woo troubles were up and running so early. But that was memory and here I was now waiting for Gerald who'd gone to put the eternal kettle on leaving me in a blade of sunshine by MISCELLANEOUS. The light was warm against one side of my face and yet the carpet seemed as if I might sink into it. I'd watched Gerald in times gone by place books in MISCELLANEOUS with a sigh as if impatient at the book's refusal to belong to a specific category. Most recently it was *The Blinded Soldiers and Sailors Gift Book*. Though it was unlikely ever to sell, he said, he couldn't bring himself to discard it any more than he could discard a puppy. I asked him if he had a puppy and he laughed and said not so much, which struck me as odd along with a number of odd things that day. He came out with mugs of tea. From the top pocket of his suit jacket poked four wafer biscuits. The sun had fixed me to the spot so in the end Gerald had to tug me from it and sit me in a chair beside his desk while he took up what he called The Executive Position. I'm anticipating a busy day, he said, what with the sun out. I'd been going to his shop long enough to warn him that whenever he'd anticipated a busy day it had been a death knell. I wondered while you're here – after the tea and biscuits of course and once I've got the Outside Shelves set up – if you'd stand by the door welcoming people as they arrive – he laughed – the exception being Mrs McKintosh, not that she will. Arrive I mean. He shook his head. Don't let a Mrs McKintosh into your life however tempting, Peter. Father's already warned me about Miss Woos, I told him. Gerald rubbed above his eye with tiredness, reminding me of the bruise. He must have seen me looking because he quietly said: Mrs McKintosh, as if this should explain. As our dear friend once wrote, he added, hell hath no fury, not that I believe I scorned her in the true sense but with the fairer sex you'll find what one considers scorning another may not, and Mrs McKintosh is of the former outlook. As he sniffed I noticed air only passed smoothly up the right nostril. The upshot is she's unlikely to darken our door again as I hinted earlier. You'll understand as you get older. So I keep being told, I said as lightly as I could. And what of Jim? Gerald's laughter was of sufficient intensity to send him backwards. Fancy you remembering, he said when he'd restored himself. Last time I came it was Jim this Jim that, I said. Well yes it was, Gerald said. Pottery, I added. That's right, Gerald said snappily. I've been praying for a while now that he might help me let go of my worries. I asked if he meant Jim. Gerald said no, God. I prayed inwardly for a world free of Jims on Gerald's behalf. Behind me in the dims of the back room the Bird Clock sounded the hour. I guessed wren correctly. I'm without a father, temporarily, I said. Gerald went still. Is he off working? No, I said. He and Mother rowed. Gerald said quaintly: Miss Woo? Not this time apparently, I said. Mrs Chaffin. Gerald said: Mrs Chaffin? Your poor mother! And here was I thinking I had troubles. With Jim? I said. Exactly, Gerald said. So say Mrs Aldridge is going round Jim's after the next class so he can show her his sketches for future pottery projects. I can't think why she hasn't asked me to go too. I hate her going to see Jim even though as she pointed out his wife will be there. The one with the bad leg? I asked. Well remembered again, said Gerald, though the thing is I don't *know* she has a bad leg or even if there's a leg or wife at all. Unable to manage further I put my tea aside and returned to the spot by *Miscellaneous*. A shock it was then to see Father and Mrs Chaffin passing along the far side of the street, he with his arm round her. I became triangular for a while. And then for another while – at least till Gerald put his Jim worries aside and rescued me – I could think of nothing but Mr Chaffin digging those fatal potatoes.

*

Strange, K said, how strong some memories are long afterwards. It's not so long geologically, I said. Though I could see how sensible it was, I didn't like her balaclava. I'd opted for no facial protection and was regretting it. Near the bank on the far side of the canal, where there were rushes, flakes of ice had formed on the water. Do you want to say more about it? K said. I told her I didn't. The memory came out of the blue, I told her, and I felt I should just say it. It can't be out of the blue as such, she said. If you look back at what we were saying or doing, you'll find what prompted the memory. When Alexander said he'd have a think too it was like I'd forgotten he was there. He was walking with Miriam behind us. Her thermal suit rubbed at every stride. I hope, I said, more or less to the two of them, you don't mind me recounting childhood when we're out for a walk. No, it's interesting, Miriam said. Who was Miss Roo again? Alexander told her (with a sigh): Miss *Woo* was the woman Peter's dad had a thing with first of all. Mrs Chaffin was the second and last, As Far As We Know anyway, he added. No need for capitals

Alexander, I told him. I was unnerved by what Ormerod called The Chaffin Interlude. It seemed to indicate even the least suspicious of us could become embroiled in goings-on though as he pointed out time and again the most shameful things are also often the most difficult to resist. I said: Thanks Ormerod, though it was one of those days I didn't much like him. I hate all that sort of thing, Miriam said with an audible shiver. Something like it happened to Harold. Him again, Alexander said. He was so say happily married for years, Miriam continued, but all the time his wife was ravishing someone. Wow, I said. Harold was devastated, Miriam went on. I heard behind me the slightest change in tempo of Alexander's footwear. Having known him so long I could tell it meant he was wishing he hadn't been born. He wished it more than any person I knew even though he'd been told by myself and others many times if he hadn't been born he wouldn't be able to wish it. Now as he cleared his throat a plume of breath overtook us before dispersing. Is there any possibility, he said to Miriam, of you and me walking more than a hundred yards without you bringing this Harold up? There was a pause in the rubbing. I don't understand, she said. I thought you and me were merely enjoying a walk together. Oh yes, well we're doing that all right, Alexander said. Suddenly he was overtaking as his breath had done earlier but unlike his breath he didn't disperse but over time became a smaller and smaller version of himself and whenever he reached a frozen puddle he paused to stamp at it with the heel of his boot. Some time later Miriam said to us from behind she felt she must have annoyed him. I'm sure it's nothing, I told her. He's sensitive that's all. Well, Miriam said, I am a *bit* worried. I don't really want to be out with people who're going to fly off the handle when I least expect it. Oh you've got a point there, I said, there's hardly a handle he hasn't flown off lately. K said to Miriam once you got to know him this sort of thing didn't happen often. It might be you've mentioned Harold without having explained to him who Harold is, she said diplomatically. At the far side of the canal, high on a branch, a heron regarded us, plump and overly solemn like a disgraced member of parliament. Miriam said she hadn't realised she needed to explain her every affiliation. Oh, I said softly, again aiming the words in the semicircle necessary to reach her, I'm sure in the world you're used to you absolutely don't need to. But this, I said, holding my hand towards the distant figure breaking another puddle, is Alexander. Historical circumstance makes him this way. The heron opened its wings solemnly. Its feathers weren't adequate for the temperature. I expect both K and me were hoping Miriam would say who Harold was so that even though she might not be willing to reassure Alexander directly, it would enable us to do it when she wasn't there. A plop mid-canal I took to be a stone tossed by her. I mean, she said, it's not like we're in an intimate relationship. We're mostly walking companions. Come to think of it he's been acting oddly for a while. Ah, I said, it might be he's already gone beyond any guns which invite jumping. K glanced at me. She was not frowning but looking as if she might if I didn't say the right thing soon. By the time he gets round that corner he'll have thought twice about rushing off, I said. He's like me in that respect. We were passed coming this way by a softly chugging long boat. A man at the tiller raised his hand. Quietly I recognised him as the Chandler and to my satisfaction realised K had failed to notice him and that he had failed to recognise her. I love the shades of foliage along here, I said. K laughed. When I asked her why, she said she'd set an obscure bet with herself I'd mention foliage at some point because I'd said similar on other occasions although, she admitted, not all of them. I kept my voice to a minimum as I asked why she had an interest in pointing out things I might have said before. Well, she said, it's one of your characteristics. That might be the case, I replied, but I still don't see why we need them aired, especially in company. I missed K then remembered she was with me. It must have been the balaclava. Me and Alexander used to wear balaclavas when we were small, I said to her. K said abruptly: Yes, I know. I went on anyway: In winter it was hard not to suck the wool round our mouths and we'd end up with chapped lips. Then of course balaclavas had an innocence which has since been lost. I like to have a warm head and ears, K said. Miriam said she preferred to feel the air on her face providing the temperature didn't go too low. My late husband loved cold, she went on. He said it was healthier than warmth. He used to say given a choice he'd prefer to live in Finland for example rather than anywhere muggy. Like India. I'm with him there, I said, though I do like it if the scenery matches the temperature which you could say it does here on the canal but when it's really cold and you're in the centre of town or something it doesn't seem natural. Thing is though, Miriam said promptly, if he *hadn't* liked the cold so much he might be alive now. It's interesting, I said, hoping it was, how easily the course of events can be altered. Let's say your husband hadn't died in the avalanche, then the likelihood is you wouldn't be going on walks with Alexander which would mean you wouldn't be here with us either and Alexander wouldn't have stormed off. Miriam laughed and nudged K from behind. I see what you mean, she said. Had not Alexander already done the storming, I might have set off myself. Things had gone downhill, I decided, because of the notion I hadn't been comfortable with in the first place that we should have Alexander and Miriam along on one of our walks. It had been K's idea. To help me – and Alexander – become sociable, though I'd explained on many occasions being sociable with more than one person at a time was difficult for Alexander and that she should leave well alone. The swing of boots over the towpath, the quack of a duck or honk of a goose, accompanied us in a bleak serenade as we moved towards the bend in the canal. I wondered if it hadn't been the argument about Harold alone which had made Alexander leave but the thermal suit. It covered Miriam entirely except for an oval hole containing mouth, nose and eyes. The rolled nature of the material gave her a corrugated appearance. Alexander tells me you two have known each other your whole lives, the suit said. This idea quickened my heart when so few seconds earlier it had plumbed with despair. That's right, I said. As babies first of all. I would have gone on then to list the other stages we'd been through since then, but felt it patronising. And I hope you don't mind my asking, Miriam said, but are you and K a couple? Alexander hasn't said. I looked towards K's balaclava. Luckily her mouth began to move. We're in a subcategory, the mouth said. I told Miriam I agreed entirely though I had to admit I wasn't always clear what the category was. You don't live together? Miriam asked. K made a sound in her throat. I'd rather hang myself from the nearest tree, she said. I know what you mean, Miriam said, drawing with difficulty alongside me. I could just about bear being in the same house as my late husband but I'm glad we both had careers which stopped us joining at the hip. I echoed the sound K had made earlier and said how odd it was, the term 'late husband', as if any minute now he'd come panting up the towpath behind us frantically checking his watch. As I looked to Miriam for approval, the face crinkled with sorrow and before long she too had sped forward, the thermal suit stooping to reduce drag. You've put your foot in it again, K said, not unhappily. I asked her what she meant by again. Again in the sense you've done it before, she said. Not today, granted, but generally, in life. Oh, I said. I didn't say more because she was right. I asked if she thought Miriam would be affected by my indelicacy for long. I don't get the impression she's keen on you, K said, so she might be affected longer than she might otherwise have been. I sighed heavily. I've never been good with late husbands, I told her. I consoled myself with a review of the towpath area giving most attention to the canal becoming still again after the disruption of the Chandler's boat. Yes this was lovely, I told myself, and as such should be catalogued for later when there would be no canals, no frost across the grass, no winter, perhaps – God forbid – no K. Anyway, I said, how do you know she's not keen on me and how can that have happened so soon after this socialising scheme began? I told you it wasn't a good idea. K said it wasn't that the idea wasn't good as such, but it might take someone like Miriam longer to realise I meant no harm generally speaking. You mean harm in what I said about her husband? I asked. No, K said. You're unsettling during early encounters. Thanks for allocating so much time to your assessments, I said, but they're not necessary. The thing about her husband shouldn't have slipped out, I grant you, but at the end of the day that's all it was – a thing which slipped out. It shouldn't be used to make generalisations about my character. K put her hand to the mouth hole of her balaclava for a few moments. You tickle me, she said. I seem to provide any amount of tickling for the entire world, I said. Anyway, K said, enough of that. We still haven't found out who Harold is or was. No, I said – though to be honest I didn't want to speak to her any more – and I don't see it's any of our business. And yet, K said lightly, if *I* mentioned a Harold you'd be beside yourself. This is partly true, I said, though thinking I'd be beside myself as you put it, is overstating the case. I was thinking of how you've been about Gareth, she said. I told her she was being unfair; that I hadn't brought him up myself for a while; and that she never took into account that if I saw she had a point in any criticisms, I made an effort to adjust. Formality was killing me. I wanted to take her hand but since it was covered in glove and since I didn't have any on myself, I held back.

*

Kandinsky's idea was that we should compose a few words to have inscribed on our imagined tombstone. Atkins said: You'll be the death of me with your death games, and then he chuckled lightly but grotesquely. Kandinsky told Atkins as far as he could remember this was the first death game he'd proposed so maybe he – Atkins – should refrain from exaggeration. Anyway, clever clogs, Atkins said, you go first then. Kandinsky pushed his slippers into the floor and consequently a little of himself up the leatherette of his high-backed chair. I was thinking, he said, of *He Came. He saw. He Failed To Conquer*. Smetham woke or appeared to at least, in his hand a bath sponge he was yet to consume. You've got that wrong Mr Kandinsky, he said. It should be: *I came. I saw. I conquered*. Thank you Mr Smetham, Kandinsky said, but I fear you were away with the fairies when the concept was originally aired and may have missed the point. May I? May I really? Smetham said with such vehemence I felt he might burst a vessel. Harry was against the patio doors, an opened copy of *Collected Poems 1934–1952* in his hands. Earlier he'd read to us – though not all of us had wanted it – *The Hunch-back In The Park*. He believed – though this was my assumption – more poetry would be conducive to our well-being. He'd explained about Cwmdonkin Park and how Dylan had frequented there. Jaundice asked what sort of word Cwmdonkin was. No one responded. So anyway, finally Smetham was instructed in the purposes of semi-comic misquota-tion and was asked then if he had any idea what he'd want inscribed on his own imaginary tombstone. How about, he said, edging the fabulous bath sponge ever closer to his mouth, *Here Lies Mr Smetham*. Kandinsky nodded. Good, he said, and containing necessary information for the casual cemetery visitor, but still not quite what we hoped for. It should be something to make your stone stand out among the others. I hadn't realised there were others, Smetham said. Oh yes, Kandinsky said, you have to imagine it surrounded on all sides by fellow dead people you want to rise above. Smetham jerked. Oh, how about *All That Was Mr Smetham Is No More*? I had a feeling Kandinsky was actually jealous of this one. No, no, he said. You're still not on track. I had half a mind myself to butt in but before I could open my mouth Major Gwillingington roused himself long enough to suggest *There'll Be Bluebirds Over The White Cliffs Of Dover*, speaking the words first of all followed by a rendition of the tune itself. Well yes, Kandinsky said when he'd finished, nice idea Major, but it isn't relevant to your death is it? She was marvellous singing that though, the Major said. As far as I could tell one sparkled eye had focused on the patio doors and Harry. Let's recap, Kandinsky said. We're looking for a few words which sum up to people who read our stone, what measure of chap we were. You might – as in the one I thought of – want to convey something wryly amusing, or you might want the short-term gravitas only death can bring. Atkins slapped his chair and said he loved gravitas with roast beef. I believe I was the only one to have perceived his play on words. Or was Kandinsky simply annoyed his topic was getting out of hand? How about *Thanks For Dropping By, Now Fuck Off* Jaundice suggested. The room – metaphysically at least – devolved into perplexed laughter. Harry shook his head and reminded Jaundice – not with any conviction – such language was not encouraged. The far doors flew open about then disclosing first a trolley and then Fiona in a chequered pinafore. Tea up, she said. Atkins stopped laughing long enough to ask why tea should be in that particular direction. More laughter, mostly from himself, including a dabbing of the lips with a soiled handkerchief. Fiona laughed too, asking then what was all this about and Kandinsky managed to explain we'd been playing a new game which he was going to call Tombstone. Fiona set about preparing teas. Tombstone? She said, what sort of game's that? Atkins told her it was Kandinsky's latest monstrosity and Fiona said she felt we could come up with a more cheerful way to pass the time and Atkins said he quite agreed but what could he do? I should explain, Kandinsky said gravely, the game itself calls for imagination and flair and is not the frippery Mr Atkins makes out. Fiona brought across my tea first of all. I took it to mean, foolishly, she loved me too. As she leaned forward I caught the aroma of her freshly washed hair. I longed to touch her cheek with the backs of my fingers. So how do you play it? She asked, the words reaching me in an angelic whisper although intended for Kandinsky. He heard the question of course. Well, he said with a clap, you have to think what you'd want written on your tombstone which would sum you up. Oh now there's a tricky subject, Fiona said as she leaned away from me. We'd been restored to bourbons. I decided I wouldn't bother dunking. A cousin of mine in Ireland had *I Could Have Danced All Night,* Fiona said. She liked musicals. Atkins thought this interesting and asked if the cousin had enjoyed any musicals in particular. Kandinsky puffed his cheeks. You ask stupid questions Mr Atkins. Yeah, Jaundice said in a rare display. Kandinsky performed one of his lengthiest ward-lawn-ward excursions. He then stood with his fingers squeezed into fists. It was sung, he said, by Eliza Doolittle after she'd danced with Henry Higgins. Atkins calmly picked up his compendium and looked at it at an angle, not intending to open it. You've fallen into my trap Mr Kandinsky, he said, through a loop made with his lips, as I thought you would. I thought he would too, Jaundice said. You see, Atkins said, I already knew it was My Fair Lady. Then why, pray, Kandinsky said slowly, did you ask if the cousin enjoyed any musicals in particular? If she wanted *I Could Have Danced All Night* on her tombstone it was obviously one of her favourites. I would have thought so too, Jaundice said. Not even one of her favourites, Smetham said – oh the sponge was close! – but *the* favourite. He or she would hardly have had a reference to a second favourite etched onto such an enduring memorial. By now tea distribution was well under way. Kandinsky had to hold cup and saucer in both hands to prevent rattling. Sometimes, he said, I fear you're all beyond help. Harry snapped shut *Collected Poems 1934–1952.* You must make an effort to be better behaved towards one another, he said sharply for him. And Mr Kandinsky – we won't use phrases like 'beyond help' if you don't mind. Jaundice beamed mostly I think because he felt this criticism would overshadow the one he'd had just now. If you're not careful Harry, Kandinsky said, you'll be veering towards the censorship of a totalitarian state. He took a sip of tea after saying this and wandered into the corner to examine the remains of the rubber plant. Fiona said I thought we might all have a sing-song later. You'd like that, wouldn't you? I could tell by Colquahoon's face he was trying to decide if he'd like that or not. It was weeks since the last. The idea had been Fiona herself would do the verses and we'd come in with the two line chorus which lay between each like jam in a sponge cake. That's not my image. It was something Colquahoon said once. He'd been inspired by the sponge the person assumed to be Mrs Colquahoon brought in that day. In the only negative thing I've heard him say in reference to her, he opened the tin when she'd gone and said to no one: There's not a problem she doesn't imagine will be fixed with sponge. A buttery vanilla sweetness fumed from the tin which had a picture of dragoons on the lid. I thought about cakes, hoping to find a way to tag something onto the end of what Colquahoon had said but fact is I hadn't ever liked cakes as such, sponges particularly. Oh my word no one's answering me Harry, Fiona said. They're in their afternoon lull, Harry said. I would have said to Harry it was unlikely our lulls were so similar they could be stuck under one heading. I say 'would have' because for no reason I could make out my mouth wasn't working. There'd been other occasions when the same had happened. Come on, Fiona said, surely you'd like a sing-song! A skidding from beyond was Kandinsky's slippers against the floor as he swivelled. You seem to think, he said sharply, all it takes are a few choruses of Old Macdonald to ameliorate us. For a while he was shocked by his own word. Then Smetham said: Aha! prompting us to direct our gazes at him to wait for whatever it was he wanted to say next. He put aside the bath sponge. I've wondered since I was a child, he said, if there really was an elderly farmer called MacDonald and if this song was based on and dedicated to him. For two pins I reckon Kandinsky would have thrust a hand backwards and snapped the remains of the rubber plant. It's sad, he said, you've been wondering such a thing for so long Mr Smetham. It probably explains – as if any explanation was needed – why you're here in the first place, quite apart from your – how shall I put it – wide-ranging appetites. I believe Smetham was hurt by this criticism. All the same he retrieved and took a bite from the bath sponge, having to pull for a long time before a piece detached. He then literally chewed this over. You've been trouble since you first came, he mumbled to Kandinsky. I have to agree, Atkins said. I've never actually seen anyone look so beady as Atkins looked just then. Beady, and sneaky. Smaller, more bespectacled. Tobias Mawk sitting nearby – though as usual not through choice – gyrated in his chair. Harry has said this is caused by an organic illness – apparently the opposite to a reactive one – though some have a torrid combination of both. If you mean by trouble, Kandinsky said calmly, that I'm willing to say what I believe and stick with that opinion unless a good reason comes along to modify it, then yes you could say I've been trouble because God forbid we should have anyone here as clear-cut and sophisticated. About now Smetham gagged on the sponge and had to be saved by Fiona who'd been sitting nearby flicking through a magazine. She used her ring finger to pass almost to Smetham's throat and tug the sponge out. I complained to Harry a few days later because I believe he could see what Smetham had been up to and maybe he should have intervened sooner though I tempered what I said with pauses and comical asides because I didn't want him to think I felt he was bad with us generally. No no, he said, you're right to point it out. I guess I'm so used to seeing Mr Smetham eat all manner of things, I didn't react in time to the dangers of this one. Is it because you're worried about Cheryl? I said. He frowned. Cheryl? He said. Cheryl who? A measured breath on my part was intended to mask a timpani of panic in my chest. I wanted to say Cheryl, your wife, even though Jugg would have found it unbearably expositive. Instead I repeated the word Cheryl, downturning the yl into a playful reminder. After a pause Harry asked if I'd given any more thought to doing a jigsaw and that if *The Haywain* wasn't my cup of tea then the other day someone had donated *La Grande Jatte* which had even more pieces – two thousand in fact. It's not so much the title of the jigsaw – or its size – I said, as the principle of jigsaws themselves. My last was *Baboons of the Serengeti*.

I didn't ever finish it. You see I've never been able to reconcile the actuality of baboons with small cutouts which, when arranged correctly, give an *image* of those baboons. All the while I was hoping Harry would say more about the Cheryl – or lack of Cheryl – incident but something in his expression warned against me making further enquiries just then.

*

The dog from up the road was half on the pavement, his paws holding back a fish and chip paper. The afternoon prickled with mist. Among the prickles, sometimes high above, scraps of blue. I'd reached the end of life. Sooner or later God or one of his emissaries would come and ask me to pack a bag or whatever was usual in the circumstances. The best imagination had the emissary taking my hand as we sped into the prickled sky. I thought through as I swung in fatherless impunity if I'd leave a note for Mother. *Hello,* one of the imaginary composings said, *this is from guess who. I hope things go well for you now and into the future. Yours etc.* This ending was one suggested at some time by Mrs Strachan. I remember because Alexander had put up his hand and asked her exactly what the future was. She'd said something about it being that which hadn't yet happened, an odd concept to some, Horace in particular, who said at break time he hadn't realised there was anything other than Now. Alexander told him there wasn't, really, but that the future was to do with Nows which came later. Horace drank his milk and said no more. The last dregs passed airily into his straw as I watched the sky. If I tilted long enough I felt I'd fall over. I was testing this out at our front gate when a figure loomed. It's done with, Gerald said failing, I felt, to start at the right place. He looked up and down the road. Is your mother in? I told him she'd said she was going to be out all day if anybody asked but she was in really. Well that makes it easier, he said. I asked him if it was Mrs Aldridge and he said is what Mrs Aldridge? and I said the reason it's done with. Well it is and it isn't, he said. Oh I said. He took off his trilby, did something with his hair and put the hat back on. That dog's having one of its days I see, he said. He thrust his head forward to indicate which dog he meant. He's maintaining his breakfast position, that's all, I said. There comes a point in any conversation with a distressed adult when you see

them become impatient with a particular element even though they themselves initiated it. The mark below and to one side of his left eye had
retained its yellowish aspect, lost its bluish one. I turned in time to see the
bottoms of Mother's slippers rise into the front window and rest against
it. That's her now, I said, pointing, but remember she's out. She does yogi
to help her cope. You mean yoga, Gerald said. But right you are, I won't
disturb her. It would be gargantuan of me to assume she's out to everyone
but her local bookseller. Please tell her I'm grateful for her lending you on
Saturday mornings and if I should ever have another shop – which I can't
see to be honest – I'll be looking for you to help again. Oh, I said. It was
my second oh. Part of me – although not a large part – was sad I'd never
found anything about poltergeists for K. I asked him what he was going
to do with the books and he said though he hadn't utterly decided yet,
Mrs McKintosh did have a large waterproof shed where he might store
them temporarily. I said a third oh. Mother's slippers swung from the
window. Just afterwards her upper half appeared. Noticing Gerald,
she shuffled sideways. Well, Gerald said, I'm at a loss as to what to say
now. It's hard on momentous occasions. Mind you I daresay I've already
provided the necessary information and perhaps it only behooves me
now to wish you, my dear Peter, farewell. You're speaking funny, I said.
He told me it was because he was upset at certain things he'd done recently
which singled him out as someone not to be trusted or respected not only
by the world but by women especially. The awkwardness was resolved to
some extent by Gravel, a walking stick in one hand. He eyed Gerald. I'm
off for that X-ray, he said, as if we'd heard of a suspected appointment
previously. Last time there was a queue. You'd think they'd have a system.
I believe they do, Gerald said, just not a good one. Gravel leaned back and
extended one arm in a signal of surprise. I've a feeling I've seen you
somewhere. Gerald said quite possibly, because he had a bookshop in
town. Ah yes, Gravel said, what's it called again? Gerald said it was called
Books! but that he was soon closing down. That's a shame, Gravel said.
I thought of coming in for a look round every time I went by on my way
to the surgery which – as the poppersqueal here will confirm – is a regular
thing. I've spotted you through the window. You enjoy tea from what

I've seen. Rather than harangue the man for not going ahead with his thinking of going in, Gerald sympathised instead with Gravel's need for medical attention. Oh I've just got one of those bodies, Gravel said. I was in an accident years ago. Haven't been right since. I was amazed to hear new information and took a hefty swing on the gate. Mother's fingers were gripping the edge of the curtain. Sorry to hear that, Gerald said. Thank you, Gravel said. Good luck with any new venture. Thanks to you, Mr Ah... Gerald said. Gravelle, said Gravel. Both he and Gerald scanned the vicinity, maybe surprised to run out of commonality so soon. Having cleared his throat, Gravel pointed his stick forward. Here we go then. Off to be radioactively examined. He gave what I believe to have been a chortle and limped forward. We watched him for a time. Then Gerald said listen Peter be sure to tell your mother thanks. I will I said. Inwardly I was sad at his deciding to end his career without consulting me but then as now I found it inordinately hard to say what I was really feeling. The energy for doing so would only arise years afterwards and then usually at night when I couldn't sleep. You should know, Gerald said not looking at me, I've decided to give it another go with Mrs McKintosh. The lower tubing of the gate softened under my shoes. I would later discover this to be a neurological response to unfortunate news. But you don't like her, I said. You like Mrs Aldridge. Gerald's head and hat made dancing movements. That's partly true, partly not, he said, though I see where you got the idea. Being happy with someone isn't everything. And let's face it, Mrs McKintosh does have the heart to pop in occasionally! This made him laugh to an Alexander extent. He had to grip the top of the gate. I was glad to be on hand when his hat threatened to fall. It would be best if you went for happy though, I said. In a perfect world yes, Gerald said, but there are practicalities too. You can't eat dreams. I was trying to imagine as I swung what a bowlful would look like. But you said you had enough money not to worry if the bookshop didn't go well, I reminded him. Gerald stopped laughing. He grudgingly congratulated me on my memory. The truth of the matter is, he said, Mrs McKintosh has talked me round. The dog from up the road twitched as if having indigestible dreams. I asked Gerald to hold on, got off the gate and walked to the back of the house. I kicked the shed, counted to ten then came back, mounting the gate as before. I thought you'd hopped it, Gerald said. I told him I was trying an exercise suggested by Ormerod that was supposed to help boys manage situations. And has it? Gerald asked. I told him I didn't know, partly because I'd already lost sight of what it was I couldn't manage. Then I remembered all at once. Really I was hoping you'd stick with Mrs Aldridge come hell or high water, I said. Gerald seethed between his teeth. How can I stick with Mrs Aldridge if Mrs Aldridge makes no effort to stick with me? Aha, I said. Aha what? Gerald said, less patient than he had been. There's nothing to go with it, I said. I was worried this was all to do with Jim but that Gerald was too proud to admit it this time. You can't go aha then stop, Gerald said. I say it sometimes to fill in, I said. Well don't, Gerald said. All right then, actually I was thinking about Jim, I said. Jim from night school. I know who he is thank you, Gerald said in a tone. And I'd rather you didn't mention him again. I just don't think you should give up on Mrs Aldridge, I said, especially when Jim isn't specific. Gerald repeated specific twice and loudly enough to bring the dog from up the road to his paws. You shouldn't use words like that at your age. It isn't natural. And more to the point you don't know what you're talking about. Ormerod had taught me specific recently along with amethyst, notwithstanding, totem-pole, ecumenical and squid. Even so I couldn't really remember what I'd meant in respect of Jim when I'd said it. Since Mrs Mackintosh came along you've not been the same, I said to Gerald, he reminding me almost at once it was McKintosh. I will own, he said sheepishly, that in Mrs McKintosh's company I become a touch unhinged as history has shown, but I had a think about it last night and asked myself if it was better to join Mrs McKintosh right now or hope for a Mrs Aldridge who might take *years* to get herself together and then all the time there's the Jim risk. My first experience with Mrs McKintosh wasn't exactly smooth but there were never *any* Jims, not even a hint. With Mrs Aldridge Jims are wall to wall. These most recent words of Gerald brought added softness to an already softened world. The dog from up the road looked this way and that before loping softly to sniff a lamp post. I remembered something Ormerod had once told me about a study someone had done to find out how many paws a dog had in contact with the ground while it was moving in that way. There was much, he said, to find out about the world in the time available and he added that though the common conception was that important things were the most advantageous to study, we must always find a place in our hearts for the inconsequential. I said: Thanks Ormerod. He brought his lips together and nodded. Of course, he went on eventually, the rules about paws differ according to what speed the dog's moving. But to be frank the only time we can be absolutely sure they have all four in contact with the ground is when they're standing still. I offered gratitude though this was the first time I doubted what he had to say. As a consequence I cleared my throat unnecessarily and turned my feigned attention to Baboons of the Serengeti.

*

Some time ago Colquahoon said yes, he'd heard of poppersqueal and believed it to originate with Dickens. I was heartened to hear him reply so promptly and tried to extend the conversation by suggesting it seemed many words and terms had. He raised the newspaper and sighed. I said anyway I thought Dickens a remarkable fellow, what with those walks to Slough to visit his lover. This was met by silence. Sometimes at night when everything else has been lost I walk with Dickens through dark polluted streets. Even so I have a job keeping pace. He was saying yes, we do have chops for breakfast on occasion and then I realised it wasn't Dickens confirming chops but my own mind. If ever that sort of realisation comes when I'm in bed it causes a surge of adrenaline, a pounding heart, an unpleasant taste. I've learned that if I wait for ten minutes or so the adrenaline clears my system and the body calms, calms enough anyway to hear the serenade of Atkins in the cubicle to my left and the Major to my right. Whoever's on duty has a system of tight-tucking, which means it's hard to get comfy once you're in. Atkins told me to count sheep. The first few nights I reached a thousand plus. Harry or whoever comes round with a torch occasionally. One night he saw I was awake – staring into the void he called it – so took a few minutes to sit with me. I told him about the sheep. He said he'd never taken to the idea at all. Cheryl, he said – at that time I didn't worry much who Cheryl was – hardly slept at night, which had several times put her job with Lambton, Lambton, Lambton & Lambton in jeopardy. He said too it meant he was always being woken. I told him I was sorry to hear that. There were few things as distressing as continually disturbed nights. He laughed, making the torch beam shake. I can tell you're going to be trouble, he said. When I asked why, he said he'd known a fair few people pass through and it was surprising how many used defensive phrases such as the one I'd used about there being few things as distressing as continually disturbed nights. I struggled against the linen. Well, I said, I don't think there *are* many things more distressing than continually disturbed nights, really. That's one of the reasons you have tablets, he said. Oh those, I said, praise be. Don't get like that, he said softly. Following the softly he got his arm between the bottom and upper sheet. Just empty your mind, he said. Next door the Major was reliving conflict. Atkins was snoring less sonorously now. I said thanks Harry. He gave a final stroke before withdrawing his arm. Remember, he said, standing up, empty your mind as well. He then laughed. It shouldn't take long, he said. He and the torch were gone. I lay awake with Judy Garland. When I say I was with her what I mean is Judy Garland as Dorothy in *The Wizard Of Oz* and how she sang in black and white with Toto trembling on the farm equipment. A plough? Anyway so say she was sixteen at the time. Sixteen and ruining a million hearts. I felt I might tell Harry of my proposed black and white system for inducing sleep, but it turned out not to be successful anyway because on the third or fourth rendition I had another adrenaline rush. I called Harry back to report it and said it didn't seem right I could have all these tablets and still suffer. Again he waited with me. At least on nights, I said, he didn't have to put up with Cheryl's sleeping difficulties. This was in the very early days of my being here. Before the Cheryl Incident, I think of it. I had a regular hope K or someone would come to say there'd been a mistake. I'd quickly realised home became most precious when you were drawn from it against your will and that to some extent an ability to imagine yourself continually returned to familiar things made life easier to bear. The clock on the upper third of the wall had luminous dots where numbers would be in the day and at the tip of the sweeping second hand sat another luminous dot, so if I wasn't careful I'd end up watching life go round. It was an illusion, Harry told me, that time moved in that kind of way but all the same we each had only so many seconds left and they were ticking. I had to say Harry, you're not helping me sleep just as my father hadn't with the petunias and Harry said sorry, he was probably tired because he hadn't had chance for a nap before coming on duty. He'd been up all day. I said: Harry you need to take better care of yourself, especially after what you've told me about Cheryl is it? He said: Yeah – sulkily I felt – Cheryl. Interesting isn't it, I said, some people pronounce it Cheryl like you've just done while others say Cheryl and he said: She doesn't like it when anyone says Cheryl rather than Cheryl and I said: I see why. People have a right to be called what they're called. He and the torch sat back in the chair as if he might be planning to make a night of it. The beam was passing across the counterpane and striking the wall at the far side. I said: Thanks Harry, thinking this might prompt him to turn it off and let me get back to Judy now the adrenaline had cleared, but he remained there a few more luminous minutes. I said it sounded like the Major was on the point of victory and Harry said yes, but he lost the battle more often than not and I asked if he knew what battle it was and Harry said he didn't. He just assumed the Major was doomed to revisit the field of conflict on a nightly basis and that he won or lost depending on an inner variable. Harry then said if he was ever on duty at night and I was discreet about it he wouldn't mind providing me with a couple of extra tablets to help the insomnia. I said didn't he mean to help *alleviate* the insomnia, and he said with an insincere chuckle, yes he had and trust me to pick up on it. It's no wonder you don't sleep, he said, and I said there were so many things to go through first like how was K and whatever happened to the dog from up the road and if I wasn't to be conscious of death when it came how come I knew I was alive now and other considerations, and Harry joked I might need more tablets than he first thought and I said and even when I've sorted those things I do like to have a think about Fiona, and he said I had a feeling you liked her, by the way you rock when she gives you tea you old goat and I said in fact Harry there's only K for me and the little thing about Fiona's purely medicinal and Harry said I don't for a minute blame you. I've had Fiona moments myself. What is it about her do you think? I said. He said: Hair maybe, face, biscuits. I said for me it was hair voice though not so much biscuits and wasn't it odd how you could love a K yet have Fiona moments, and Harry said: I believe we need to stop telling ourselves off about every little thing especially at our time of life, though I guess he'd said 'our' to soften the blow. I said: Harry – or something like that – Harry, you do realise, don't you, how thin the membrane is between you there in the ordinary world and us in here. It would take only a careless fingernail to rupture it permanently.

*

Did you open it? I turned from my work, which was in fact me in the cubicle with a pen tapping blank papers. Henderson's hair shone in the overhead light. I gave a few swings. Open what? I said, though I already had a notion. The Eternity Sweet. We left one for you, Henderson said. It sounded like a musical composition. Henderson however wasn't the sort you could joke with about stuff like that. I nodded towards the drawer where I'd hidden the praline. I haven't actually, I said. Till now I've been enjoying the occasional speculation as to who might have left it. Now I know it's you and – I guess – Mrs Henderson, a little of the excitement has gone. Aha, Henderson said, once you've read inside the wrapper you'll change your tune. I'd been feeling relaxed till he'd arrived. Earlier on Alexander had popped in carrying files, and had said he hoped I'd had a good weekend because he'd had an awful one. He'd suggested to Miriam they might discuss their friendship and she'd told him that after his behaviour on the canal she was thinking that not such a good idea. It seems I'm destined not to have an interesting time like everyone else on earth, he said. The look in his eye suggested in view of this maybe I'd be good enough to let him explore his K feelings and I'd put a look into my eye that warned him off the plan, so he'd soon taken his files and left. The Office was less stuffy than it had been. Sutton had greeted me with gusto as I'd arrived. Now Henderson had rattled my expectation this was to be a better day. I've been discussing you with my wife, he said. We agree if you gave yourself to the Lord you'd be happier. But would he? I said. I was about to apologise when Henderson reminded me neither he nor Mrs Henderson assigned gender to the object of their worship, though for purely working purposes at church and sometimes at home for simplicity they said he too. So you *do* ascribe gender to the object of your worship some of the time, I said. The lack of a God shows in you as anxiety and pickiness, Henderson said. He came to sit on the corner of my desk. Only then did I see a triangular sandwich in one hand. To take the pressure off myself I asked if it was Emmental yet and he said no, Cheddar, glancing at it sadly afterwards. But then he must remember he was lucky in this day and age to have cheese at all, he went on. I keep thinking I'm a fan of Stilton, I said, though I wouldn't eat it full time. No one's asking you to surely, Henderson said. It's quite rich. Yes, I said. This was one of several cheese conversations we'd had. It seemed this one was to have as little success and longevity as the others. So maybe when I've gone you could have a look inside the wrapper, Henderson said. It'll change your life. I'm not sure I want it changed I said, not in that way at least. You're always stiff and out of sorts, Henderson went on. The Lord could help you. Oh don't get me wrong, I said, as if Henderson had suggested he might be about to, I like the idea of there being a Lord but I can't bring myself to be as enthusiastic as you – and Mrs Henderson. It would be the making of you, Henderson said. I happened to be gazing towards the distant rectangle of light blue. Thanks, I said. Having remembered the expedition K and me had that time, I wished she was there instead of Henderson and the sandwich. Of course, he said suddenly, it can only be called Stilton if it's made according to a strict code within the counties of Nottinghamshire, Leicestershire or Derbyshire. I didn't know that, I said. Thanks Henderson. I'd wondered just before reaching 'Henderson' if I should put 'mister' beforehand. I'll plunge into my next Stilton with renewed vigour, I added. He slid off the desk. The Lord doesn't want people who aren't civil, he said. I asked him if it was calling him Henderson that had annoyed him but no, it was the tone I'd used when saying about plunging into Stilton. It's true I find sarcasm irresistible when the chips are down. Henderson reminded me about the praline once more – suggesting that my opening of it was even more urgent than he had at first thought – and left the cubicle in turn leaving me to feel I'd been unkind. I took hold of the pen and rattled it against the pile of paper. Phone K don't phone K. If I did phone I'd have to make my way to the foyer where Sutton would keep an eye on me, calculating to himself what the phone system would record exactly – the amount of time I stood waiting for K to answer. History had shown she was unlikely to. In that case, I thought, why bother going to the foyer at all? There were calculations to collate, statements of intent to verify, synopses to proofread. I leaned back, causing the pen, which was still in my hand, to make a line on the paper beneath. In the unfathomable distance a passenger jet passed across the sky. I'd had a dream of life drawing towards the lip of a waterfall. I'd told Alexander about it come to think of it and he'd joked about me needing a stronger paddle. I sort of missed him being here now Henderson had gone. Sure no one was imminent, I slid open my bottom drawer and drew out the praline. Sometimes when I'd decided to do a thing some inner force – Ormerod calls it The Indecision Web – makes it difficult for me to carry it through. I was thinking if I opened the praline I'd be doomed to mention it to Henderson next time I saw him. If, on the other hand, I didn't open it I'd be in a position of having to explain why, given his insistence that I did. I felt I'd been blackmailed into a response even though my preferred one would have been not to have received a praline in the first place. Yes, I wouldn't ring K because of her refusal-to-answer tendency and anyway I was fed up suddenly of having to do anything in front of Sutton. My only recourse just then was to find once again in the landscape the light blue rectangle. We'd imagined on the way to it nut trees and red squirrels, the squirrels being added by K while I'd thrown in cowslips and a young dog. In reality I was embedded on a swivel chair wishing home time would come.

*

The world was pinned up in an elongated form that years later we learned was the Mercator Projection, and Mrs Strachan was rapping a stick against the North Pole. Who can say what Geography is? she asked. Miss, said Horace, it's where you get countries and stuff. Mrs Strachan huffed. The huff induced coughing, which took a while to die. *Stuff*, Horace?

What do you mean? Miss, said Alexander, he means it's the science of the surface of the earth and its inhabitants. That's what I meant Miss, Horace said. He grinned at Alexander who'd been reading from a book below desk level. And who can say what shape the world is? Mrs Strachan asked. Horace – trying to make up – said it was round. Mrs Strachan said in some senses it was, but the answer she'd been looking for was spherical. Yes, Horace said, that's what I meant, pherical. Fatty prevented us from learning more – about the world's shape at least – by vomiting. It ran along the pencil grooves, filled the inkwell and poured to the floor. Probably he hadn't come to be called Fatty at that stage, but it's hard to filter him from the changes of subsequent years. It was suggested we went to the playground while the mess was cleared by the janitor. I stood by the coke bunker. K came to see how I was getting along. She knew I feared vomit. I told her it had made me feel ill myself but that it wasn't as bad as I first feared and maybe that meant I was coming to terms. Oh I don't mind vomit, she said. Unless it's milk vomit. My phobias aren't selective, I said. She had her hair divided into halves, each of which ended in a ribbon. It made her look as if she was pleased. I asked her – because I was afraid of illness generally – if she'd detected anything in Fatty's manner earlier. I didn't want it to be the case he had a bug and that there was a risk we'd all get it. She said she'd seen him eating white chocolate before assembly. She wasn't sure if the chocolate had made him vomit but it had to be a suspect. I said I wished I was the sort of child who could see someone vomit then say I felt the chocolate eaten earlier had to be a suspect. K said she'd said it like that because she knew I enjoyed convoluted sentences. She didn't use the word convoluted. I'm attributing it in retrospect. He eats many sugary things, she said. He was gorging chocolate mice on his way to school yesterday. Smithson would say that would be his mum's fault, I said. Gorging as a love substitute. K reminded me that for the purposes of evenhandedness and enlightened attitudes I should have said his dad *and* mum's fault. Okay then, I said. The playground itself turned watery. Leaves blew across it from trees and bushes beyond the fence. The school cat was chasing the larger ones. Did you finish the Baboons? K asked. I said no, I had some small areas of Serengeti to go. I was alarmed to see Fatty come outside with one of the other boys. He took a tennis ball from his pocket and started kicking it against the school wall. I told K he couldn't have a bug if he could play football so soon. Yeah, K said. It must be the sugary things. They'll be bad for his heart because he has to lug so much of himself about. I loved her when she'd said lug. Before I could tell her, she said it couldn't be easy being called Fatty and really we should use his real name. I said and what would that be? though I was joking. Paul, she said. Funny name, I said. It doesn't feel long enough. Just after kicking the tennis ball against the wall once more Fatty rose a foot or two above the ground, leaned forward and unleashed another torrent of vomit. The sloping asphalt caused some of it to run towards a drain by the entrance. Funny, K said, how you can vomit because of sugary things without there necessarily being evidence of what exactly on the ground. Tell me when he's finished, I said. It's down his jumper and trousers as well, K said. Isn't Mrs Strachan here? I asked. No, K said, but the janitor's standing by. I don't know how she knew he was standing by; how she differenti-ated that status from others he engaged in. The odd thing was how Fatty looked happy between bouts and how, if it hadn't been wedged against a ruffle of vomit, he would probably have gone to retrieve the ball. I said some of this to K, who said not everyone had problems with vomit, even though all but the hardiest had moved to this far side of the playground. K wondered how best to put across the smell. She mentioned rotting milk although no, that didn't fully explain it. And the lumps? Where did they come from? From Fatty, I said grimly. By being grim I was hoping to cheer myself. The sound of retching was followed by further splashing. My heart was beating quickly. We were bounced at by Alexander. Fatty's got chronic something, he said. The teachers are on about it. I asked him if it was catching. I didn't hear anything about that, Alexander said. He half turned as if to appreciate Fatty's next bout. The janitor's covered what he threw up in the classroom with sawdust, Alexander said. Apparently this soaks up the juice so the solids can be shovelled easily. Alexander seemed to share an invulnerability towards vomit with K. Don't know what they'll do with this lot out here. Probably get a hose to it, he went on. Yeah, K said, swill it into the drain.

Kandinsky wanted the patio doors left open. Atkins again demanded they be closed. Kandinsky said he would have words with Harry if Atkins kept on. Atkins informed Kandinsky he felt it was a degree or two less warm today and that a draught was coming through. He then asked him to look at the Major shivering. Don't give me that, Kandinsky said, he shivers whatever the weather. I might have known you'd prove yourself irretrievably self-centred, Atkins said. He reached from his chair, snatched up his compendium and put it down again. It was the action of someone who wanted to draw greater attention to his own sorrows. I'm grateful no one asked me what I felt because I wouldn't have been able to say. I was remembering K coming back from what she called a dip. You should go in, she said. It's lovely. They wouldn't have put pollution warnings in the gift shop for no reason, I told her. Alexander was a hundred yards further along. Miriam was breaststroking offshore. Plus, I said, I don't relish being half-naked with people. K rubbed her hair with a towel. I didn't see any pollution, she said. She glanced round. And Miriam's obviously not bothered. It gathers suddenly, I said, not knowing if it did. I don't expect it'll do us any harm anyway, K said. It was only an amber alert. I don't know why, but I replied with: Yeah, right, and hauled myself onto the shelf of rock behind me. Alexander was having difficulties too. He'd been saying earlier he didn't yet know if the times he spent with Miriam constituted a relationship. I fancied as he watched her he was on the lookout for clues to his status. I don't know how many times we've been here, K was saying, and still you haven't been in. The water's always cold, pollutants notwithstanding, I said. K told me as usual that once I'd been in a minute or so the cold would pass. The best thing's to plunge, she said. That's all very well, I said. You're a plunger. We could even conclude you plunge into life itself while I more often stroll its beaches testing a toe here, a toe there. As K rubbed her hair the flesh on her upper legs shook. From looking at them, thinking myself impolite, I searched for Miriam's bathing cap and soon rediscovered it moving parallel to the beach in tiny increments. Maybe we'll get out the Frisbee when Miriam's back, K said. I told her I couldn't wait. K sighed. I heard it through the rubbing.

I waited for her to say wasn't it time I cheered up, but then I supposed I didn't need her to given I could imagine it. I'm not sure anyone plays Frisbee any more, I said. It's had its day. Don't be daft, K said. Frisbees are timeless. They go back to a game with a cake-pan in the nineteen thirties, I said, hoping this might end my unappreciated days. It had actually been Alexander who'd told me this earlier when I'd revealed to him there was a danger we'd be forced to have a game at some point. He went on to say the word Frisbee was a trade name and that strictly speaking we should call them flying discs. It intrigued me Alexander had at his disposal information about things he didn't even like. If it comes to a vote, he said, make sure you side with me. If it's fifty-fifty, you never know, they might cave in. I'm rubbish at flying disc games anyhow. Don't, I said, call them flying discs because of what you've just told me. No one'll mind if you say Frisbee. In fact they'll welcome it. It made us feel not quite men because Miriam had driven here with K beside her in the passenger seat and us in the back. K and she talked occasionally, in bouts you might say, while Alexander and me craned slightly forward to hear. But usually we gave up and stared out of our own windows watching a blur of the world. I brought myself back to the beach by shifting against the rock. I'll take your word for it, K said, but you won't get out of playing easily. I feared that might be the case, I said. It would have been too hopeless then to cite Alexander's reluctance also. He didn't so much look at as examine Miriam's bathing cap as it progressed through the sea. I was mightily pleased on the whole because he didn't seem as interested in K today. Anyway, K said, you could do with the exercise. That's partly what makes you grumpy. I'm not grumpy, I said. When I said I wasn't grumpy it brought home to me how grumpy I was and yet there didn't seem to be enough reason for it. Finished with her towelling, K went round the rock I was sitting on to change into her clothes. I called that I'd keep one eye out for peeping Toms till she came back. Really, I heard her call back, it's only when you hide bodies they become interesting. I've read something to that end, I said. All the same I'm glad you're taking the rock option. I slid off, alerted K to my intention and wandered to Alexander, joining him as it were at the shoulder in his Miriam scan. You're staring, I said to him.

I could tell from back there. You don't want her to think badly of you. I'm merely enjoying the sea, he said. If you look through history you'll find most people do when they're adjacent to it. Come on, I said, I can tell you're uptight. Why not join me for a stroll till Miriam comes back? She'll thank you in the long run. Alexander looked at me momentarily. All right then, I suppose – yes – I do have an eye on her, but it's only because of the rip tide and the pollution. Me and K were talking about that, I said. She doesn't think it'll be harmful. The pollution I mean. Just because someone thinks something isn't harmful, Alexander said, going quiet then because he couldn't think how to proceed. A newly walking child toppled towards us while her mum followed ready to catch her. We were babies once, Alexander said suddenly. I had a sun hat like that. With frills. We both did, I said. I like the way he's waving his arms about as he comes forward, Alexander said. It's a toddler thing to do. It is, I said, though I'm not sure it is a he. I'm saying he to simplify matters, Alexander said. I don't like using 'it' with babies. But clearly she's a girl, I said. Notice the vague definition about the brow ridges. Oh all right, she, Alexander said. After a pause I said: If I was that age again one of the things I'd be enjoying would be sand under my toes. Oh me too, Alexander said. It's also nice to have a mum behind you though I suppose as we get older we should have some kind of God to take her place. Just this week, he said, old Henderson at work gave me an Eternity Praline. Yeah, I've had one, I said sadly. Isn't he a complete bastard, Alexander said. Henderson I mean. I don't think so, I said, neither in a literal nor a figurative sense. He's only trying to pass on the joy he and Mrs Henderson evidently experience. Well I can't be doing with it, Alexander said. I like misery. Me too, I said. I thought the praline was from an admirer initially. An admirer! Alexander said brusquely. What about K? I'd said too much. Had it been from an admirer, I said – which obviously it wasn't – it wouldn't have made me guilty of anything. We're unlikely to go through life with no one taking an interest in us. Alexander laughed. You'll note, he said, we're talking about admirers and what have you even though we know the pralines weren't from one. It's like we've filtered from the conversation the things we're not interested in – Henderson and pralines

– and latched on to a topic we do enjoy – admirers – all be they not applicable. Can you say all be they? I asked, at the same time having one cruel eye on the incremental Miriam. No idea, Alexander said, but I'm trying to make it a rule that if I say something it means it can and will be said. That's forthright of you, I said. Indeed, Alexander said. It might be though after the dreaded car journey down here I'm trying to imagine myself having a bit of power. It was wrong of Miriam to have K in the front instead of me. I don't think you can say it was wrong per se, I said. The word 'wrong' has a moral twang. It might not have been the best idea for you and me, but it wasn't wrong as such. And men are unutterably dull in cars. We'll have to see, Alexander said, if we can't change seating arrangements on the way back. No offence but I don't want to spend another two hours in the back with you. And it'll be worse in the dark. I agreed it would be worse as at last Alexander gave in to my prompting to have a stroll. We had to weave to avoid a chap spelling HELP with his heel. He was on the P and doing well. A small girl nearby clapped occasionally. Alexander said the chap was most likely her dad and a hero to the little girl whatever he did with his heel. Why HELP though? I asked, assuming it to be rhetorical. I suggested to Miriam I might do MIRIAM earlier, Alexander said. She looked daggers at me. I'm not surprised, I said. It might well have been the death knell of any advance between you. Alexander sighed. I had a feeling you'd say that. But I just wanted her to know I was feeling more than ordinary friendship. We'd slowed even though we'd been going slow to begin with. Funny, this relationship business, I said. I often wonder if it would be as important if we had a few acres of land to plough with oxen. Oxen reminded me of Jugg. It could easily be he was in the ether watching for linguistic excess. I'm glad to have seen her in a swimming costume, Alexander said. Do you think that's bad of me? Don't be daft, I said. It's only natural. Genetically you'll have been screaming to look. Yes, Alexander said, but I was also disappointed to realise how *much* I'd been looking forward to it. Were you? What? I said, looking forward to it or disappointed to realise *you* were? The first, Alexander said. I can't say I was looking forward to it or not looking forward to it, I said. But yes, I'll grant you she has a pleasing figure. Alexander grunted. No one but you would say figure. It's so non-committal. I glanced at him. It's non-committal, I said, because I'm not interested in whatever shape she might be. I can't help thinking about her dead husband whenever I look at her, Alexander said. You can be sure he's kissed every inch. That's as may be, I said, but as you pointed out, he's no longer with us. We chuckled at the euphemism. The chuckle lasted ten or fifteen yards. We realised too we'd fallen into a slow march to boot. Where's K anyway? Alexander said, glancing round. Changing behind the rocks, I said. Alexander said oh and glanced round again. He told me he'd been reading an astronomical report that said they'd detected galaxies one hundred billion light years from earth. What I've been wondering is this, he went on. He bowed his head and looked into his palm. Yes? I said. Well, if you assume we're in the middle… I interrupted to ask the middle of what? and he said that if there are galaxies one hundred billion light years in that direction – he pointed left – and other galaxies one hundred billion light years in *that* direction – he pointed right – that means we're in the middle of a two hundred billion light-year expanse and I didn't think the universe was that old frankly. The way he'd said frankly suggested he was angry at something for this possibility. I don't expect we'll ever know, I said. We need to find an astronomer, Alexander said. I looked around myself in a show of trying. I then heard myself say yes two hundred billion light years was a long time. Alexander took out both hands. Given, he said, light travels one hundred and eighty-six thousand miles per second then over the course of one hundred billion years it would travel… He breathed heavily through his nose. Let's work it out when we've got a calculator or stumbled upon that astronomer, I said. Otherwise my head hurts. The sun had caught the crest of Miriam's swimming cap. Her right hand rose and flapped momentarily, I presume to greet us. Miriam just waved, I said. You weren't looking. She does things when I'm not, never when I am, Alexander said. I really do think if you abandoned the idea of a love relationship with her altogether, I said, it would make one more likely. That's the thing, Alexander said. I'm not sure I want one, not really, but it's odd how hard it is to work out if you *really* want one till you've got one. Something in this made him select a nearby pebble and hurl it. A dog raced to retrieve it and soon dropped it at Alexander's feet. The effort of stopping quickly bunched sand between its claws. Alexander walked on. Typical, he said. I've had similar troubles myself, I told him. We slow-marched for a while. The beach had failed to live up to what had been secretly expected of it. At least she comes places with me, Alexander said eventually. That counts for something. I've had other women friends who look at you like you're mad if you suggest the coast. Though I chose not to argue, I was sure he hadn't really had other women friends at all. I think it's not only good of her to come but also kind of her to suggest using her car, I said. You're right, Alexander said, but it's not purely unselfish. She's said many times being the driver makes her feel in control. Her husband once drove her into the countryside for a day out but left her stranded at a picnic site after they'd had a row. She had to make her way home ten miles on foot. It was early on in their courtship. She told me she was surprised to realise zoologists had tempers. Oh yes, I said, statisti-cally they're right up there. You know the worst? Alexander said. I didn't bother saying what because I knew he'd carry on anyway. When I thought of her making her way home alone, he said, I felt glad he'd died in an avalanche. I was reading about avalanches the other day, I said. There's a science to them. If you get one sort of snow they happen all the time. Another sort and the chances go down. It's a poorly funded area of research because statistically – again – they don't often happen anyway. Don't go where there's any snow would be my advice, Alexander said. He was occasionally on his toes to track Miriam. I warned him again of the dangers. It's happening automatically, he said. I just think to myself I won't be doing that again and then I do it. So you think she has a nice figure? Really? I didn't say nice, I said. I said pleasing. And before you say any more I mean it scientifically, taking into account things like propor-tion. It's wrong of us to assess her in that way at all really, Alexander said. I mean if we knew she and K were sizing us up physically we'd be morti-fied. I'm not sure mortified, I said, but yes perhaps we'd find it narrow-minded. Anyway someone said we don't fall in love with people we find attractive so much as find attractive those we fall in love with.

231

Oh? Alexander said as he descended from his latest toes, who was that? I asked him, naturally, who was what, and he said the person who told me and I was obliged to confess it was one of those occasions when I'd attributed one of my own beliefs to a third party to avoid any possible backlash. Well mate, Alexander said having slapped my shoulder, you won't be getting any from me. I thought it was quite good. Thanks, I said. We began without having to say to one another a shallow curve that was unconsciously intended, I suppose, to bring us closer to the sea as well as taking us back the way we'd come. K was sitting on the rock shelf. She had, as Alexander pointed out, a flying disc in one hand. We tried spectacularly to transmogrify our march back into a stroll. Miriam's not out yet anyway, I said, and K wanted to wait for her. This'll be my chance to see her shrivelled, Alexander said. I told him he was in danger of becoming sexist or misogynist – I wasn't sure which – and he said merely he'd still feel the same about her even if she was shrivelled but that he was just interested in knowing anyway. Like with himself, he said in his defence, he developed a sore nose whenever he was near – let alone in – seawater and he hoped he'd be excused for that by any potential partner. The body does have a way of spilling secrets once you're caught up with a woman, he said and I said I hadn't realised he was already caught up and he said he thought he must be because he kept having squiggles in his upper chest and I said surely he could think of a better way to describe them than squiggles and he said on the contrary he'd realised since knowing Miriam squiggles were just the thing. If it's as you say, I told him, perhaps you should come clean with her. This might be in contradiction to what I was saying earlier but I hadn't realised it was so serious. Oh yes, Alexander said. I've got three bed positions. On my back to consider the World. On my right to go to sleep, but on my left – I save it up – for thinking about her. We're much alike you and me, I said, although generally I wish I wasn't like anyone – except obviously with me it's K rather than Miriam and unlike you I don't have a fixed World position. K has said sometimes she sleeps flat on her front with her arms at her side and I said to her didn't that block her nose but she said apparently not. I used to think all sorts when I woke up, Alexander said, but now the word Miriam comes and it sticks till I get myself out of bed and put the kettle on. He paused. Do you really not have a fixed World position? I find it vital otherwise World considerations interfere with me trying to get to sleep. What I've said isn't quite true, I said. I do try to think about the World in just one position but occasionally I find it gets taken over by what to you might be much smaller things. The Hagendorff Syndrome for example. And what's to become of me. Oh yeah, Alexander said, I'd forgotten. That's my point, I said, but Doctor Mainwaring's said time and again I mustn't underestimate the range of its effects. Surprising how easily then the World falls into third place. I was noting how as we came closer to the water and whenever my foot pressed down, the sand became lighter and the lightness flared outwards. It was helping me forgive myself for citing something Doctor Mainwaring had never said, but I was sure was truth. So anyway, Alexander said, I lie there thinking about Miriam. I guessed it was serious because when it isn't I try to think about a person and the thought soon changes into something else but with Miriam even when I start out trying to think other things they turn into her. In she comes with her hair and her smile. I even visualise her neck as we have imaginary embraces. If I can't say figure, you can't say embraces, I said, impatient suddenly. Then again, Alexander went on, I've noticed that if I see her profile from about forty-five degrees she isn't half so attractive. To you, I said. That doesn't mean she wouldn't remain attractive at all angles to someone else. I hope you don't mean you, Alexander said, hanging back. I've apologised for the K business I don't know how many times. No I don't mean me, I said. I was just surprised to hear you talk about her in that way and was theorising about other men to nudge you towards some insight in that area. But it's true, Alexander said, his voice rising. She just isn't the same from forty-five degrees and I'd challenge anyone to argue if they checked her out. I wanted to bring this particular conversation thread to an end so asked instead what sort of things he thought about at night under the heading of the World. He said he started out on natural disasters (when applicable) and global injustice, then usually found himself narrowing it down to issues specific to this country. Do you think, I said, you'll still have a World component if you finally get it together with Miriam and share a bed with her? Alexander grinned as if the possibility hadn't occurred to him. How would I know? he said. I haven't spent the night with a woman. I simulated amazement. What ever? I said. I have intimated as much before, Alexander said. I told him I'd always assumed he'd been just trying to protect his secrets. He reminded me I hadn't spent the night with a woman either and I had to remind *him* that wasn't strictly true because of the times me and K had been up talking till late and had fallen asleep in the same room. Oh that doesn't count at all, Alexander said.

*

Ham, said Atkins. No, said Kandinsky, chicken. No, no, definitely ham, Atkins said. He took up his compendium as if to close the matter down. Kandinsky was laughing as he asked Atkins if it was off the bone or the re-formed stuff. For a while Atkins tossed the words silently then said you won't get far in life making fun of people. Kandinsky said: I'll have you know I have a degree in Horticulture. Fat lot of good it did you, Atkins said, scowling at his compendium. It was an hour or two after lunch. Jaundice had earlier said loudly and repeatedly he was bored. Smetham said yes, he was as well. So the mood had swollen till I imagine we each thought why yes, we all were. What was it with Wednesdays? Harry had agreed to the principle earlier of procuring a new ball for the table tennis table to replace the one ruptured by Tobias Mawk, but there was often a large gap between the principle of a thing being agreed upon and it becoming established. Colquahoon had said that though he had no intention of playing himself, wouldn't it be judicious for Harry to procure say six balls so that if other acts of vandalism took place, there wouldn't be any waiting? I believe everyone looked at Fiona when she arrived with the tea in expectation of her lightening our situation. She remarked on the general glumness as she began pouring. It's because we're bored, Jaundice said. And Atkins keeps going on about human flesh tasting of re-formed ham. You could tell Atkins was impatient with what he saw as everyone's intolerable mental state. He put the compendium noisily aside. Firstly Mr Jarndyce, he said, I don't keep on about anything – I merely offered the topic to relieve our tedium and secondly

I didn't say anything about people tasting of *re-formed* ham. That was Mr Kandinsky's idea of a joke. I meant good ham. Ham off the bone. Fiona said she felt it might be better to talk about something less controversial. The reason I made an attempt at humour in respect of your topic Mr Atkins, Kandinsky said, is because it certainly wasn't the kind to ease the mood. And whatever we say we're unlikely to reach a definitive answer to the conundrum anyway. Colquahoon leaned round to say years ago his next-door neighbour had eaten his own wife. Kandinsky was the first to recover. All of her? he asked. Colquahoon cleared his throat. They say that was his intention, but he'd only roasted and eaten one arm before the police caught up with him. Atkins said it was a shame he wasn't here now. We could have asked him directly what people taste like. Ah yes, Colquahoon said, but a wife wouldn't taste the same as a stranger. Would it be like having your usual shepherd's pie at a different restaurant? Smetham asked tentatively. When no one answered, I'd say it was because they didn't want to get him enthused gastronomically. Fiona had her softest lilt when she said: Who'd like a game of charades later? Only Major Gwillingington raised his hand, and then with additional palsy. He almost always raised a hand in answer to questions. Kandinsky reckoned it was military training. Right you are then, Fiona said, again softly, I'll ask another time. Take no notice of us, Kandinsky said, we're in a pickle today. Don't include me in your pickles, Atkins said. Actually Fiona I was thinking just now how it might be that I'm in a coma and I'm imagining all this, you included – sorry – and that one day I might wake up as a stockbroker married with three children and a house in Henley-on-Thames. Do you think it's possible Fiona, do you? Kandinsky made a sound in his throat. Really Mr Atkins, it's rude to suggest Fiona might not be real then ask questions of her. He looked round, as if trying to gauge the level of support for his comment. Smetham said he knew Fiona was real because she'd just poured him a cup of tea. When Kandinsky adjusted his glasses it was the first time I registered he wore any. Now, now, Mr Smetham, he said, much as I dislike Mr Atkins's opener on this topic, you have to see, surely, it's not about you knowing if poor Fiona's real or not. If Mr Atkins is imagining you in his coma, *neither* of you are real. Atkins nodded. As much as I object to Mr Kandinsky's aggressive demeanour, he said, I must support what he has just said. But I can feel heat through my cup! Smetham said. Kandinsky was out through the patio doors and back again. He walked that day like an animated toy soldier. He later revealed (as if he'd been saving it for the right moment) he was having pain in both hips. My mother had that, Smetham said. You want to make sure you don't go far in damp weather. I'm hardly likely to, am I? Kandinsky said. I'd never heard as loud a sigh as Atkins issued then. Getting back to the coma theory Fiona, he said, I've often lain awake worrying about it. Don't get me wrong, he went on, I wouldn't entirely mind finding out *some* of us in here weren't real, but if it was you I'd be devastated. This comment coincided with Fiona handing Atkins his cup of tea. He blew her a kiss. Jaundice asked what would happen if we were all in comas. If we were all in comas we wouldn't be having this conversation, Kandinsky said forcefully, adding: This is the worst Wednesday I can remember. Colquahoon said that yes, for the whole of his adult life he'd found Wednesdays difficult too, but that this one was exceptional. It's probably because, Atkins said after a sip of tea, Wednesdays are between weekends. I hate it, Kandinsky said, when Mr Atkins states the obvious Fiona, I really do. Atkins was incensed Kandinsky should refer to him in the third person when he was there having tea. But I thought we were in comas, Smetham said. Though he made no direct move, I'm sure he was eyeing up the vicinity for something other than tea to consume. We hadn't so far had our bourbons. Fiona varied the way she handed these out. Sometimes they came with each tea as it was presented. Other times she'd finish the teas and go round separately. When she got to me with tea, and at the same time as smelling her, I asked her discreetly why Harry had been so odd about Cheryl recently. When Fiona asked who Cheryl was, a sensation threatened my brain. In the end I said never mind, forget it, and Fiona being Fiona she left me with my tea and went to do the next cup. I was thinking to myself through the afternoon: Note to self – don't mention Cheryl to Harry any more or anyone else for that matter. To this note to self I added a small burst of laughter that surely didn't belong there. I referred to you in the third person Mr Atkins, because it saved me having to be unpleasant to you directly, Kandinsky said. But you've no reason to be unpleasant in the first place, replied Atkins. I was merely suggesting the most obvious reason for Wednesdays being difficult. Smetham said more loudly than he normally spoke: If I was in a coma I wouldn't be eating this bourbon. Kandinsky stood over Smetham, who cowered in his chair. It's not about you being in a coma, he said. It's about Mr Atkins being in one. Fiona asked why anyone had to be in a coma, which Colquahoon agreed was a fair point. It might also have something to do with us not having fruit bowls to do on a Wednesday. Rarely for him, Atkins got up and walked out to the patio, even then down on to the lawn. My guess was he'd gone slowly to avoid anyone feeling he was storming, but there was such deliberation to his movement, it was like that's what he was doing anyway. Kandinsky went to the patio doors to watch after him. Now we'll get some peace, he said.

*

Warblers, woodpeckers, thrushes, finches. Smithson put the pamphlet aside. Good combination, he went on, forty-five acres of woodland and wildlife and three hundred years of the dead. A low sun cast shimmers of copper across trees and over headstones, many of the headstones at angles brought about by years of soil movement. Smithson tapped the pamphlet. At night there are bats, badgers and foxes. Spooky. I told him there was no such thing as spooks and so therefore no atmosphere or location we could rightly describe as spooky. He ignored me. And could there be a more restful place? he said. He widened his arms to embrace it. Just up over the ridge, he said, pointing, stand Monuments of National Importance. I read it just now. In the pamphlet. Things are often up over the ridge, I said, although it was an utterance from an older version of myself. In a metaphorical sense at least, I added. Smithson adjusted his theatrical pipe. I understand what you mean, he said, though I find your precociousness unpalatable. Blame Jugg, I said. Smithson picked up the pamphlet again. This time of year, he said, people come here to view the burnet, the saxifrage, the field scabious. He put the pamphlet down. This was somewhere the late Mrs Smithson and me walked, oh not often, just half a dozen times during our life together and then mostly in the winter when she'd dare me to explore the dark with her. Like you, she had no fears of that kind but knew I had one or two tucked away despite Therapeutic Specialism. He'd patted the top pocket of his tweed jacket. Is this why we're here now? I asked. Partly, he said, partly. Each partly had been made up of a sigh. But I was also hoping to draw our attention to death and to find out what it is you don't like about it. A robin on a twig almost directly above us sang robustly. Ah, Smithson said, one of our finest feathered friends. I told him Father used to say they'd sit on the handle of his spade urging him to get on with the digging because they knew worms would be unearthed. I doubt robins know what's going on in detail, Smithson said, but yes, I guess you could extract the principle with a boiling down of the components. He started to laugh. In the midst of death he'd discovered the very engine of life. When he'd recovered he asked how things *really* were with me and I said they weren't so good what with home having fallen apart and he said well that's grim at your age and I said yes. It reinforced in me to some extent the futility of exchanges between people. Had the exchange not taken place I seriously wondered if I'd have been any the worse for it. Is this Jugg involved? Smithson asked. His question was a tapered flag with indifference at its narrowest end. I couldn't believe we'd been through so many sessions without my having mentioned him. I explained briefly who he was and Smithson apologised for having got the wrong end of the stick and I said it was bound to happen from time to time, what with sticks having two ends most often, and Smithson laughed again so heartily, he fell sideways from the bench having imagined, I suppose, there was a rail there. A woman coming by with an infant in a pushchair and a small white dog helped him up and asked if he was all right, and Smithson said he'd overdone hilarity and the woman made a joke herself about not expecting to find hilarity in such a place and the reason, she said, she was bringing her daughter here was to familiarise her with the concept of death so it wouldn't come as a shock and Smithson was crossing and uncrossing his legs as he explained how, as a Therapeutic Specialist, he was having to deal with the effects of Death Denial in his clients on a daily basis. It's partly why I've brought Peter here, he said. Snap then!

238

the woman said with a look on her face as if she was about to. She eyed
me for a moment before asking if I was his and he said no, not as such.
We were here in an official capacity. Since he wasn't allowed to reveal the
exact nature of our relationship, I guess he was hoping the woman would
remember what he'd said about his being a Therapeutic Specialist, link
this to official capacity and draw an accurate conclusion. The baby girl
in the pushchair – and to an extent the dog too – writhed as if pleased
to see me. Mum's here too of course, the woman said, nodding towards
the forty-five acres. We're killing two birds with one stone. The robin
used its twig as a springboard to launch itself. It flew to another perch
some distance away. Soon I could make out its song among other songs
surrounding us. I was briefly at Gerald's oilcloth table. Smithson seemed
to appreciate the woman's joke, rocking once as a result. My late wife
and I used to explore here at night, he said, just to give me what she called
the willies. Sorry to hear she's no longer with you, the woman said. Oh
I'm beyond acute pain, Smithson said, though I do miss her especially
when I come to places we walked. You're bound to, the woman said.
Mum always said she didn't mind death because at least it would give her
chance for a lie-down. She was hinting about what hard work us kids had
been, not to mention my dad. Smithson indicated the landscape. Is your
dad…? he asked. The woman said no, he was still terrorising the neigh-
bourhood on a mobility scooter. Ah, Smithson said, that's good to know.
Not the terrorising. The baby girl raised her feet against the pushchair's
restraints, drew her hands into fists and kneaded her cheeks. I began to
think about how people become adults having been children and how it's
mostly noticed by people who've been away a long time or in retrospect
by those looking through photo albums. I then found myself watching
for slow-worms having heard about them in the pamphlet but being not
sure what one would look like. The baby girl laughed when I looked at
her after looking at the ground. It was a game while Smithson worked
through his conversation. My Boo! made the baby girl laugh again
and the dog jump. The dog wore a tartan bow. Well, the woman said,
we'll get going. Try not to fall off any more benches. I'll do my best,
Smithson said. The woman walked forward. The dog rose on to its

paws and began walking too. The baby girl made no show of minding whatever might happen next. Smithson sighed as they moved away. Nice woman, he said. I said yes she was and did he know when we were going to have chance to discuss my situation? It's best to creep towards things rather than jump at them, Smithson said. It's something the late Mrs Smithson used to say. In fact I remember the first time. We were up there. See that beech? We were sitting at the base of it. There are several head-stones nearby. Really old ones. Mrs Smithson had been listening like the fine person she was to the list of my current frustrations – I'm speaking professionally you understand – and that's when she said about creep-ing towards things rather than jumping at them. She wasn't referring to my frustrations, obviously, but to the components of those frustrations, which I won't go into here. She then said – have you heard the phrase Peter? – softly softly catchee monkey? Yes, I have heard of it, I said. From Ormerod. He has said many believe it to have originated with Lord Baden-Powell, who is said to have picked up the phrase while in Ghana with the Ashanti people. Smithson shuffled a little uncomfortably. Well maybe you'd like Ormerod to be your Therapeutic Specialist, he said.

*

By now Bulwark was able to sit in the chair beside his bed, meaning visi-tors had to use one brought in from the corridor. He put aside the small leather-bound book he'd been looking at. *Tristram Shandy*, he said and I, thinking to get things off on the right foot, said no thanks. I had one before I came out. Bulwark scowled, apparently not caring I was giving up part of Saturday to visit him. You must have heard they got the Dean, he said. Yes, I said, a dawn swoop at an address in Lincolnshire according to the paper. We stared at each other, maybe wondering if it would be appropriate to smile. I had to make do in the end with a shimmer in the extremities of Bulwark's facial hair. Have you seen anything of Maureen since? he asked. She's on sick leave, I said. I have to confess I feel guilty, Bulwark went on. If I hadn't had feelings for her none of this would have happened. Oh come on, I said, you don't know that. Maureen might have had admirers before and maybe the Dean was at the end of his tether. I'm hoping she hasn't had a relationship with any student but me actually, Bulwark said. Sorry, I said, sounding as sorry as I could, but I'm not sure she was in a relationship with you however much you feel you were in one with her. Ah now there you're wrong, Bulwark said. The largest part of a relationship takes place even before the relationship has officially started. But yours didn't officially start, I said. I know, Bulwark said with an edge, but that doesn't mean the largest part of it didn't happen. And how would you define this largest part? I asked. He said he was fed up being interrogated by people. People being who, I said and he said you, and I said that's more like it. He craned upwards, looking towards my hands. No cherry creams? The shop was closed, I said. You could have gone to another, Bulwark said. I told him yes I could have, but something in me said: Don't bother, carry on. It's odd how the mind does that, even when you know overriding it would be preferable. Whatever the case, we are without cherry creams. I didn't think you liked them much anyway. The early days of being shot can stem the appetite, Bulwark said. I was thinking what a relief it was to have visual perspective because the plane passing through the pale sky was comfortably small. So what else has been happening? Bulwark asked. Any sign of Jennifer coming in? You hinted she might. Yes, I said bowing my head, I did. Thing is, you remember Bernard Swann? Bulwark asked if I meant the tall stoopy fellow with curling ginger hair and I said yes I did and he said what of him? and I said well, sorry to be the bearer but I'd heard he and Jennifer were seeing one another. Typical, Bulwark said. When he leaned over I felt he might be going to grab *Things To Cheer You Up*. Instead he took a beaker and drank from it. Despite how careful he was, water droplets adhered to his beard. You'll know now why I was cautious, he said. He wiped beard and mouth with the back of his hand and put the beaker back. Swann? he said. He's one of those people I always had a bad feeling about. I shrugged. You're reading too much into it. I don't remember noticing anything between them before. Bulwark rubbed his nose, having recently located it. He said: Remember Induction Day and Maureen herself saying to us first-years there was a ten per cent chance of us eventually divorcing the person on our left and I was at the end of a row? Yes, I said. If it's any comfort I had Swann. He was stooped then too but less curly. Well things haven't got much better since, Bulwark said. Culminating in *this*. A pat at the bedclothes I took to be his attempt to indicate the wound. Mr Opopopopapalous says being shot as a result of a romantic attachment, coupled with the troubles below I was having already, could easily result in a lifetime's impotence. Yes, I said, I can see how they might tie in. Luckily there are books, books and books, Bulwark said. It's not necessary to live with someone, have children, a shed et cetera. I wasn't expecting you to say shed after children I told him. The bullet's deepened your eccentricity. No offence. Bulwark said none was taken. Then he leaned over again and, yes, this time he took hold of *Things To Cheer You Up*. There's a section in here on Boating, he told me. I said to Mum last time she was in how great it would be if we could all afford boats and she said it was suggested probably because the book had been compiled by a wealthy landowner from the Lake District in the 1930s who knew nothing of lowly people. This Mulligan fellow. Bulwark tapped the book where the compiler's name was. But then you never know. If I do get compensation a boat might be on the cards. Then again I say things like a boat might be on the cards but you can bet I won't get one. For a start boats are cumbersome when you're not boating. We haven't got a garage or even a big enough drive. Mum has a friend she plays bridge with who's got a sizable garden so maybe at a push she might let us put it there. Listen, I said, maybe the best solution's not to think boats at all till you actually get one, assuming you do at some point receive compensation. You're right, I suppose, Bulwark said, we're getting ahead of ourselves. I asked him if he'd managed to come up with a cigarette strategy and he said now he was more mobile he was able to wheel himself or be wheeled down to the front entrance where, though it was frowned upon, smoking was tolerated. I had a feeling when he'd said 'be wheeled' he was hinting a smoke would be welcome right now since I was here. Though I find being anything but steeped in self-interest difficult, I put this plan to him and, as I suspected, he readily agreed and was out of his bed, into his dressing gown and on to the wheelchair with a speed reminiscent of the unwounded. Shame we don't have a lake to go round, I said. We thumped through the double doors and along a short corridor thick with nursing staff till we reached the far end and passed through more doors into a hallway with stairs at both sides and a pair of lifts. Take that one, Bulwark said, pointing his foot. It occurred to me as we were passing into the left-hand lift – which thankfully had no one in it – how much lighter and more positive he was now he'd been shot. I've been thinking about the Said Book, he said. I stood behind him as the lift descended, holding both handles of the wheelchair. It had PROPERTY OF ST KATHERINE'S across the back. As the lift slowed my stomach rolled and I had a sense of wanting to strike Bulwark from above with something large and solid. We passed out of the lift into the main foyer. Realising I wasn't going to comment, Bulwark added that he'd been thinking the book could be semi-autobiographical, amusing and historically inaccurate. I get the impression you're putting in early disclaimers to stop anyone being critical if it doesn't cut the mustard, I said. Not only that, I said – and don't take this the wrong way – but have you done enough in life to make the semi-autobiographical part readable? It's true I haven't done much, Bulwark said. School. Scouts. Amateur Dramatics. College. Maureen. That's about it. My point exactly, I said. Though I believe people should be interested in you as a human pure and simple the chances are they won't be interested enough to part with cash. And even if they are, I can't see them struggling on beyond page two. You'll be *Ulysses* without a Molly. After a while Bulwark looked round and up. What about the shooting? I forgot it. Being murdered by an enraged Dean is interesting surely? I agree, I said, but there's a lot to get through beforehand if you go chronologically. I'll start with the murder then, Bulwark said proudly. We'd eased into the cool morning, and headed for a wall along which smokers had gathered, many in dressing-gowns, one holding at his left side a wheeled oxygen cylinder. I parked Bulwark's chair facing the traffic. If you start with the shooting you might excite the readers, I said, only then to disappoint them. You're underestimating my readership, Bulwark said. They won't need a shooting on every page. I was looking over at a butcher's shop. A man in an apron and a straw hat was laying chicken breasts it looked like on to a sheet of paper in his left hand while a woman watched. Not every page, I said, but probably they'll need more than

243

scouts and amateur dramatics. And school don't forget, Bulwark said. His nicotine gratitude filled the vicinity. Alexander was coming along the other pavement, Miriam beside him. She stopped to look in the butcher's window. Alexander came to a halt but didn't look in the window himself. He put his hands in his pockets and scanned the street. I noticed him notice me, though for a moment he seemed to dismiss what he'd seen because of the medical context, but then he must have accepted it was me after all and unconvincingly raised his hand. I raised mine. With one eye on the two of them I asked Bulwark who he felt his readership might be and he said he wasn't sure what demographic he'd aim the Said Book at yet, he'd better write it first, and I said absently I felt that to be a good idea and he became even more cheerful in his smoking. There's a friend across the street, I said. Alexander. I might not have mentioned him. Oh really, Bulwark said. Yes, I said. The one by the butchers with a woman. They go for walks. I hadn't noticed her, Bulwark said. Hey, good outfit. I believe it to be thermal, I said. The butcher had finished the chicken breasts and retreated deeper into the shop. He appeared to saw something. Miriam eased from the window, a steely light passing over each of her padded ribs. Alexander moved on after her as she headed up the street, choosing to make no further acknowledgment of me. There was an unspoken agreement between us that we could safely ignore each other if either of us was in the company of a woman. When you've finished gawping, Bulwark said, we were discussing the Said Book. I wasn't gawping, I said, just wondering if they might come to say hello. People are reluctant to do that when there are hospitals, Bulwark said, his voice giving the impression this was a wisdom frequently expressed. Alexander wants to go out with her far as I can tell, I said. But she – well she isn't keen to change parameters. She was married once to a zoologist. He died in an avalanche. Bulwark drew on his cigarette. As I looked down I detected a tightness in his shoulders. I could do with an avalanche for the Said Book, he said. You were right. My life so far isn't blockbuster material. You've done well though, academically and what have you, I said, hoping to cheer him. That's not quite true, Bulwark said. If I don't go back to college I'll have nothing to show for it. Seriously, I said to him, it's my opinion college is actually beneath you. I mean come on, a lot of it's about having a memory. I wasn't sure I agreed with myself but couldn't be bothered to start again. Besides, I went on, you'll still have it all up here even if you do leave. Up here involved a patting of Bulwark's hair. Discreetly, afterwards I wiped my hand down the back of my trousers. Between me and Alexander were lanes of traffic and a throng of strangers. Afterwards I planned to see if K wanted to do anything. She'd been on my mind. I did though find it hard to ask if she wanted to do anything. It was more in my nature to wait for her to contact me. Smithson had said it was because I couldn't bear the prospect of rejection even on a mundane level, and then as I was about to reply he said and please no more of your mother leaving you on that bus and I said to him I hadn't been going to mention buses and he said yes you were. But anyway, I'd go against my nature and give K a call later. I could tell by her voice if she was in a mood to do things and if I detected she wasn't I could always just chat on the phone and pretend I'd already lined up something for myself. The thing is – and I knew it deeply as I looked upon Bulwark – I rarely had things lined up and K probably already knew this, though I guess she'd be too polite to mention it. That's one of the things about K. She'll leave you at the mercy of your rationalisations. And I said one day to her would you do that even if the rationalisation might lead to something harmful? and she said she thought she would in the interests of allowing the world its freedom and allowing what should come naturally in the wake of life. I told her she was being terribly thoughtful for someone shampooing. She raised her head to check herself and my reflection in the mirror and said she'd been surprised to see me in the bathroom with her but had decided not to make a fuss. Well, I said, it's not like you aren't decent. I'd been in the living room for ages but had wandered in on a whim, knocking with the nub of my finger but hardly loud enough. I didn't hear if she said come in. So probably I shouldn't have. But then I saw she was washing her hair and felt it was okay. Have you left the living room for a reason? she said. I said: Not really. I'd been there twelve minutes and had wondered if there was a problem. She asked if I'd been timing her and I said not as such though I did end up watching the clock on the mantelpiece. I had momentary imaginings of her slipping out of the towel to draw a bath. Saw me getting in with her and washing her hair in that way instead. She did however ask me to rinse it using the plastic jug she kept on the bath rim. This I did, testing the water each time to make sure it was warm enough but not too warm and drawing my hand through her hair as I poured. Why did you come round in the first place, she said among water, it's not like you to turn up unexpectedly. I was on my way to the shops and thought I'd call in, I said, for a change. Part of me wishes I hadn't because you seem busy. I wouldn't call washing my hair busy, she said, though I do have to go out later. With each pouring the hair became less soapy. The water tickled my fingers. Anywhere nice? I asked. A few of us are having pizza before tonight's meeting. That sounds fun, I said. How many's a few? It's hard to be precise with AA people. We'll take it as it comes, K said. This seemed to be my last pouring because a pressure against my hand was K wanting to raise her head. Then she took a towel from the rail and rubbed her hair with it. I'm not good at being in a bathroom with a woman if I have nothing to do. Hoping she wouldn't catch on, I folded my arms. Probably Gareth's going, I said. Well, she said, her voice shaking as if it was being rubbed too, he said he'd try. My heart sank. I expect your heart's sinking, she said. Not at all, I said. I'm happy you're having pizza. Happy too if Gareth goes or if he doesn't. Life's too short. A look suggested she wanted me to leave the bathroom. I passed back into the living room, roamed the furniture a while, checking for example the dryness of the soil in the mother-in-law's tongue, picking up then putting down each photo of K in Paris, the certificate – in a brass frame – of her parachute jump, and then I retired to the sofa. I found sitting difficult, at least in a way I decided would look natural if anyone came in. Fingers on thigh. Thumb on nose. Hands behind the head. Or maybe left ankle on right knee.

*

I was wary of saying Gerald aloud, not because I worried the shock might affect him but because I couldn't remember if I'd used his first name in speech before. He was squeezing a teabag against the edge of a cup. I chose eventually to feign a clearing of the throat. He paused mid-squeeze then resumed squeezing, perhaps having slyly identified the origin of the sound. I'm making myself a hot drink, he said expositively. Would you like one? I said I wouldn't. Having finished with the teabag, Gerald applied milk. I was becoming uncomfortable with my stance, which had involved initially a head round the edge of the door frame hoping to amuse him if he caught sight of me, but since finding him with his back turned I hadn't been able to unstick myself. I'm surprised to see you, Gerald said as he eventually sat down. I said I was surprised to find him open given his plans last time. If you thought I'd be closed, why come? Gerald said. I could tell he was pleased to be able to muster logic in his emotionally broken condition. I'd been able to perceive this due to the unruly hair that hadn't seen shampoo or comb. I saw the lights on as I came by, I said. And what of your mother? Gerald said. I explained she didn't know I was here yet or indeed anywhere because I'd run away and had left a note to say I was en route to Ormerod's and could be years. And does Ormerod's mum have somewhere for you to be? Gerald asked. I felt this to be the wrong question. It belonged later in the conversation. If Ormerod had a mum, she'd be delighted, I said. The first sip of tea instigated a widening of Gerald's eyes. You shouldn't run away really, he said. It happened by itself, I said. Yet you had time for notes, Gerald said sarcastically. He raised his brows and half-nodded as he finished speaking. I've never liked it when people do that. I sat diagonally opposite him. The Bird Clock's gone, I said. Gerald turned as if to check my accuracy. I supposed he'd taken it home for safekeeping. After a short pause he said Mrs McKintosh had been given it. I had a feeling that reminding him he'd promised to leave it me in his will would put me at an emotional disadvantage. Gerald picked up his cup in both hands and looked across the top of it. I heard chirrups as if my mind wanted to make up for the clock's absence. So it's bye-bye Mrs Aldridge too, I said. Gerald nodded, and then said not at all. Why nod then? I said. He said he'd been wanting to convey that though something bad had happened, something good had happened as a consequence. Right up to the moment I was going to throw my everything in with Mrs McKintosh, he said, there was nothing I wanted more. But then as I was in her living room waiting, as it were, for our life together to begin I realised I didn't want it after all. Probably you'll soon feel the same about this running away business. I told him I didn't quite yet feel like that but suspected I might, especially since sitting at his table. But please don't call it the running away business, I said. So anyway, Gerald went on. Mrs McKintosh had a thing about the Bird Clock so I took it as a softener when I went to tell her it was all off. She punched me right here. I leaned up to see where he was pointing. Then she threw the clock after me down the path. Now of course I want to go straight round Mrs Aldridge's to confess about being a fool over Jim at night school even though she doesn't know I was jealous in the first place. Beware of stupidities as you get older, he said. Beware them. For that moment stupidities were a type of insect found among tall grasses and, having imagined this, I was there among grasses myself, hearing from elsewhere the movement of the sea. Gerald must have noticed from the corner of his eye because he strayed from his cup to ask if I was all right. So it's Mrs Aldridge again? I said. Yes, Gerald said, facing forward, even though she hasn't realised it hadn't been her at any point. And of course there's no reason for her to know. He raised his brows and half-nodded again, though not at me as such. I heard a rupturing of birdsong as the clock hit concrete. I'm glad you didn't get round to putting your books in Mrs McKintosh's shed, I said. You need sometimes to go from where you are and look back before you can reappreciate it, he said. Books were beginning to pall, but now – after those few moments in Mrs McKintosh's living room – I'm wanting them again. I don't think you should leave the shop door open while you're in here though, I said. People could waltz in and take them. Funny, Gerald said, waltz in. Ormerod taught it me the other day, I said. Then on this occasion he's to be congratulated, Gerald said. And yet we don't say people tangoed in. With your help they might, I said. Yes, Gerald said. Who knows but that the repeated practice of an idiosyncrasy might lead to it becoming commonplace. His mouth opened as an oblong to receive his own rectangular suggestion. You haven't put the outside bookshelves outside, I said. To be frank I've been awash, Gerald said, and even though the outcomes have been better than I could have hoped, I'm shocked any of it happened in the first place. The quiet that followed I feel was about us seeing if we could remember what *had* happened. Life could be like that, Ormerod said. Sometimes when tough things came to an end it was like they hadn't even started.

*

Harry will often stand the other side of the patio doors looking in. Whenever I catch him at it I raise a hand, not only in continued acknowledgment of the service he renders but also as a reminder I'm here at all. Once when I did it Colquahoon followed as it were the direction of my raising. No point bothering with that, he said over his *Times*. I've no intention of losing every social grace, I said bitterly. Bitterness often happens when I address Colquahoon. Kandinsky had been in one corner, biting his nails. He said it was because he'd lost sight of himself as if he was a child in a department store. I could see Atkins thinking what retort to make, but though the words were in his eyes, he didn't say them. Instead he clapped and said how about I Spy? Jaundice laid aside his mirror long enough to ask if it had come to this. Atkins said he'd make it interesting because the initial letter of the object chosen by the person on it should be four letters of the alphabet behind or in front of what it really was. Even better, Jaundice sighed. The words sank into his mirror. For example, Atkins said, if the object was spoon you'd say I spy with my little eye something beginning with O or W and the listeners would know it would begin with K or S. In this instance they'd realise it couldn't be the fourth letter *after* W because the alphabet isn't long enough. Spoon, Smetham said. Atkins squared himself. We know it's spoon because I told you, he said. That was only an example. Harry was passing back through when he asked – as an aside – if we might not be better off playing normal I Spy. Atkins said a challenge would do everyone good but by then the door to Harry's office had clicked behind him. I'm always less secure when he isn't around. Kandinsky again abandoned his nails enough to ask Atkins what he thought he was playing at because nobody in their right mind would bother working out every time what letter was being referred to and then guessing what object. You're just not adventurous, Mr Kandinsky, Atkins said. He made a sound as if someone'd punctured him. Colquahoon said that though he admired Atkins for wanting to innovate, he, like Harry and Kandinsky, thought it an innovation too far. And besides, he said, what's to be gained? Well, Atkins said slowly, we played it at home one Christmas and there was uproar. Good uproar or bad? Kandinsky sneered. We always have lots of family round, Atkins said. It proved to be our most popular game, even more so than pin the tail on the donkey. Kandinsky asked if Atkins and Family planned their fun in advance. I'd say Atkins had picked up on the sarcasm contained in the words Atkins and Family, but fair play to him he chose not to bite. He said indeed yes, a planned Christmas is a happy Christmas. On the morning in question we have a lie-in, opening gifts et cetera, then in the afternoon guests arrive and we eat. After this, let Fun Commence. Kandinsky made a sneering noise. Don't invite me to your place then, he said. From my angle it looked like his cupped hand had passed into his cheek. Believe me Mr Kandinsky, Atkins said, if indeed there ever are more Christmases you won't be in receipt of an invitation. And what do you mean by et cetera? Kandinsky said. Who has et cetera on Christmas morning? He jerked his chin towards Jaundice thinking he might be an ally, but Jaundice was too close to his mirror to spot it. He probably means Sexual Relations, Smetham said. He'd had nothing unusual to eat for days, having been on a new regime Harry was supposedly supervising more rigorously. He already seemed brighter. Some leaves that had blown into the patio from elsewhere a while before had disagreed with him. I mean nothing of the sort, Atkins said, and I'll thank you Mr Smetham to keep a civil tongue. There's nothing uncivil about sexual relations, Smetham said. Lots of people have them Christmas morning. Kandinsky separated his hand from his face. So do *you* Mr Smetham? Do I what Mr Kandinsky? Smetham asked. Do you have them Christmas morning? Kandinsky said. Atkins interrupted to say when Kandinsky used the word *do* it implied sexual relations were a current procedure in Smetham's life, but one look at Smetham was enough to cast doubt. I have had them Christmas morning Mr Kandinsky, but not for years, Smetham said. Jaundice wanted to know if he meant he *only* had them Christmas morning. Everyone laughed, though I'd say from what I could see of Jaundice's face he was being serious. How many times have we had reason to be grateful for Fiona's arrival? Why have you gone quiet you rascals, she said as she came in. Believe me you don't want to know, Atkins said, though as you might guess, the topic originated with none other than Mr Kandinsky here. I'd have said it was Mr Smetham actually, Jaundice said. That is, if you're referring to the sexual component. Kandinsky sighed. You see Fiona, Mr Atkins was trying to get a complicated game of I Spy going and somehow this got us round to the subject of Christmas morning. But Mr Jarndyce is correct in his suggestion Mr Smetham was responsible for introducing sexual relations. Fiona set about preparing tea. Her hair was held back by a silver butterfly clip. I won't ask how you got from Christmas to sexual relations, she said, enunciating each syllable of the term. You'd better not let Harry hear you. Where is he by the way? He was out on the patio, I said, but has since veered. I'd said this because I hadn't contributed so far. Harry's whereabouts was a safer topic. He'll be in the office then, Fiona said. I was more or less ready when she brought my tea and loomed in. I imagined an inner me leaning forward to kiss her cheek. I've wondered what sort of outer life I'd have had if I'd given in to every inclination proposed by my inner. I used to talk about it with K. She was of the opinion that in my case additional selves were best ignored. I see we're maintaining bourbons, Colquahoon said, holding one of the biscuits inches from his nose and going cross-eyed. That's right, Fiona said. As she turned towards Colquahoon, the lower half of her uniform tightened across her hips. The man at the market said there wouldn't be any more shortages for the foreseeable future. Then we must give thanks, Kandinsky said, his brows raised. I was simply proposing, Atkins said, we played I Spy with a twist, Fiona. Someone chooses an object as usual, but then says it begins with a letter that is four letters earlier or later in the alphabet than it really does. I gave spoon as an example. Jaundice nodded. I can vouch for that, he said. We can't have spoon every time otherwise there won't be any point playing, Smetham said. We're still not playing officially so far Mr Smetham, Atkins said. These are just more examples to give Fiona an idea of what's going on. So yes, Fiona, if it's spoon you say I spy with my little eye something beginning with

O or W. It widens the game you see. Smetham said right then, he'd start. I spy, he said, with my little eye, something beginning with B. Atkins asked Smetham if he was sure about it being B and Smetham said never in all the years he'd been playing I Spy had anyone asked if he was sure about the letter he'd stated. Well you see Mr Smetham, Atkins said, you didn't seem certain of the rules earlier so I was checking. You following this Fiona? Kandinsky said. Mr Atkins's idea is that by saying B, Mr Smetham will have chosen an object four letters before or after the one stated. You'll note of course that because he's said B, the object must actually begin with F simply because there aren't four letters *before* B. Even though you criticised my invention, Atkins said, it hasn't gone unnoticed Mr Kandinsky that you've grasped the principles well. Just because I grasp them doesn't mean I like them, Kandinsky said. I was explaining for Fiona's benefit. Oh don't worry, Fiona said. I don't expect I'll play anyway. I was never any good at I Spy when it was ordinary. It won't be the same without you Fiona, Atkins said. We don't have enough women. Colquahoon sat up and looked round. No women would be more accurate Mr Atkins. Yes, Atkins said. And we rue the day. You rue it if you like Kandinsky said, but I like a woman-free zone myself, no offence Fiona. Fiona said not to mind her and they should just carry on with the game. If I have time later, she said, I'll pop back for a sing-song. It was like Major Gwillingington roused himself specifically. Let's not have any fucking sing-songs today, he said. I reckon if I'd been in Fiona's position, I would have found it hard to decide what to do in circumstances where some wanted a sing-song and others didn't.

*

I only ever went to one AA meeting with K, and only then because it was 'open' and this, she said, meant people who weren't in recovery were allowed along and the reason I was going at all was because someone had asked her to do the share that night. Though she'd agreed at the time, she was now darkly reluctant, adding, to my surprise, she didn't really care for anyone there and never would. Even though we still had over half a mile to go, my heart pounded about Gareth R. I was between wanting to avoid the meeting and wanting to be there for K. Above the rooftops hung the comet's fanlike tail. It came through our solar system every ten thousand years, K said, so we should make the most of it. It was a crunchiness of pavement underfoot given the frosted conditions. Don't sit near the front when we get there, she said. If you're in my line of vision it'll put me off even more. I said I would specifically go straight to the back row and then make sure I positioned myself directly behind the largest recovering alcoholic I could find. It was a good road and as we went I speculated one day we might buy a house like these and live unhappily with a dog. You'd have to look after him though, K said as if I'd had one already and had proven neglectful. I'd like that, I said. It's one of the pot lucks for dogs when the fates are deciding who they'll end up with. If there are children in the house you need a bouncing type though where there are old people – I saw one the other day – it's best if you have something older, a dog who's happy to have been to the shops and library but who's now content to be going home again. I doubt we'll get to that stage anyway, K said. My heart shrank. I don't quite know what you mean, I said. Well, K said with authority, let's say you're too embroiled in habits that aren't compatible with mine. I expect you've noticed. Well yes, I said. It's occurred to me we hardly ever want to do the same things and when we do there's often controversy. Controversy's a bit strong, K said. From the angle of her face I guessed she was checking the comet. Something about it made you want to look at it over and over. She lowered her face to explain that yes, though she felt controversy was too strong, it was true we often had awkward moments while trying to have nice days out. It's a good term though, isn't it, I said, nice days out? I bet Gareth has them. And before you say anything, I'm teasing. I was, so to speak, parodying my own paranoia. It acts as a vent if ever I'm faced with a situation where I might come across the said person for real. I was giving secret homage to Bulwark when I'd called Gareth the said person and a pleasure about myself, about K and about the comet made me walk with one foot in the gutter, the way Alexander used to. When I asked you to come this evening, K said, I knew at some point you'd mention Gareth, although I accept in recent times you've made progress putting him aside. I said:

I feel it's reasonable to mention a lion when approaching the lion's den. What wasn't reasonable of me was those times I mentioned lions when there were no lions to hand. K looked at me, either because of my foot in the gutter or the wildlife. Anyway, I'm coming, that's the point, I said and K said she felt that to be true so I said I was glad she felt it was, although to be honest, she added, she didn't care if she herself went or not. The road we were passing along became taut with frost. We noted on three occasions cats staring through curtains on the ground floor. K said we should regard cats as paragons of blind acceptance. I had a feeling I knew what she meant but asked her to explain anyway, thinking it would help take her mind off the share and maybe ease her nerves. Well you know, she said, you never get the impression cats are wishing they weren't in windows. I was stuck for several steps because I couldn't think how to respond or if, indeed, a response was necessary. In the frosted night I heard the comet crackle. I was saved in the end because K left cats as a topic to say if I didn't want to mingle when we got to the meeting that was fine, but she would have to before and after her share because that's what people did. Myself I've always found I promote the notion of mingling more when for the moment it's theoretical, so to speak, inasmuch as we weren't yet at the venue. If it's what people do, do it, I said. Just pretend I'm not there. Like I said, I'll find a chair somewhere. They do tea, K said and sometimes this meeting has biscuits. I'll see how I feel, I said. Remember too, she said, if Gareth *is* there it'll be because he's attending to recovery. It won't be to irk you. I laughed a little, for what reason I wasn't sure. It might have been the irk or this one foot in the gutter stuff. Noticing this time a scowl on K's part, I brought the foot up to join the other. Soon we were at ease. If I had the time I'd study the rhythms between people who know each other well. I'm going to have a roll-up, K said. Yes, smoke away now, while you have chance, I said. I don't think I've ever told you, but I like it very much. When I held my hand open towards her left side it was as if I was giving her permission to begin smoking and, horrified at this suddenly, I turned my gesture into something else though I couldn't have explained it if challenged. The comet won't return for another two and a half thousand years, she said as she was rolling. Makes you wonder. It does, I said. It's not even that big, she said. And yet it's roughly four and a half billion years old. Fair play to it, I said. I glanced up. How long, I said, do you think you'll be mingling after the share? Just so I know. Oh ten, fifteen minutes. We're never long. We have to close the hall by half past. Some people go off for a coffee afterwards. I walked along behind and then beside her. This is great, I said. You going to do the share. Frost. The comet. Life's okay if you break it down into minutes. K said: AA members are advised to live one day at a time. I know, I said. When I mentioned minutes it was about dealing with heightened fear. Day at a time for normal, minute at a time for emergencies. I felt again it was the comet's fault for bringing me this topic. I crossed behind K till I was next to the privet we were passing. Seriously I hope it goes well, I said. I'm not sure a share can go well as such, or badly come to that, she said. I've a feeling I imagined him just then, which must be why Alexander appeared alongside K. Thought I recognised your backs, he said. I'm off to Miriam's. I probably would have said Thank God if I'd been in a world free of rules; instead I remarked on the cold and said surely he and Miriam weren't going for a walk in this. No, Alexander said, we're watching *Brief Encounter* at her place. The one with Trevor Howard and Celia Johnson. We know who's in it, K said. Alexander said: This Harold bloke lent her the DVD. K said: Did you find out who he was in the end? She seemed vaguely affronted. Not as such, Alexander said. But I don't care any more. K asked him why and Alexander said because Miriam was inviting him to her home he felt the relationship was about to go up a notch. He hopped mid-stride. Hopefully you'll still find out who Harold is though, I said. If he's lending Miriam the DVD it'll be a perfect time to bring him up. You could be right, Alexander said. We'll see. I half noticed initially then fully noticed he'd slipped his hand through the hook of K's arm. I worked out it was probably because he was pleased about Miriam and to my own surprise I managed to let go about it. I'm never sure though when my mind tells me I've let go if I actually have. Sometimes casual touching springs up years later. Perhaps there's no such thing as letting go really. I'd ask K some time. She said after a breathing-out through her nose: *Brief*

*Encounter* eh? I said I reckoned Alexander was right that if Miriam was inviting him not only to her house but also to watch a romantic film, the chances were she was entertaining the idea of upping their relationship. K felt it was worrying I could make such deductions. It was something men did she didn't like and even though it was me who'd only just said it, I told her I didn't like it either. It was a mistake. K preferred me to be wrong sincerely than right on the basis of what she felt because otherwise she could have no faith in anything I said. When I glanced up it was to imagine how the earth had been when the comet last passed. Are those freesias? K said. They surely are, Alexander said. Bought this afternoon. From Buds A Go-Go. They were on offer. They're force-grown so they don't have any perfume, but I felt it would be a gesture especially if things go the way I hope. Be careful, I said. Hoping has a way of undoing what you hope for. Thanks Peter, he said, but from the start I've had a feeling me and Miriam would get together at some point. Even that would be strange for you, K said. You haven't exactly been prolific with women. Another hop from Alexander. I know, he said. I've had to get a book out of the library. They have books on it? I asked. Alexander said he'd been up most of last night reading and making notes. The main thing is not to scare them by making sudden movements, he said. I suppose flowers are all right though, K said. Yes they are, Alexander said. I checked. Well I utterly wish you both well, I said, feeling genuine warmth. Thanks mate, Alexander said. I couldn't remember him calling me mate before. Is she doing food? K asked. Oh she said something, but I was in such a state I can't remember now if she is or she isn't, Alexander said. I've had a pizza in case. My stomach makes noises when I'm nervous otherwise. Funnily enough Peter it was Henderson who gave me the tip. He goes to a special church. They spend most of the service meditating. He was embarrassed he said that if he hadn't eaten enough, his stomach rumbled and others in the congregation were either complaining to him or making jokes about it. He went to see a dietitian. She said that though eating something will generally lessen the effect, the *best* thing he could have – ideally about an hour beforehand – was pizza. So I've had a pepperoni with extra anchovies. As if to conclude his own sentence, he sniffed in vain at his freesias. That was a lot more information than I was expecting, K said. But I suppose it's sensible in any event to make sure you've eaten something in case there's no food at Miriam's. I said to him I felt he should have asked her outright. I will next time, Alexander said. That is if there is a next time. I might make a hash of things. Oh you, K said, don't start worrying before you've even got there. When else am I going to do it? Alexander said. I expected to see him smile but when I checked there was nothing. I also took the opportunity to survey the looseness or otherwise of the hook in which K was allowing his hand to rest. In some ways I felt it an odd thing anyway, because I'd only ever seen women with their hands in *men's* hooks. And I had a memory, which I may well have invented, of K saying she didn't like that sort of thing because it looked subservient on the woman's part although in this case of course the subservience was all Alexander's. I guess, I said, the difficult time will be after the film. If ever anyone invites you round for something specific it's a job to know how long to hang around after the specific thing has finished. K laughed. Take no notice of this one, she said, referring to me I believe. I don't think you'll have any trouble knowing what to do or when to do it. Actually I'm with Peter, Alexander said. I remembered then Smithson suggesting if ever I was in that sort of situation I should pre-empt events by making a decision to leave anyway. If the person hadn't wanted me to leave they would be left hoping for more at some other time, and if they had then nothing was lost and no one had to suffer. Meanwhile we walked coldly on, me wondering exactly when Alexander was going to head off. Once he was at the tail end of the pleasure he'd had over what K had said, he asked us where we were heading anyway and K said she was sharing at a meeting more's the pity and Alexander said: Oh, that's something I'd like to do one day. Not share. Go to one of your meetings. Cold was sneaking even more effectively through my coat. I made an exaggerated shiver to put across the point. Where does Miriam live anyway? K said, which I was pleased about because I more or less wanted to know. Dalrymple Street, Alexander said. Though I couldn't verify it I was sure in his voice lay the vague pleasure derived from being on the way to an address where someone

257

you've taken a fancy to lives. It's only one notch less satisfying than saying their name. Number thirty-two. Green door she said. Gnomes. You're only half a dozen streets from the meeting, K said. While I'm sharing you'll be ploughing through *Brief Encounter*. I've got a confession about that, Alexander said. When she said which film we were going to watch and asked me if I'd seen it, I said no. I was scared if I said yes she might have said well let's not do it this time. You were a bit silly there, K said. I don't expect she would have done that. I know, I know, Alexander said. Me saying I hadn't seen the film went against the advice of that book from the library. Now I'm going to have to remember not to say anything about the film that might give away I've seen it before. They're right, you know, about how one small untruth can soon grow out of all proportion. I said to him, having brushed my hand through the adjacent privet, okay, but who are 'they'? Oh you know, that book, Alexander said. There's a section on how beginning a relationship with honesty will be a help as it goes on. It says many people feel a small untruth here or there will avoid some difficulties, but it stresses that as sure as eggs are eggs any untruths will eventually come to light. I was on the next privet by now. I asked him if it really said as eggs are eggs and he said no, that was him paraphrasing because it was an old book and some of its terminology was outdated and I said probably eggs are eggs is outdated itself and K said: Don't you two start. Alexander said he wouldn't class it as starting and I said certainly not, rather it was just an entomological discussion, and K said she felt I meant etymological because otherwise it was insects and Alexander said he'd spotted that too but hadn't wanted to embarrass me. I said there was no need for embarrassment anyway because they were tricky terms and there was no shame in mixing them up this once though I'd make sure it didn't happen again. Alexander said it was unlikely to come up in the near future at any rate. At this point we swung round as one to the zebra crossing, causing a 38a to draw up for us. As we were crossing, K gave me a look I took to mean there was no need to mention mother abandonment or the Rumanians now. So yes, Alexander said, she said come round and we'll watch *Brief Encounter*. I'm not sure I liked it that much to be honest. And let's face it, Celia Johnson's no oil painting.

I hardly think that's relevant, K said. You can be so shallow. We'd reached the far pavement as Alexander said yes he could be and he was worried about it in case shallowness slipped out during the evening. Probably the less you say the better, K said, punishing him I guess. I was saying if Celia Johnson was ordinary-looking surely that was one of the points of the film, which was that this sort of thing could happen to anyone. I could tell this upset K so I said Trevor Howard wasn't great to look at either. It was one of those occasions I couldn't decide what I felt about things. I could see why K was annoyed at how the conversation was going, but felt powerless to hold it back. I suppose I have Alexander to thank for rescuing the situation though I'm sure he wouldn't have seen it like that. Anyway, he said, I'll be bidding you goodnight. Oh why's that? K said. I hated the disappointment in her voice. I'm far too early, Alexander said. I like to allow time for emergencies and since none have come up, I find myself pre-emptive to the tune of forty minutes. He laughed to indicate this feigned grandeur. Where are you going to wait? K said. It's a bit cold to be outside for long. Oh there's that vegetarian cafe round the corner, Alexander said. I'll hang out there. I shook his hand. I hope it goes well when eventually you get to Miriam's, I said. Me too, he said, shaking, and let's hope the duodenum behaves. He unhooked himself from K and gave her a hug, I was relieved then to see him make his way into the darkness. So there was Alexander, I said. Funny he popped up. He does now and then, K said, glancing back. He's a popper generally. Myself I hope he doesn't get together with Miriam because I find her a bit harsh, I said. Whenever I said anything like this to K I had an anxious few moments hoping she'd support the opinion. He does seem to be doing most of the work, she said. I wondered why when people talked about someone who'd just left they often looked in the direction they'd gone off in. I said: And what if he's wrong about her being ready to up the relation-ship? Yes, K said, he's certainly looking at things through rose-tainted glasses. I like 'tainted', I said. I made it up, K said. Linguistic fluency bodes well for your share, I said. Well yes, I see what you mean, K said, but you've got to remember it's not the way I say it that matters. It's any honesty and humility that'll mean most. Not that there will be a fat lot.

I agree with that too, I said cautiously. K told me it was one of my problems that a fear of being controversial made me agree too often, and though it worked well with people I'd only just met those who'd known me a while were able to see eventually I had hardly any opinions of my own. Wow, I said, a broadside. I don't mean to be hurtful, she said, but it is true. I said: If someone fires a cannon at you does it matter that the fuse was lit accidentally? Anyway I expect it's because you're anxious about the share. Hold on, she said, though I didn't quite mean it the way it came out you shouldn't go making one of your interpretations. We were a good way towards our destination, becoming quiet for a moment. I took another look at the comet. You know K, I said at last, despite everything I'm glad to be walking with you. She asked what I meant by despite everything. Oh, I said, I don't mean despite anything about you, what I meant was despite life being tough lately. She said she didn't think it had been particularly and I said neither did I and I couldn't think why I'd mentioned it. You're crazy, she said. And don't go on about the Hagendorff Syndrome. I said I hadn't intended to say anything about it and that sometimes she was quick to judge and she said if I liked she'd mention that in her share, and I said oh no you mustn't say anything on my account, and she said actually she'd been joking and one day she hoped I'd understand her humour and I said it would probably take a lifetime, and then strangely – so much so my heart swelled – she touched my arm and said how about going for a drink after the meeting? and I said yeah sure and she said we don't have to go far and as we walked on I mused upon the fact I hardly ever turned her down when she suggested something even though she turned me down most of the time if I did. I'm glad we won't be having coffee with anyone frankly, I said. Couldn't bear the sleepless night for one thing. Where shall we go? How about that pub down by the waterfront? She said. The one with the Indian outside. Are you sure? I asked, too high-pitched. It's a pub after all. Yeah, she said. For a change. Let's just go for it. And I'd like us to have a talk. General or specific? I asked. She said both and I said that's something to look forward to and I explained that when I had to go through a social situation it always helped if I knew at some point I'd be alone with whoever it was again. We walked past the Methodist Chapel where stood either side of the doorway two wilting potted shrubs. It occurs to me how important symmetry is, I said. K sneered. What made you think of that? she asked. I glanced back and said it had been the Methodist shrub pots. K said it was like me to call them Methodist shrub pots when they were just shrub pots. Now and then the language of the world threatens to unravel, I said. Jugg did warn us about it.

*

Atkins asserted that since he was conscious only of his own self, then so, only for as long as he was alive, was everyone else – Kandinsky included. In effect, he went on, I've got the world in my hands. It dies with me. He seemed pleased to have got in a dig at Kandinsky without sounding too obvious. But, Kandinsky retorted, since I know *I'm* alive it might well be me. Did you think of that? Yes I did, Atkins said gravely, but I have no proof you're anything more than imagination on my part. There was a song, Smetham said, it's on the tip of my tongue. Atkins sighed before asking what he was on about. Smetham said: It went: He's got the whole world in his hands. Years ago. When we lived by the river. Kandinsky wiped his nose with the back of his finger. Since none of us are familiar with the fine details of your life Mr Smetham, it's of no use to say when you lived by the river. In summer you'd get a lot of people walking in front of the house, Smetham said. There was a footpath. And we had no fence. A couple of tame geese used to waddle up from a house further along and quack at everyone. You do mean *quack* I suppose? Kandinsky said. He sounded impatient. I used quack, Smetham said, because I wasn't sure what the sounds of geese are called. Atkins felt honk would do. Yes, Mr Smetham, try honk. You say quack to almost anyone and they'll associate it with ducks. His compendium was being groped for. He'd often resort to it if at any point he felt there was a risk of getting out of his depth. Jaundice laid aside his mirror. There was a joke, he said. I can't remember the start of it but it ends with a farmer saying: Sorry sir, but I assure you the water only came halfway up my ducks. I remember that joke as it happens, Kandinsky said, but I hope we're not going to have one of those situations where we drift off topic. What was it then Mr Kandinsky?

261

Atkins said. What was what Mr Atkins? Kandinsky asked politely. The joke, Atkins said, abandoning the compendium. I won't go into it now if you don't mind because of the aforementioned, Kandinsky said. He went out through the patio doors. After half a minute, sighing, he came back. Thought I heard something, he said. What? Smetham asked. Not sure, Kandinsky said. Colquahoon chuckled. It was something he did occasionally – coupled with a tiny snap of his *Times*. I've an idea that just as Kandinsky came back in we each looked startled – Colquahoon excepted – by the certainty nothing would happen from then on unless we somehow rescued what was turning out to be the flaccid narrative of our afternoon. Then I realised in part it was due to the fact Fiona hadn't yet turned up with the tea trolley. It must have been so deeply embedded in our expectations that when it didn't happen we tumbled from the event horizon into a black hole. It was proven more or less when Atkins looked at his watch and glanced at the door. After this he took up the compendium and laid it in his lap. Spurred on, Kandinsky found the nearest vacant chair and slouched into it. I absolutely know you're not the only being in the universe Mr Atkins, he said, because I know I exist. Atkins had barely had chance to open the compendium. He let displeasure cross his face. I wish I was confident in your abilities to understand if I elaborated, he said to Kandinsky, but I wouldn't want to make you feel confused and or inadequate. Kandinsky closed one eye and rubbed it. And or inadequate, he repeated to himself. I like it Mr Atkins. And or. Colquahoon had released his *Times* to take up and unwrap a toffee. Banana. Smetham said – as if to take the heat out of the moment – yes, along by the river it was when that song came out. He's got the whole world in his hands. Laurie London with the Geoff Love Orchestra. Trust you, Kandinsky said, to remember the name of song singer and orchestra and yet eat tablecloths. Thank you for that reminder sir, but a cure's currently under development, Smetham said with a degree of pride. Well let's hope it's completed before you consume the cosmos, Kandinsky said. It was out of character, I felt, to say such things to Smetham, and I could only put it down to Kandinsky's general lack of victory in the duel with Atkins. It sort of sticks in my mind, Smetham said. Things do. Other things don't at all. Atkins asked if he meant the song and Smetham said, no the house by the river. It was one of those places you didn't fully realise how happy you were there till you moved somewhere else. And yet, he said and then he paused, probably waiting for Atkins to say and yet what, which he did. Smetham explained in summer the sound would come downriver of the ferry crossing. It was operated by one man in what was basically a rowing boat. A chain attached to both banks of the river passed through hoops at either end of the boat so the ferryman could haul rather than row everyone across without the current drawing them downstream. Oh the chain's elusive clanking, Smetham said, looking up obliquely. He went on to propose there's often one sound and one alone that encapsulates the ambience of a particular time. I daresay many of us were wondering what Smetham could have consumed to create such lush reminiscence but then again I could see there was truth in what he'd said and set about wondering what sounds in my own life could have that effect. The song was written, Smetham said, by Obie Phillis, a Cherokee Indian. Jaundice asked if that also wasn't the name of those small cigars and Colquahoon untoffee'd himself enough to say you're going bonkers old boy. I hadn't heard anyone say old boy for a time, but was unsurprised that when it finally came, Colquahoon had been the one to say it. Kandinsky reminded us Harry himself had warned us against using bonkers. I'll use whichever word I like, Colquahoon said.

*

Ormerod told me he guessed wonders were afoot. Good I said, because there haven't been many. They'll come only if you don't anticipate them though, he said. He could be like that, Ormerod. Thanks, I said, and hopefully soon you'll tell me something that doesn't have a caveat. Good word, Ormerod said. Where'd you find it? Gerald used it, I told him, and I remember it distinctly because at first I thought he'd said cravat and he had to put me straight. I understand why you thought I'd said cravat, he told me. When *he* was young however, and *he* first came across caveat, he thought it was something to do with cats because he'd heard something like it though a wise uncle of his said no, he was thinking of civet. I told Gerald I felt it more reasonable I should mistake caveat for cravat than he should mistake civet for caveat, these two words having less in common sound-wise and structurally, and Gerald said yes, he'd actually been trying to make me feel better but hadn't had time to compose a more decent lie. You'll have to stop doing that, I said. After a pause I asked him if he'd really had a wise uncle, and he said though he'd had an uncle, he wouldn't go so far as to affix the adjective to him. We were in the back room by then and giggled into our teas. I hadn't the heart yet to tell him he'd forgotten to take the bag out of mine. It was the sort of thing I didn't tell him if he was having a bad Mrs Aldridge day. Sometimes the slightest incident could send him over the edge. Luckily I was saved by his curiosity. What's that poking out of the top of your cup? he said, leaning over. The teabag, I said. You forgot to remove it. Sorry about that, he said. The odd thing was he didn't then suggest he took the cup to the sink to effect a repair. This was left to me to do though I was hardly at an age to accomplish it smoothly. I took it as further evidence he was having a prolonged Mrs Aldridge. Sometimes it really hurts, he said as I was sitting back down. I mean I'm not expecting the earth of her, but if she would only give a bit more. During the word bit he created a tiny space between thumb and first finger. Having remembered something Smithson had mentioned I said didn't Gerald think if he had a bit more – I didn't bother with the thumb and finger – he'd then inwardly define what even more constituted and hanker after that? Gerald looked stunned for what seemed a week or so. He then leaned up and looked at my tea again as if to do so would take us back to a time where teabags were the prime concern. I'm thinking of holding a book bonanza, he said eventually. It's where we have a lot of books on a particular day and people can come in in droves and look at them hopefully with a view to buying. I asked him how therefore his book bonanza day would differ from a normal day in the shop other than in the concept of droves, which though desirable was unlikely. Any more of this, he said, and I won't feel good about having you here. I'm going through something incontrovertible, I said, though that hardly seemed to explain. There's more to life than elongated words, Gerald said, especially if you can't rely on using them in the right context.

This was a moment where I felt his shirtiness was about Mrs Aldridge really, but thought it safest to keep this to myself. I'm glad you didn't get rid of it, I said, looking round to indicate the entire bookshop. He looked round too. It was a close thing, he said. If ever you have one and you fall foul of a Mrs McKintosh, hold on to it. Even if your bottom drops off. I will, I said. Though I doubt the latter. Being simply affirmative with Gerald often prevented reams of less necessary conversation.

*

We were along the infinite road on our way for K to share her experience strength and hope though she wasn't sure she had any. For her, she said, the world had darkened recently. I walked several paces in bewilderment and tried to change the subject by asking what exactly was meant by experience strength and hope. Those, she said, are the guidelines for what should be in a share even though many include a number of other things because people in recovery for the most part are naturally loquacious. I enjoy that word at least, I said, though opportunities for using it don't come often. Jugg would have liked you. It was one of those evenings where the nearer we got to where we were going, the further we were. I spent a minute or so thinking about Alexander and how he must feel with *Brief Encounter* coming up. Only now he was full of pepperoni would Miriam have prepared food. It was part of a syndrome explained by Smithson – and so say originated by him – where life was continually balanced in an ironic fashion by what he called an Impish God. He told me he'd written a pamphlet on the matter and that if I was interested I could have two for the price of one and in that way I could maybe let Ormerod have one or someone like him. I told him there wasn't anyone like Ormerod and he said there I went again because he was only being figurative and I said – boldly for me – I wish you wouldn't. My heart contracted as I imagined him underground, not even a fluid by now, and unable other than in memory to charm or frustrate the Therapeutic world. I heard K ask suddenly if there was anyone at home, realising she meant me. She could always tell if I'd drifted off. It's in your shoulders, she said, glancing at them. I told her – making it up as I went along – I'd been diving into memory, going deep one moment, not so deep the other but always having to come up for breath and that perhaps death was where you went down but didn't surface at all and K said I could have bet you'd bring up death. You did ask if anyone was home, I said. You shouldn't do it unless you're prepared for whoever answers the door. I laughed for a while, once having to lean into a privet for support. When I'd recovered, I caught up with her. It'll soon be over anyway, I said. Then you'll feel more relaxed. Thanks for that observation, she said, although it hasn't helped. My pleasure, I said. We walked on. I told myself along here was Miss Woo country though I wasn't sure. I tell myself things sometimes because they sound good. The comet helps though, K said, using a tone that suggested it was the only thing that did. I told her I was glad, and glanced up. I remembered Ormerod suggesting I should never say the sky was peppered with stars so I was thinking to myself well what would be a good word? He said I should look for one with no romantic or poetical associations. Strewn's another, he said. Avoid it at all costs. I wasn't happy. Strewn had been next in line. In your defence though, he said, it's hard finding a word relating to the distribution of stars that *doesn't* have romantic or poetical associations. Thanks, I said. But then I suppose, he added, you could resort to the phrase *distribution of stars* like I just did. I told him I felt distribution of stars went too far the other way. Maybe you're right, he said. There was one of our famous pauses then, long enough for me to remember I was actually with K. I asked her if she still felt dark. She said she did. Darker. Darkest. I told her I couldn't remember her ever saying she felt such things and she said it had been building for a long time. I didn't tell her I was shocked because I felt it would stop me from sounding as if I was. Is there anything I can do? I asked. She said there wasn't, and that it was a lonely feeling. She went on to say the loneliness reminded her about a chap she'd read about who'd died for several minutes and when he was brought back by the hospital operating team he'd told them being dead was like being behind a very *very* thick pane of glass, trying to alert people he could see but not hear on the other side. I told her that though I'd heard stories about people who'd had near death experiences the fact is they weren't *really* dead so it was hard to tell if the same would happen if they weren't due to come back. I then pointed out as warmly as I could she was bringing death up this time, even though actually I'd been working hard not to mention it for her sake. You spend, she said, a lot of time trying not to mention things. I said it was a syndrome. Another one, she said. Meanwhile the moon's outer edge was diffusing through its immediate sky. I wondered whether to say to K it was a nice moon, though I had vague memories of having said it years before and she'd said something like you can't say it's a nice moon as if there's more than one. You must say *the* moon is nice if anything. Okay, I said at the time, the moon is nice, and yet I didn't feel I sounded as if I meant it. K must have picked up on it judging by the look she gave me. I coughed to bring myself back to the moment. Turned out we were still on our way through Miss Woo country – tubular gates, owls, fathers, paving slabs, ponds, dogs, privet. Don't think I'll do the meeting after all, K said. She stopped abruptly enough for me to have carried on another two paces. When I asked her what she meant, she folded her arms and asked me what did I think she meant? A piece of me was grimly excited at the prospect, and yet I said I felt she should go, if not for herself then for all the others, who'd be wanting to hear. Gareth and what have you. Suddenly it's all ridiculous, she said. How about straight for that drink instead?

*

Our spirit sneaks off to explore, say, the universe, drifts back later and here Colquahoon remains with his *Times* and Fiona, bless her, hasn't arrived with the tea. Nor Harry with that damned trolley. Smithson said there's no way of knowing what is or isn't true, and that any choice thereof is at best a biased selection. I told him I'd enjoyed the thereof and he said he had too. I kind of wish it was him opposite me, not Colquahoon; he might rip apart the absolute stillness. Oh, inadvertently it would have to be. I will take however Harry's advice and try to stay in the moment. Focus on the tip of a slipper, one of Colquahoon's perhaps, then dare my eyes to stray. A bit much, the additional tartan and those quadrants of elastic. I've been resentful since coming here that his are private slippers while mine are standard issue. Cerise it said in the booklet. Maybe to help me out – though goodness knows how often he has the opposite effect! – Colquahoon explained cerise was French for cherry and I said I knew that even though I didn't. Mine are Argyll Highlander, he said. Really? I said. Yes, a special edition, he said. I glanced at them, as you do when someone says their slippers are special. They create an interesting juxtaposition with the pattern on your dressing gown, I said. Yes, he said, we did try to get Argyll Highlander in this too – saying 'this too' he held lightly and briefly the dressing gown's collar – but though they had had them in the past they didn't have any then and wouldn't do so for the foreseeable future thanks to a downturn in the dressing gown market. Never mind, I said. I felt the softness of my response might make up for any bad thoughts I'd had about him, though there have been many others since. So yes, Argyll Highlander. I should have asked him if all of this means a Scottish heritage but I haven't got round to it thus far. The intention maybe would be to charm him with my imagined Loch Lomond and cubist cardigan. Ten to one he'd huff and say there I go making assumptions on the flimsiest evidence and I'd be forced to say I hardly thought tartan dressing gown and tartan slippers, albeit of dif-fering clans, flimsy evidence. He'd chuff and chortle, opt for a toffee and leave me wishing I'd said nothing, which is often the way. I could almost safely assume anything I say in here would have been better unsaid, that no progress will have be made by my having voiced it. I believe it was Ormerod who quoted an obscure essayist he'd come across in a charity bookshop: Why use words at all when they so often cause a breakdown in communication? I smiled at that one though quietly I had to agree. The best moments so far have been those with no language in them at all. Like now. The stillness. Eternal stillness.


END